LIFE BEHIND
THE WALL

Other books by Robert Elmer

The Shadowside Trilogy

Trion Rising (Book One)

The Owling (Book Two)

Beyond Corista (Book Three)

The Case for Christ for Kids Series

Off My Case for Kids, with Lee Strobel

Visit www.robertelmerbooks.com

LIFE BEHIND THE WALL

BY
ROBERT ELMER

ZONDERkidz

ZONDERKIDZ

Life Behind the Wall

This title is also available as a Zondervan ebook. Visit www.zondervan.com/ebooks

Requests for information should be addressed to:

Zonderkidz, 3900 Sparks Drive SE, Grand Rapids, Michigan 49546

This edition: 978-0-31074265-4
Candy Bombers: 978-0-310-70943-5 Copyright © 2006 by Robert Elmer
Beetle Bunker: 978-0-310-70944-2 Copyright © 2006 by Robert Elmer
Smuggler's Treasure: 978-0-310-70945-9 Copyright © 2006 by Robert Elmer

Published in association with the literary agency of Alive Communications, Inc., 7860 Goddard Street, Suite 200, Colorado Springs, CO 80920, www.alivecommunications.com.

Zonderkidz is a trademark of Zondervan.

Editors: Kristen Tuinstra and Kim Childress
Art direction: Cindy Davis
Cover design: Cindy Davis
Interior design: Ruth Bandstra

Printed in the United States of America

QG 11-11-14

14 15 16 17 18 /QG/ 20 19 18 17 16 15 14 13 12 11 10 9 8 7 6 5 4 3 2 1

To Ronda,
my wife and writing partner

A NOTE FROM THE AUTHOR

I want to write stories that grab a reader and won't put them down. I like action and adventure. So a few years back, when I was speaking at a school, I thought I'd test-drive an idea.

"What would you think," I asked my young students, "if you woke up one morning to find that your city—your neighborhood—was divided right down the middle by an impassible wall?"

The kids responded! Nobody wanted to be separated from friends and family that way. No one wanted to be kept out, or kept in. And yet it happened in Berlin. This city would be the perfect stage for a series of stories that I hoped would not only grab our attention—but also our hearts.

Naturally these stories are filled with all the action, adventure, and history I can cram into each chapter. But at the same time, that ugly concrete wall reminds us of deeper truths. How do we move past bitterness to find forgiveness? What do we do, when we just can't? And how do our mistakes rub off on those around us?

The characters in these three stories had to wrestle with those questions. And in the end, they had to face the truth of Ephesians 2:14, which tells us that *"He is our peace, who has made the two one and has destroyed the barrier, the dividing wall of hostility."*

So I hope you have enjoyed reading this series, as much as I enjoyed writing it. Thanks for coming on the adventure with me. Remember that the wall, in more ways than one, is history.

–Robert Elmer

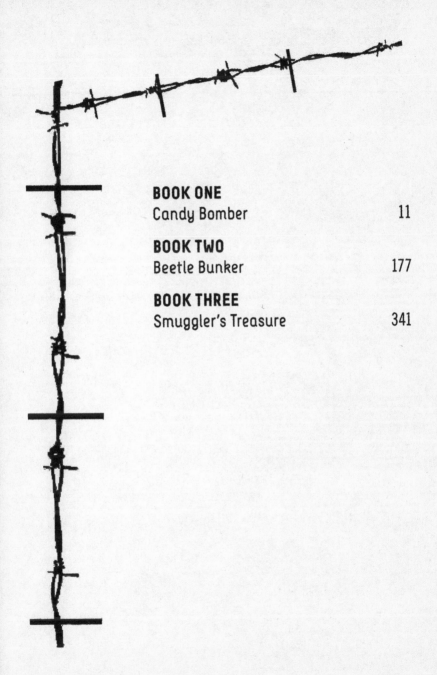

CANDY BOMBERS

CONTENTS

PROLOGUE

Nick held Trouble's collar and scanned the runway on the other side of the chain-link fence, just to be sure. From here the Bighorn County Airport looked tons bigger than any old Wyoming airstrip. Maybe because it had started out as a military air base in the 1940s before it became a home for smoke-jumping and forest-firefighting planes. It stretched way out past Little Dry Creek, like a big city air-port, only Greybull was no big city.

He counted a dozen bright orange planes parked around the oversized hangars. They used those planes during fire season, not April. And not on a Saturday morning, when the mechanics and everybody else were probably sleeping in.

Then he squinted at the five old cargo planes, their aluminum skins glimmering with the first rays of morning sun. The one on the end was the coolest—a mothballed four-engine C-54 Skymas-ter transport with a silly flying baby painted on its side. The *Berlin Baby*. Funny name for a plane. But all the planes still wore their stars proudly, even though the years of blistering seasons in Wyoming had faded the old girls.

"Come on, Trouble." He crouched as low as he could and sprinted to the shadow of the C-54's wings. He waited for a moment to make sure nobody saw them. Okay. In one smooth move Nick pulled himself up the rope ladder and swung inside the open hatch of the big Skymaster.

Trouble barked as soon as he disappeared, the way she always did. As in, *Don't forget me!*

"Shh!" Nick tried to quiet her down as he added his pack to his book stash. He took in a whiff of air still smelling of clouds with a hint of airplane fuel. Just right. And that was probably the best part about this place: the smells and the wondering and the dreaming. How many times had she been around the world, and how many miles had slipped under her wings? What kinds of cargoes had filled her huge dark insides, now littered with ripped nets, ropes, and lumpy canvas tarps? And who had flown her during the past forty years, before Nick had secretly taken over command?

Next came Trouble; Nick reached down to the clothesline still knotted to his belt. He had tied the other end around his little mutt's body like a harness, and it was no trouble to hoist his cargo into the plane with him. The dog had done this dozens of times. So once inside, Trouble curled up in her usual spot behind the co-pilot's chair while Nick secured the hatch and settled into the pilot's seat. He imagined that his view of the distant snow-capped Bighorn Mountains to the east might look almost the same if they were airborne. *Let's take it up to thirty-two thousand. Throttle up. Heading oh-eight-niner.* Trouble glanced up and wagged her tail, thunk-thunking the plane's metal skin. At the same time, a much louder thunk nearly lifted Nick out of his seat.

"Hey, you in there!" *Bam-bam-bam.* "Out! Get out!"

The hair on the back of Trouble's neck stiffened, and she tilted her head at the noise. But with Nick's hand on her collar she didn't bark.

"Good girl," he whispered.

"Do you hear me?" came the foghorn voice again. *Bam-bam-bam.* "Get out of there, or I'm gonna call the sheriff and have you arrested for trespassing."

He would too. Nick had heard the stories about the caretaker. So, like a pilot with a pre-flight checklist, Nick ticked off his options:

Option One: Surrender and come out. Pray for mercy. Hmm. Maybe not.

Option Two: Sit right there and say nothing. But the first place the sheriff would look for him was right there. Which left him with—

Option Three: Hide in the cargo hold. *Really* hide.

"Don't make me wait all day, kid. I know you're in one of these planes."

Aha! *One* of these planes? If the old guy wasn't sure which one, Nick knew he still had a chance of not being discovered. So he slipped off his shoes, picked up Trouble, and tiptoed into the shadowy belly of the airplane. The flashlight gave him a wimpy little flicker, but it still had just enough juice to guide him back past the navigator's table to the cargo hold.

But where to hide? He crawled to the line of wooden crew seats, wedged himself below one, covered himself up with a piece of canvas, and waited.

"Come on, kid!" The voice sounded a little softer this time, moving away. Nick lay back in his hiding place with the bottom of a fold-down wooden seat just inches from his face. And he noticed something.

What's that? He pointed the light up to check it out. Somebody had carved a name into the bottom of the seat. Well, that was rude. But kids did that to old school desks all the time.

Was it really a name, though? Maybe, if you could see past the little stain, which looked like old dried blood. First came a capital *E*, then an *R*, except it was squiggly and hard to make out.

Erich something? The rest of the words didn't look English.

What kind of weird graffiti was that for an old Air Force cargo plane?

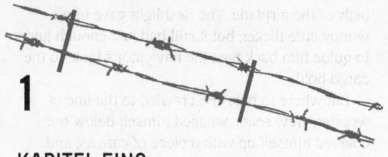

1

KAPITEL EINS

BERLIN, GERMANY

SUMMER 1948: 40 YEARS EARLIER...

Erich stopped his carving for a minute, listening to everything going on outside the plane. So far his plan was going *almost* the way he'd hoped.

Step one, sneak onto the American plane that was unloading supplies at Berlin's Tempelhof Airport. That had been no problem with all the confusion of the airlift—with hundreds of planes coming and going all day and night. In fact, the British and the Americans had been flying in for weeks, ever since the Russians had blocked off Berlin, surrounding it so no supplies could come in or go out by land.

Step two, find a stash of food. Maybe some dried fruit or flour. A few potatoes. Whatever. The Americans would never miss it. They weren't doing this because they cared about the people of Berlin, *nein*. No, Erich was sure of it. It was just part of their war, this *cold* war they fought, the English and the Americans and the French, against the Russians.

Step three, slip away without getting captured by the enemy. And if he could pull this off, everyone back in the neighborhood would call him a hero. Erich the Hero. He liked the sound of that. See? The world war might have been over for three years, but thirteen-year-olds could still do risky—and important—things.

But this plane held no food, nothing. So he decided he'd just leave some kind of record behind. Proof that he'd been here, that he'd been brave enough to do what he'd told everyone he would. Maybe his cousin Katarina and the others would never see it, but he would know, and that would be enough. Keeping one eye on the exit, just in case, he crouched low and used the dull point of his penknife to carve a few words into the bottom of the wooden seat.

And no, he didn't feel guilty, or like a vandal, though Katarina would have yelled at him. After all, this airplane belonged to the enemy. Even though the war had ended, the men who flew this plane had rained fire and death on his city.

And on his family.

And on his father.

Yes, Erich Becker was here to try to even the score, any way he could. Even when the knife slipped and jabbed his finger. *Ouch!* Forget the trickle of blood; he continued for a couple more minutes until he had finished. There. He folded up his knife, crawled to the exit door, and looked around. All clear? He slipped out and landed like a cat on the hard-packed airport runway.

Safe for now. Erich adjusted his cap down lower and wished for a few more shadows so he could blend into the German work crews—men who swarmed over each incoming plane to pick it clean of cargo. No one seemed to notice when he hurried along with everyone else. A truck screeched by him, full of men on their way to unload an approaching C-54. Its pilot followed close behind a guide jeep bearing a big FOLLOW ME sign. If nothing else, the Americans knew how to run an airport.

"Let's go, gentlemen!" A man in uniform windmilled his right arm at the approaching truck, pointing to a place on the pavement where he wanted the work crew to wait. Another man wearing dark green coveralls and white gloves stood at attention in front of the plane parade, directing the latest arrival with twirling hand motions. The plane taxied into position, its four propellers spun down, and the side hatch popped open—all at once. Erich tried not to stare at the finely tuned ballet, where each dancer knew just when to jump, and how high.

Instead, he studied the pavement and held on to his hat as a final gust of propeller backwash hit him, hunched his shoulders, and did his best to look ten years older and six inches taller. Only, which plane would have food in it? Which could he try next? Not the one at the end of the lineup, where the crew raced to unload bin after bin of coal. He skirted around that one while still trying to look as if he were going somewhere on purpose. And that might have worked fine, if he hadn't rounded the next plane ... and run square into a brown-uniformed soldier.

"*Bitte, bitte.*" Erich choked out an apology as he caught his balance. "Excuse me."

But that wasn't enough for the soldier, who grabbed Erich by the shirtsleeve and waved a friend over to join them.

"*Bitte bitte* nothing." The soldier scowled and didn't loosen his grip. "You can't be wandering around here. Which crew are you with, anyway?"

Erich tried to back away, couldn't, and decided the safest answer would be rapid-fire German. He was going over to the *flughafen*, headquarters just as ordered, he said. In a terrible hurry. *Schnell!* But the soldier only held up his free hand, motioning for him to stop.

"Whoa, whoa. Around here we speak English, fella. *Verstehen?* Understand?" He looked a little closer, and his eyes widened. "Hey, wait a minute."

This time Erich did everything he could to wiggle away, twist out of the grip. But the more he tried to flee, the tighter the man squeezed his arm.

"Hey, Andy!" That must have been his friend, now trotting over to join them. "Look at this. This ain't no worker. I just caught me a street kid! How do you think he snuck in here?"

Erich knew he was dead. Take him back to the *kirchof*, the graveyard next to the airport, and bury him.

"Beats me," answered Andy, a dark-skinned man wearing dark green coveralls and a baseball cap with the bill turned up in front. "But you better get him out of here before the captain finds out, or we're going to have some explaining to do."

"Yeah." The first man frowned again and began to drag Erich toward the main terminal building. "You speak English, kid?"

Erich wasn't sure he should answer yes. But he couldn't help staring at the dark soldier as he stumbled away from the airplanes. He'd seen black men before a couple of times, mostly Africans, but only from a distance. Never this close up. Erich had to focus his ears to understand what this man was saying. The edges of the words sounded as if they'd been rounded off, and Erich liked the smooth warmth of them.

"What's the matter, kid?" Andy flashed him a smile. "You look like a deer caught in the headlights."

Erich swallowed hard and nodded, not sure how a deer could find itself in such a place, or he in this one.

"Out this way." The first guy pointed at a gate in the fence where trucks and jeeps came and went past one of the airport's main terminal buildings. "And don't you ever let me catch you trying to sneak in here again, you hear?"

"I hear." Erich finally managed a couple of words, which made the man named Andy laugh.

"You probably understand every word we've been saying, huh?"

"Not every word." Erich shook his head as he hurried out the gate, rubbing his arm where he'd been squeezed by the first guy. But Andy called after him.

"Hey, wait a minute."

Erich didn't wait.

"You like Hershey bars?" asked Andy.

Erich froze but wasn't sure if he should turn around. It was a trick. Had to be.

"Hershey's?" the man repeated. "You know, chocolate?"

That did it. Erich looked over his shoulder, just to be sure. The tall man reached out, offering a brown-wrapped candy bar. Erich couldn't ever remember having a Hershey bar all to himself. A bite, once. Never a whole bar. His stomach danced at the thought.

"Come on," said Andy. "Take it before I change my mind. You've got to be hungry, right?"

Erich could already taste the chocolate, sweet and warm and rich. He turned back to accept the gift, expecting the man to pull it away at the last second. But no.

"Dankeschön." Erich looked up at the man whose skin seemed as dark as the chocolate he offered. "Thank you."

"Andy!" someone yelled from inside the *flughafen*. "Need you back here!"

"See you around." The man winked at him as he turned to go. "Only next time, you stay outside the fence, okay?"

"Andy!" The voice did not belong to a patient man.

"Aren't you going to eat it, kid?" Andy asked as he started back through the main gate. "I thought everybody liked chocolate."

"Ja." Erich fingered the treasure, knowing how wonderful it would taste. It had been given to him, had it not? Didn't he have every right to enjoy it? He paused. "Yes. But it will be for ... Oma, Grandmother."

And before he could change his mind, he slipped the precious Hershey bar into his shirt pocket, turned, and sprinted away.

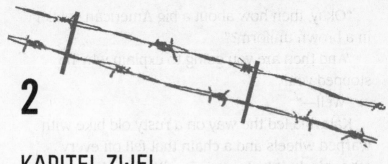

2

KAPITEL ZWEI

GOOD EXCUSE

"I told you, I didn't steal it." Erich pedaled up Potsdamerstrasse, Potsdamer Street, as fast as his old bike would let him. "I can't believe you would even *think* that of me."

"Sure." Katarina checked over her shoulder and slowed down as they entered the spooky wasteland of the Tiergarten—once a beautiful, green city park but now sheared of all its trees by bombs and firewood scavengers. Some of the grand statues still stood, headless, high on their columns, ruling over rubble and ruins. Others had long since toppled to the gravel pathway. "But I don't think your story's going to help us explain what took us so long to get home."

"We'll just tell them the truth. A big green lizard monster grabbed me and wouldn't let me go. I was ... kidnapped!"

Katarina wasn't buying it.

"Okay, then how about a big American soldier in a brown uniform?"

"And then are you going to explain why he stopped you?"

"Well—"

Katarina led the way on a rusty old bike with warped wheels and a chain that fell off every other block. Which was actually fine, since it gave them a chance to catch their breath. Meanwhile, Erich did his best to keep up on Frankenbike, a monster he'd wired together from the skeletons of several dead or smashed bicycles he'd discovered in bombed-out buildings. At least traffic seemed lighter now, after dinner, so that was good. Shops had closed for the day. But his front tire—the one that didn't fit quite right—wiggled a little more than it had earlier that evening, and he had to keep jiggling the handlebars to keep it lined up right.

"You going to make it?" she asked him. They had skirted the Soviet sector of the city, districts to the east where Russian soldiers were in charge. Here at the eastern edge of the American sector, jeeps with American soldiers—like the ones at Tempelhof—passed them every couple of blocks. The cousins would reach Oma Poldi Becker's flat in a minute or two.

"Yeah, I'll make it. It's just this stupid wheel." He gave it one more good shake, jerking back his handlebars and planting the wheel squarely on the pavement. That should fix it.

And it did—sort of. The next thing he knew the front wheel bounced out ahead of him, even as he continued to pedal. Without a front wheel, the front end of his bike nosed down and jammed the fork into the street, launching him chin-first to land—OOMPHH!—spread-eagle on the pavement. The frame of the bicycle tied itself into knots around his legs, bending him into an impossible pretzel.

"Erich!" Katarina kneeled next to him, but her words only buzzed in his ears. "What happened?"

What happened? He slowly untangled himself from the bike and tried to sit up straight.

"Wheel decided to go solo, is all." And sure enough, it still bounded down Bernauerstrasse. "It wanted a new life as a unicycle."

"Quit being silly."

"Who, me? I'm all right." By that time he'd collected himself enough to stand up. That seemed to be a good sign: all his arms and legs worked. His elbow and right knee looked a little scraped. The worst part: his jaw.

That, and the warm red stain on his shirt.

"No, you're not." Katarina pointed at his chin and wrinkled her nose. "Oooh, gross. You're bleeding all over the place."

Nicht so gut. Not so good. He cupped his chin in his hand, trying to keep from making more of a mess all over everything. That helped a little, but he had broken open his chin more than just a little.

Good thing they were only a half-block from Oma Poldi's place.

"Can you walk?" Katarina wanted to know.

He nodded, still cupping his chin tightly. And he supposed they looked a bit odd, him holding his chin and dragging what was left of Frankenbike, her juggling his runaway front wheel while pushing her bike.

"Don't make a big deal out of it," he told her. "It's just a little scrape."

Or not. Five minutes later their Oma Poldi dabbed carefully at his chin with a damp washcloth and told him it most certainly was *not* just a scrape. Katarina turned green and looked the other way.

"Does that hurt?" Oma studied him with her sharp blue eyes. Everything else in her body had wrinkled or twisted: her face and her hands, for instance. Her knees, she said, from spending so much time on them, praying. Her cheeks had aged even more in the last few years, like prunes that had been left out in the pantry too long. And at times she coughed so hard and so long that Erich and Katarina thought she might never be able to take another breath. Just a little tickle, she told them, but Erich's mother had called it chronic bronchitis, which sounded a lot more serious than just a tickle.

But she had nursed her share of children and grandchildren back to health, patched plenty of skinned knees and broken arms. She caught her breath and repeated the question.

"No, Oma." He shook his head and winced. Not as long as he didn't move or breathe or try to open his mouth. Otherwise, no problem.

"Then what were you doing out on the street at this time of night?" Of course she wanted to know everything as she patched up the gash on his chin with a slice of medical tape, cut into careful little pieces, just like a doctor would have done. And maybe she wouldn't tell her daughter-in-law, Erich's mother. Or maybe she would. But her question reminded him of something, and he reached down into his shirt pocket.

"I went to get you this." He presented the prize—a little broken, a little squashed, but all there. And for just a moment her eyes widened, the same way Katarina's had.

"Where did you get that?" she asked him, but she had to know the answer. Only the Americans—

"A soldier gave it to me." Erich still held the Hershey bar out to her, hoping the wrapper had stayed clean. "He was as dark as the candy. You should have seen him."

"He *gave* it to you?" She raised a knowing eyebrow and looked over at Katarina just to be sure. Katarina nodded.

"Take it, Oma." He held it out. "When was the last time you had chocolate?"

For a moment she let herself gaze out her apartment's single window, with her view of the tall steeple of the once-beautiful *Versöhnungskirche,* the Reconciliation Church, not much more than a block away.

"When your father was still—" she began, and her voice trailed off. Even she could not say the word *alive.* "Well, he would work on his sermons, and on his way home Saturday afternoon, a half bar of chocolate for his old mother he would bring."

It hurt Erich to smile as she shook her head and came back to the here and now.

"But that was before you were born, of course. Before the war ... and all this."

All this. A city in ruins, where most of the men were dead or disappeared, and where women worked all day shoveling rubble and clearing collapsed buildings, bucketful by bucketful. *Rubblewomen,* they called them. Like Erich's and Katarina's mothers.

"Then you should have it, Oma." He held it out once more. She wasn't making it easy. "Please."

"On one condition only." She finally held out her hand, then took the chocolate and divided it into three parts. "That you kids will share it with me."

Of course there was no arguing with Oma Poldi, and no way to get her to nibble more than a couple of squares of the rich chocolate. Erich closed his eyes and let it roll over his tongue, again and again, before he finally had to swallow. And when he opened his eyes again they watched the Russian soldiers on the street below. One of the thick-armed guards had stopped a row of people as they stepped off the S-Bahn streetcar. He rummaged through their shopping bags and removed what he wanted: a loaf of bread, several packages of cigarettes, a kilo of coffee. They meekly took back their empty shopping bags, stared at their shoes, and hurried off.

Is this what his father had meant by "blessed are the meek, for they shall inherit the earth"? Well, there wasn't much left to inherit, not in this Berlin. Only what the Soviet soldiers could steal from people coming in from the other side of town, the western side. And, as the Soviet blockade wore on, that supply was getting thinner and thinner.

Just like Oma Poldi.

In this section of Berlin they kept starving old women alive with hand-me-down bars of American chocolate, smuggled across the invisible line between east and west.

"It's not getting any better, Oma." Katarina was the first to break their silence. "Why don't you come live with us, over in the American sector?"

Oma carefully licked her fingers, making sure to get every chocolate smudge. She seemed to think about her granddaughter's question for a moment before answering.

"How could I leave?" She stared out the window

once more. "You know my grandfather grew up in this building. Your father and uncle, even. I belong in this place where God has called me."

And there could be no arguing with that, chocolate or no chocolate.

"And besides," she added, "your father and his brother loved the people in this neighborhood. Some of them are still left here. Frau Schnitzler. Poor Ursula Ohlendorf. They all went to church at the *Versöhnungskirche*."

The church, the *kirche* that now lay quiet and empty and ruined.

Just like Oma Poldi. She could hardly speak anymore. Still she kept Erich in her sights.

"They all heard your father preach against the Nazis, against the evil. I honor my sons by staying, now. So this is my place. This is where I will live and die."

"Oma." Erich nearly choked on his last bite of chocolate. "You're not going to—"

But he knew she was going to, even if he brought her a chocolate bar each day. She needed much more than snacks to survive.

"Of course I am going to die, when God wills it." She reached out and mussed his hair, and the effort must have drained her. She leaned back in her chair and closed her sunken eyes. "Now go on home. You're a sweet boy to be bringing your old grandmother sweet treats, even if you're a bit clumsy on that old bicycle of yours."

He'd almost forgotten about the accident and his blood-stained shirt. He still had some explaining to do at home.

"I'll be sure to let your mother know that you were visiting here," added Oma. "And a bit late it was."

Erich rose and nodded, reached over and kissed his grandmother on the cheek.

"Let's go, Katarina." And he was out the door before his cousin, bounding down the stairs two at a time. "I'm headed back to the airport."

"What are you talking about?" Katarina stepped on his heel as they hurried through the landing to the door out to Rheinsbergerstrasse.

"Tomorrow, that's what I'm talking about. I'm going to try again."

3

ERICH BECKER'S PRIVATE WAR

"Yes, Erich, I'm glad you were visiting your grand-mother yesterday." Erich's mother barely got the words out as she sat at the small kitchen table the next evening, her head in her hands. "Sitting there in that dark apartment all alone. Almost starving, and goodness knows the Russians don't care what happens to old people in that sector, much less if they get anything to eat."

It was true. Erich licked the back of his spoon to make sure he'd cleaned up his serving of thin cabbage soup, though it didn't begin to put a dent in his stomach-clutching hunger. The kind of hunger that just ate and ate at him, that sapped his energy and made him want to just stay in bed all day. Come to think of it, though, maybe it was a good thing they'd had soup tonight; it had taken little effort to chew. His jaw still hurt when he bit down, but no one needed to know. He touched the bandage on his chin and looked up at his mother, who had closed her eyes.

Was it just his imagination, or did his mother look almost as old and wrinkled as his grandmother? No blood relation, of course; Oma was his father's mother. But since the Americans had killed his father in the war, it seemed his mother had aged a whole generation, maybe ten years for every one.

Her hands had been the first to go: cracked and bleeding, covered now with calluses and blisters from holding her shovel. Her nails had nearly disappeared, too. But who could stay young-looking while shoveling bricks and rubble all day, clearing the city of ruined buildings?

It was, she told him, the only job she could find. And though it paid nothing, it helped them get extra ration cards, so that was good. But at what price? And who had dropped the bombs that had destroyed all those buildings in the first place?

She never wanted to talk about whose fault it was, or who had killed Father. Sometimes in the middle of the night, though, he heard her crying. And now, with her eyes closed, she moved her lips as if answering all his questions.

Why did they drop so many bombs on us, then divide our city?

Where will we find our next meal?

How long will Oma live?

Finally her lips stopped moving. The dull hunger

still gripped him, still made him dizzy and sleepy and angry all at once. Of course they'd prayed for help; how could they not? And if crying or screaming would have helped, he would have done that too. But not today.

Their single stub of candle flickered and sputtered, and still his mother didn't move, only held her chin and let her long dusty hair flow freely. *Good for her*, Erich thought. *She's sleeping.* He licked his fingers and quietly tried to snuff the flame—*fsst!*

"Ow!" he muttered; the feeble little flame fluttered back to life. "I thought I knew how to do that trick."

Brigitte Becker blinked and shook her head in the half-dark, as if waking from a dream.

"Oh!" She straightened up and checked her hair. "I must have dozed off."

"That's okay. Thanks for breakfast."

"Mm-hm." She nodded and began to push out her chair, and yes, he'd said *breakfast*. It took only a few seconds for her to freeze, though. "Wait a minute. It's not … Oh, you!"

She smiled for the first time all evening, a shy grin that spread slowly across her tired face. And that was the best reward of all.

"Erich Becker, you're more like your father every day. He would do the same thing to me. Tell me the silliest lies with a straight face, then when I believed him, he would grin and—" She paused, dishes in hand.

"Mom, I don't remember him very well anymore." Six years ago felt like a lifetime. "I can't even remember his face, except for the pictures we have. I'm sorry."

She set down her dishes by the sink and rested her hands on his shoulders for a moment.

"Don't be sorry. You were much younger. It was a long time ago."

"I do remember the last time I saw him, when I took his lunch to him at his study at the church." He paused. "Do you remember the last thing he said to you?"

His mother's face went serious again. She turned to the small window over the sink that revealed the narrow space between their apartment building and the next one.

"I don't know why I asked that," he told her. "It just slipped—"

"He was talking about books, always talking about his books." She bent down to the bowl in the sink, splashed water on her face. The candle made her shadow dance on the wall, weird and larger than life.

"What kind of books?" he finally asked.

"Luther. He told me he'd been reading a volume of sermons by Luther. That he very much liked it."

"Doesn't every Lutheran pastor read Luther?"

"I suppose." She nodded, hugging the dish towel

to her chest, remembering. "But this was different. He said that if anything ever happened to him, I should not forget a book called *Dr. Martin Luther's Sämtliche Schriften.*"

"*Collected Writings*?" In other words, a book of sermons and short essays. "That was his favorite?"

"I think so." She dabbed at the corner of her eye with the towel. "He said he would explain it to me, but he had something urgent he had to do at the church first. So I still don't know what he was talking about. It didn't come up for another couple of days; we were so busy. And then the air raid—"

Erich knew the rest of the story, the bombs that fell near the church, how they never found his father's body, all that. But not the part she'd just told him.

"You never told me that before. That part about the book."

"It's the first time I've thought about it in years, Erich." Finally she turned back to face him. "I never thought it was important to anyone else. Now, as I was saying before I dozed off, I do appreciate your visiting your grandmother. But you must be more careful on that old bicycle thing of yours."

"Just a loose nut holding the wheel. I fixed it fine."

"Maybe, but your chin is not fixed so easily, and the stain in your shirt didn't come out all the way."

"You don't need to worry about me, Mom."

"I still don't like the idea of you wandering all over the city. It's not safe these days."

"Safer than before. I was thinking of going to see Oma again tonight."

She started to say something, then nodded quietly, took a half-cup of flour, and poured it carefully into a handkerchief-sized piece of clean brown wrapping paper she'd saved. Everything was saved, used again and again. She folded up the corners and tied it off with a loop of string, also saved.

"Then, my good pastor's son, you will take this to her, as well."

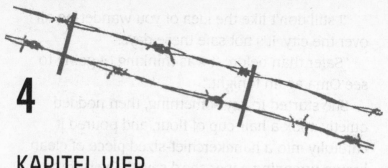

4

KAPITEL VIER

UNDER THE FENCE

"But it says 'No Trespassing,' Erich." Naturally Katarina would feel the need to remind him. Cautious Katarina. She ran her finger along the big block lettering in the early evening shadows. The sign was wired crookedly to the eight-foot chain-link fence, just below the coil of barbed wire. "By order of—"

"I can read English as well as you can, Katarina." He found a hiding place for his bike behind a tombstone, good enough for a few minutes until he got back. Through the fence and across the runways he could make out the glow of floodlights at Tempelhof Airport, where twenty-four-hour crews unloaded emergency supplies from American and British cargo planes. Around them, the city circled the airport, forcing pilots to come in low and slow over bombed-out neighborhoods.

"Well, I think we should just turn around and go

home, before we get in trouble and it starts pouring rain. This place is creepy."

"Yeah, the monsters and the spies are watching us, huh?"

Everyone knew about the spies. Men who watched everything the Americans did and reported it all to the Russians, in exchange for a few ration cards. Men who counted the planes taking off and landing, and probably a lot more than that besides.

"You just make it into a joke, Erich. But it's not—" Katarina started to leave as a jeep carrying two American soldiers bumped toward them across the huge expanse of landing strip on the other side of the fence.

"Down!" he hissed and pulled her behind a taller tombstone. Without warning, they tumbled blindly into an open pit.

"Oh!" Katarina scrambled to her knees. The jeep whined past them, its headlights casting long shadows across the graveyard for a brief moment.

"Bomb crater," Erich decided. Good thing for them no one had yet repaired this end of the St. Thomas Kirchof, the St. Thomas Cemetery. He hadn't seen it before, even in the daytime when he'd come to scout the place out. This would make a good hiding hole, though it seemed a bit weird, considering where they were. He realized he'd have to move fast before another patrol came by.

"You sure you won't come with me?" He rolled

out of the waist-deep crater and crept over to the fence. This *was* the fencepost, if he remembered right. He yanked at a corner of the chain-link wire where it attached to the metal pole. No luck. Had someone fixed the loose piece of fence? He moved on to the next one. It had to be here.

"Seriously, Erich, I still don't think this is a good idea."

He would expect her to say that. Meanwhile, he found the right spot and peeled the corner of the chain link back a couple of feet. He looked up at her and pulled the little package of flour from his shirt pocket, the one his mother had wrapped.

"You think this half-cup of flour is going to do Oma any good?" Erich held up the package.

"That's not the point."

"It isn't?" Erich felt the back of his neck redden. "Why don't you tell me the point?"

She crossed her arms before answering. "I don't think this is about trying to survive, Erich. I think it's about ... trying to get even. You want to do whatever you can to get back at the Americans. This is the private war of Erich Becker."

"That's crazy." Erich crossed his arms to match hers. "*Wahnsinn.*"

But why did she always have to be so under-his-skin right?

"Look, Erich. We both know we have to do something to help Oma. But this isn't the way."

"You said that before. But I'm not just going to

sit around waiting for her to starve to death while we figure out plan B. Is that what you want?"

"That's a dumb question. I just can't go along with your plan this time."

Erich sighed and ran a hand through his light, short-cropped hair.

"Look, I'm sorry, but I don't know what else to do. So I guess you can come with me, or not. I think I have it figured out this time, but I could still use your help."

She looked at him and swallowed hard, but finally pressed her lips together and shook her head no.

"You may think you have it figured out, Erich, but that doesn't make it right."

"Fine." He tossed the little package at her and turned back to the fence. "If you could just deliver this for me, I'd appreciate it. Tell Oma I'm coming back with a crate of Hershey bars."

That's right. And maybe no one else had noticed this loose piece of fencing; it wasn't quite big enough for an adult to skinny through. But an underfed German kid like him?

He ducked as another big American cargo plane took off. He felt his chest rumble as the huge bird gathered speed and roared east over the bombed-out apartment buildings, shaking any glass windows left in the Neukölln neighborhood. The supply planes left Berlin every three minutes, as regular as a good Bavarian cuckoo clock. He couldn't help smiling—before he remembered his mission.

No! He gritted his teeth and reminded himself how much he hated the men who flew those planes. The same men who had dropped the bombs. The same bombs that had killed his father. The same father who had always promised that God would protect them.

And then he didn't smile anymore.

Instead, he took a deep breath and held it, looked up the runway and back. All clear.

"Hold it open, please," he told her. "I'm going in."

"No, Erich." She crossed her arms. "I can't help you steal."

"Come on, Katarina. You make it sound like I'm some kind of criminal."

Her shoulders fell when she sighed.

"You're not a criminal, Erich. But you don't need to do this."

"And if I don't, we line up for our one lousy loaf of bread for five people, and Oma gets skinnier and skinnier. If the Americans hadn't—"

"Don't start blaming the Americans for our problems again."

"But can't you see what fakes they are? First they try to kill us all, and now . . . now they think they're our new best friends, just because they toss a few cigarettes to the beggars on the street corners. You ever tried to eat a cigarette?"

Katarina made a face. "They're the ones

44

bringing the food, Erich. They didn't have to do that."

Erich smacked his forehead with the palm of his hand.

"Don't you get it, Katarina? They're still the enemy. They will always be the enemy. And when they're the enemy, the old rules don't work."

"But for how long, Erich? And we're supposed to love our—"

"Don't preach at me. Besides, it doesn't matter. You're too worried about the rules, when we need to be worried about helping Oma."

"Okay, but that doesn't mean you can just sneak in there and steal whatever you want. What about everybody else in Berlin who's hungry? Can you look me in the eye and tell me this is the right thing to do?"

Erich closed his eyes and rubbed his forehead.

"I don't know if it's the right thing or not. I only know that I have to try."

"We'll get the food some other way." She wasn't giving up so easily. "My mother gets some more ration cards in a few days. We can share, the way we've been doing. If they catch you—"

"Nobody is going to catch me."

Yeah, but if he didn't hurry over to the supply planes, he'd lose his chance.

And his nerve. So he would crawl under this fence, with Katarina's help or not. He flattened himself out like a worm, poked his head under the chain link … and the wire caught like a trapdoor, square on his back.

"Ow!" Great. Now he couldn't move forward, couldn't back up, couldn't quite reach back. The wire had skewered him pretty well. "Katarina! I'm stuck. The wire's digging into my back. You have to—"

He didn't have to finish; she lifted the corner of fencing so it unhooked from his shirt.

"Thanks." He wriggled through the rest of the way on his belly. Getting his only shirt dirty didn't matter. He dusted off and straightened up on the other side.

"I'll be right back."

"I still don't think—"

He didn't let her finish. Instead, he hunched low and sprinted along the edge of the fence. As long as the jeep patrol didn't come back too soon.

"Can I have your bike if you don't make it?" she called after him.

"Sure. Sell it for a thousand *reichsmarks*." He grinned. There's the old Katarina. "You'll be rich."

But he almost tripped over his own feet when he glanced back one last time. In the distance, just behind the *kirchof,* he noticed a light flicker in the window of one of the apartments. Nothing unusual about that, only—

"What?" Katarina must have seen the look on Erich's face, and she turned to see for herself. Too late, of course.

But before the light went out, Erich was sure he saw the shadow of a man bringing a pair of binoculars to his eyes. Even in the dark there was no mistaking.

Someone was watching them.

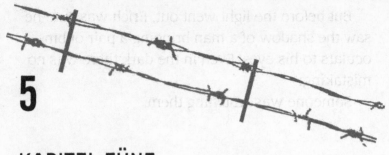

5

KAPITEL FÜNF

CORNERED

Don't breathe ... Erich blended into the shadow behind the American transport plane, waiting for just the right moment as the pair of American mechanics strolled by, their heels clicking on the tarmac. One told a mumble-mumble joke, and the other laughed.

Erich waited.

But this time he knew who to look for, when to look for them, and where the floodlights would betray him. Mechanics hurried by as the planes came rumbling in, right on time, while flight crews and unloading crews scurried from plane to plane. He was pretty sure even Andy, the friendly black American with the chocolate, would not be very happy to see him again so soon.

"Ready to roll again in twenty minutes?" one of the flight crew asked his pilot. The two men paused in front of a truck, barely three feet from where Erich hid.

"Yeah, if we can get the ground crew to get the lead out. This one's full of food."

This one was called the *Berlin Baby*, a name painted on the side by some soldier-artist who had included a funny picture of a diapered baby with wings on his back and coal smudges on his face. Hadn't he seen this one before?

But Erich didn't have time to admire the artwork; he knew he would only have a matter of seconds before the unloaders arrived. So as the men moved away he slipped under the plane and clambered up the rope ladder, as if he belonged there.

Slip in, borrow some groceries, slip out.

But he paused in the airplane's doorway as Katarina's words echoed in his mind.

You may think you have it figured out, Erich, but that still doesn't make it right.

Oh, brother. He gripped the side of the door, trying to take the next step, but he couldn't get his feet to move or his hands to stop shaking. What? And out of nowhere a thought popped into his head.

What would Dad have thought of Erich the Thief?

He knew the answer and sighed. After all these years, the conscience he thought had died with his father ... well, maybe it hadn't died all the way. It wasn't because he was scared, but—

"I can't do this," he whispered, and for an unguarded moment he rapped the inside of the dark airplane with his fist.

But that didn't help. And it didn't help that a jeep was heading right for his plane. Too late! He dived into the plane's belly and out of sight behind a dark pile of crates, wondering what he was going to do now. This wasn't the plan.

Even worse, another worker must have found his way to the plane, right on Erich's heels. Give me a break! Once more Erich held his breath; he was getting pretty good at that. He heard a grunt as someone hauled up inside the plane, then a shuffling sound as the worker came nearer.

"Erich?" came a voice. "Erich, I know you're in here."

Erich blinked back the surprise. Katarina?

"Shh! Back here!" He tried to signal her deeper inside, but he wasn't sure she could see him in the dark.

"Back where?" She stumbled toward him just as the engines turned over and fired to life.

What in the world?

"This one's done, guys." An American bellowed from just outside the door as the engines revved. Americans seemed to do that extremely well. Bellow. Erich had no problem hearing the orders: "Button it up and get on out of here."

What had happened to all the food the men had been talking about outside?

"Wait a minute!" Katarina turned to the door, but Erich caught her wrist just in time and pulled her down to his hiding place.

"We're dead if they find us in here," he shouted into her ear over the roar of the engines.

"We're dead if they don't," she shouted back. "We have to—"

"Hold still for a minute." His mind raced. "We'll think of another way."

Meanwhile, another American shoved a large wooden crate through the double doors and hopped aboard. He pulled the doors shut behind him and threw a strap around the crate before hurrying through the near-empty cargo hold to the forward compartment. The food flight must have been some other plane. Erich held a hand over his cousin's mouth, just in case she had any ideas of calling for help. Maybe they could get back to the door before they took off.

"Whoa! Hang on," he told her. The plane jerked forward as engines revved and they started down the runway. And instead of nearly reaching the door, Erich tumbled and slid through the empty hold, a bowling ball flung down the alley.

"Easy for you to say." Katarina joined him as they tumbled into a heap in the tail section. But by that time they couldn't have bailed out of the plane even if they'd wanted to. All they could do was steady themselves as the plane gained speed, turned, gained even more speed. And it must have been enough for the crate to work itself loose and tumble against the inside of the plane. A moment later he could hear it sliding back to crush them.

"Your legs!" It was the only thing Erich could think of. "Stop it with your legs!"

So they both sat in the tail of the American plane, legs out, waiting for the crushing blow that never came. Instead, the plane lifted off and banked left. The box must have hung up on something halfway back through the plane.

"Let's just keep an eye on it." Erich sat ready to catch the loose cargo with his shock-absorber stance. So did Katarina.

"How did you ever find me here anyway?" he wondered.

"You weren't hard to follow. I thought maybe you needed somebody to keep you out of trouble."

Erich might have laughed if they hadn't been in so deep. Sneaking onto an American cargo plane? Bad enough. Flying off in one? He wondered what the soldiers would do to them when they finally landed at the other air base, or when he and Katarina were found out. It would be nothing compared to what his mother would do to him when he got home.

If he got home.

Right now, though, they had to deal with the Americans. One of them appeared at the door to the cargo hold a few minutes later, probably looking to see what had fallen. He pulled a dark blue baseball cap a little lower over his forehead and carefully made his way toward the back of the plane, gripping handhold loops as he did.

"I thought we tied this stuff down!" he yelled back at the open door. Erich couldn't tell how many others there were—probably at least two flying the plane—but they had already lit a couple of dim overhead lights in the main cargo hold. *Nicht so gut.* Not so good. Katarina looked over at him, and neither of them said a word.

"A wonder we didn't lose these crates through the back end when we took off." The airman talked over his shoulder as if the others could hear him, which they most likely couldn't. From a few feet away Erich could barely make out the man's words.

In any case, the soldier's eyes followed the pile of boxes, still half-secured, back to the loose box snagged on a side door handle, and finally farther back to the two young Berliners huddled in the shadows. Okay, here it came. For a moment Erich thought the guy might jump out of his skin.

"Lieutenant!" He never took his eyes off the kids. "You're not going to believe this. I think we've got us a couple of passengers."

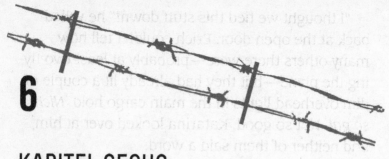

6

KAPITEL SECHS

THE DEAL

"You want to explain to me what you two are doing aboard this airplane?" the pilot growled, and Erich knew that no jokes were allowed here. A younger co-pilot studied them from the right seat, while the man who had discovered them stood guarding the cockpit door, arms crossed.

Not that they had anywhere to run.

"It was—" Erich wanted to be sure he used the right English words. It was one thing to listen to the Americans and British speak, quite another to speak for himself.

"It was all a mistake." Katarina finished the sentence for him. "I was looking for Erich. He is my cousin. We were getting off the airplane, but the plane started moving. We didn't know what to do. We didn't mean to be on the airplane when it took off."

Which was a pretty good try, Erich thought.

"Yeah, I can see how a person might get

confused between a C-54 and the S-Bahn tram downtown." The co-pilot pulled a checklist from behind his seat, as if this sort of thing happened every day. "Can't you, Lieutenant?"

"Humph." The lieutenant wasn't smiling yet, just gripping his steering wheel and staring straight ahead. "Still doesn't explain what you kids were doing on the plane in the first place."

"I was hungry," Erich blurted out. What did they have to lose by telling the truth? The pilot raised his eyebrows as he went on. "And my oma, she is not well. She has not a good ration card, so we must bring her extra food. She has to eat, or she'll die."

"Her and a million other Berliners," the pilot snapped. "So you thought you could just push your way to the front of the chow line, huh?"

"Easy, Lieutenant." The co-pilot acted like a referee in a soccer match. "He's just a kid. Don't you have a son back home?"

Erich was still trying to figure out what "chow line" meant. But finally the pilot's scowl eased up a bit.

"Yeah, about their age." He glanced over at Erich. "What are you, kid, fourteen?"

"*Dreizehn.*" Erich knew the English number; he just wanted to be sure. "Sirteen."

Or "thirteen," if you stuck your tongue out at the "th" sound the way the Americans did. They studied each other for a long moment, the pilot and the stowaway. And still Erich wondered how they would get out of this one.

"By the way, I'm Sergeant Fletcher." The smaller, round-faced man in the right seat nodded at the long-faced pilot. "Lieutenant Anderson's the serious guy in the pilot's seat, and Wilson there is in charge of the maps."

The other men barely nodded as Erich and Katarina introduced themselves.

"Did you fly bombers also?" Erich had to know. Maybe his chin stuck out a bit at the question, maybe it didn't. But the co-pilot whistled.

"Whoa, Lieutenant. I think I know where he's going with this."

The pilot nodded and checked the sky ahead, and Erich noticed the muscles on the back of the man's neck tighten.

"What are you trying to do, Erich?" Katarina whispered to him in German, obviously so the men wouldn't understand. "Have them throw us out of the plane without a parachute?"

Erich stood his ground.

"Er, he likes airplanes." Katarina gulped and tried to explain. "I think maybe he just meant—"

"I know what he meant," the pilot interrupted. His eyes narrowed as he turned back to the challenge. "And yeah, kid. If you really want to know, I flew sixteen missions over Europe. Don't think anybody likes the way it turned out, and I'm sorry about that. Is that what you were thinking? You think I liked dropping bombs?"

When Erich bit his lip and nodded, the pilot turned back to his instruments, mumbling something about Krauts and their lousy war that wouldn't end.

"Gotta admit, I like this duty a lot better," the co-pilot put in, sounding much more cheery than he probably needed to. "Not as many people shooting at us, and the natives are a little friendlier ... well, most of the time."

"Yeah." The pilot kept his gaze steady. "Piece of cake. All we have to do is stay right in the middle of a twenty-mile corridor between Rhein-Main base and Tempelhof, hold at exactly 170 miles an hour, exactly six thousand feet, exactly three minutes behind the last bird and three minutes in front of the next one. And all to feed a bunch of Krauts."

"He's a real nice guy," said the co-pilot with a wink, "once you get to know him. But you two. Anybody back home that's going to be worried about you?"

Erich crossed his arms and said nothing as Sergeant Fletcher asked them question after question, the way a policeman would. Where they lived. Their mothers' names. Where they went to school.

"Stop answering his questions," Erich told Katarina, but she wouldn't listen. The co-pilot wrote it all down on his clipboard.

"I have a feeling your mothers aren't going

to be too pleased to hear you stowed away on an Air Force plane," Fletcher told them, scribbling yet another note. "And by the way, you know what the U.S. government does to stowaways?"

Erich stiffened. But they didn't have a chance to ask before the pilot broke in.

"Hold on, Rhein-Main. How close?" The lieutenant pressed the earphone against his head a little tighter and leaned to check out the front windshield.

"What's up?" asked the co-pilot, snapping to attention and pulling up his own earphones.

"Rhein-Main tower says there's an unidentified aircraft coming right at us, four o'clock."

The words had hardly left the pilot's mouth when a gray streak fell out of the sky, cutting right across their nose. Katarina shrieked and Erich gasped, but the two men hardly flinched.

"Yeah, we see him," the lieutenant spoke into his microphone. "Saw him, I mean. Russki fighter shaved a few of our wing feathers off, is all. Thanks for the warning."

Erich was still trying to catch his breath. Kill him now, or kill him later, what difference did it make? Sergeant Fletcher hadn't finished what he'd started to say about what they did to stowaways.

"Oh, and by the way, tower," the pilot added, "we have a couple of visitors with us that you're going to want to know about—"

Erich looked at Katarina and wished she hadn't followed him to the airport, wished she hadn't said anything to the Americans. Now they knew everything. What kind of trouble waited for them on the ground?

"I'm Sergeant Fred DeWitt." A fresh-faced man in a sharply pressed brown uniform greeted them as they climbed down from the Skymaster to the wet pavement below. "Hold it right there."

Erich grabbed his cousin's arm and braced himself. So this was it. But instead—

"No, no," said the man, whose toothy grin was slightly crooked. "Relax. Here, look at the camera, and don't grit your teeth like that. Smile."

Smile? Is this what they did to all their condemned prisoners? Shoot their pictures before they carted them off to prison?

Pop! The dark-haired man's camera caught them with its flash as they huddled next to the plane, trying to stay dry in the drizzle. But smile, he would not. *Nein.*

"*Furchtbares Wetter heute, nicht?*" the man with the camera asked them in flawless German. Well, *that* got Erich's attention in a hurry, and yes, it *was* horrible weather today, as the man said. Even Katarina stopped shivering to take a closer look.

Some kind of trick?

"*Das tut mir leid,*" he told them. "I'm sorry. I

didn't mean to scare you. I just thought they told you everything."

"There's no telling him nothing, DeWitt." Sergeant Fletcher landed on the pavement beside them. "He's a hard one. And I get the impression he's not all that keen on Americans."

"Thanks for the tip, Sergeant." DeWitt gave the other man a friendly half-salute. "I think I'll be able to handle it."

"Good luck." The co-pilot glanced up at the darkening sky and wiped a sudden splatter of cold rain from his face. "Lieutenant Anderson and I didn't get very far with him. But hey, come to think of it, you speak the lingo pretty good, don't you?"

Their host shrugged as a truck approached to load them back up. The co-pilot stepped aside.

"Well, so long, kids. Hope you find your way back to where you belong."

Katarina nodded politely, but Erich couldn't bring himself to wave at Sergeant Fletcher as he trotted off. Okay, he'd acted friendly. But that meant nothing. And Erich still couldn't just forget who these people were, or what they had done. Katarina looked at him out of the corner of her eye but said nothing. By this time, though, Sergeant DeWitt looked ready to go too.

"Will we be able to go back to Berlin?" Katarina asked, looking back up at the plane. DeWitt laughed, though the question didn't seem funny at all.

"Sure we'll get you back. I've just been assigned to take care of you while you're here in Frankfurt. We haven't been able to contact your families yet, but we're sending a messenger to your homes in Berlin. And we have a plan to get you home."

So that was what all the questions on the plane were about, Erich thought.

"By the way, you ought to be thanking me for getting you out of hot water. Brass was going to send MPs to get you when word got out. I talked them into letting me handle this for a PR project."

Hot water? Brass? MPs? PR? Up to now, Erich thought he'd understood most of what the Americans were saying.

"You are a soldier?" Katarina looked at him with a questioning expression.

"Oh, right." He looked down at the bulky box camera hanging from a strap around his neck. "Guess I'd be wondering too. I'm a reporter with the *Stars and Stripes* newspaper. So yeah, I'm a soldier. Maybe not like some of these other fellows. Came in through the reserves, never saw combat. They found out I had a bad back. So they gave me this camera and told me to go out and write news stories, if you can believe that. I studied history at college, so I guess they thought, *Here's a college boy—*"

He paused for a moment and gave them a sheepish grin, as if he'd suddenly realized he'd been talking too much.

"Das tut mir leid," he told them once more. "I'm sorry. That's probably a whole lot more than you want to know."

Erich still said nothing. What else could they do but follow this man through the drizzle to his car? He seemed about the same age as their mothers.

"Anyway," he told them, "long story short, I've been looking all over for a great human-interest angle for this whole airlift thing, a way to put some real faces on the operation. A good PR angle. Public relations. You know, making sure everybody out there understands what we're doing. So when I got the call from Ops tonight, I knew we had something. You're perfect."

They both looked at him with a blank "huh?" expression.

"Unless you wanted to spend some time with the MPs? You know, military police?"

"Oh, no." Katarina raised her hand.

"I don't think so," Erich agreed.

"That's what I thought you'd say." DeWitt grinned as he reached for the door handle of a gray military sedan. Katarina took the backseat; Erich the front, though he kept his arms crossed. "So I'll take you back to Berlin myself, but we're going to be taking a lot of pictures and asking a lot of questions. Fair trade?"

No trade. Erich knew he couldn't trust this man. But he had to know—

"How did you learn German so well?" he asked.

Because this was way more than just "Guten Mor-
gen, Frau Schmidt" (Good morning, Mrs. Schmidt)
or "Wie geht es Ihnen?" (How are you?). The man's
accent didn't make him sound like a Berliner, but
he could have passed for a Bavarian, easy.

"Oh, right." DeWitt started up the car and put it
in gear. "I was raised by my grandparents in Cleveland, Ohio. Thing is, they both came from Munich,
so they never spoke a word of English to me."

This was getting a little more interesting.

"So I guess you could say I was raised German,"
continued DeWitt, "which sure comes in handy
over here, but it caused me all kinds of grief back
home in the States."

"What kind of grief?" Katarina wanted to know,
then brought a hand to her mouth, as if she'd
asked too much.

"Hey, wait a minute." DeWitt's easy smile spread
across his face once more. "I thought I was the
reporter around here. Why don't you let me ask
you a few questions this time?"

So as they drove through the dark streets of
Frankfurt, he asked them about their home and
about their life in Berlin. And Katarina gave him
the happy version, the one without the hunger
pains and the war, without the nightmares and the
bombing, without the ugly things they somehow
survived but wished every day they'd never known.
Erich knew it was much better to tell those kinds
of stories—rather than the gritty, real ones—like it

was better not to pull off a scab before the wound had healed.

A few minutes later they pulled up to a three-story apartment building, windshield wipers still keeping time.

"You'll be staying here tonight," DeWitt told them. "In my apartment."

"Not an army prison?" Erich wondered, but of course not. DeWitt didn't even carry a gun.

"No, the base doesn't have enough beds right now. Barracks are all full. Although if you'd prefer, I could probably find you a small German jail to sleep in."

Erich shook his head, but the soldier with the camera wasn't finished.

"Listen, I know it's been hard," he told them. "I have relatives over here too, you know. Pretty distant, but my grandparents told me all about them. So if you ever want to tell me your *real* story, I'd be glad to listen. But I understand why you told me what you did."

So he knows what really happened. Without another word, Erich followed his cousin out of the car, back into the rain. And he wondered what else this man might know, this American who was also a German.

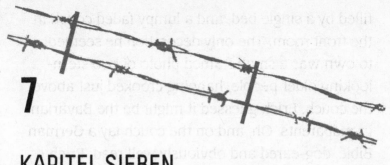

7

KAPITEL SIEBEN

THE STORY

Erich stopped at the door to the apartment. It had once been very nice, with fine wood trim and fancy stained-glass windows. The apartment even shared a bathroom down the hall with four or five other tenants. Imagine that, indoor plumbing! Now the gray and the dust had taken over, just as it had back in Berlin. Someone had tried to sweep the stairs, but even so the plaster ceiling still rained war dust on everything.

"You are not married?" Katarina asked when they'd climbed the stairs to the sergeant's apartment. One look could have given her the answer. Not messy, exactly, just a little like ... a bachelor's apartment.

"Nein." He folded his hat carefully and set it down on the front table. "No."

At least he was neat. But his apartment held only a typewriter on a rickety card table, several piles of papers, an empty kitchen, a small bedroom filled by a single bed, and a lumpy faded couch in the front room. The only decoration he seemed to own was a small framed photo of two stern-looking older people, hanging crooked just above the couch. Erich guessed it might be the Bavarian grandparents. Oh, and on the couch lay a German Bible, dog-eared and obviously well read. Erich figured this was another trick to make them think the American could be trusted.

"So here's the deal," DeWitt told them, opening a tiny coat closet and pulling down clean towels for them. "The *fräulein* will sleep in the bedroom. I have a clean sheet for you. The men will sleep out here. Breakfast is at oh-seven-thirty tomorrow on the base, so make sure you're ready to go by seven fifteen. We'll take a few more PR photos there after breakfast, maybe of you guys standing next to the airplanes, and then catch a flight into Berlin by oh-nine-hundred. That means we land at Tempelhof by eleven thirty. A few more pictures that afternoon around the city, and we'll have you back home safe and sound in plenty of time for dinner. Any questions?"

They both shook their heads no as he grabbed a toothbrush from a glass on a shelf and started for the door. The bathroom, Erich remembered, was shared by the entire floor.

"Sorry I don't have any extra toothbrushes for you. Wasn't expecting this kind of company." He paused and pointed at the couch. "You're welcome to read my Bible while you're waiting, though."

With that he popped into the hallway, leaving them in the strange room in a strange city, wondering how this had happened to them.

"This is all my fault." Erich paced the floor just in front of the closed door. "I shouldn't have let you come."

"It wasn't your decision." Katarina ran her hand across the German Bible. "And besides, I couldn't leave you to fly here by yourself, could I?"

"No, but it was kind of—" He didn't dare use the word *fun*. "Well, I mean, did you ever think you were going to get to ride in one of those planes, ever in your life?"

"Never. But I wonder what our moms are thinking right now."

Erich had been wondering the same thing. "I hope they get the message soon."

"That's not going to keep us from being in huge trouble."

"You're right about that," said their host as he reappeared at the door. "But we'd all better get to bed now. Tomorrow's going to be interesting."

Or *crazy*, perhaps, like this entire adventure was crazy. *Wahnsinn,* insane, like the chase dream Erich had later that night, after everyone had fallen asleep. The men chasing him had no faces, only guns and parachutes, and it was just like the dreams he'd had ever since the war that never seemed to end had started, only in this dream the soldier who finally landed on his head was an American, like—

"Wake up!"

Someone grabbed his shoulder and shook him awake. Erich could only cry out and punch at his attacker. He connected with something hard: a cheekbone, maybe. But the enemy only grabbed him by the wrists and held him. So this is how the torture would begin, but not without a fight.

"Erich!" the man's voice hissed at him in the dark. "Settle down, kid. *Ruhig!*"

Erich couldn't think of too many reasons to settle down, but finally he realized where he was. It was still pitch dark, and a door creaked open behind him.

"Erich?" Katarina asked in a small, sleepy voice. "What's going on out there?"

The neighbors must have heard everything too.

"Herr DeWitt?" An older woman's voice came through the hallway door. "Mr. DeWitt? Is everything all right in there? I heard screaming."

"Everything's fine, Frau von Kostka. I apologize for my guest. He's just having a bad dream."

"Ah, *ja*. It sounded like a battle, and your guest, he was losing."

"I'll bring you a couple of extra potatoes tomorrow, Frau von Kostka. *Gute nacht.* Good night."

"Knowing that will help me sleep better—as long as there are no more battles."

They heard Frau von Kostka shuffling back down the hall as she returned to her apartment. Katarina closed her door again too. And Erich sank his head back into the arm of the couch as DeWitt returned to his pile of blankets on the floor.

"Do we have a truce, kid?"

No truce. Erich pressed his lips together. *But—*

"I'm sorry I hit you," he finally managed. "You're not going to write about this in your newspaper, are you?"

"That depends on how much you pay me."

Erich wasn't quite sure if the guy was kidding, not at this hour. Midnight? Three a.m.? Outside he heard a plane take off in the distance. They weren't very far from the air base.

"Sorry, kid. Just trying to make a joke."

Erich didn't answer as he stared up at the dark ceiling. And it sounded like Fred DeWitt wasn't done asking questions yet.

"I know there haven't been a lot of things to joke about in Berlin lately. Did you have to leave the city during the war?"

Erich thought about not answering, about pretending he'd gone back to sleep. But he had to tell the American something.

"Thanks to you, we did. We were almost killed too."

"I'm sorry to hear that. What about your father? Was he—"

Erich spit out his answer to the dark, which was somehow easier than face-to-face.

"My father was drafted into the army when I was seven. My older sister was nine."

"He was in the *Wehrmacht*, the army?"

Erich paused before deciding to answer.

"A chaplain. He never shot a gun in his life. But just before he had to leave, he went back to the church where he was a pastor, I think to bring home a few things. Then your bombs started dropping. He never made it back." No one said anything for another long minute. DeWitt finally cleared his throat, though, and his voice sounded far away.

"I'm very sorry to hear that."

That's what they all said. But Erich wasn't through yet.

"They told us we had to leave, my mother and sister and I. The bombs were coming day and night, all the time. The city wasn't safe. But you know that part of the story."

Fred DeWitt didn't answer.

"My oma was supposed to leave too, but she was too stubborn. Always stubborn. My mom nearly went crazy about it. We have no idea how Oma survived all the bombs, except that none fell on her building. She always talks about angels."

Still no answer from DeWitt.

"But they took us to a little village a hundred miles north, to get away from American bombs."

Erich made sure he reminded DeWitt the bombs were *American*.

"Is that where you stayed the rest of the war?"

"*Nein*. A few months before it all ended, the government took us away once more, except this time we had to travel in cattle cars, which was horrible because we all got lice from the old straw we had to sleep in."

"I've never had lice."

"It's like torture; they bite you all over. And you get these big welts. But that wasn't all. We stayed in a farmer's barn for a couple of months, and then we nearly froze to death, until my mother decided we should go back to Berlin."

Erich took a deep breath, and it truly seemed like someone else was telling the story, not him. He only felt numb now, nothing else, and he didn't care who was listening. The tears had all been cried, the feelings all felt, and the only thing left was the dull anger. But still he went on.

"So we walked all night and all day, and the roads were full of people who had the same idea we did. Everybody just wanted to get home, no matter what. We could die out there, or we could die back home. Except we didn't know we were walking straight into the Russian battle zone. During the day the Russian planes came flying over, shooting their machine guns at us. We had to dive into the ditches, only some of us didn't—"

His words caught, and he took a deep breath. His voice fell to a whisper, even softer than before.

"—some of us didn't make it. A man that we knew, a milkman from back home in Berlin, he helped my mother and me bury my sister."

There. Was that the kind of story the American had expected? But now Erich had to keep going.

"So we stayed in an abandoned castle for a couple of days, stayed there with only the servants. But there was nothing to eat so we had to keep walking, ten or fifteen miles a day. I had to carry our suitcase, until we found a baby carriage we could use. The baby had died. Don't know why we didn't too."

"And the Russians?" DeWitt found his voice again.

"The Russians came almost every day, just stopped us and pointed their guns at us, took whatever they wanted. What did we have left? Some of those guys had watches all the way up their arms."

"Pirates. But you finally made it home."

"What was left of it, after the Russians—well, we had to hide for a month until the Americans and the British and the French came. But my mom says we were lucky to find another place to stay in. Our old house was a pile of bricks."

"Look, I know I keep saying this, but I'm really sorry."

But Erich didn't say anything else. Couldn't. He

just lay with his eyes open in the dark, listening to the planes taking off and landing, fighting back the sleep and the dreams of the men and the parachutes, chasing him, chasing him—

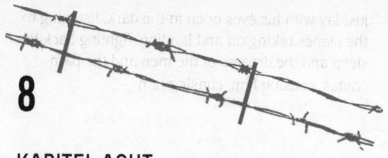

8

KAPITEL ACHT

JUST AN ACCIDENT

"Would you look at that shiner!" Fred DeWitt bent in front of his shaving mirror, squinting at himself.

Erich stretched and pulled the covers back over his head, wondering if he'd really told all his stories in the dark, or if it had been a dream.

Probably a dream. And what was a "shiner," anyway? He peeked out between his hands.

Oh. Now he remembered, and the knuckles on his right hand seemed a bit sore to match.

"You see that?" DeWitt turned toward him and pointed to the dark purple halo of a bruise around his eye. "I haven't had a black eye like that since I was a kid. Good thing it's not going to be me in those pictures."

Erich kept an eye on the man shaving as he slipped on his clothes.

"You're not mad?"

"Who, me?" DeWitt chuckled. "Nah. You didn't know what you were doing. Did you?"

"Coming out!" Katarina knocked from inside DeWitt's bedroom before she came out, but she stopped for a moment in the doorway, staring.

"See what your cousin did to me last night?" DeWitt balanced his army cap on his head and slicked down his hair. "I should have put him to bed with boxing gloves."

"It was an accident," Erich mumbled as he followed DeWitt out the door. Katarina still gave him a funny look, as if she weren't sure she should believe him. But they hardly had time to talk about anything as they followed the sergeant to breakfast.

Erich wasn't sure why DeWitt called it a "mess" hall, since the floors looked clean enough to eat from, and he might have called it a dining hall. But the noise, and the men, and the food!

"Extra big helping of scrambled eggs for my friends here, Sam." DeWitt pointed them out to a large black man standing behind a long counter crammed end-to-end with steaming stainless-steel platters of scrambled eggs, sausages, toast, and a kind of porridge. Erich wasn't quite sure what to do when DeWitt pulled his plate and tray in closer and the cook dished up a huge helping of everything.

"You sure you can handle all that, kid?" asked the cook.

Erich checked his plate, now piled high with breakfast, and he almost grinned. Almost.

"I can handle it."

So could Katarina, for that matter, who put away nearly as much as her cousin, thank you, *dankeshön*. And they were almost through their fourth piece of toast with butter and orange marmalade when DeWitt looked at his watch and scooted back his chair.

"Sorry to cut things short, kids." He wiped his mouth with a napkin. "But we have some snapshots to take and a plane to catch."

Well, that was fine, but Erich still had eggs on his plate. He shoveled as much as he could into the next few bites. If only he could take home even a piece of toast—

"Jussaminute." He held up his hand for them to wait, gasped for air, and felt some of the eggs go down the wrong pipe.

Nicht so gut.

"Ahh-HAACK!" As Katarina pounded him on the back, he couldn't help turning his head to the side and spraying out the half-chewed eggs—

—right on top of a pair of shiny black military shoes.

And no, he really did not want to look up and see whose uniform he had just decorated. Better to slide under the table now. But as he caught his breath he had no choice.

"Er ... Captain Matthews." DeWitt sounded a little edgy. "These are the German kids I told you about. The ones we're doing a story on."

Erich finally gathered the courage to look up at a frowning man in uniform, who looked down at his egg-speckled shoes.

"And we're terribly sorry about that, sir." DeWitt held out a napkin. "But actually, we're a little late, and we'd probably better get going."

DeWitt grabbed Erich's arm as he apologized once more, and they scooted out of the mess hall.

"Don't we have to take our trays back to the kitchen," wondered Katarina, "like everybody else?"

"Not now," mumbled DeWitt. "Just follow me."

They walked over to the airfield, where they spent the next half hour standing beside air crews, saying "Cheese."

"He's just making me more hungry," whispered Erich, "talking about cheese all the time." And Katarina scolded him when he pulled three big packages of Juicy Fruit chewing gum from his pocket.

"Where did you get that?" she asked as they waited for DeWitt to talk to a pilot about their ride back to Berlin.

"Those guys over there gave it to me when we were taking all those pictures. Said I looked as if I could use it. Do I look that desperate to you?"

"Not so much today. Today you just look full. Did you get enough eggs back there? Enough to eat?"

Actually, yes, today he felt full, for the first

time in … well, a long time. He looked down at
the candy in his hands but stuffed it back into his
pocket again when he noticed someone watching
them from outside the airfield's chain-link fence.

"What are they looking at?" he wondered aloud.
But he knew without asking. And it wasn't just one
or two kids now, but three, five, ten of them.

All staring. He tried not to return the stare, tried
to ignore the little question that chewed at the
back of his mind, the question that swirled in the
pit of his stomach and made him want to shrink.

"Almost makes me feel guilty."

Katarina looked at him with a crinkled nose, as
if she didn't understand.

"Do you have a fever, Erich Becker?" She
reached over and felt his forehead with the palm
of her hand, the way a mother would do. "You've
never talked about feeling guilty before."

He felt his pockets to make sure the gum was
still there. Oh, and the Hershey wrapper from
the candy bar he'd eaten himself. At least he had
another one to bring home with him, for Oma, the
way he had promised. But—

"But I ate all that breakfast," he answered. "That
was more than we have in a whole week back
home. For sure a whole lot more than what Oma
gets. Didn't that cross your mind?"

"Of course it did."

Still, he couldn't keep from staring back at
the crowd of kids on the other side of the fence.

Meanwhile, DeWitt motioned them over to a plane near the middle of the lineup.

"Here's our ride," he told them as the last coal-smudged worker came out of the hold, slapping the dust off his hands. "All loaded and ready to fly."

As they stepped closer, a little door in the belly of the plane opened, then shut again with a snap. Not a door, exactly; more like a mail slot.

"What's that?" Katarina wondered aloud.

"Pre-flight," answered DeWitt. "They're just checking everything to make sure it works. That's the flare chute, for dropping out emergency flares."

Erich wasn't sure he liked that word, *emergency*. Hopefully they wouldn't need anything like that. But as he climbed inside the plane, he looked back toward the fence one more time, and he felt the gum in his pocket.

And he started to get an idea.

"Well, if it isn't our friendly local stowaways!" Sergeant Fletcher came out to greet them in the crowded cargo hold. It was stuffed to the gills with bulging burlap sacks. He grinned and slapped Erich on the back. "Ready to head back home?"

"Just a few more photos." DeWitt explained what they'd been doing as they took their places behind Lieutenant Anderson, who grunted and nodded at them as he went through his pre-flight check. Fletcher didn't seem to notice his grumpy pilot.

"Did you see that horrible mess?" He pointed with his thumb at the back of the plane. "I thought

we were doing just fine carrying flour and pow-
dered milk. But somebody got the bright idea to fill
us up with sacks of coal. My clean airplane!"

The lieutenant kept flipping switches but paused
a moment to catch his co-pilot's attention.

"Pre-flight checklist, Fletcher."

"Right, sir!" Fletcher grabbed his trusty checklist as they worked, flipping switches and pulling
knobs, adjusting levers, checking and rechecking
each step. The pilot would bark things like "Bypass
valve down!" (whatever that meant), and the co-
pilot would echo every word. Erich watched, though
he did take a moment to poke at the flare chute just
behind the pilot's seat. His idea could work.

Ten minutes later the four engines finally roared
to life, each one in turn, sending storms of smoke
swirling behind them. Throttle up. All four engines
spun up to full power as the plane lurched and
bumped through puddles on its way to the head of
the takeoff line, then forward faster faster faster,
until they nosed up and left the muddy airfield
below.

"Think you'd ever like to fly a plane like this
someday?" DeWitt asked Erich above the roar of the
engines a few minutes later. Erich nodded before
he could catch himself. Well, what did it matter? He
looked over at the bundles of parachutes tucked
under a seat. He couldn't do this by himself.

"Do you have any handkerchiefs, DeWitt?" Erich
pulled the gum from his pocket, and the American

gave him a puzzled look. "All we need are a few handkerchiefs and some string."

By the time they approached Tempelhof Airport, Erich and Katarina held three handkerchief parachutes ready, each one tied with string at its four corners and each one carrying a pack of Juicy Fruit.

"Hold one of the chutes up for me." DeWitt aimed his camera at Katarina, and the flash went off. "Perfect. In fact, this whole idea is perfect. Don't know why I didn't think of it myself. This is going to be front-page."

"I didn't mean for it to be on your front page," mumbled Erich. Maybe he'd made a mistake.

"Just don't get in my way," growled their pilot as they once again neared the city.

"You're sure the chutes won't just land on the roofs of one of those ruined apartment buildings?" Fletcher wanted to know.

"Kids will find them," Katarina told him. "Especially over the Russian sector. They watch the planes."

"The Russian sector?" Lieutenant Anderson frowned. "Nobody said anything about the Russian sector. We drop stuff over there, and we're going to stir up a hornet's nest of trouble."

"Oh, come on, Lieutenant." DeWitt folded the parachute back up and carefully wound the string around it before handing it back to Katarina. "It's just candy. What can it hurt?"

"I'm telling you, it's a bad idea."

Erich bit his lip, wondering if the lieutenant might be right. What *would* the Russians do if they saw little parachutes coming down on their territory? But by that time DeWitt was grinning and snapping photos nonstop as Anderson and Fletcher worked to bring the plane in low and slow over the city. The lieutenant called for their before-landing checklist, and Fletcher knew the drill.

"Heater switches off," barked the pilot.

"Off."

"Main tanks on."

"On."

And so a little lower, even lower than the tops of some of the crumbled apartment buildings. Katarina, who knew the Russian sector as well as anyone, served as spotter. She chose Fletcher's window and gave them a running review of the city below.

"Wait a minute, Katarina." Erich watched the roofs below and felt his stomach turn flip-flops. "We'd better not do this."

"Too late," she told him. "We're coming up on the Tiergarten! And oh, there's the Brandenburg Gate! We're going so fast. The *Versöhnungskirche* is coming up. I see the steeple, near Oma's apartment. That would be a good place. Is the little door open?"

DeWitt pried open the little door and *whoosh!* Even at landing speeds, the wind rushed by the plane outside. And for a moment Erich panicked as he thought of what it must have been like for the men who dropped bombs over this same city, not so long ago.

"It's fine." DeWitt didn't look worried. He just held one of the gum parachutes ready and looked up. Katarina held up her hand and counted down from three.

"*Drei, zwei, eins . . . now!*"

"Chutes away!" Erich and the American stuffed the three bundles out, one after the other, and Erich wondered how much trouble they would be getting into because of this silly idea, or who would find the treats. One of the hungry kids on Rheinsbergerstrasse, probably. DeWitt whooped, then straightened up when Lieutenant Anderson shot a glance over his shoulder.

"Done yet?" asked the pilot. "I don't want those things snagging my landing gear or nothing."

"No snags," answered DeWitt. "But that won't be the last time we do this."

"No kidding?" Fletcher glanced out the window, and DeWitt pointed at him.

"Absolutely positively. You, my friend, are going to help us with the biggest gum drop in history."

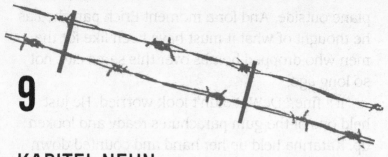

9

KAPITEL NEUN

FIRST MEETING

"You've never been in a taxi before, have you?" De-Witt grinned at them in the back of the car.

Was it that obvious? Erich tried not to look so stiff as he watched Urbanstrasse go by. Imagine! Riding in a taxi for a walk home that would take only twenty minutes, at the most! He wondered what the kids in the neighborhood would think when they saw him and Katarina with the American soldier.

"My father took a taxi, before—" Katarina's voice faded, and it reminded Erich he wasn't the only one who had lost family during the war. Outside their window, though, it looked as if the war had never ended. On the corner a half dozen street people nearly mobbed a man as he set out a garbage can with restaurant food scraps. The grin left DeWitt's face.

"We bring a little extra food to my grandmother

every week," Katarina told him, as if that had something to do with it. "But still she is hungry."

"It's tough everywhere in the city." DeWitt nodded and looked away from the scuffling and shouting. An older man had claimed a handful of potato peels and was doing his best to fight off the others. "But we'll see if we can bring her something."

"She lives in the Soviet sector," Erich told him.

"Oh." The man's face fell even more. "That's not good."

"We've tried to talk her into leaving." Erich thought it never hurt to ask. "Maybe she would listen to you."

"Wish I could help you." DeWitt shook his head slowly. "But there's really nothing I can do. I can't even cross the line, the way you kids can."

Maybe true. Still, it seemed as if the American should do *something* to help Oma.

"This it?" DeWitt looked out at the battered apartment building. And no wonder he asked. The building next door had been hit by a bomb during the war, taking it from four stories down to one and a half. Much of the outside wall between the two had crumbled as well, taking with it most of Frau Landwehr's living room on the third floor of their building and forcing the *frau* to find another place to live. The rest of their building seemed to sway in the wind, and only half the windows had survived. Herr Eickmeyer on the fourth floor had a great view of Tempelhof from his open patio (which had, before the bombings, been his kitchen).

"Second floor," Erich announced as he jumped from the taxi. "Follow me."

Katarina paused by the curb for a moment. "Want me to come along?"

"Maybe that's a good idea." Erich looked up at their window too. "My mom won't kill me if you're there."

"We did our best to explain to your mothers," DeWitt told them as he bounded up the short flight of front stairs. "But I can't guarantee anything."

Except that he would be charming and funny and make it sound like a grand adventure—in perfect German, which of course led to the story about growing up with his German grandparents in Cleveland, Ohio. Erich's mother listened to his story, wide-eyed, and then apologized many times for not having any coffee to serve her American guest.

"I'm so sorry, but I traded our last ration for bread, and—"

"I understand." He twisted his hat in his hands as he sat on their most comfortable living room chair, the one with the stuffing escaping the sides. "And now I hope you'll understand about your children. I mean, about your son and your niece. They were only trying to find food for their grandmother."

"Yes, I know." Frau Becker lowered her eyes. "We pray for her every day, but—"

"Erich told me about her." He nodded and looked as if he understood, while Erich's mother glanced up once, blushed, and returned her gaze to the worn rug. "And I want you to know that I appreciate kids who care the way they do."

She nodded as he went on.

"Although next time they go flying with us, we'll want to make arrangements first."

This time it was Erich's and Katarina's turn to stare at the rug.

"I'm very sorry they put you through all this trouble." Erich's mother was still apologizing.

"Not at all." He shook his head. "As it turns out, my editor is pretty excited about all this. We have some incredible photos so far, and the wire services are already picking up the story. Erich and Katarina are going to be in papers all over the world."

"This is what I sent you to do?" Frau Becker looked at her son sideways, but the twinkle in her eyes told Erich he was probably safe. Hopefully Katarina still had the measure of flour for Oma, as well.

"But only if it's all right with you," DeWitt told her. "I want to be sure we have your permission."

"Of course." Frau Becker smiled.

"And I want you to have this." DeWitt held out a

bulging cloth sack. "Just to thank you for letting me work with the kids."

"Oh, my goodness!" Frau Becker's eyes lit up even more as she pulled out cans of Spam, condensed milk, and peaches.

"Just a few things from the commissary that you probably can't get around here lately. Maybe you can share them with your mother-in-law."

Frau Becker hid her face in her hands and cried, which only seemed to confuse the American.

"I didn't mean to upset you, Frau Becker. I just—"

"You're very kind," she interrupted him. "It's just that I haven't seen this kind of food for so, so long."

And it didn't seem so strange, then, when she laughed softly over the food, the kind of laugh that says, "I can't believe this is happening to me," and asks, "Am I dreaming this, really?"

But Erich enjoyed the sound; in fact, he couldn't remember the last time he'd heard his mother laugh. For sure before Father had died. And he knew just how she felt as he quietly lifted the peaches, to be sure he wasn't just seeing things. Real American peaches, packed in syrup from Oregon, United States of America. He tried not to drool. After so many months of eating hard bread crusts, he wasn't quite sure how to deal with all this food, this real food. Just as he wasn't quite sure how to deal with this American.

Because, wait a minute—the man had to want

something. They all did, and as DeWitt talked about his German grandparents again the thought came crashing back on Erich like a door slamming in his face. Of course. No one gave away food for free, just because. Erich could have kicked himself for letting down his guard, for believing it, for not seeing the strings attached.

"Look, I have a three-day pass for this assignment," DeWitt said as he rose to his feet and fitted his hat to his head. "If it's all right with you, I'd like to see if we can get some more pictures of the kids and the gum drops, maybe from the ground this time, if we can get some other planes to do the drops too—"

"Gum drops?" Erich's mother didn't quite follow.

"Oh, I'm sorry." DeWitt chuckled. "I didn't tell you about that."

And as Katarina told the story of the candy parachutes, Erich backed away slowly, trying his best not to get caught in the web his mother had stepped into. Surely he'd made a mistake helping this DeWitt. Even Katarina looked as if she'd let down her guard, lured on by all the food. Who wouldn't be? But Erich wanted to shout: "Don't you see? This man isn't what you think he is! He's an American, and you can't trust people who bomb us one day and pretend to be our friends the next!"

But nothing would come out of his mouth, so he just slipped to the edge of the room with his arms crossed and his mind racing. There had to be a

way out of this trap. Meanwhile, DeWitt told them
he'd be back the next afternoon at three, flying
over with more gum, and would the Reconciliation
Church still be a good place to drop them?

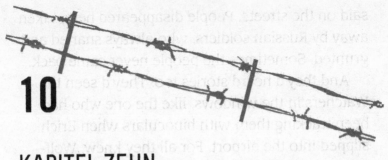

10

KAPITEL ZEHN

HEAD-TO-HEAD

"Well, he's not my aunt's *friend,* exactly." Katarina did her best to backtrack, but the next afternoon the kids in their oma's neighborhood weren't buying it. "He's just an American newspaperman, and he's doing a story on the gum drop. That's what we're helping him with. That's all."

"You're helping an American?" An older boy named Wolfgang scowled at them with his big hands on his hips, then looked around at the group of kids who had gathered. Though he stood a head taller than most of them, he hadn't ever really been a bully before—just a pain. Now he acted like both. "Did everybody hear that? Katarina and Erich are working for an American soldier!"

"I'm not," Erich said as he crossed his arms, but no one heard.

How else were they supposed to answer? Erich didn't forget where they were; in the Soviet sector of Berlin, you had to be very careful what you said on the streets. People disappeared here, taken away by Russian soldiers, who always snarled and grunted. Sometimes the people never came back.

And they'd heard stories too. They'd seen the Watchers in the windows, like the one who had been tracking them with binoculars when Erich slipped into the airport. For all they knew, Wolfgang was feeding the Russians information too.

"It's just for a newspaper. Just some pictures." Erich tried to make it sound like no big deal, but so far it wasn't working.

"Then where did you get all the food, if he's not your mom's *ami*?"

Wolfgang leaned on the last word, *ami*, and everybody knew about *amis*. The American boyfriends who visited the homes of the women who had lost men during the war. The soldiers who came to visit with food, or cigarettes, or sometimes fancy clothes.

"Katarina told you he's not my mom's *ami*." Erich stood up to Wolfgang and clenched his fists. No one had the right to talk about his mother like that. She hadn't done anything wrong.

"Prove it." Wolfgang stood where he was and kept the mocking grin pasted on his face.

"We don't have to prove anything to you." Katarina wasn't backing down either, bless her heart. This bigmouth was talking about her aunt, after all. "All you have to do is stand right here in the *strasse* while the American planes fly over, only don't get run over, of course, and in about fifteen minutes you'll see."

They hoped. DeWitt had promised he would be on the flight from Rhein-Main arriving right at three o'clock, hadn't he? And while Erich didn't trust the American's word for a minute, now probably wasn't the best time to say so.

"I'll see *what*?" Wolfgang laughed. "Is your mom's *ami* going to wave at us as he flies by?"

"You'll see." Katarina sounded more sure of herself than a girl had a right to be.

"Humph." Wolfgang still wasn't convinced, but so what? "He's going to have to do something pretty special, because in a few days the capitalists are going to be leaving the city with their tails between their legs."

"What's a capitalist?" asked a little blonde girl named Ilse.

"He means everybody but the Russians," explained Katarina.

"But that's stupid." Erich kept his arms crossed as he looked straight at Wolfgang. "Who told you that?"

"My teacher. We're going to be learning Russian too. Pretty soon it'll be the world's language. Is your mom's *ami* teaching you English?"

Erich might have hit him then; Wolfgang deserved it. But Katarina pulled him back by the shoulder, and his hands flew up for balance.

"It's not worth it, Erich." Katarina was probably

only trying to help. Trying to keep him from getting into trouble. Trying to help him turn the other cheek, the way it said in the Bible.

But either Wolfgang hadn't read that verse or he didn't care. Because a moment later he tackled Erich and they tangled on the street, arms and legs flying. Katarina was there too, yelping and elbowing her way into the middle of the fight, while all the other kids gathered around and chanted, *"Am-i, am-i, am-i!"*

Or something just as brainless. It all just sounded like a roar in Erich's ears as the blood pumped in his head and he tried to stay alive. His chin throbbed with pain all over again. And he felt a punch connect to his ribs, then another. He heard the larger boy's grunt, felt Wolfgang's hot breath and forearm choking him. But the strange thing was that once Wolfgang had tackled him, all the hot, angry feelings dribbled away. Erich only wanted to keep from being choked to death.

"Am-i! Am-i!"

What was wrong with those kids? They cheered as if they were watching a soccer championship, only this match was over as quickly as it had started. Erich felt the lashes of the cane, saw Wolfgang roll away and scramble to his feet before running off with his crowd of squealing rats. Then Erich heard the scolding voice of his oma over everything, as in, "What in the *world* is going on here?" and "What are you thinking, attacking my grandchildren? Hoodlums! Go home!"

She helped Erich to his feet with a firm grip on his ear. Katarina saw the kind of help he was getting and jumped up without any help, thank you. Then he had to explain what happened as Oma herded them back to her apartment.

"No grandchildren of mine are going to behave like this."

"But—"

"Is that what you want people to know you for? For street fighting?"

"No, Oma, but—"

Finally back in her apartment, she settled into her easy chair as if the effort had taken more than she had to give. And it had. She dropped her cane to the floor in front of her and coughed long and hard, so long and hard that Erich thought about running to fetch a doctor. Her face turned blue, and her hands shook as if she had been the one beat up, not Erich.

"And this — ," Oma finally managed, sort of catching her breath. "This is the kind of Christian example you want to set? They'll know you are a believer because of the way you use your fists?"

"No, Oma." Erich patted her on the back; what else could he do? "But he said Mom had an *ami*."

Their grandmother stiffened at his words and looked over at him, her eyes barely open but now blazing and alive. "Oh, so he said that, did he?

Well, then I hope you gave him a good poke in the nose."

With that she closed her eyes and rested her head back against her pillow. But her breaths sounded even more short and shallow, rattling and deathly. Erich straightened his shirt and looked over at Katarina. The look on her face told him she knew too. It was going to take a whole lot more than Fred DeWitt's food to help their Oma Poldi survive the summer.

As they thought of Fred DeWitt, the rattling windows told them an American plane had come in low once again, winging over the city toward its touchdown at Tempelhof. Erich and Katarina couldn't help looking out the window, staring at the dozens of little white parachutes that blossomed in the sky over their city.

"He's really doing it." Erich's jaw dropped open, and he counted ten, fifteen, no, at least thirty little parachutes. Most drifted directly down onto Rheinsbergerstrasse, where they'd been fighting just a few minutes earlier. Well, yes, this *was* where they'd told him to drop them, but—

"Did you think he wouldn't?" Katarina glanced back to check on their now-sleeping grandmother.

"How should I know?" Erich just shrugged. But as they watched, he had no doubt what was happening below them. A handful of the neighborhood kids jostled and jumped to catch the parachutes as they drifted to the street. Who had ever seen anything like this before? The kids giggled and laughed at the candy rain of chocolate and gum and other sweets—until an ugly snub-nosed Soviet army truck came flying around the corner. One little girl barely made it to safety as the truck screeched to a stop in the middle of the street and two soldiers jumped out.

"Hey!" Erich almost leaned out the window to shout, then thought better of it. "Those soldiers need to get their own candy."

But the men shooed the kids away like flies and scooped up as much of the treasure as they could. The good thing was that some of it had fallen out of reach onto a nearby rooftop, and some had disappeared into a pile of rubble. A couple of parachutes even got hung up high in the bell tower of the *Versöhnungskirche*.

Still, the blank-faced soldiers managed to corral most of the booty. Some they tossed into the front seat of their jeep; some they held up to the light of the sun to study a little more carefully. Well, sure, it might look like a candy bar, and it might taste like a candy bar, but it could still be an American trick. A nuclear bomb shaped like a piece of gum, perhaps? And even if it wasn't, no telling what would happen to these children if they were allowed to eat a few sweets, especially when they were starving to death.

"Look at Ilse." Katarina giggled and pointed at

the little girl on her knees, peeking around the truck. "She's trying to grab a piece before it's all—"

Erich saw her. Too bad one of the soldiers did as well. He stomped on the candy chute with his big black boot before poor Ilse could quite reach it.

"Hey." Erich groaned, but of course they couldn't have helped her, even if they'd been down on the street. They could only watch as the soldiers picked up the last few candy chutes, barked at the kids to clear the street, and then roared away in a cloud of thick black smoke. No doubt the Soviets would protest this to the American military leaders very soon.

Finally the smoke cleared. Kids came out from their hiding places once more, careful at first, then dancing and hollering and waving their prizes like trophies of war. The soldiers hadn't been quick enough to grab everything.

"Look what the *ami* dropped for us!" yelled a little guy named Rolf, skipping in circles and holding out his parachute. He popped the gum into his mouth and started chewing as if his life depended on it. "Katarina was right! *She was right!*"

So she was. Ilse had grabbed a piece of chocolate and started skipping around with the rest of them, waving her prize in the air. She stopped once in a while to smell it and hold it up, studying it almost as the Soviet soldiers had.

Only one of the kids wasn't dancing. Wolfgang just stood in the middle of the dance, staring up at

Erich and Katarina with his hands on his hips as if it were all their fault that such a wonderful, horrible thing had happened on Rheinsbergerstrasse. Shouldn't they be sorry for bringing this capitalist candy down on everyone's heads? Erich couldn't help feeling a chill creep up his spine before the other boy finally turned and marched down the *strasse,* looking very much like a soldier himself.

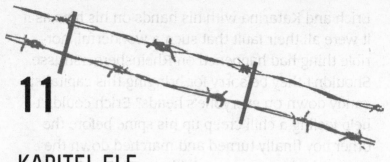

11

KAPITEL ELF

LUTHER'S KEY

"This is wonderful to have you all here, so wonderful," Oma said, looking at her family the next Sunday. Her eyes glittered with tears, and her voice trembled when she spoke, as if the words might shatter before they reached the ears of the people sitting around her little kitchen table. They'd walked over together after church. Oma had set out her only lace tablecloth and a small tapered candle she'd saved for a special occasion. She had chairs for herself and the two mothers, wooden boxes for Erich and Katarina, and a sturdy pile of books for Katarina's seven-year-old sister, Ingrid. It didn't matter that they knocked elbows or that the chairs teetered dangerously. As Oma said, "Ein gemütlich abend ist." And a festive evening it was. Especially with all the food they had brought with them, most of it hidden under their clothes to avoid attracting the attention of soldiers on the street. Yes, a feast!

"A whole can of American Spam meat," Oma wheezed, "and those berries—"

"Cranberries," Erich's mother told her, picking up the can from its place of honor on the table. "It's something they grow in America. The sergeant said it is festival food in his country, for their special giving thanks dinner."

"*Cran*-berries." When Oma said the word it sounded more like *krrrahn-behr,* and they all had to laugh. The problem was, that only set off Oma's coughing once more.

"Have you been to the doctor again, Oma?" Katarina's mother asked. Concern wrinkled her round face. She tried to offer a glass of water, but Oma only shook her head no.

"They tell me there is nothing to do about it, but to go home and die." Oma plucked the handkerchief from the pocket of her apron and breathed through it like a mask. "The young Russian medic even told me to try not to breathe, since that would only make it worse. Ha! Do you think he was serious?"

Even as sick as she was, she could still tell a joke on herself. But Erich's mother wasn't laughing.

"I'm serious, Oma," Erich's Aunt Gerta said. "The doctors we have over in the American sector are much better. A little medicine could help."

"Maybe it would. Maybe it wouldn't."

Erich knew his aunt could say nothing else to her mother-in-law. They didn't want to get into *that* argument again, about leaving this house or this neighborhood. And they would not argue about being friends with the American soldiers, either, not unless they wanted to upset Oma, make her start coughing again.

"So tell me," Oma began, managing to change the subject. "This DeWitt, he is your friend?"

Erich couldn't remember seeing his mother turn so red before.

"I don't think we could call him a *friend* exactly, Oma."

That's for sure, thought Erich, taking a bite of meat and rolling it around in his mouth.

"I don't want you to think wrongly of me," Erich's mother whispered.

"Wrongly?" Oma shook her head and rested her hand on her daughter-in-law's shoulder. "You've cared for your family through all this time, and now you've come back to care for me. You will do the right thing once more. Just like Ruth."

Ruth from the Bible. Naomi had lost her husband and two sons, but her daughter-in-law, Ruth, stayed by her, even when she didn't have to. Come to think of it, maybe his mother really *was* like that. But when the subject changed to serious stuff like ration cards and food lines, Erich decided it was time to let the adults talk. After clearing their dishes, he and Katarina headed outside.

"You remember that story too?" Katarina asked

as she and Erich tripped down the *strasse* toward the church.

"You mean about Naomi and Ruth? I'm a pastor's kid, remember?" And that made him think of something his mother had talked about once, something he'd been meaning to do. He told Katarina his plan and looked up at the *Versöhnungskirche* bell tower, just around the corner on Ackerstrasse.

"Are you sure you want to go this way?" Katarina asked.

This way would lead them right past Wolfgang's house.

"He's just the neighborhood watchdog." Erich tried not to notice the eyes that watched them go by. "I don't understand why he cares so much about where everybody goes."

Katarina shrugged her shoulders. She didn't seem to mind as much as he did.

"Maybe he's training to be a Russian spy."

They both laughed, while Erich looked back once more to make sure Wolfgang hadn't followed them.

But getting away from Wolfgang wasn't the hard part.

The hard part was actually making their way through the church building, once they'd pushed open a splintered door, past piles of bricks and chunks of stone.

"Wait a minute." Erich paused for a moment at

the back of the sanctuary, where the late-afternoon light spilled in from above. Even more filtered down around the bell tower, where he could see two of the gum drop parachutes, tangled in the spire.

No one had yet cleared the rubble from this part of the church. Snow and rain from the last few years hadn't made things any better. It was going to take a lot of work to make this a place where people would come to worship again.

A lot of work. Gaping holes reminded Erich of the beautiful stained-glass windows he'd loved to stare at, back when he was little.

"Erich, I'm totally confused. Do you remember where your father's study—"

They both jumped when something fluttered just over their heads, but Erich had to laugh.

"Just a couple of pigeons."

They watched a pair of birds circle once inside the sanctuary before they found the hole in the roof and disappeared outside. A couple more cooed and purred in the shadows, the way pigeons do. And though Erich had been inside the old church building hundreds of times before, he still paused to find his way.

"It's weird." He shook his head. "Everything's so different from what I remember. Scrambled and jumbled and wrecked."

"I don't like it." Katarina kept her arms crossed as she picked her way over a pile of bricks. Her shoes crackled on the broken colored window glass. "We're in big trouble if any of the Russian guards find us."

"Would you stop worrying? They don't ever come in here."

He hoped not, anyway. Once Erich had his bearings, he led the way over a collapsed section of wall and down a side hallway. Here and there they had to stop and crawl over piles of plaster rubble and cracked building stones and pieces of splintered beams.

"Careful." Erich helped his cousin over a pile near the end of a dark dead-end hallway and looked around. At the doorway to his father's little study, the charred door now hung by just a single hinge. Inside, a half-burned pile of papers and books had been swept into the corner, as if by a giant hand. Pigeons in the far corner stared at the intruders. Only one piece of furniture survived—his father's solid walnut desk—but it was mostly charred and had been crushed on one side by a fallen ceiling beam.

"Wow. It looks so different in here," Katarina whispered.

It seemed right to whisper in a place like this, like at a graveyard. Erich nodded then fell to his knees and began digging through the pile of papers and books.

"Your mother has never been back, has she?"

"Are you kidding?" He shook his head no. "Seeing all my father's stuff like this would kill her."

And what really was left? Nothing you could call a memory, exactly, not like what he was looking for. Only shredded records and damaged books. As he dug deeper, most of the paper fell apart at his touch. Deeper still, he found a few books that had survived with only a ripped spine or a blackened cover.

"Look at this." He held up a copy of an old theology book, mostly whole, and another that had been buried. That one had his father's name in the front, handwritten. He set it aside to take home. And the deeper he dug, the more books he found. Mostly in German, but a few in English, by authors like Dwight Moody and Brother Lawrence. And then—

"Luther," he whispered, and he held the book up with two fingers. Compared to most of the other stuff in the pile, it still looked okay. He blew the dust off and read the title on the cover.

Dr. Martin Luther's Sämtliche Schriften.

Collected Writings, the book his father had talked about just before he died.

But Erich wasn't sure what he would find inside: A note? An inscription? Maybe nothing but Luther's sermons. If nothing else, Erich would at least save this one, though it reeked of dust and mildew like everything else in the pile.

"Open it up!" Katarina leaned over his shoulder. Another book for her collection? She'd probably want to read it.

But not this one.

Erich whistled when he opened the book and discovered its hollowed-out insides. But hollowed out on purpose. Each page had been carefully cut, leaving a square hollow in the middle big enough to hide—

"It's a communion cup." Erich picked it out and held it up to the light. The silver cup looked tarnished and a bit smaller than usual—not much bigger than a cup that might hold a soft-boiled egg. "The kind pastors take with them to visit sick people."

"But why did he hide it in this book?" Katarina wondered. Erich had no idea, but he noticed something else inside the hollowed-out section.

"A little key!" The kind that might open a suitcase or a jewelry box.

Katarina pointed at it. "Just like in a mystery book."

"Huh?" Erich didn't follow.

"You know. The hero finds a mysterious key, and nobody knows what it fits until the end of the story, and then they find a treasure in a pirate chest. But you don't read those kinds of stories, do you?"

"Nope." Erich grunted, glancing around. "And I don't see any pirate chests in here."

"That's just in the stories, silly. There has to be a good reason your father hid this key in a place like this."

"And then he tried to tell my mother about it." This was beginning to sound more and more like one of Katarina's stories, after all. They'd have to do a little more searching to see if this key fit anything in the ruined study. But as Erich picked up the little key by its faded blue ribbon, they heard voices echoing down the hallway from the sanctuary.

"Shh!" Katarina tilted her head, as if that would help her hear better. She listened for a moment before whispering: "They're speaking Russian."

And they were getting closer.

"You sure?"

"We need to get out of here."

Erich didn't argue as he slipped his two new treasures into his pocket. He would come back for the books. But surely no one had seen them sneak inside the church, had they?

Wolfgang!

"This way." Katarina found her way past the half-crumpled desk and through a gaping hole in the wall of the study, back to the hallway. "Hurry!" Erich looked back to see a Russian soldier catch sight of them as they slipped around a corner. Erich stared at him for just an instant—long enough to see the man's black eyes and square jaw. He looked more like a shark than a man, and Erich felt more like a fish about to be eaten for lunch than a thirteen-year-old. Well, he had never seen a shark, but he'd seen pictures in school.

"You there!" shouted the Shark in thick-accented German. "Stop!"

Sorry, not this time. Erich and Katarina flew down the hallway and around two more corners, up a short flight of stairs, and right through a flock of pigeons.

"Whoa!" Erich held up his hands as dozens of wings batted him in the face. Katarina did the same, but was quicker to vault over a broken door to a back exit. A moment later Erich brushed the feathers out of his face as they burst outside and sprinted down Ackerstrasse, back toward Oma's apartment.

He didn't dare look back.

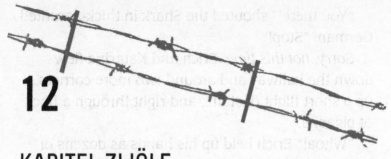

12

KAPITEL ZWÖLF

EMERGENCY CALL

FOUR WEEKS LATER...

"Oh!" Erich mumbled to himself as he opened their front door and stepped back to let Fred DeWitt inside.

Four times in four weeks.

But the airman pretended not to hear.

"Hey, bud!" DeWitt was all smiles, as usual, as he stepped into the tiny living room. And as usual he carried his bribe: another bag of food. "Your mom around?"

Well, that was a dumb question, and Erich let him know as much by looking around the room as if she might be. By way of a short hallway, the kitchen joined the living room, where his mother had set up a sheet curtain around her bedroll for privacy. She had pulled it back neatly before she left, though, and tied it off with a piece of colored yarn. Erich's blanket lay rolled up in the kitchen next to where he slept on the floor, and the little kitchen stood empty.

So no, she wasn't home. Obviously.

Neither of them said anything for a long, awkward moment. Of course, it wouldn't have been awkward if the guy would just leave them alone, if he would just leave Erich's mother alone.

"I guess that's a no." The sergeant didn't seem to let it get him down. "You expect her back very soon? She's off work, right?"

"She's out standing in some line to get more of that cornmeal stuff."

The stuff that made Erich want to throw up. The stuff that answered the question: what's worse than having nothing at all to eat?

"Oh. Well, listen, I feel bad about that." He set down his paper sack on the folding card table in the kitchen. "So I brought you some more stuff. Another can of peaches. You like those, right? And some canned tuna. You ever had tuna fish sandwiches?"

Erich stared at him blankly. He didn't mean to be rude, but he just couldn't pretend to be this man's friend, no matter how often Katarina told him he should try.

"Hmm," DeWitt said and then went on. "Anyway, you just mix it up with some mayo, see?" He paused. "Right; you don't have mayo. Well, you don't have to mix it up with anything. You can just serve it straight on a piece of bread."

Another pause as he thought that one through too.

"Right. No bread, either. Well … you don't need to add anything at all. You can just eat it straight out of the can. How does that sound?"

Erich shrugged and the American smiled.

"There you go. It's all I could bring you right now, but I'll get some more on my ration card next week, soon as I can."

"Thanks." Erich nodded, still holding the open door, hoping the man would get the message.

Instead, DeWitt crossed his arms and leaned against the wall.

"Listen, I know we got off to a rough start, and—"

Erich didn't look at the man. He studied his shoes as DeWitt continued.

"—and I don't know exactly what happened here, but maybe we can start all over, huh? I introduce myself, you introduce yourself, like we never met, see?" He put out his hand. "Hi, I'm Fred DeWitt from Cleveland, Ohio. Pleased to meet you."

Erich didn't shake the outstretched hand of the man from Clevelandohio; he just bit his lip and, without thinking, looked up at the photo of his dad on the wall. It looked like the one in Oma's apartment, only in this one his father wore his pastor's robe, looking proud and excited and grinning from ear to ear. Erich's mother had told him it was taken the day his father was ordained as a pastor.

"Ohh, I get it." DeWitt nodded as he lowered his hand, but he didn't get it. The American didn't get anything. "You think I'm trying to elbow my way in here and steal your mom away, is that it?"

Erich didn't answer. He looked down again and could almost see his own reflection in the guy's black military shoes. And he kept his arms crossed as DeWitt stumbled on.

"Listen, Erich, I don't have any . . . That is to say, I'm not . . . I'm just trying to—"

Trying to what? Erich waited while the American tried to untie his tongue. But it wasn't as much fun to watch as Erich might have expected. With a sigh and a "Skip it!" DeWitt finally gave up and headed for the door.

"Oh, by the way." He reached into his shirt pocket and pulled out a folded newspaper clipping. "My picture—I mean, *your* picture, you and your cousin catching that parachute candy that we got Fletcher to drop out of his plane? It got picked up by the *New York Times*, which, if you don't know, is a really big deal. Page three"—he tapped the clipping—"right next to the article about how the airlift brings this Cold War right back to the Russians."

"Oh."

"Look, I just want you to understand I wasn't trying to use you and your cousin for a big story.

I'm not trying to get you mixed up in the politics of this whole thing. That's just the way it turned out, and I apologize for making you … I don't know."

"What kind of politics?" Erich didn't quite follow.

"Oh. You know, the Russians against the Americans stuff. The Cold War. Well, look around you." He pointed out the window at a C-54 dropping from the sky on its final approach to Tempelhof. "That's the Cold War, right there. Us versus them. Like it or not, we're right in the middle of it."

That part, Erich understood. Maybe more than DeWitt knew. But the American wasn't finished.

"It's just that the pictures turned out better than anybody expected, and now my editor wants more. A follow-up story on the kids of the Berlin Airlift, right? People back in the States are eating it up."

Erich had to think about that one for a moment. The sergeant was always saying things in a funny way.

Eating it up?

DeWitt held out the clipping once more. "So, anyway, I thought you'd want your own copy. For your scrapbook, huh?"

"Thank you." This time Erich forced himself to be polite, but he couldn't think of anything else to say, and he didn't have a scrapbook. DeWitt rubbed his forehead for a moment and stepped into the hallway, which turned out to be perfect timing.

"Fred!" When Erich's mother saw DeWitt at

the door, she nearly dropped her little parcel of rationed cornmeal. A smile lit up her face. "I was hoping you'd stop by. Will you stay for din—"

That's when she must have realized what she was holding.

"Oh, I mean ... if you don't mind cornmeal soup."

DeWitt glanced briefly at Erich and shook his head no.

"Thanks, uh, but no. Nothing against cornmeal, actually. Just wouldn't be right to eat your food. And I, uh, I have to get back to the base. But I left a couple of things on the kitchen table ... thought you might, well—" He turned again to go, this time for real. Frau Kessler from across the hall poked her head out her door, checking to see what the American was doing. Erich's mother frowned, mostly at Erich.

"He's just leaving, Frau Kessler. And thank you, Fred." She started to wave with her free hand, then changed her mind and folded her fingers one by one before poking Erich in the ribs.

"Ow!" Erich yelped, but he knew what his mother wanted him to say. "I mean, thank you, Fred."

He wasn't sure DeWitt heard him, anyway. And he wasn't sure why he went to the living room window to watch the American step onto the sidewalk, look both ways, and hurry down the street.

But that's not what caught Erich's attention. He

might not even have noticed if he hadn't seen the man move inside the old gray Mercedes.

Actually, it looked like two men. One in the driver's seat, the other putting on his hat and slipping out the passenger door to the far sidewalk. And when the passenger looked straight up at the window, Erich was quick enough to back away—but not before he got a pretty good look.

"Can't be." Erich caught a quick breath as he backed even farther into the living room and tried to think of what to do. Good thing his mother had already gone into the kitchen to see what DeWitt had brought them. Because he was willing to bet a whole can of peaches that he had seen the man before, back in the ruins of the *Versöhnungskirche*. Even from across the street, it was hard to miss the square jaw and dark eyes.

The only thing was, the man didn't have on a Russian uniform this time. In the American sector of Berlin, he'd better not. No telling what would happen to him if he were caught. Erich understood this part of the Cold War.

He just didn't understand why the Shark was following Fred DeWitt.

If it really *was* the Shark. Erich would have liked another look, just to be double-sure. But when he checked again, the car had gone. And thirty minutes later Erich had other things to worry about when he answered the urgent pounding at the door.

Erich cautiously opened the door. "Herr Kessler?"

The red-faced apartment manager pushed his way inside.

"Frau Becker!" Herr Kessler headed straight for the kitchen. "You'll want to hear about this urgent telephone message right away!"

"Urgent?" She looked up from the dishes in the sink. "Who sends us an urgent message?"

"That's just it!" Herr Kessler only got this worked up when the plumbing plugged up or the coal ran out. "He sounded Russian. But he didn't give his name."

"Well, that doesn't matter. Just tell me what he said." Erich's mother offered the man a sliver of canned peach on a plate. He licked his fingers after downing the treat, looking for more payment. And he got it. After all, the building manager and his wife, the spy, owned the only working telephone in the entire apartment building.

"He just said that he had visited your mother-in-law in her apartment and that she was in critical condition, that you should come quickly because the accident had been quite serious."

"Accident? Quite serious?" Frau Becker gasped and set the remaining canned peaches down on the table. "What did he mean by that? Did she fall? Does she need to go to the hospital?"

"I just take the telephone messages, Frau Becker." Herr Kessler kept his eyes on the can.

"Although it does seem as if he said something else, perhaps. You don't happen to have any more of those American peaches, do you?"

"Mom!" Erich whispered, too late. His mother had already offered their building manager the last of the fruit.

"Help yourself, Herr Kessler," she told him. "It's the least we can do for your kindness."

"Dankeschön." He smiled and inhaled the rest of the treat in one swift move before scratching his bald head. "Thanks so much. Now I remember."

"What do you remember?" Erich had to know too. "What did the doctor say?"

"Erich!" His mother scolded him while Herr Kessler wiped his mouth with the back of his hand.

"That was all, actually. He said nothing more before he hung up. I remember it clearly now."

Erich would have thrown the empty can at the man if his mother hadn't held him back.

"We're grateful to you, Herr Kessler." And two minutes later they were on their way to Oma's apartment once more, after leaving a message for Katarina's mother. At least the Mercedes hadn't returned to its parking spot across the street. Still, Erich checked up and down Oranienstrasse as they hurried to catch the S-Bahn, one of Berlin's streetcars.

"They'll be along," his mother told him. "They" meaning Katarina and her mother. "I think they're still waiting in a line somewhere."

Like everyone else in Berlin. But they would
make it to Oma's soon. Erich checked over his
shoulder once more, just to be sure no one else
was following them.

13

KAPITEL DREIZEHN

HELMUT WEISS, CHURCHMOUSE

"Brigitte?" Oma Poldi's face showed her surprise as she opened her door wide and motioned for them to step inside. "A pleasant surprise."

"Wait a minute." Erich's mother stopped short in the doorway. "What are you doing out of bed?"

"Bed? It's only eight o'clock, child. A summer night in August, and it's too warm to go to bed early. I may be old and sick, but—"

"No, but is the doctor still here? We came as soon as we could."

"Doctor? What doctor are you talking about?"

"The doctor that called our apartment house an hour ago," Erich explained. This was getting too strange. "The one who told Herr Kessler to tell us that we should come right away, that you might die."

Oma Poldi, in her flowered pullover dress,

looked as though she might start coughing any minute. But near death?

"You didn't actually talk with this ... this doctor?" asked Oma.

Erich's mother shook her head no. "Only Herr Kessler, who passed along the message."

At this Oma Poldi leaned her head back and laughed, which was probably a mistake, as it set off her coughing. They had to wait several minutes while she caught her breath once again.

"I wonder if you gave him something for his trouble?" Oma finally asked, still wheezing.

"Of course."

"Nearly a half can of American peaches!" Erich put in.

"There, you see?" Oma had it figured out, this mystery. "Kessler is no fool, only a liar and a thief. He sees something he wants, and he finds a way for you to give it to him. So he makes up the story about me on my deathbed, which is not so far from the truth, after all, so you believe it. He makes up this pretend doctor, and the pretend urgent telephone call. You are in his debt. 'Oh, *dankeschön*; thank you so much, Herr Kessler. You will have some peaches, *bitte*?' Humph! Not such a mystery."

"That makes sense," replied Erich's mother, "except Herr Kessler didn't know about the peaches before he pounded on our door."

"If not peaches, then something else," replied Oma.

"But what about when we found out the truth?" Erich wondered. "Did he think we would just come home and say, 'Oh, well, that was a funny joke'? What would he do then?"

"Maybe he didn't think it through that far." Oma shrugged. "Men can be like that, you know."

Maybe. Erich still had a hard time believing old Herr Kessler was that good an actor, though. And he worried about who had really called them, and why. He couldn't shake the image of the Shark outside their apartment. But as far as the ladies were concerned?

"Well, never mind," said Oma. Then she offered to make tea for them, and they shared the few crackers Erich's mother had brought along.

"I'm going outside for a few minutes," Erich told them. He checked his pocket to make sure he still had the key. "To see if Katarina is coming."

Or maybe their friend Wolfgang would be waiting for him.

It didn't matter either way. Waiting for Katarina and her family gave him time to search his father's study again. This time without the Russians on his tail. He hurried outside, munching his half-cracker, keeping one eye over his shoulder.

Was that man a half-block behind following him? He couldn't tell. But when he stopped at an *apotheke,* a pharmacy, the shadow also stopped.

And when he sped up, the shadow also sped up. He passed two Soviet guards, laughing and smoking on the corner of Ackerstrasse. They stood at attention as the shadow passed by them.

Not a good sign. And Erich could not forget where he was: in the Soviet sector.

Why did I come out here alone? he asked himself.

He sprinted around the corner in front of the church, ducked into an alley, and counted to *neunundneunzig*, ninety-nine. A mother walked by pushing a stroller. A couple of old people, going slow. A group of four young women, probably off work for the day. But no shadow.

So okay. He darted across the alley and approached the ruined church from the back, where he and Katarina had made their escape the other day. No one seemed to notice on a Thursday evening; everyone probably just wanted to be home. He pushed past a temporary fence and slipped inside.

And if it had seemed dark before, this time ... he held his hand out in front of him and felt the way with the toe of his shoe. At least he'd come prepared, with a candle stub and a single match. He would save them, though, until he approached his father's study once more. There! The candle flickered and cast a pale puddle of light, a meter to every side.

Once more he stood in his father's study, the same way he had when he'd been five or six, only it had seemed so much bigger then. Now it hardly seemed the same place. Then, his father would sit at his desk, writing sermons. His bookshelves covered the walls. Now, nothing looked right, and he could find nothing that would fit the key. Not even close. What did he expect? A magic door? After several minutes of fruitless searching he sighed and leaned against the wall.

"Why did I come here?" Hot wax dribbled onto his finger, and when he jerked back, the candle blinked out—just as a hand came down on his shoulder.

"I have no idea, preacher's boy. Why *did* you come here?"

Erich might have died right there if the man hadn't held on to his shoulder. And honestly, he tried to scream, but nothing came out of his mouth except a chattering "yaa-yaa-yaa!" Too bad Katarina wasn't here this time; she could have let loose with a real screech.

"Relax." The man spoke softly, as he might to a scared animal. He stepped back and lit a small candle lantern of his own. "You're not in trouble, not with me. Now, the Russians who were following you the other day, that could be another thing."

"You, you know who I am?" Erich croaked as he tried to get a closer look at the man's wrinkled face. But he had seen hundreds of men like him in Berlin. Scarecrows, really, with sad, hollow sockets for eyes and sunken cheeks that made them look like concentration camp survivors. The skin around his arms hung loosely, as if he had once filled out his frame much better.

"You don't remember, of course." A shadow passed across the man's expression as he looked up and around. "I used to clean this building, keep the furnace lit, dust the altar. That kind of thing."

Once he got used to the man's toothless lisp, Erich could follow the words plainly. And yes, he *did* remember, though faintly. A large round man who laughed, an old man even back then. The maintenance man, Herr—

"Helmut Weiss." He nodded when he said it, the way a doorman or a train conductor might. "Glad to serve you."

Glad to serve me? As if he had stumbled upon some long-lost family butler. But yes.

"My mother—" A ghost of a thought tickled the edge of Erich's memory. "My mother used to pack little *pfeffernusse* cookies for my father's lunch. Well, they weren't really *pfeffernusse*, since we didn't have any sugar or eggs. But she tried. I would bring them at lunchtime, and we would leave some for you on a plate."

The man chuckled and closed his eyes. "You *do* remember."

"But what are you doing here? And how did I not hear you come up behind me?"

In other words, what kind of ghost had he met in this spooky old church?

"I live here, young Master Becker." He carefully scooted a twisted book aside with his foot. "Actually, not in this room, but in another, that is, in the basement. I've learned to get around."

Erich shivered to think of someone actually living here, someone watching him and Katarina as they walked through the building, someone slipping through the shadows.

"Isn't it cold and damp?"

"I don't mind so much, living as a churchmouse. No one bothers me. And the pigeon eggs, well, they're small, but tasty. Perhaps you'd like to try some?"

"Nein, danke." Erich shuddered and tried not to look at the man's haunted face. "No, thanks. I was just looking for—"

But he couldn't finish the sentence, and his hand went to the key once more. Maybe Herr Weiss could help him. Maybe not. Erich wasn't sure if he could take the chance. Better to ask questions than tell secrets. The old man held up his lantern and looked at Erich more closely.

"You look just like your father, you know." That seemed an odd thing to say in a place like this, in the ruins of his father's life and work. "Your father was a good man."

"He was, until the Americans did all this." Erich couldn't help kicking at a stray piece of plaster. "Until they killed him with their bombs."

Herr Weiss said nothing for a long moment, only

breathed in through his mouth, making a raspy wheezing sound.

"This is what they told you? That your father was killed in a bombing raid?"

Erich felt himself tense up, as if he'd put up his fists. Who was this man, really? What was he saying?

"Isn't that what happened?"

Herr Weiss turned deadly serious, and the look on his face made Erich shiver.

"Listen to me, young man. Your father was not killed by an American bomb, and his death was no accident."

"What do you know about that?"

Did Erich really want to know? This was getting ridiculous, this strange meeting in a ruined church. Was this man crazy? But once more Herr Weiss turned quiet, and when he spoke again, Erich had to lean closer to hear him.

"I can't tell you the whole story, but this much I know: your father was involved with something ... something against the Nazis. A plot of some kind. Something very dangerous. They came to ask him questions many times. And the last day you saw him?"

By that time Erich was nearly face-to-face with the man, hanging on every word.

"He was not killed here in the bombs. *They* took him away."

Erich didn't need to ask who *they* were. The

Gestapo— Hitler's secret police. So it wasn't the Americans, as he had believed for so long?

Erich finally broke away, shaking his head. "I don't believe you." He stumbled backward and sat down hard on a pile of books. "You're just making up stories."

Herr Helmut Weiss looked at him with his sad, sunken eyes. He held out his hand to help Erich to his feet.

"I wish I were, Master Becker. I wish I were."

So did Erich. Maybe it was the sad shock of what Helmut Weiss had told him. Or the look in his eyes. Either way, Erich could not stop the tears, as if they had been stored up for all these years. Now he knew, and he wished he didn't. It had been easier just being mad at the Americans.

He turned away and buried his face. And as his shoulders shook with sobs he felt the horrible weight of this new truth. Love your enemies? Easy for Katarina to say. But he'd been so good at hating these people, maybe too good. Now, if he was honest, he couldn't think of a reason to keep it up, anymore.

I miss you, Papa.

After a couple of minutes, he gulped for air and tried to dry his eyes on the dusty sleeve of his shirt. When he felt ready to stand, he reached for Herr Weiss's outstretched hand—just as the man stiffened and turned his head.

"What's wrong?" Erich didn't hear anything. But like a bat in a cave, Herr Weiss seemed to know.

"Someone's come in the front doors." His whisper blew out the candle. "You will leave the back way again, as you did the other day. Quickly!"

There would be no argument with Herr Weiss, who disappeared the same way he had appeared—without a sound. Erich had no idea how someone could be so quiet. He felt his way out of the room, praying that whoever had entered the church would make more noise than he did. Once again Erich left the Reconciliation Church with more questions than answers.

14

KAPITEL VIERZEHN
BORDER STANDOFF

"Too bad you couldn't have asked that man more questions." Katarina kept her voice down that late-summer night as they walked ahead of their mothers by a few steps. Another half-block and they'd be back in the American sector, almost home.

"Well, you should have been there, then. I didn't have a chance." Erich dragged his feet a little, which wasn't so odd, considering everything that had already happened that night. And though it would have been nicer if they'd had the money to ride a tram this time, it really hadn't taken long for them to walk the mile and a half from Oma's apartment. Just long enough to tell Katarina everything that had happened in the church—from the stranger in the shadows who had followed him, to the odd church janitor who had told him about his father.

Her eyes grew wider with each detail as they neared his apartment building on Oranienstrasse.

They could almost see it, on the other side of the line between the American and Soviet sectors, which sort of wandered through this neighborhood. Except for the signs, you couldn't always tell just by looking where one sector stopped and the other began.

But Katarina held back.

"What's wrong?" asked her mother, bumping into them from behind. Katarina pointed up ahead.

"Someone," she whispered, and Erich followed her gaze to see someone sitting in the shadows of the apartment building's front steps.

"Is that Fred?" Frau Becker's step lightened. "I hope he hasn't been waiting for us all this time."

Well, he might have. But whoever had been there disappeared just as a car parked on the Soviet sector side came to life and raced at them, its lights on full bright. They jumped out of the way, but the old gray Mercedes bumped onto the sidewalk. Erich's mother held her hands in front of her face as the car shrieked to a stop. A man stepped out to meet them.

"Pardon the interruption, Frau Becker." The uniformed man stepped in front of them to block their way. Erich gasped when he saw the square-jawed outline and the black shark eyes, the twin row of buttons on his uniform jacket and the peaked military hat. No telling what rank this man was, though clearly he was some kind of officer. "We've been wanting to speak with you and your son for quite some time."

Well, then you certainly made the grand entrance, didn't you? Erich didn't dare speak the words.

But his mother didn't shrink back. "Who are you? And how do you know my name?" She kept a hand on her purse and the other on Erich's arm. Katarina and her mother held back in the shadows. And the dim glow from a nearby streetlight caught the man's toothy grin as he bowed his head slightly.

"Captain Viktor Yevchenko, at your service. And if you've forgotten where you are, I'd be happy to remind you." He still blocked the way, only ten feet away from the American sector. Ten feet away from freedom.

"We know where we are," Erich answered him.

"Then perhaps you also know that in this part of the city *we* will ask the questions. And for the time being, you will consider yourselves our guests."

"A guest would get an invitation, right?" Erich blurted out. And even though his mother shushed him, he had to know. "You're the one who called today. The phony doctor. Isn't that true?"

A wild guess? The shark eyes twinkled for a moment, and Captain Yevchenko grinned again as he looked at Frau Becker.

"Your son is very bright. We'll have much to discuss, the three of us. You other two—" He snapped his fingers at Katarina and her mother, dismissing them as he would a servant. "You will go home now, please."

"We're not leaving our family." Katarina's mom planted her feet.

Which was awfully nice of her to say, just maybe not the best timing. Erich glanced over at his cousin, and for a moment he thought they shared the same idea. They could outrun him. But what about their mothers? She shook her head, and he knew she was right.

As if reading his mind, a uniformed Russian bodyguard stepped from the car. Even in the dark, Erich could see this was the kind of guy who filled out the uniform pretty well. His neck looked as wide as his head. And he made sure they could see the blunt gray rifle slung over his shoulder like a guitar, his finger on the trigger. So much for the idea of running away.

"Oh, yes, you will leave." This time Captain Yevchenko wagged a finger at Katarina and her mother. "Immediately, please. Your friends will be back home in no time at all."

"I demand to know what this is all about!" Erich's mother dared to raise her voice, though the Russian hardly blinked, only pointed his square jaw at her.

"You're quite a talented actress, Frau Becker. But let's stop playing the innocent bystander, shall we?"

When she didn't answer, he went on.

"Or perhaps your son should tell you what he's been doing searching through forbidden buildings and restricted areas. Did you know about that? Surely you already know about his association with the American agent, since you seem to have frequent contact with the spy yourself."

"The spy?" she whispered.

"Humor me just a little, Frau Becker. We're talking about the American who drops propaganda by parachute into the Soviet sector. The one with the camera who is responsible for so much anti-Socialist propaganda. He's using you for his own purposes, woman. Or maybe you don't see past the cigarettes and the nylon stockings he brings you."

The words hit Erich like a slap in the face. DeWitt. This was all about Fred DeWitt. Did the Soviets really believe the American was a spy, or were they just sore at him for making such a big deal about the gum drop, making them look bad?

"Now, please," he went on. "It's late, and I have been waiting far too long." This time he grabbed Erich's arm and pointed to where the guard stood by an open car door. "You will come with us now."

"Let go!" Gun or no gun, Erich wasn't going to just get into the car without a fight. He dug in his heels and squirmed, whipping his arms around and trying his best to land a good punch. Captain Yevchenko was more than ready for him, though. And his arms were longer than they had looked, plenty long enough to hold Erich off. He simply twisted the collar of Erich's shirt until Erich fell to his knees and gasped for breath.

"You're making this rather difficult for everyone, Erich." Captain Yevchenko wasn't even sweating. "Now straighten up and act like a man. You can help us."

"Noooo!" Naturally his mother came to the rescue, but by that time the bodyguard had stepped up with his gun and jabbed it hard into Erich's side. "Oh!" Erich doubled over with pain as tears came to his eyes. And Frau Becker would probably have grabbed the rifle if the bodyguard hadn't hit her across the cheek with the back of his gloved hand, sending her tumbling to the ground.

"Nobody hits my mom!" Erich tried to face the man but felt his legs buckle beneath him. He didn't think Jesus had this kind of thing in mind when he said to turn the other cheek. Or did he?

"That's enough." This time the command came from an American. And Erich had to say that for the first time ever, Fred DeWitt's voice sounded wonderful. Beautiful, even. Erich curled up and hugged his side, trying not to sob or throw up, while his mother held her arm around him.

"Sergeant DeWitt!" Captain Yevchenko sounded glad to see him. "I was wondering how long it would take for you to join us. This is good. I'm sure we will have a fruitful discussion on matters of mutual interest. If you come a little closer, you might find that we can help each other."

"Tell your thug to back away from these people." DeWitt didn't sound like he was in the mood for a fruitful discussion.

Captain Yevchenko sighed. "Ah, but I think you're forgetting which side of the border you're on. Remember that over there, you can do nothing. You can't set one polished boot over here. In fact, I can't even seem to hear you, and that's quite a shame, isn't it?"

"Then maybe you can hear this."

Everyone froze when they heard the plain *click* of a gun, ready to fire, a sound that seemed to echo through the now- deserted street. Erich looked up slowly to see that DeWitt still stood planted in the American sector. But the serious military handgun he pointed at Captain Yevchenko could surely hit its target from ten feet.

"Now, let's do this slowly," came DeWitt's steady voice again. "I want your friend to set his rifle down on the street, and both of you to get back into your car."

"You have no right! We're simply attending to state security matters." Yevchenko's expression had turned to stone.

"It's a little tough to find the exact border in some places, don't you think?" DeWitt's aim remained steady. "I might cross over by mistake."

"You're not serious. Now let's just—"

"You don't want to find out how serious I am."

DeWitt's voice told anybody listening that he wasn't kidding. And after a couple of strained words from Captain Yevchenko, the Russian weapon clattered to the pavement. Erich didn't want to touch the rifle, but now that he'd caught his breath he didn't mind kicking it away, out of reach. It stuck barrel-first into a heavy steel grate of a gutter storm drain, which gave him an idea. Ignoring the burning pain in his side, he got up and grabbed the wooden stock, yanking up with all his strength. As he'd hoped, the steel grate held the business end of the rifle in place, and he had just enough leverage to bend the end of the barrel slightly. He pulled it free and tossed it back toward the car, twisted and useless.

"I always thought it would be fun to be able to shoot around corners," Erich told them. "Now you can try it."

DeWitt raised his eyebrows but held his own gun steady.

"The gun is of no consequence." A black fire still glowed in Captain Yevchenko's eyes, and he lowered his voice so that only the two of them could hear. "But I do fear for your safety, young man. And that of your American friend."

With that, Captain Yevchenko picked up the useless rifle and returned to the car with his bodyguard. And though each breath felt like the stab of a fire poker in his ribs, Erich knew he had to help his mother to safety. Katarina and her mother scurried away, as well.

"Don't tell me you read a book like this once." Erich took his cousin by the arm as they hurried to the safety of the Beckers' apartment. DeWitt would follow them, while the Russians' car left with a squeal of tires and cloud of smoke.

"No." Katarina wasn't saying much, just shaking her head. She looked almost as pale as his mother. "I haven't ever read anything like this."

"Are you all right, Mama?" He looked to his mother, who had collapsed in tears on the stairway halfway up to the second floor. DeWitt bounded up to help them back to their apartment. Erich pretended his side didn't hurt as he brought a damp washrag for his mother. Her cheekbone was already turning purple where Captain Yevchenko's thug had hit her.

"Don't let those jerks scare you." DeWitt had to be trying awfully hard to sound so cool and collected. "Although you probably shouldn't go visit the Soviet side again anytime soon."

Erich knew he'd better tell them where he'd seen the Russian pair once before, here on their own street, in the middle of the day. But as he watched DeWitt, he couldn't bring himself to say it. Another question burned his tongue.

Since when had DeWitt the newspaperman started carrying a gun?

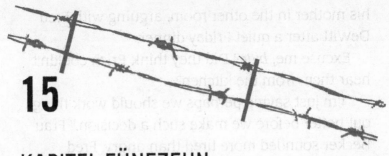

15

KAPITEL FÜNFZEHN
THE ANNOUNCEMENT

THREE MONTHS LATER . . .

One good thing about their little apartment: from their kitchen window (and even a little bit from the living room), Erich had no trouble following the parade of C-54's coming in for landings at Tempelhof, which he thought was a lot more interesting than doing math homework. Especially when they'd let go with a load of candy parachutes once every couple of days for three whole months: September, October, and November. Even his mother liked to watch and remind them how much she loved chocolate, and would *someone* run out there and get her some?

So it didn't matter how noisy the planes turned out to be. On the other hand, a lot of other noises came through their thin walls just as easily. Herr Meyer belching below them. Frau Braun's yappy dog next door, who barked at shadows. (There had been a lot of shadows in November.) And now his mother in the other room, arguing with Fred DeWitt after a quiet Friday dinner.

Excuse me, *bitte*? Did they think Erich couldn't hear them from the kitchen?

"I'm just saying perhaps we should work things out better before we make such a decision." Frau Becker sounded more tired than angry. Fred DeWitt just sounded confused.

"I don't understand. Yesterday we agreed, but now today?"

"Fred, you understand what I'm saying. It just seems like everyone is against us."

"Name one person."

"Your grandparents in Ohio. That's two. Also my mother-in-law, when I checked on her last week. She smiles and says it's all fine, but I can tell."

"You went over there again?"

"I had no choice, Fred. No one followed me. Maybe they've forgotten."

"I still don't like it."

"Even so, you ask who is against us. What about your commanding officer? And I didn't even mention Heinz."

"Oh, Heinz; come on. Since when do you have to get an okay from your older brother to get married? He's Communist, for crying out loud."

Erich caught his breath at the words. One, because his mother never talked about Uncle Heinz. All Erich knew was that his mother's brother had worked in Moscow for a few years, and they hadn't heard from him, well, until now. Definitely the black sheep of the family.

And of course the other thing that stopped his heart was the "M" word. Make that the "H" word in German. *Heirat.* Marriage. Had Erich really heard them right?

Erich's mother didn't answer right away. But when she did she sounded far away and weepy.

"I'm sorry, Fred. Everything's happened too fast. I know we need to trust God, and we can't worry so much about what other people are saying. But still. When your commanding officer says that he'll do everything in his power to prevent you from marrying a German woman, doesn't that concern you?"

"Bigots don't concern me. All that concerns me is serving God and marrying you."

"You'd better be careful how you talk about your commanding officer, Sergeant DeWitt." But she giggled when she said it. By this time Erich was pretty sure they'd forgotten he was in the apartment. He wasn't sure if he should clear his throat so they'd hear him, move closer to the wall so he could catch every word, or plug his ears and start humming to himself. Option A, B, or C.

He chose option A, except he knocked into one of the kitchen chairs on his way to the short hallway between the two rooms.

"Oh, Erich!" His mother looked up at him with

wide eyes when he picked himself up and stepped into the living room. "I thought you were outside."

"Well, I was this afternoon," he reminded her, "but then I came in for dinner. Remember?"

Remember, Fred DeWitt came over for dinner, the same way he had been doing for the past several months? Remember the can of American pork and beans he'd brought with him? Her face flushed for a moment as Erich headed for the door.

"Maybe I'll go see what Katarina is doing," he mumbled.

"No, wait, Erich." DeWitt had been pacing by the threadbare sofa. "Your mother and I have something we need to tell you."

Erich didn't like the way that sounded, not at all. *Your mother and I.* He gritted his teeth and braced himself against the wall, the way an old guy might if he were expecting a heart attack. This would be worse.

"I already heard." Erich looked at the floor. Why did it come as such a shock? Maybe Fred DeWitt wasn't such a bad guy, after all. For an American, that is. Ever since the standoff with the Russians, Erich had learned to see some of the man's better side. DeWitt seemed to care about them. He'd been to church with them, said he loved Jesus, and Erich didn't have any real reason to doubt the man's word, other than the fact that he was an American. At least DeWitt always acted like a gentleman around Erich's mother, which was more than he could say for some of the other soldiers he'd met.

And his mother seemed to like him. A lot. This is what people did who really liked each other. Erich couldn't get himself to use the word *love,* though, not for anything. Just couldn't, because he still guarded a part of his heart somewhere, still kept the door closed and locked. But this was his mother's heart they were talking about. His didn't matter.

"You didn't hear the whole story, though, Erich."

"What's to know?" He pinched his lips together so he could spit out the words a little easier. "You want to get married. You should get ... married."

His mom glanced at DeWitt before turning back to him with a "please listen" in her eyes. All right, then. For her.

"I'm resigning the service," DeWitt told Erich. "I'm not going to re-enlist."

"Oh." That wasn't quite what Erich had expected to hear, but all right. "So what are you going to do?"

"Not just *him,* Erich." Erich's mother tilted her head to help get her point across. "Us. It's what *we're* going to do from now on. And we want you to be a part of that decision."

"Wha-what kind of decision?" Erich felt his heart race as he began to understand. As if he were in a tunnel and he saw the train coming straight at him. Because if Fred DeWitt wasn't going to be in the Air Force anymore, he would go home to Clevelandohio. And not just *him*—

"We can get married here in the *missionskirche*," his mother went on. The Lutheran Mission Church. Of course not the Reconciliation Church, where his parents had been married, where Erich hadn't been since last summer.

"And then what?" He turned away so they wouldn't see his tears, which welled up out of nowhere. "Are you going to go to the United States? Is that what you're saying? Leave Berlin?"

"Would that really be so bad, Erich?" his mother's voice pleaded now. "You know this hasn't been an easy time, or an easy place to live. Not during the war and not since."

"But things have been getting better, haven't they? And Oma always says this is home, no matter what."

Erich crossed his arms, remembering how stubborn his grandmother could be. Stubborn about living. And stubborn about dying.

Well, he could be just as stubborn.

"Did you hear what I'm trying to tell you?" His mother's voice faded back to the present. "I . . . that is, we want you to be as excited about this decision as we are."

Erich swallowed hard and nodded. Next they would tell him how much he would like Clevelandohio. Well, maybe so and maybe not. But in his heart he knew this was not a battle he would win, wasn't even sure it was a battle he wanted to fight anymore. A few months ago, maybe ... probably. Yes. But not now. And when he looked back at his mother's hopeful, tear-brimmed eyes, he knew he would not hurt her by digging in his heels.

"You understand what your mother is saying, don't you, Erich?" DeWitt looked him straight in the eyes, expecting an answer that Erich didn't have words for yet.

"I still have a lot of things to figure out."

What else could he say? His mother started to shake her head, warning DeWitt not to push anymore.

"I understand." The man rested his hand on Erich's shoulder. Big mistake. Erich shook free and headed for the door before he said something dumb, something he would be sorry for later.

"You don't understand anything." *No, no, no.* He bit his tongue. He'd only meant to think it, not say the words out loud. But his tongue seemed to have its own mind.

"Wait a minute, Erich. We're not done here."

"Fred, no." This time Erich's mother took DeWitt's arm, but the military man wasn't through.

"I don't know about you," Erich snapped, and wished it hadn't come out sharp enough to cut, "but *I'm* done."

Erich pulled at the door. *Out, out.* Anywhere but here. Before his mother started crying. Didn't

DeWitt see? But DeWitt didn't see; he just parked his toe to stop the door.

"Why do you always think I'm stupid, Erich? You really think I haven't lived at all? That I don't know what you're thinking?"

"I don't think you're stupid." Erich tugged at the doorknob. "I just don't think you understand me. You speak German, but—"

"Yeah, well, you're not the only guy on the planet who ever lost his dad. Did you know mine left when I was twelve? So I think I know just a little bit of what you've been going through. If you'd just stop running away—"

Erich stared at the door as DeWitt's words echoed through the room.

"I didn't know that," he finally breathed and let the doorknob go. He felt low enough to crawl under the closed door. Instead, he wandered over to the window.

"You weren't supposed to. But I'll tell you, kid ... maybe we have more in common than you think."

"Maybe." And this time he didn't tense up just because DeWitt rested a hand on his shoulder. He tensed because of what he saw on the street below, through the window.

"Erich," his mother told him, "I know it's a big adjustment. We can talk about it some more later."

But Erich hardly heard her as he backed away from the window. After all these months, why now?

"The Russians," he whispered. "They're back."

"Are you sure?" DeWitt moved to the side of the window and peered out from behind the curtain. "I don't see anything now."

Erich peeked again, and the car had disappeared. Was he seeing things?

16

KAPITEL SECHZEHN

LAST GOOD-BYE

This time Erich didn't care if the Russians followed him or not, or whether he had really seen them or not. What did he have to tell them, anyway? They were wasting their time, following the wrong person. He ran with his head down, faster and faster until his lungs could not keep up with his legs, and he finally had to stop and breathe. By that time a drizzle had soaked through his shirt, but he didn't care about that, either. Didn't care about the tears that ran down his cheeks and mixed with the rain.

He had been right about one thing.

He did still have a lot of things to figure out, a lot of things to think through. Would going with his mother and DeWitt to Clevelandohio really be so bad? He sighed. Maybe not. DeWitt said that in Clevelandohio people didn't go to bed hungry. In Clevelandohio, the buildings weren't all bombed out and empty. In Clevelandohio, everyone drove their own automobiles, and there were no Russian soldiers in Clevelandohio.

So maybe Clevelandohio would not be that terrible, after all. He wiped away another stupid tear, hoping no one saw him on Ackerstrasse, near the *Versöhnungskirche*.

His church. But movement on a pile of rubble next to the church caught his eye as the sun peeked out once more. An alley cat, probably. Or not. A second later he saw Wolfgang tumble down the pile without a word and run in the opposite direction, down the *strasse*, and around the corner.

Well. Not that he'd wanted to chat with Wolfgang anyway. But what had sent him running? He looked up and down the *strasse* once more before he slipped through the gap in the fence and found his way back into the *kirche*.

For the last time?

Quietly he picked his way down the hall, wondering what it took to get Weiss the Church-mouse's attention. If he tiptoed, surely the man would not hear him.

But what was he doing here? Hoping for wisdom from his father? Saying good-bye? He stood in the entry to his father's study, and once more he could not help feeling very small and young and stupid. The key in his pocket didn't fit some special treasure. What was he thinking? It just reminded him of what he could not have. He pulled out the key, squeezed it in his fist. And without thinking about it, he flung it across the room.

Good-bye. And I'm sorry for the way it turned out. Sorry I didn't keep my promise to take care of Mom as well as I should have. Sorry I failed. He couldn't say the words out loud, but he meant them all the same, and he turned to go. Even though—

No. Even if it didn't fit anything, the key had belonged to his father, had been held by his father. He would keep it. He'd take it to America and keep it with him always. Erich turned back and stepped over the rubble to the wall where the key had landed with a *plink.* Had it bounced under the collapsed desk? He got down on his knees to look for it. A little bit of gray light filtered in through the hole in the ceiling here, just enough to let him see—

—a small keyhole on the underside of the desk! It was where his father would have once parked his knees. How had he not seen it before? Only now that he had found the keyhole, what about the key?

"Oh, brother." He searched a few more minutes with no luck. *Maybe the key didn't land near the desk,* he thought. *Maybe it went down inside the hollow plaster wall and dropped down to who-knows-where.* He backed out from under the desk, bumping his head with a crack as he did.

"Owww!" He squinted in pain, but the hollow

cracking sound wasn't so much his head as the desk itself. Maybe—

He lay down under the desk again. Using the heel of his hand, he slammed as hard as he could into the wood panel with the little keyhole, his father's hiding place. Let the Churchmouse hear him; he didn't care.

Crack! He tried again and again, and each time the wood gave way just a little more. Two more times, three, and the seam began to open. Four times, five, and his hand ached from the hammering, until the small door finally gave way. A little cloth bag fell onto his chest.

He could not move, his heart hammered so. But after checking to make sure the rest of the little compartment was empty, he finally crawled out from beneath the desk and emptied the little bag onto the floor. He felt like a pirate there in the ruined building, pouring out a small river of silver *reichsmark* coins in the last light of the day.

Thirty-three, thirty-four, thirty-five ... He counted again, just to be sure he wasn't imagining it. Katarina would surely tell him she had read a story like this once, and it seemed far too unreal. Real people didn't find thirty-five *reichsmarks* in a compartment of a splintered desk, did they? He wasn't sure what such a treasure was worth today, but it didn't matter. Surely his father had meant for it to help him and his mother in an emergency, even in a small way.

Now it all made sense! Look in Luther for the key, and the key opened the little coin stash under the desk. Except his father didn't have a chance to tell them the whole story before he'd been killed by the Nazis. Not the Americans. Not the air raid. Not the bombs.

Well, no matter how much it was worth, his mother could use the money. Maybe it would buy them a new suit of clothes when they made it to Clevelandohio. Or a new car? He focused on scooping the coins back into the little bag, until he noticed that a cloud had slipped in front of the sun, darkening the room.

Actually, not a cloud. Erich looked up to see the Russian officer with the shark black eyes, hands on his hips, bigger than life. There would be no slipping by this man.

Captain Viktor Yevchenko, at your service.

"Erich Becker." The man dusted off his hands as if he had been infected by stepping inside the ruined house of worship. "I'm very pleased to have finally caught up with you ... after all these months."

Pleased was not a word Erich would have used within spitting distance. He palmed the coin bag and slipped it into his pocket as he stood. In time?

"Why have you been following me?" asked Erich.

Captain Yevchenko sighed and rolled his eyes.

"Perhaps you've already forgotten our meeting

on the street a few months back? Though I regret the negative impression I must have made on you and your family."

"You hurt my mother."

"An unfortunate misunderstanding." Captain Yevchenko held up a hand. "Pasternov was reprimanded for being so rough with you, and I apologize. I hope it will not be necessary again."

"Right." Erich squeezed his lips together in a silent prayer and wondered what he was supposed to say to that. How about "I need to go."

But Captain Yevchenko didn't move out of the way, only pretended they were having a pleasant conversation. What *did* he want?

"Now you're wondering why I'm here, perhaps." From this angle he looked almost sorry to be there. "I think you will understand very soon. Now turn around."

Erich blinked. What?

"I said turn around! Please. I don't want you to be hurt."

Erich had no idea what would happen next. He only knew that he couldn't just stand there and let it happen. Why couldn't Katarina have been here this time? He lunged for the door, but the Russian must have been expecting it. As Erich hollered and kicked, Captain Yevchenko spun him around, pinned his arms against his back, and forced him to his knees, leaving Erich gasping for breath.

"I am so sorry," the man apologized once more

as he taped Erich's wrists together with electrical tape. Then he wound the tape around Erich's head and over his mouth. "This will only be for a short while. Is that too tight?"

Erich leaned up against the wall, still stunned by the ferocious wrestling moves that left him helpless and silent on the floor. And why? He glanced up at the man for a clue.

"Please let me assure you one more time." Captain Yevchenko lowered himself to Erich's level. "I regret having to put you through this. It's just that we need your help right now."

Erich didn't bother trying to argue the point, not with his mouth taped shut. He was still trying to breathe.

"In fact, I have two girls, not much younger than you, back home in Moscow. Two lovely girls with no mother; now they stay with my sister."

For a moment he sounded like a real person, and for a moment his black eyes softened as he spoke of people he cared about. So the Shark had a soul, though he hid it behind the anger of his next question. "And do you know who killed their mother?"

Erich could guess. This had something to do with what the German army did. Captain Yevchenko took a deep breath and sighed.

"But I leave the past behind. Now we build for the future, and we have much to look forward to. It is now only the Americans who stand in our way."

He raised his voice, as if giving a speech. "They stand in the way of a unified Germany. And they stand in the way of a unified Socialist world."

So now it was the Americans against the Communists. This Cold War that DeWitt always talked about. But Captain Yevchenko still had his point to make, and he lowered his face to look straight at Erich. Erich could close his eyes, but it would do no good.

"Your only mistake, Erich Becker, is making friends with the wrong man, with the wrong side. The side that can never win. Your American spy friend, Sergeant DeWitt? You might know who he really is, or you might not. That is not the point, because now we are left with only one way to deal with him. I have been waiting for this chance for many weeks."

He straightened up once more, washing his hands in the air.

"And I give you my word, you will be free to go after we deal with him."

What did this mean, this dealing *with DeWitt?* Erich shivered at the thought and wondered what he had to do with it, tied up like this. He tried to wiggle his wrists, now tingly and numb, when a pair of feet appeared at the door.

"Comrade Wolfgang." Captain Yevchenko turned to meet the boy, and Erich could only gasp when he remembered how Wolfgang had seen him coming down the street.

Comrade?

Wolfgang the Lookout stood at the door with no expression on his face, as if he saw people tied up like this every day. Meanwhile, Captain Yevchenko pulled a small pad and pencil from his uniform pocket and wrote something, thinking for a moment, then looking to Erich.

"*Allein* is the right word in German, is it not? By himself with no others? Yes, of course. *Allein*, alone. The sergeant will come *alone*, immediately, to guarantee the safety of the boy." He looked up from his note. "This is something he will understand, will he not? Let us hope so."

Erich could hear no more of this, but when he tried to get to his feet, Captain Yevchenko pushed him back to the floor. And so Erich could do nothing but lie with his face in the shreds of his father's library. He looked up in time to see Captain Yevchenko tear off his note and hand it to Wolfgang the Robot, Wolfgang the Zombie, who said not a word.

"Hurry, now." Captain Yevchenko patted his comrade on the shoulder. "We don't want Erich to be uncomfortable on the floor."

Erich would have screamed if he thought it would do any good. Instead, he worked his wrists, trying to loosen the tape. And just an inch from his face, behind a pile of shredded books, he spotted the little key.

17

KAPITEL SIEBZEHN

COME ALONE

At least Captain Yevchenko hadn't noticed his father's collection of coins. That should make Erich feel a lot better, lying facedown in the ruins of the *Versöhnungskirche*.

Oh, and knowing where the key was made Erich feel better too.

Right?

He grunted as he wriggled his wrists, trying to keep the blood flowing to his hands. Maybe in the process he could loosen his wrists a little too. But Yevchenko had strapped the tape on too tightly for that. Still, he almost had to smile, imagining what Katarina would have said if she'd been here.

I read a book like this once. And she would probably tell him the story of a man who undid his wrists, pretended to be asleep, and then thunked the prison guard on the head when he came in the cell to give the man a bowl of thin soup. That's how it happened in the adventure novels.

Only not this time. Erich's hands went from tingling to pins-and-needles numb. After a few minutes he started sneezing from the moldy dust. And though he worked at it for more than a half hour, it was no good trying to chew through the layers of tape strapped across his mouth.

Captain Yevchenko paced the hallway. *How long will they keep me here?* Erich wondered. *What if DeWitt isn't around? And even if he is, will he really come to the Soviet sector, alone ... just to save me?*

He heard a faint scurrying sound, a scratching in the corner, which could mean only one thing.

In a moment he'd be nose-to-nose with a rat.

Lord, how did I get into such a mess? Erich closed his eyes and prayed, not knowing how God would answer, or whether God would think this mess he'd gotten himself into in a ruined church was a horribly sick joke. And the worst part was, it looked like it was going to get a lot worse before it got better.

If it got better. He kept his eyes squeezed shut, waiting for a nibble at his nose or the tickle of a rat whisker. Without opening his eyes he blew through his nose, over and over.

Shoo, rat! Get away!

He shivered at the thought, blew a little faster, as if burning coals had brushed his lips: *foo-foo-foo.*

Where was it? He heard the scratching sound

once more and opened one eye halfway, just to check.

What? The rat had turned into a very human face belonging to the churchmouse janitor, Helmut Weiss. He peered straight at Erich through a gaping hole in the back wall and gave him a strange look. Well, anyone would have to wonder, after all that *foo*-ing. But where had the man come from?

Never mind that. Captain Yevchenko had returned to the study, washing his hands in the air once more. Weiss shook his head and melted back into the shadows.

"What are you doing in here on your face?" asked the captain, pulling Erich up by the shirt collar. "That can't be very comfortable."

He propped Erich up against the wall like a rag doll and grinned. So much for chewing through the tape on his mouth. So much for wiggling his hands free and overpowering his captor. So much for even pulling his wrists around under his feet so he'd have his hands in front of him.

So much for anything. This was obviously not one of Katarina's happy-ending adventure novels. Because in this adventure, Fred DeWitt was probably walking into a trap, Erich was the bait, and there was nothing he could do about it. Captain Yevchenko glanced at his wristwatch.

"I imagine our friend should be arriving soon."

He wasn't far off. Ten minutes later they heard footsteps coming down the hallway, crunching on broken glass. A grim-faced DeWitt—not wearing his uniform—arrived at the door just ahead of the gun barrel pointed at his back.

"You checked him for weapons, I assume?" Captain Yevchenko pointed his own pistol at DeWitt, and Pasternov, the silent bodyguard, nodded, turned on his heels, and headed back down the hallway. Yevchenko turned his attention to his new guest.

"Sergeant DeWitt!" Yevchenko greeted him like an old friend. "You're even more foolish than I dared hope. And prompt, as well."

DeWitt wasn't playing the game; he hurried over to Erich and began to pull off the tape that wound around his head. Erich didn't mind losing a little hair, not at all.

"You okay, kid?" DeWitt whispered as he removed the last of the tape and helped Erich to his feet. Erich nodded and rubbed his wrists. Yes, he was okay. But now what?

Captain Yevchenko was obviously having his fun with this.

"Imagine! Here you are in the Soviet sector without your uniform on. You'd be demoted down to corporal if your superiors found out, wouldn't you? Perhaps thrown in the brig, jailed for a few months?"

"You got that right," growled DeWitt. He wadded up a handful of electrical tape and threw it at

Yevchenko's feet. "But I showed up. Now you let him go."

"Of course." Captain Yevchenko still looked amused. "I already told him I have no interest in harming anyone. He's free to leave."

Well, that was fine. But Erich decided he couldn't let Yevchenko off so easily.

"Did you hear me?" The Russian raised his voice. "Leave us!"

Still Erich didn't move, except to park himself beside DeWitt. He didn't even have to think about it. He wasn't leaving the man behind. DeWitt was beyond help over in the Soviet sector, and he'd be in deep trouble if he were found out. Erich's glance darted around the room. If he could find a piece of wood, he might have something to defend himself with.

"Listen, Yevchenko." DeWitt must have remembered the name from their last meeting. "Maybe you've got me mistaken for somebody else. I don't have anything to tell you. My enlistment's up in a couple of weeks, so I'm done with the service. I'm just a journalist, okay?"

"Just a journalist." Yevchenko spit back the words. "A journalist who happens to organize a *subversive* parachute-dropping campaign over the Soviet sector."

Subversive? As in dangerous? The way a traitor was dangerous? Erich marveled. DeWitt didn't think so, either.

"Didn't know you guys would get so bent out of shape about a little candy," he replied. "We just wanted to cheer the kids up a little."

"And you are just a journalist, you say, yet you also work as an American agent?"

"Oh, come on." DeWitt dropped his shoulders. "You guys would think my ninety-two-year-old grandmother was a spy."

"I know nothing of your grandmother. But in my country, we shoot people like you."

Erich's blood ran cold when he saw Yevchenko's finger on the trigger. And he heard in the man's voice how serious he was. Just as serious as DeWitt's low warning.

"It's time you get out of here, Erich." DeWitt didn't take his eyes off the Russian's gun. "Go home now, and don't look back. Tell your mother—"

"No." Erich wasn't sure what was going to happen. All he knew was that he could not leave now if he wanted to. Who would help them, any-way—over here? "You tell her yourself."

For once Erich didn't mean it the way it sounded. Only that he could not carry a message from a dead man. A dead man that he cared about.

"Erich!" DeWitt's voice took on a harder edge. "I didn't come over here to see you get hurt. You need to—"

"I'm sorry, DeWitt. But I'm not leaving." Erich

crossed his arms and planted his feet. "Not unless it's with you."

That did it. Yevchenko glared at Erich. And Erich tried not to stare at the man silently slipping up behind Yevchenko, a broken board raised over his head like a club.

Helmut Weiss.

Yes, he'd been silent as he'd slipped up behind the captain. But the little janitor's weapon looked too big for him to hold. And as he pulled back just a little farther, ready to swing, a piece of glass snapped under his foot.

"What?" Captain Yevchenko glanced over his shoulder, probably expecting to see Wolfgang or his assistant. When he didn't, he snapped his gun hand around, too quickly for Erich to grab it. Without thinking, Erich launched himself headfirst at Captain Yevchenko, clawing and grabbing. At the same time, Helmut Weiss bellowed as he swung the club over his head. DeWitt dived for Yevchenko's feet as the captain's gun fired wildly.

Even if he'd been shot, Erich wasn't sure he would have known right away. All he knew was a wild moment of wrestling, of grabbing the gun, another shot, yelling all around, and another dull thud as Herr Weiss connected with his target.

Then all was deathly quiet as they untangled themselves from the mess of arms and legs on the floor. Captain Yevchenko lay still on the ground, unconscious but still breathing, an angry red welt appearing on his forehead. While DeWitt got to his feet, Herr Weiss stood panting over his victim, eyes wide with horror, blood staining his shirt just above the elbow.

"Herr Weiss!" Erich blurted out. "You're shot!"

But Herr Weiss didn't move. "I've never done that kind of thing before," he gasped, ignoring the wound in his left arm. "Is he dead?"

DeWitt took charge again, and Erich felt his arm nearly pulled out of its socket as the sergeant pulled him from the floor.

"He's not dead, and neither are you," DeWitt told them. "But we all will be if we don't get out of here now!"

Still Helmut Weiss stood over the limp body of the captain.

"Listen, pal," DeWitt told him. "I don't know who you are or what you're doing here. But trust me, it's time to leave, and—"

And it seemed a very odd time to notice, but there on the floor lay the bag of coins, just out of Captain Yevchenko's reach. It must have fallen out of Erich's pocket during the fight. He reached over to pick it up. Maybe it wasn't the huge treasure he'd expected, but that didn't matter now. DeWitt watched, curious.

"God go with you, Erich," Herr Weiss said. He dropped his club then shook Erich's hand. "You know the way out."

164

He did. But the bodyguard must have heard shots. And what had happened to Wolfgang?

"Don't worry," Herr Weiss added as he saw Erich's expression. "Just go."

Erich nodded. And then Helmut Weiss limped into the darkness as quietly as he'd come.

Erich and DeWitt, on the other hand, weren't out of the building yet. And as footsteps thundered down the hallway toward them, closer and closer, Erich knew what to do.

"This way!" he whispered.

18
KAPITEL ACHTZEHN
CELEBRATION

THREE WEEKS LATER ...

"There, you look fine." DeWitt straightened Erich's bow tie, which in a past life had been a piece of his mother's dress. "Never seen a finer-looking best man."

Erich nearly didn't recognize himself in the mirror they'd set up in the back room of the Berg-mannstrasse *missionskirche,* the Lutheran Mission Church. Hair slicked back with a little dab of Bryl-creem hair gel. Freshly pressed shirt. Long pants even, borrowed from Pastor Grunewald. Never mind that the pastor stood three inches taller and the pants had to be rolled and safety-pinned at the hem. Even his shoes looked as if they'd been given a military spit shine.

Just like DeWitt's. The American wore his brown dress uniform, creased at all the seams and fresh from the cleaners. Same as his Air Force buddies, ten of whom had showed up early. Strange how many stood by the doors, though, their eyes on the street, arms crossed. Somehow they didn't quite look as if they were waiting for wedding guests.

Katarina, on the other hand ... well, she knocked before poking her head in the door. "Are you boys ready yet?"

"Ready when you are!" answered the groom-to-be, and he gave his own tie a nervous yank. He could look as cool as a magazine ad, but Erich knew better. Under it all he could see the man's hand shaking. The jokes only helped to cover.

"You didn't invite our friends the Russkies, did you?" He winked at Erich.

"Did you want me to? Haven't seen them for the past couple of weeks."

"Just want to make sure they don't crash the party."

"Maybe they're tired of following us."

"I hope so." DeWitt checked out the window. "But hey, what kind of talk is this for a guy's wedding day?"

"The pastor's waiting," Katarina reminded them before disappearing again. At least she sounded like Katarina. The rest of the girl, Erich wasn't sure. Aunt Gerta had sewn her a yellow dress with a frilly hem and had braided her dark hair into a bun.

"I've never seen her dolled up like that," DeWitt said as he followed her out the door, then he held up a finger of warning. "You keep the guys away from her, okay?"

"Not a problem. But ... DeWitt?" He felt in his pocket for the little cup he'd been carrying around for the past few months. The only physical thing that still connected him with the memory of his father.

"Yeah?" DeWitt looked back over his shoulder.

Erich felt the knot in his stomach but held out the silver cup before he could change his mind. This would be for his mother as much as for the American, he told himself. And it was his job to take care of his mother, wasn't it? God would want him to do this ... this crazy thing. "I want you to have this."

"Are you serious?" At first DeWitt didn't seem to understand, not even as he rolled the little cup around in his hand to read the inscription:

"Presented to Rev. Ulrich Becker, Reconciliation Church, 12 June 1936." He looked up again, a question still on his face. "This belonged to your father, didn't it?"

Erich nodded.

"Why are you giving it to me?"

Erich swallowed down the lump in his throat.

"Just keeping a promise."

So DeWitt accepted the gift. The day might have been perfect, if not for the bittersweet knowledge of who was missing. Fred's Air Force friend Joe Wright stood with the groom, hardly knowing a word of German but smiling for the whole ceremony. Katarina's mother took her place next to the bride, and a handful of people from the little church joined them. But Oma was not there. That was expected, and Erich could understand why she had stayed home. Not because of her health. She'd begun to feel a little better these last few weeks. But because of who she said she would become at this ceremony.

An ex-mother-in-law, if there was such a thing.

"No, absolutely not." Mrs. Fred DeWitt put her foot down, just a few weeks after the wedding. "It's much too dangerous."

Dangerous because autumn had turned to winter and fog hung over the city nearly every morning? Or because they'd heard stories of C-54's forced off course, even fired on?

"I'm going, Mom." He looked at her and tried to sound as grown up as he could. "I have to."

"It's all right, Brigitte." DeWitt could talk her into just about anything. "I'll be with him the whole time."

She sighed and turned away, her arms crossed. Yes, she was outnumbered now, two to one, and maybe deep down she didn't mind.

"Just don't tell me anything about it afterward."

The two men grinned and headed for the door. And Erich couldn't help smiling even more as he waved at Katarina, who had come to see them off that cold Saturday afternoon, hitching a ride in Lieutenant Anderson's Berlin Baby. The plane looked a little grimy for all its loads of coal but still purred as loudly as ever. And this time the plane ride would be different, very different.

"Hear you're a married man now!" Jolly old Sergeant Fletcher still co-piloted the plane, even after all these months. He looked about as grimy as the rest of the C-54, but he gave them his wide smile and a slap on the back for DeWitt. "Way to go, guy."

"Pre-flight checklist!" barked the pilot. Lieutenant Anderson hadn't changed a bit, either.

"I'm on it." The sergeant pulled out his clipboard as the others settled in for a quick flight to Rhein-Main and a Frankfurt dusted with early season snow, hopeful Christmas candles in its shop windows. A few hours later Erich enjoyed the wreaths on many of the shop doors; he hadn't seen any in Berlin for years.

"So what are we going to get her?" DeWitt asked as they stepped down the newly shoveled street together. Erich stopped at a shop window to look at a box of chocolates and knew the answer.

"You doing the honors this time?" Sergeant Fletcher wanted to know, and DeWitt bowed at Erich with a flourish of his hand. The plane lurched as they approached Berlin once more.

"Wait a minute." Erich tied the corners of the

next handkerchief as quickly as he could. "I still have a few more."

"Tempelhof in three minutes." Lieutenant Anderson put the plane into final approach as DeWitt opened the flare hatch. "Just make it quick, Sergeant. I don't want those things—"

"—snagging your landing gear!" Erich and DeWitt finished the pilot's warning at the same time, which made them both laugh. But the *Berlin Baby* wasn't slowing down for anybody; they'd have to work quickly. DeWitt handed the box across.

"Need some help?"

Erich shook his head no. "Not this time. But thanks."

No, not this time. He could do this. So Erich took a handful of carefully folded parachutes, ready to let loose as the wind whistled below them. He shivered as the cold December wind stiffened his fingers.

"Woo!" the sergeant chirped. "Somebody opened the barn door! A little chilly out there."

It didn't matter. This time Erich didn't think about the *other* bombers, the bombers during the war. He didn't think about anything except dropping candy to the kids on the ground. They would release right over Oma's apartment, as they'd agreed. So DeWitt glanced up through the forward windows to get their position before he started the countdown.

"*Drei, zwei, eins* ... Let it loose!"

And Erich did.

HOW IT REALLY HAPPENED

History books tell us that the Cold War began in 1948. World War 2 had ended, but the countries that had defeated Nazi Germany didn't get along. Soviet (Russian) forces took over the eastern half of Germany, while Americans, British, and French occupied the western half.

The problem was, the capital city of Berlin was stuck like an island in the middle of the Soviet territory. And about three years after the official end of fighting, the Soviets decided to seal off Allied-occupied West Berlin from the outside world. No trains or trucks would be allowed in.

What could the Allies do? Give up and go home, leaving all of Berlin to the Russians? No. Instead, the United States, Britain, and France joined to provide a massive 24/7 air supply line known as the Berlin Airlift. Between June 26, 1948, and September 30, 1949, Britain and the United States flew in 2.3 million tons of supplies to keep the western part of the city alive. Day after day they kept it up, even when no one thought it was possible.

It was a huge, and sometimes dangerous, job. And it was a hard time for the people of Berlin, who had already been through so many tough times during the war. But with the world against them, the Soviets gave up fifteen months later and once more allowed supplies in by traditional land routes.

The gum and candy drops really did happen, thanks to an American flier named Gail Halvorsen. His bravery and compassion showed the world that Americans wanted to help, any way they could.

The Reconciliation Church, the *Versöhnungskirche,* was also a real place, stuck in the no-man's-land that would grow up along the border between east and west. This border would divide a city and a people more and more over the next forty years. But the story of the people living around that remarkable church is not over—

QUESTIONS FOR FURTHER STUDY

1. In the opening chapter, why do you think getting a chocolate bar was such a big deal for Erich? Explain what he was going through.

2. According to Erich in chapter three, whose fault was it that his father had been killed? Do you see why he felt that way? What made him so bitter about life?

3. In chapter four, both Erich and Katarina wanted to help Oma Poldi. Why did they disagree, and who do you think was right?

4. Why did Erich change his mind about stealing food (chapter five)? Why did he still get in trouble?

5. In chapter eight, how did Erich and Katarina feel when they saw the kids on the other side of the fence? What would you have done, if you were Erich and Katarina?

6. The story about the gum drops is true (chapter nine), except in real life it wasn't Erich and Katarina who started dropping candy on the city. Who did, and why? (You'll need to do some research on this one.)

7. In chapter eleven, Oma compared her daughter-in-law to a person written about in the Bible. Who? And why would Oma say that?

8. What really happened to Erich's father? In chapter thirteen, how did Erich's ideas about the Americans change?

9. Who was Wolfgang really working for (chapter sixteen)? Why do you think he would do that?

10. Which church did Erich and his family attend in chapter eighteen? What is different about this church, compared to other churches in Germany?

BEETLE BUNKER

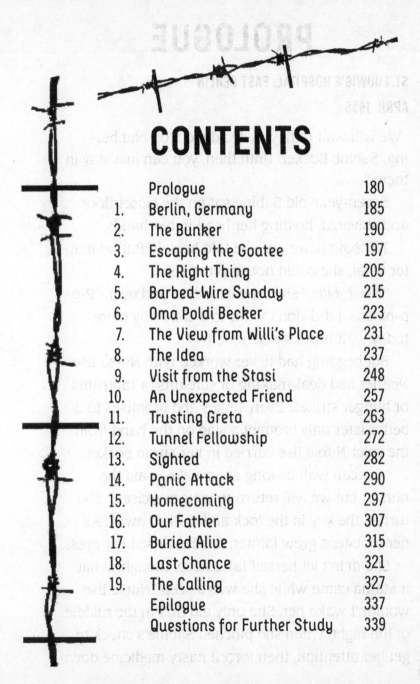

CONTENTS

PROLOGUE

"We will wait until you decide to stop blubber-
ing, Sabine Becker. Until then, you can just stay in
there."

Seven-year-old Sabine sat on the closet floor
and shivered, holding her head in her hands.

Tomboys never cry, she told herself. But no matter what, she could not stop the sobs.

"*B-b-b-bitte*," she repeated, over and over. "P-p-
p-please. I d-d-don't want to d-d-do any more
today.... It hurts s-s-so much—"

But begging had never worked with Nurse Ilse.
Neither had deal-making or screams or tantrums
or hunger strikes. Even smiles and promises to do
better later only brought a slap on the hand from
the ruler Nurse Ilse carried in her apron pocket.

"We can wait as long as you like," said the
nurse, "but we *will* return to your exercises." She
turned the key in the lock and walked away. As
her footsteps grew fainter, Sabine closed her eyes.

She didn't let herself fall asleep, though. What
if Mama came while she was asleep? Nurse Ilse
wouldn't wake her. She only did that in the middle
of the night, when she pinched Sabine's cheek to
get her attention, then forced nasty medicine down

her throat. It was supposed to make her polio better.

Sabine bumped her head against the inside of the door and shivered. She prayed to her mother's Jesus and talked to her own made-up friends—like the characters from the books Mama read to her. Sometimes she wasn't sure which was which, though she would never dare admit that to Mama.

At least for a little while she was away from Nurse Ilse. Here she could escape to her pretend world, the place where she could walk and run, just like all the other kids.

Only not forever. Nurse Ilse came back a few minutes later with another threat, this one worse than locking her in a closet.

"If you continue to raise such a fuss, your mother will never be able to visit again. Never. Do you hear me?"

"I don't believe you," Sabine answered defiantly.

Maybe next time Mama will finally take me home again, Sabine thought.

Rheinsbergerstrasse. Home. To Oma's crowded apartment on Rheinsberger Street in East Berlin. Where she'd lived all her life with her mama and her ancient grandmother, Oma Poldi Becker, and her half brother, Erich. He was twenty years old and wanted to be a doctor. She tried to remember his stories about hiding on an American airplane with his cousin Katarina when he was thirteen. He even said they flew to an American air base with

Sabine's father, who had been an Air Force sergeant. Sabine wasn't sure she believed it all, but of
course it made her jealous of Erich. He had known
her American father, while all she had were stories
about his sense of humor—and about the plane
crash.

If I could go home today, she decided, *I'd never
complain about Onkel Heinz and Tante Gertrud
again.* Her uncle and aunt had moved into Oma's
apartment a couple of years ago. It made things
a little crowded, but Uncle Heinz had shown her
how to tell the difference between a Mercedes and
a Volkswagen. She knew she wasn't supposed to
care, because she was a girl, but she did anyway.
He could get bossy sometimes, though, and he
belched a lot. Especially when he drank beer.

Even Aunt Gertrud's ranting and smoking
wouldn't seem too bad, if only—

"Out, now!" growled Nurse Ilse, startling Sabine
as she unlocked the door. "You have a visitor."

Sabine blinked at the bright lights but smiled as
the nurse carried her back to bed. Wait until she
could show Mama—

Her mother stood in the doorway of the hospital
room only a few minutes later, her mouth and nose
hidden behind a blue hospital mask but her eyes
twinkling with tears. She had to wear the mask
and a hospital gown just like everybody else, so
she wouldn't catch Sabine's polio.

"Sabine!" Mama held out her arms as if to hug her only daughter, which of course she could not.

"I've been waiting for you all week, Mama." Sabine couldn't help grinning from ear to ear. Maybe polio could turn her legs to limp noodles, but it could not keep Mama from her weekly visit. Sabine knew that more than anything. And now it was time for the surprise she and Jesus had been working on for days, in secret, when nobody was looking.

Watch this, Nurse Ilse! Sabine grabbed the corner of her sheet, and a moment later she rolled her left shoulder so her weight would carry her off the edge of the bed.

"No! What do you think you're doing?" Nurse Ilse fumed as she dropped her clipboard. But Sabine would swing her legs around and show them she wasn't disabled any longer. See? Just as she'd hoped, her bare feet cleared the edge of her bed and hit the cold, slick tile of the hospital floor.

Now, Jesus! she prayed silently. *Please, now! Make my legs strong!*

Only maybe she should have prayed out loud. She later decided that must have been what she did wrong. What else could it have been? Not enough faith, she decided. She should have said something out loud, the way Jesus did, like, "Rise, take up thy pallet and walk!" Only Sabine wasn't sure what a pallet was.

And as both her mother and the nurse lunged for her, Sabine's knees wiggled for a moment.

Then they buckled and sent her sprawling face-first to the scrubbed tile floor.

She remembered how the yucky smell of floor cleaner made her throat burn and her stomach turn. But she remembered nothing else. When she woke up, she found herself tucked tightly once again into her bed, her prison of sheets. How long had it been? Two minutes? Ten? Her cheekbones throbbed with pain as if someone had slapped her. She knew that feeling. But she did not open her eyes, only lay still and listened to the two women arguing in the hallway.

"You don't seem to understand how serious this is, Frau Becker. If you don't leave now, I'm going to have to call security."

"But that's my *daughter* in there."

"Your daughter will be fine, no thanks to you. Now—"

"Wait a minute. How was this my fault?"

"If you continue to fill her head with religious nonsense, I'll have no choice but to file a report. You see what it's done today. She actually seems to believe what you tell her about"—she spit out the words—"this *God* healing her legs."

Sabine didn't hear her mother's response. But she was ready to throw her bedpan at the evil nurse. Nurse Ilse went on, threatening to find a more suitable home for Sabine after her hospital treatment—if the "religious nonsense" didn't stop.

And even polio could not stop Sabine's tears.

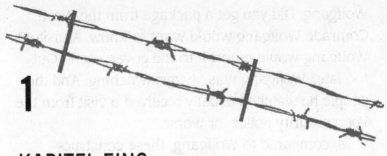

1

KAPITEL EINS

BERLIN, GERMANY

MAY 1961: SIX YEARS LATER...

"Not again!"

Sabine groaned when she rounded the corner, adjusting the crutch clamps around her wrists and arms. Up ahead, it looked like construction workers had begun tearing up Brunnenstrasse once more. Maybe this time they wouldn't stare at her as she limped by on her walking crutches, more like canes that strapped to her forearms. In the past six years, since getting out of the hospital, Sabine had heard all the cruel jokes. So what? She could walk okay, now, even with the brace on her right leg that no one saw. And she couldn't stay home the rest of her life, just like she couldn't stay in the hospital. This was 1961, after all.

So she gripped the handles of her crutches a little more tightly, took a deep breath, and stared straight ahead. She would ignore them, just as she always tried to ignore the neighborhood spy,

Wolfgang. Did you get a package from the West? Comrade Wolfgang would want to know. A visitor? Wolfgang would report it to the government. Out too late? Wolfgang was always watching. And the people he watched usually received a visit from the *Vopo* security police, or worse.

Ja, compared to Wolfgang, these construction guys seemed pretty tame. Or she hoped they were. But no spy and no construction workers would keep her from visiting her brother, Erich, at the hospital where he worked. If she had to circle around the block on Bergstrasse, that would probably add half an hour to her walk. Not this time.

To the right, a large older apartment building cast a ragged shadow across the street. The top two stories had collapsed in an American bombing raid during the war, leaving crumbled piles of stone and rusting, twisted steel. That had happened years before Sabine was born, but things didn't change very quickly in East Berlin. Not like in the western half of the city.

But not to worry. It looked like the construction crew up ahead had taken a break. One of the men sat in the back of his truck, hands clasped behind his neck, eyes closed in a midday nap. The early summer sunshine hit him in the face. Fine. The others had left their pile of water pipes on the sidewalk, blocking the way with a sign that read "CAUTION! NO ENTRY!" in big block letters. But who knew when they would return? Everyone seemed to have cleared out for lunch. A typical hardworking Tuesday in the Soviet sector of East Berlin.

Limping past the warning sign, Sabine glanced down. Flimsy boards covered part of a gaping hole in the sidewalk. An unsteady ladder slanted down about ten feet to an exposed pipe. From top to bottom, they'd laid a canvas tarp out like a slide.

Careful, she cautioned herself as she stepped past the sign. Without warning, a board gave way, launching her right over the edge. Sabine could hardly yelp as she fell; the best she could do was to plant her crutches on the tarp, like a skier sliding down an alpine slope.

But a good deal less graceful. She lost her balance and slid down the slope on the seat of her pants, crutches waving like windmills. The tarp pulled loose, and an avalanche of dirt followed her down, down, down—she slammed into a crumbling brick foundation wall, crutches first. Ouch.

"Ack!" Sabine coughed and struggled to breathe. She'd bent the tip of one crutch, but it was still usable. The brace on her leg had loosened up a bit, but no problem there, either. Had she broken anything? Her arms moved all right, though she'd twisted her right elbow a bit during the tumble. If that was all she'd injured, she'd been spared.

Thank you. She breathed out the words in a quick prayer and struggled to rise. Had Wolfgang seen her fall? She hoped not. No telling what the workers would do to her if they found her down here. How soon would Erich come looking? He knew the route she would take, but he might just think she'd forgotten about visiting. And he might be too busy to worry about her.

A couple more loose bricks fell with a *thunk*.

She clutched her head for a moment, trying to decide what to do. She couldn't climb up the rickety ladder without help. And for certain she didn't want to meet up with any angry construction workers—not after she'd ignored their warning signs. Maybe she should just see what she'd stumbled onto.

And *ja,* she could just imagine what her mother would say about *that*! "Sabine Becker, I thought little girls were supposed to play with dolls, not—"

Not explore old ruined buildings? Well, that's what famous explorers did. So why not her? And why not here in Berlin? She couldn't discover ancient civilizations, but this might be the next best thing. She used her crutch to knock away a couple more bricks, then...there! Look at that! She peered into the little cave she found that had just opened up at the bottom of the workers' dig. More like a basement, actually. Through the dog-sized opening she could make out the dim outline of cement walls and floors, maybe connected to the old apartment building upstairs. She knew that no one had lived in this bombed-out building for years.

She whispered a shy "Guten Tag?" into the

darkness and waited for the echo of her hello
to return. And she shivered at the draft of stale,
musty air that hit her in the face. *Hmm. Is this what
it's like to discover a pharaoh's tomb?*

Faint slivers of sunlight streamed down from
above, filtered through cracks in the upper floors.
Maybe she could find another way out, up through
the ruined building's basement. That way she
could escape before anyone found her. *Okay*, she
thought. *Here goes.*

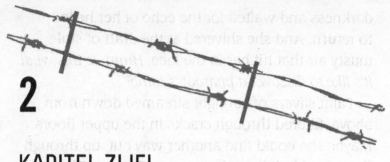

2

KAPITEL ZWEI

THE BUNKER

For the first few minutes, Sabine felt her way like a blind girl with a cane, taking care not to place her crutches in holes in the floor or cracks in the cement. And as her eyes slowly adjusted to the cellar, she began to realize what this place was, really.

"A bunker," she whispered to herself. A bomb shelter. Deep cellar. Storage room. Definitely much more than your everyday basement. The ceiling had collapsed here and there, leaving piles of charred timbers like twisted toothpicks. That had opened it up just enough to let in filtered light here and there, through the floor of the ruined building upstairs. But what was all this stuff?

In the first room, she ran her finger along the top of a metal drum, stacked against a wall with a dozen more. It smelled faintly of fuel, maybe gasoline, though when she hit a drum with the end of her crutch, it rang empty.

"Doesn't look like anyone's been down here

since the war." Her quiet words echoed in the cavelike main room and the others that opened into it. Each was separated by a heavy-duty metal door, almost big enough for a streetcar to drive through. When she pushed on one, it gave way with a loud complaint of rusty metal hinges.

Wow. She picked her way slowly through other shadowy rooms, each one more interesting than the last. In the next room, someone had piled wooden crates full of rusty metal cans clear up to the ceiling. Sabine picked up a can that had been punctured in the bombing raids and held it high to catch a faint ray of sunshine.

Trinkwasser. The emergency drinking water had long ago gone dry. She wondered what it might have tasted like, though, or even if it would still be any good after all these years. But there were more rooms to explore.

In room number three she could make out a small radio receiver on the floor; it had slipped off an overturned table at some point and looked pretty beat up. Sabine tried all the switches. Nothing.

She found the biggest surprise in the last room. She smelled the stale air and sneezed. More stinky fuel? Not exactly. She peered at the shell of a small car, perched on cement blocks, collecting a thick layer of dust.

"Well, there's not much left of it," she told

no one in particular, "but it looks like an old Volkswagen."

Uncle Heinz would have been excited to see this. From the looks of it, this had to be a World War 2 Beetle, the kind with a convertible top that folded down. Sort of like the Volkswagen sedan she saw on the streets over in the West, in the American and French sectors of the city. This one was missing the back seat, but it still had the two front seats, a steering wheel, an engine in the back (mostly in pieces), and a windshield (totally cracked). All four of the wheels were missing, though. Well, what did she expect? But the big question was—

"How did they ever get this thing down here?"

She looked around for a big enough opening, but the far wall had crumbled; it ended in a pile of dirt and concrete chunks. Had this been an underground parking garage, as well as a bomb shelter? Maybe. She slipped into the driver's seat and spun the wheel. Ha! Wouldn't Erich love this too—driving a twenty-year-old army staff car around Berlin—

But no. Only a few people she knew of owned cars in the Soviet sector. And they only drove noisy, smelly little cars called Trabants—Trabis—made in East Germany. She sighed and bounced on the seat a little. A spring started to pop through.

Oh, well. Maybe she would come back to this place. With a couple of candles and a nice blanket to cover the rotten seats, it could make a perfect reading retreat. A place to get away. If she could just find a way to get in and out of the bunker.

Hmm. That could be a problem. But as she poked around the other rooms a bit more, she wondered why she couldn't find a ladder. "Or," she mused as she checked a dark corner, "a stairway!"

There! She looked up at a circular staircase and tested the first step with her crutch. It protested loudly. Okay. Shifting both crutches to her left hand, she did her best to hold her weight up by gripping the railing and taking each step slowly. Up to the second step, then the third—

Minutes later, she pushed up at the boards that covered the only other way out.

"Come on!" she grunted, using the ends of her crutches as hammers to loosen the trapdoor. "Open up!"

Not very ladylike, perhaps, but it worked. After a couple more hits, one of the boards gave a little, even splintering in the corner. She could peek out through the crack into the ground floor of the ruined, empty apartment building above her. She saw a bit of peeling rose wallpaper. Now she knew where she was, sort of. And what to look for. She gave the board another jab for good measure, forgetting where the edge of the steps—

"Au!" All she could do was hang on to the railing as she slid halfway down, fireman-style. Her feet followed behind, hitting every step hard. She eased herself all the way to the floor. Well, she came down a little faster than she went up, didn't she? In the process, she'd lost a crutch, which had clattered down to the cement floor before her.

Which probably wasn't a bad thing. By the time she had recovered her lost crutch, she heard a voice echoing through the bunker.

"Suh-BEEE-nuh!" Even from a distance, she could make out Erich's call. "Sabine! Are you down here?"

"Erich!" she answered back. She squinted as she limped through the bunker and neared the hole in the foundation. "I'm right here!"

"I see that." Erich still wore his white hospital smock as he peeked inside. "The question is, what in the world are you *doing* down a hole like this? *Bist du verrückt?*"

"Nein, I'm not crazy!"

By that time, several construction workers had joined Erich at the top of the hole to see what was going on. Sabine looked down at herself as she thought of how to explain. Good thing she'd been wearing her brother's hand-me-down pants, the ones her mother never let her wear to church. A dress in this situation would have been a disaster.

"But," she finally added, planting a hand on her hip, "I could sure use a hand out of this hole, please."

Which came swiftly as Erich hurried down the ladder and helped her back up, one step at a time.

"I started to get worried when you didn't meet me at the hospital at noon," he told her. "You weren't back at the apartment, either. Then when I ran by this hole, I saw workers looking down. They said they'd heard a noise. Like something collapsed. That was you?"

"Probably sewer rats," she told him. "I had to fight off a few."

Erich just harrumphed; he knew when Sabine was kidding. And Sabine knew Erich had probably been running up and down the streets, searching for her. The athletic twenty-six-year-old hospital intern was always like that. Erich the Rescuer. Erich, always protecting her. She felt like a rag doll as he lifted her back to the street while the workers gathered around to stare.

"Quite a discovery, eh, boys?" Erich said as Sabine held her crutches out to either side like wings. "A perfectly preserved Egyptian mummy. Living down in the sewer for ten thousand years. She can even still talk!"

A couple of the men chuckled as she dusted herself off and pointed to the broken board, the little platform that had dumped her into the hole. "But really, you guys ought to fix that. A person could get hurt. I mean, I was walking just fine before I fell in there. Now look at me. I need crutches."

See? She could be a comedian too. As long as her older brother was there to cover for her. She smiled at Erich before starting back toward home.

"Thanks for coming after me, though. It was kind of dusty down there. Made me sneeze."

Erich scratched his sandy hair. "So did you see anything?" His curiosity must have gotten the better of him.

"Oh, you know, the usual Nazi treasure, gold and stuff, hidden for twenty years."

Which (except for the gold part) was partly true. But Erich wasn't buying it.

"Listen, Sabine, you've really got to be more careful." He followed her, but Sabine didn't slow down. "There are holes and old bunkers and broken sewers like that all over the city. It seems like every time they start a construction project or tear down another bombed-out building, they find something strange underground. If I didn't come to find you—"

"I could have gotten out." Still she didn't slow down.

"Oh, come on. And look at yourself. What are you going to tell Mutti when you get home? That you were out playing in the sandbox? You're a mess!"

Sabine stopped and looked at herself for the first time. The knees of her brother's cast-off pants had ripped, and she was coated with dust. She knew Erich had a point, especially when she looked up at Wolfgang's window and saw him watching them through his binoculars. She scowled at him but couldn't help feeling like a bug under a microscope. And yes, he would likely take notes and probably call the authorities. But worse than that—

Her mother would not be pleased.

3

KAPITEL DREI

ESCAPING THE GOATEE

"Sabine, stop reading that stupid storybook and pay attention to the broadcast!" Uncle Heinz's words startled her, but he'd barely opened his eyes as he reclined. Oma Poldi's old flowered couch sagged under his weight. Sabine wasn't quite sure how he managed to fit on it. But he had claimed it for his own, and she rarely saw him anywhere else.

Aunt Gertrud moaned from her chair in the corner, black shades covering her eyes and a smoldering cigarette dangling from her lips. So maybe it didn't look like a good East German socialist worker thing to wear. But she said she could "see" her migraines even with the blinders on.

"*Bitte,* Onkel Heinz…please." Sabine knew it would do no good. She could count on only three people in this world—and he was not one of them. But Oma was confined to her bed, as usual, while

Sabine's mother and brother were still at work. Her uncle belched like a bullfrog (no "excuse me," or anything) and wagged a pudgy finger at her the way he did when no one was around to defend her.

"Don't Onkel Heinz me. I'm doing you a favor. In fact, you're going to thank me when you go back to school tomorrow and you can tell the teacher what Comrade Ulbricht said in his speech. Every good young Communist needs to know this."

"I'm not a good young Communist." She lifted her book even higher to cover her face. "I'm a Christian, and I don't like the Goatee."

The Goatee was their nickname for Walter Ulbricht, the leader of Communist East Germany, and it was all his fault. The man trimmed his beard like that; what did he expect? The way Sabine saw it, he deserved every nickname they could give him.

"Have a little respect, eh?" Uncle Heinz puffed his cheeks. "One of these days, I'm not going to be able to help you anymore. You and your mother both. If she weren't my sister—"

She'd heard that line before. Next he would remind her, again, of her duties to the state, what faithful Communist working masses were supposed to do every day. Just like the big red banners that draped East Berlin's drab buildings said: Work hard. Stay away from spy-infested West Berlin. Support the people's factories and the German Democratic Republic. Meet your work quotas.

Never mind that Uncle Heinz, the good Communist, spent most of his time right here on the couch. He wasn't even really related to Oma, his sister's mother-in-law. But he and Aunt Gertrud had invited themselves for a visit to Oma's apartment and had never left.

Sabine kept reading *Black Beauty*, a horse story she'd especially liked the first two times she'd read it. And she did her best to block out the put-me-to-sleep drone of Comrade Ulbricht's speech, broadcast on the official East German state radio station. Suddenly the novel flew from her hands.

"What did your onkel tell you?" Aunt Gertrud glared down her long nose at Sabine; she'd pulled back the sleep mask and had parked it on her forehead. Sabine thought all she needed was a wart and a black hat to complete the look. And maybe a broomstick.

Black Beauty lay on the floor, facedown. Sabine sighed and stooped to pick it up. Aunt Gertrud would never dare act like this when Sabine's mother was around.

"But we've heard it all, Tante Gertrud. He goes on and on about how terrible the capitalists in the West are—the decadent Americans and their puppets, the West Berliners."

"Well, of course they are."

Oh, dear. Sabine wasn't going to try to understand what the screaming men were saying. Comrade Ulbricht and his friends just repeated what the Russians told them to say. She believed that the only puppets were right there in East Berlin.

"He says much more than that," Uncle Heinz told them, lifting a finger to his lips. "You just have to listen."

"Can't I change it to the station that plays Frank Sinatra songs?" Sabine wondered aloud. Aunt Gertrud glared once more and settled back into her chair, pulling the sleep mask back over her eyes. Sabine pretended to listen while waiting for her chance to run. Her mother wouldn't be home for another two hours.

At least it wasn't hard to tell when Uncle Heinz fell asleep again. His hands twitched once, and his lips and cheeks puffed out like a blowfish. On the radio, Comrade Ulbricht was just getting warmed up.

"The enemy is trying to use the open border between the German Democratic Republic and West Berlin to undermine our government and its economy—," he droned on. "Aggressive forces and subversive centers—" blah-blah. "Serious losses in our workforce—" more blah-blah.

And Aunt Gertrud's mask still covered her eyes. Sabine took the chance to quietly limp to the dining room table and grab her book.

If she was extra careful, maybe—

In the kitchen, she found a couple of candle stubs and some matches, which she slipped into her little backpack. She also grabbed a couple of scraps of bread as she quietly made her way to the door.

"You're not leaving, are you, child?" Aunt Gertrud screeched. "You know how upset your mother was last time, with all that dirt and—"

"Be back in just a few minutes, Tante Gertrud." Sabine didn't slow down to explain, didn't wait for the door to close behind her as she hustled down the hall and down the outside steps, into the late afternoon sunshine. Never mind that Wolfgang would probably see her. She glanced up at his third-floor window and sighed with relief. Empty.

"Sabine!" Aunt Gertrud's screech followed her outside. Sabine bit her lip.

"You should listen to your tante." The quiet, menacing voice made her jump. Wolfgang, his arms crossed in challenge, stepped out of a doorway to block her way. "A person like you could get hurt."

As if he cared. Comrade Wolfgang would be pleased only when they came to take Sabine and her family away, as "Enemies of the State."

"Danke for your concern," she said, trying not to let the fear creep into her voice. But as she passed the gangly man with the wrinkled shirt and tousled black hair, she could smell the darkness on his breath. Or was it just that he hadn't taken a bath in weeks?

"Sabine!" Aunt Gertrud's voice faded behind her as Sabine grabbed a stair railing for balance, then hobbled toward the ruined apartment building on Bergstrasse as fast as her noodle legs would carry her. Someday, she told herself, she'd run without her dumb crutches. For now, she worried that Wolfgang might follow her.

But he didn't—this time. And as she passed Number 14, she heard the familiar woof of the dog that no one claimed. He bounded out of an alleyway.

"Hey, Bismarck!" She smiled with relief and bent down to scratch his ear. She didn't mind that he had been named after a famous war hero, or that he sometimes tried to run off with her crutches. "Sorry I don't have anything for you this time."

But the German shepherd mutt had already sniffed out her backpack and knew better. He parked himself on the sidewalk, right in front of Sabine, and sat up on his hind legs.

"You little beggar." Sabine dug into her backpack for the treat, a small crumble of dried cheese. "You can't follow me around the whole neighborhood."

But unlike Wolfgang, he did, all the way down Bernauerstrasse and past the tall steeple of the once-beautiful *Versöhnungskirche,* the Reconciliation Church on Ackerstrasse. Finally they came to the bombed-out apartment block, where Sabine hoped to find the entrance to the bunker. Wolfgang would have lost interest in her by now, wouldn't he?

"It's hidden in the floor," Sabine explained to her friend, who sniffed around the ruins. Come to think of it, the dog might be good to have around. Just in case.

"What do you think?" she asked Bismarck, who scampered across piles of rubble and concrete, with no problem at all. If only she could borrow his legs once in a while.

Finally she struggled into a room with peeling rose wallpaper. *This must be it.* Bomb blasts from long ago had left gaping holes in the walls and ceiling, and Sabine could see right out to the American sector. She dropped to her knees and searched the floorboards for any sign of the trapdoor—the one that blocked the circular staircase below. Bismarck helped with a few sniffs.

"Thanks, boy." She ran a hand across the rough, weather-beaten floor. "It's not as easy to find as I hoped. Maybe you can—ouch!"

Something sharp poked her finger, like a sliver. *Au!* But that was okay if it was the board she'd split the other day, pounding on the door from beneath. She followed the board and saw the splintered corner of the trapdoor. Yes!

She set to work prying it open with her crutch, pulling out the nails, lifting it up. *Whew!* She could see how the hidden trapdoor had stayed hidden for so long. Nervously, she checked over her shoulder once more. No telling if a friend of Wolfgang's had followed her here.

"Here we go!" she told her friend. Bismarck turned circles and barked as Sabine lowered herself down. The dog jumped down after her. From the top of the staircase, she held the dog's collar and waited for her eyes to adjust.

"Let me show you something." She stooped low and closed the trapdoor over their heads. "I think you're going to like it."

Bismarck didn't wait, he just bounded down the stairs she had to take one at a time. He wagged his tail at her and ran off to sniff. She whistled at him, keeping him close as she set up her reading retreat in the Volkswagen staff car. First she lit her two candles, setting them just behind the shattered windshield. They lit her area pretty well, actually, and Bismarck even jumped aboard for a ride. After circling a few times, he made himself comfy in the back of the car, while Sabine curled up on her blanket in the front.

"Not bad, huh, boy?" She pulled out her book and returned to the chapter she'd been reading when Aunt Gertrud had snapped the book away. Without a breeze, the candles barely flickered. Sabine listened to the quiet of her own breathing...and the dog's. Pretty soon she just closed her eyes.

"What's going on?" She sat up with a start. The candles had nearly burned down, but Bismarck still kept watch. "How long did I sleep?"

Bismarck nuzzled her arm and thunked his tail as if to say he was ready to get home too.

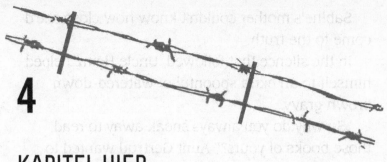

4

KAPITEL VIER
THE RIGHT THING

"Where in the world have *you* been?" Sabine's mother wiped her hands on a dish towel as her daughter slipped into a chair at the little kitchen table. The others stopped eating long enough to frown at her. And Aunt Gertrud looked over at Frau Becker to see what she would do next.

"Sorry I'm late." Sabine's mind raced to think of the right way to say it. Cabbage and potatoes looked as if they had long ago collapsed into a cold heap in the middle of her plate. "I was...I mean, I—"

Her mother's lifted eyebrows looked as if they were saying, "Yes?"

"I was reading, and I fell asleep." Sabine blurted out the truth. Maybe not the *whole* truth, but—

"Not again, Sabine." Frau Becker reached over and brushed a stray wisp of hair from Sabine's face. "And look at you. You look as if you've been...digging ditches or something."

Sabine's mother couldn't know how close she'd come to the truth.

In the silence that followed, Uncle Heinz helped himself to an extra spoonful of watered-down brown gravy.

"So why do you always sneak away to read those books of yours?" Aunt Gertrud wanted to know. "Isn't our company good enough for you?"

"Gertrud, please!" That put Sabine's mother on the defensive. "I can handle this."

"Just like you handle her staying home from school all the time? Just like you coddle her? 'Oh, my poor baby can't walk, we mustn't distress my poor baby.'"

Frau Becker's eyes filled with tears the way they had so many times before, but Gertrud wasn't done yet.

"What I don't understand is why you even stay here, if you hate East Berlin so much. Why don't you just pack your bags and run back to the West, the way all your friends are doing?"

As if they could just do that—without risking being arrested for trying.

"You can't talk to my mother like that!" Sabine stuck her chin out and would have said something else, but her mother shushed her.

"You know very well why we stay, Gertrud." Frau Becker's voice sounded as still as Gertrud's sounded shrill. "Not because we enjoy being locked up in a police state, or because we're forced to stay, which we are. But because I've already lost two husbands, and I will *not* just run away and leave her. Even if I could. Do you understand what I'm saying? I made her that promise even before I joined—"

She stopped short, but that wasn't good enough for Gertrud.

"Go ahead and say it."

But Sabine's mother only shook her head.

"Then I will finish for you. Before you joined the Communist Party. Why don't you say so?"

Sabine held her breath. *Could it be true?* Her mother finally looked up with tears in her eyes.

"I'm not proud of it. But it was the only way to get help for Sabine. They said they would take care of her…her treatment."

"And now look how well she gets around." Gertrud swept her hand at Sabine.

"No. They gave her crutches, and that's the end of it. They broke their promise. But maybe the Americans would be no better, so I will not break mine."

Aunt Gertrud shrugged as Frau Becker went on.

"And since we're the only ones left to take care of Oma, we remain—for now. It's that simple."

Of course *Oma* meant Sabine's grandmother, who lay ill in her bed most of the time. But Aunt Gertrud would not back down. She held her forehead with both hands.

"Aw, it just gives me a headache. You and

that foolish promise again. You know she can't hold you to it. And we all know she belongs in a *genesungsheim*."

"That's enough, Gertrud." Uncle Heinz looked up from stuffing his face, but she shook him off. Sabine's mother leaned over so her nose practically touched her sister-in-law's. Aunt Gertrud didn't blink. "Let me tell you something, Gertrud, just so you don't forget." Her voice trembled this time as it rose. "As long as I live, and as long as Oma lives, she will never be put away in a rest home, out of sight. Do we understand each other? And what's more—"

A bell tinkled from Oma Poldi's room, just as someone knocked on the door. Frau Becker paused and looked toward Oma's room then toward the front door.

"Go see what your grandmother needs, please," she said to Sabine. "I'll get the door."

As Sabine balanced on one crutch and offered her ailing grandmother a glass of water, she could hear everything in the front room—from her mother's polite *"Guten abend"* to the visitor's *"Wie geht es ihnen?"* But as soon as the pleasantries of "Good evening" and "How are you?" were out of the way, the visitor got down to business.

"I understand about her weakness." The woman's voice sounded as if she did not—or maybe that she did understand, but didn't care. "However, your daughter still needs to attend classes *every* day. And I don't know why she refuses to join the *Junge Pioniere*. Perhaps you have not encouraged her?"

Obviously one of the *rektors* from her polytechnical *schule* had come. And she wanted Sabine to join the Young Pioneers? Perfect, if you liked Communist pep talks (like Comrade Ulbricht's) or enjoyed shouting Communist slogans and parading the streets with flags and banners. No, thanks.

"It's just that—" Sabine's mother sounded far away. "Well, since the school year is over in just a few days, and she is so weak sometimes....It's very hard for her, with her legs—"

Sabine didn't make a sound. But that's what it always came down to—her gimpy legs that refused to work the way they should. However, just this once, she didn't mind—as long as it kept her out of the Junge Pioniere.

Sabine noticed Oma Poldi had closed her eyes again. By the peaceful look on her impossibly wrinkled face, she hadn't heard a word.

"Beginning of year, end of year, there is no excuse. Weak or not, she *will* attend her classes more regularly, or else—"

The threat from the *rektor* hung in the air like thick smoke.

Or else what?

"She reads good books," Frau Becker put in. "Many good books. I believe she has learned as much from reading as...well, she is quite a bright girl."

"If she is as bright as you say, she will be wise to join in the Pioniere. And when she turns fourteen, she will go through the *Jugendweihe* dedication ceremony and graduate to the *Freie Deutsche Jugend*."

Not the Free German Youth! Sabine wanted to yell. *I'm being confirmed in the church instead!*

"She'll receive very good training in the FDJ," added the *rektor*.

Brainwashing, you mean. Sabine bit her tongue to keep from yelling it.

"I will discuss it with her," Sabine's mother whispered.

"Discuss?" The visitor sounded like a lawyer in a courtroom. "You simply tell her what is expected, Comrade, and that will be the end of it. Most young people eagerly anticipate going through the *Jugendweihe*. They dedicate themselves to socialist ideals. Far superior to the old religious ceremonies, don't you agree?"

Frau Becker said nothing, but Sabine could almost hear her mother's teeth grinding.

"And what's this?" the woman went on. "You allow her to read *this* kind of book?"

Oh, no. Sabine winced, remembering that she had left *Black Beauty* on the table.

"Why, yes, I mean, no, I—," Sabine's mother stammered.

"You must know this is not an approved book."
Sabine could hear the poison dripping from
the woman's words. "You don't want your child
learning the wrong ideas, do you? Western
propaganda?"

The wrong ideas? Sabine felt her ears starting to
burn. The only wrong ideas she'd heard lately had
come from her Communist teacher.

"I'll do you a favor, then." Suddenly the woman's
voice sounded lighter. "I'll dispose of this book
for you, and we'll just consider it a small mistake.
But then I'll need your guarantee as a parent that
Sabine will attend classes again tomorrow, without fail. Do we have an understanding?"

Sabine dared to peek around the door, just
enough to see her mother standing with her back
to the wall, biting her lip. Aunt Gertrud sat across
the room, silent, knitting, a smile curling her lips.
Her team was winning.

"Was I not clear, Frau Becker?" the teacher
demanded.

"Ja, perfectly clear." Sabine's mother turned
away, her shoulders slumped with defeat.

But that's my book! Sabine's mind screamed.
Before she could change her mind, she swung herself into the room.

"Well!" The *rektor's* eyes widened as she
watched Sabine wobble-march straight toward
her. "I thought perhaps you were resting. I hadn't
expected to see you."

No, and the woman could not have expected the thirteen-year-old to rescue *Black Beauty*. Of course, Sabine had also surprised herself.

"Please pardon me for being rude." Sabine's heart beat wildly as she snatched her book and swallowed hard before backing up. "But I'd be happy to let you, um, *borrow* my book when I've finished reading it. The horse has just been sold to a new owner, you see, and I'd really like to know what happens next. Please excuse me."

She turned back toward the safety of Oma's room. She imagined the *rektor* gasping, or maybe that was Aunt Gertrud.

She stopped in the hallway but didn't dare turn around.

"You don't have to worry. I'll be at school tomorrow."

There. She hid in Oma's room, barely daring to listen until their visitor had left. The front door slammed with a satisfying *thump*. Good.

"Sabine—" The girl jumped when her mother quietly rested a hand on her shoulder.

"I'm so sorry, Mama." The words tumbled out before she could stop them, but didn't they always? "I didn't mean to get you in trouble, but I just couldn't let her come in here and talk to you like that. When she said she was going to take my book, I—"

"Shh." Her mother gently turned Sabine around

and touched a finger to her lips. "You don't want to wake Oma."

Oh. Right. Sabine whispered another apology. How many times could she say "I'm sorry"?

"Child, you don't need to apologize." Her mother leaned closer. "I'm the one who should apologize to you."

"For what? I know you do what you think is best. You work every day. You take good care of Oma. You let me stay home from school sometimes. You—"

"That's right, I do. But only because I feel guilty that you have to go to that horrible state school. All they want to do is train you to be a good Communist." But then she smiled, and for a second, her eyes sparkled. "But did you hear that poor woman? '*Black Beauty* is not on the approved list of books.' It's a horse story!"

Sabine proudly held up the treasure she'd rescued—for now. And they giggled together like sisters, two rebels with a cause. As long as they could keep their Bible and their books—

They sobered up quickly, though, when Oma Poldi groaned softly and stretched her chin and shoulders, as if waking up.

"I knew God had a reason for bringing us to the eastern side of the city." Sabine's mother looked down at her mother-in-law. She'd taken care of the woman every day for as long as Sabine could remember. They'd moved to Oma's apartment in the Russian-controlled sector of Berlin so long ago that Sabine couldn't remember living in the American sector. "And I still believe he does. Oma needs us. And her ties here are so strong. She raised her family in this apartment. You know her son, Erich's father, was a pastor here, and Oma still feels called to stay here. But Sabine, I often wonder if I did the right thing for *you* by bringing you here. Can you forgive me?"

Sabine squeezed her mother's hand.

"You don't have to worry about me, Mama. Sometimes I hate this place and the Vopos with their guns, keeping us here. But I don't believe a word of what they tell me in school."

Still the question nagged her: Why, exactly, had God brought *her* here? How could he use someone like her in a place like this?

As she shuffled out of the room, she promised herself that, no matter what, she would find the answer.

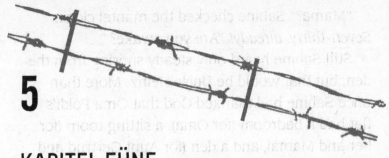

5

KAPITEL FÜNF

BARBED-WIRE SUNDAY

THREE MONTHS LATER...

At first, August 13, 1961, felt just like any other summer Sunday morning. The sun peeked through Sabine's window, waking her. She sat up on her cot and stretched. Soon she would have to be up and dressed, ready to walk with her mother to the church in the American sector. She shivered to think that Wolfgang the Watcher would surely notice and report them to the authorities again. Or worse. How long before they'd be arrested, the way so many others had been?

She hoped Erich would join them after his shift at the hospital. Puzzled, Sabine realized she didn't hear any movement from her mother's side of the room. No breathing or rustling. Nothing. She stared at the sheet that formed a curtain between their beds.

"Mama?" Sabine checked the mantel clock. *Seven-thirty, already!* "Are you awake?"

Still Sabine heard only steady snoring from the den, but that would be Uncle Heinz. More than once Sabine had thanked God that Oma Poldi's flat had a bedroom (for Oma), a sitting room (for her and Mama), and a den (for Aunt Gertrud and Uncle Heinz). Erich kept a bedroll in the corner, but half the time he slept at the hospital. So it wasn't unusual to see his roll folded and stowed in its place under the chair.

She reached for the curtain, not expecting to see her mother's sheets and blankets folded and stowed.

"Mama?" she whispered again, wondering where she'd gone. Feet pounded up the hall stairs, then to their front door. *The Vopo!* But Erich burst in, huffing and puffing.

"Get dressed, Sabine!" he ordered. "You're not going to believe what's going on out there!"

"What are you talking about?" Still shaken by her vision of being hauled away by the police, Sabine didn't move.

It took several tries for her breathless brother to explain in a way that made sense.

"Concrete posts. Barbed wire." His cheeks still flamed bright red. "Vopos all over with machine guns. They're running a fence right down the middle of Bernauerstrasse. They're really doing it! Right down the middle of Berlin!

"The *Volkspolizei* have even set up water cannons and machine guns on rooftops to keep the crowds away. Some folks are just curious, but lots are angry."

Sabine came to life and threw on some clothes, curious and a bit afraid to see the "People's Police" in action. Outside, Erich led the way through a cluster of quiet neighbors. They joined their mother, who looked stunned.

"Oh, Sabine." Frau Becker wrapped a protective arm around her daughter. "Sorry to leave you sleeping. Erich brought me down here about a half hour ago. I didn't want to wake you up if it turned out to be nothing."

But this was *something*. And Sabine could only stare in shock as the workers and Vopos and East German soldiers worked to put up an iron curtain between her world and the world outside.

"They cut off the U-Bahn at midnight," Erich told her quietly, turning away from the glare of a Vopo nearby. "Shut it down. Plus all the telephones, and streetcars, even pipelines. Nothing passes from East to West anymore. Or from West to East, either."

No more trips across the line to shop, to attend church, to visit friends, or even to hang out in the Tiergarten, a park Sabine loved.

"Too many people have managed to escape," whispered an older man standing next to them. Sabine could see his pajamas peeking out from underneath his clothes, and his gray hair stood straight up. "That's why they're caging us in. Like some kind of zoo animals, we are."

They all fell silent as a tractor lowered another concrete post into a hole in the middle of the street. Grim workers followed like spiders with their barbed-wire web, stringing it between posts set too close together for a person to squeeze through.

Sabine gasped as a half dozen West Berliners suddenly charged from the other side. The lead man held a shovel, as if to attack the new wall. Sabine gripped her crutch handles even more tightly.

"They're going to get killed!" she whispered. But the charge didn't even make it to the fence. Three Vopos with wickedly sharp bayonets on the ends of their Russian-made rifles blocked the advance. One of the soldiers shouted a warning before he fired into the air. And every eye on both sides of the new fence stared at the face-off. The six men skidded to a stop just inches from the tips of the bayonets.

The crowd gasped. Sabine's mother covered her daughter's hand with her own so tightly that Sabine could barely feel her fingers. Who would move first? A long moment later, the protesters raised their hands in surrender and backed away from the soldiers' threats. Most of the crowd gathered on their side of the new wall backed away too.

"You're not to go near those Vopos or that fence," Frau Becker warned her children. "Do you understand?"

Sabine nodded silently and tried to hide her angry tears. Yes, she understood. All too well. But how could they just stand back and let this happen?

"Why are they doing this to us?" Her voice rose a notch. Her mother tried to comfort her and lead her back home. Sabine stiffened and planted her crutches on the sidewalk. "And why didn't we leave before this thing went up?"

"Shh, Sabine. Now is not the time."

"No, now it's too late. We waited, and we waited. And now we'll never get out of here."

Erich joined their mother in steering Sabine back to the safety of home. But Sabine had to know.

"Why didn't we just take Oma with us? Why did we stay here with her? Look!"

"Sabine, shush."

"But, Mama! We should have—"

"You're getting worked up over something you can't change. I thought you understood. Your brother can't abandon his patients at the hospital. And Oma is very...determined to stay."

Determined? More like stubborn.

"Because?" But Sabine knew the answer.

"Because God placed her in this neighborhood. Maybe us, as well. You know she never asked us to stay. But we agreed that we would never abandon Oma."

Sabine knew Oma's faith led her to do what she believed, and her mother did the same. She wondered if she could be as trusting. But still she could not help staring over her shoulder at the ugly, frightening fence going up in the middle of their neighborhood. She could not help staring at the soldiers who defiantly pointed their guns and bayonets at them — as if she and her neighbors had done something wrong!

She wanted to curl up and cry, to run at the fence — screaming — as the brave but foolish men had, to throw a brick at the wall. Something! Anything! Instead, she let her mother and brother lead her home like a lamb, back to the apartment where Oma Poldi probably still slept.

When they checked on Oma, she hadn't even moved. A half hour later, Sabine left her mother and brother at the table to see if Oma wanted to eat yet.

"Oma?" she whispered, drawing a little closer. "Are you ready for a little breakfast?"

But Oma couldn't answer, and one side of her face looked funny. As she tried to sit up and speak, she slid off her pillow and nearly tumbled over the side of her bed.

"Oma!" Sabine nearly screamed as she grabbed Oma's sleeve to keep her from falling. "Erich! Come quick. There's something wrong with Oma!"

Later that night, Sabine paced outside the doors of St. Ludwig's Hospital, where Erich worked and Oma now rested. Not dead, *Gott sei Dank*. Thank God her mother had sent her in to see if Oma wanted breakfast.

"Are you sure you don't want to come inside and wait?" Erich called through the entrance. She could see his face in the little pool of light from the entry lamps. When she shook her head and kept walking, he jogged out to join her.

"Look, I know how you feel about this place. The bad memories and everything. That's why you won't come in, right?"

Oh, and she hadn't even told him the worst of it. She'd never told *anyone* about the worst days of her stay there. About the dark side of Nurse Ilse. About the beyond-painful therapy that the nurse seemed to enjoy. About the shouting and Nurse Ilse's threats. About the closet. Especially not about the closet. Even now she couldn't answer Erich.

"I'd probably feel the same way, if I were you."

But Nurse Ilse was long gone. Why did Sabine still feel so afraid? Finally she stopped, leaning on her crutches. Her big brother was only trying to help. And she had to know.

"Is Oma going to die?"

"Come on inside. The doctor explained everything to Mutti."

"I don't want to go inside to talk to Mama. Is she going to die? Just tell me!"

Erich raked his light hair off his forehead and leaned against the brick building. Yes, the air felt warm, but not warm enough for him to sweat like this.

"All right, listen. She had a stroke, and she's probably paralyzed. We don't know if she's going to live through the night. *That's* why you need to come inside."

"A *stroke*." Sabine repeated the word, wishing this day had never happened. First the horrible fence, then Oma. And now she couldn't stop shivering.

"So are you coming?" her brother asked.

Sabine crossed her arms and looked up at the hospital. A boy flattened his nose against a second-floor window, watching her through enormous black glasses. But a moment later, he'd disappeared. Erich looked up to see what had caused her questioning expression.

"Sabine?"

He hadn't seen the boy, maybe about her age, but downright skinny. His haunted look made Sabine shiver even more.

"Yes, I mean—" She stumbled over her words.

"So are you coming, or are you going to stand out here all night?"

When she studied the pain in her brother's face, she knew what she had to do—never mind the ghost of Nurse Ilse. She took a deep breath, nodded slowly, and started for the door.

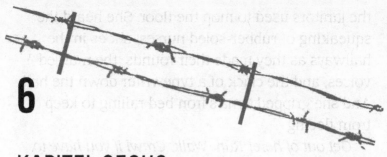

6

KAPITEL SECHS

OMA POLDI BECKER

Sabine's grandmother looked nearly the same as she always had, resting in bed, breathing quietly. She lay in the last bed in a row of ten, so when they came to visit they could see out the window to the street below. But after a day and a half, Oma had hardly opened an eye.

"Oma—" Sabine willed her grandmother to be well, to get out of the hospital bed. She wondered if Oma would ever speak to her again. She already felt a hole, once filled with Oma's warmth. They had smiled together, had shared secrets, and had prayed together.

And that was hard enough, but the hardest part—though Sabine would never admit it aloud—was seeing everyone in the hospital, and remembering. It seemed as if she had never left. When she closed her eyes, she felt the fear of Nurse Ilse's threats, of being imprisoned in the bed or the closet. She smelled the peculiar antiseptic the janitors used to mop the floor. She heard the squeaking of rubber-soled nurses' shoes in the hallways as they made their rounds, the muffled voices, and the clack of a typewriter down the hall. And she gripped Oma's iron bed railing to keep from fleeing.

Get out of here! Run. Walk. Crawl if you have to. Her head spun, and for a moment, she felt like she might pass out as she gasped for breath.

Footsteps approaching brought her back to the present, and she turned to see Erich, his white intern's smock flowing behind him. Pushing away her fear, she looked him in the eye and held her finger up to her mouth.

"Shh. Don't wake her up," Sabine whispered as she pointed to their mother, slumped on a waiting-room chair in the corner. Erich nodded and silently joined Sabine next to the bed.

If he saw it, he's not going to comment on my panic attack, she thought with relief.

"Onkel Heinz stopped by," he whispered. He bent a little closer to listen to Oma's breathing and checked his wristwatch. He wasn't a doctor, yet, but Sabine could tell he'd be a great one. "Mutti talked to him for a minute, but he left before you got here."

"Oh." Sabine didn't mind that she'd missed him. *Good.*

"He's still *celebrating* the new fence, that wall...if you can believe that." Erich shook his head in disgust. "As if it's something to get excited about."

"People are still escaping, though, aren't they?"

"Most people believe it's too dangerous, now." He lowered his voice further, as if someone might hear them. "The guards, the Vopos, they're crazy. Give them guns and they turn into monsters."

Sabine thought about what Erich said, then decided it wouldn't hurt—

"Erich, can I ask you something?"

He lifted an eyebrow. "If it's quick. I have to get back to Dr. Woermann's rounds. We're doing surgery this afternoon."

"Have you ever thought of trying to escape to the West?"

He brought a hand to his forehead, as if he'd been hit by a sudden headache.

"You're not serious, little sister."

"Yes, I am. The wall's made me really think about it, and what it means to be free, and I was just wondering if—"

"Hold on." He held up his hand for her to stop. "I don't think we should be talking about this right now."

Sabine had to lean toward him to hear.

"Why not?"

"*Why not?* Because you can get hurt. Just forget it. Don't even talk about it. There are too many—" He sighed. "There are too many ways to get in trouble asking those kinds of questions. But listen, when Mutti wakes up, tell her I'll be home late tonight."

"Aren't you always?"

He winked at her and hurried off, the big brother, the doctor-to-be, leaving her once again with her fears. She suddenly realized he hadn't answered her question.

"Our apartment building is right next to the new wall," said a voice in the shadows, which made her jump. "You should see it. They woke us up Saturday night, when they started pounding in the street and putting up the posts."

"Oh! You nearly gave me a heart attack."

"Sorry. But we're in the right place for that, aren't we?"

Is that supposed to be funny? Sabine couldn't see who belonged to the voice, then a boy about her age stepped out of the shadows. He squinted at her from behind an enormous pair of black-rimmed glasses. And then she knew.

"You're the kid in the window," she told him. "I saw you staring at me and my brother the other night."

"Me?" He wrinkled his forehead as if trying to remember. "I wasn't staring."

"You were too staring."

"Well, then not on purpose."

"You were staring accidentally?"

"My mother's here, and I visit her a lot," he told

Sabine. "I just look outside sometimes to pass the time."

"Oh. And you make big spots on the window with your nose too."

"Well, I didn't see anybody," he said defensively.

Sabine hadn't noticed how thick the boy's glasses were until he turned away.

"Wait a minute." She held up her hand. "Are those glasses...I mean, can you—"

"See? Hardly. If I take them off, I'm practically blind."

"What about with them on?"

"With them on, I'm practically blind."

He chuckled and pointed at her crutches.

"What about those things? Are you—"

"Disabled? You should see me try to walk without them."

"Can you?"

"Not really," Sabine admitted.

"Are you a patient here?"

"Used to be. But I haven't been back here since I was a little girl. I'm here visiting my grandmother. My name's Sabine, by the way. Sabine Becker."

"And I'm Willi Stumpff. Nice to meet you."

"Did you say your mother's here?"

"Yep. She had a baby, but it came too early. Mom had a hard time with the baby, and the doctors want to keep an eye on her while she heals. They're not sure about my little sister, either."

"Wow. I'm sorry." She looked over at Oma again.

227

"*Ja*. Everybody in my family is praying for her, but—" He chuckled again and looked around, as if somebody might be spying on them.

"But what?"

"But you'd better not tell my Junge Pioniere leader. I think he believes Christians are dumb or something."

"You're in the Pioniere, and you're a Christian? What about all that hip-hooray they do at their meetings, listening to all that Communist 'for peace and socialism' stuff?"

He chuckled again, and the big glasses slid down his nose. "It's just easier that way. If you knew my parents, you'd know what I mean. I'm not a Communist, though. Just don't tell anybody, or I might get into trouble."

So why is he telling me, a stranger?

As they talked some more, Sabine decided she liked Willi Stumpff's openness. She learned that he and his family attended the Lutheran church, which helped explain about the people praying for his mother. And it didn't take long to figure out that he really couldn't see much farther than ten feet. That explained why he'd seemed to stare right at her the other night but hadn't recognized her close up.

"So you can't really see what's going on outside your window?"

"I can hear things really good. Like—"

He paused and pulled her to the side.

"Like the nurse coming up behind us," he whispered. "She's a Communist, and you should stay out of her way."

Oh. Sabine didn't look as the woman in uniform hurried past.

"I can see shapes okay," he went on. "My mama sometimes tells me what she sees. Or she did, before the baby came and she had to stay here. She describes things so well, it seems like I can see them too."

"So what do you...I mean, what does your mother see out your window at home?"

"Oh, we have a great view of the Spree River, and the new fence runs right below us. You know, the wall they're starting to build. You can practically touch it."

"Wow. I can't imagine what it would be like to need someone to tell you what's right outside your own window."

"Guess I can't imagine needing crutches to get around," Willi responded. So there. Maybe they had a lot more in common than either realized at first.

"Yeah." Sabine smiled. "I guess having crutches makes it a little harder to drive."

"You mean like a car?" Willi's eyes widened in surprise. He didn't know her well enough to know she was joking. But come on, they were only thirteen, right?

"Army staff car." She folded her arms and nodded. "Volkswagen. It's mine."

Well, technically, maybe... not. Unless you lived by the law of finders-keepers. But she didn't tell him that part. And his eyes started to look like magnified saucers as she described the underground bunker and "her" car. She neglected to mention some of the minor details, like the missing wheels and the engine that sort of lay in pieces on the ground. Other than that, she could probably drive it right out of there, if she wanted to.

"Really?" Willi still couldn't believe it. "This I have to see."

She thought for a moment. Could she really trust this boy? Then again, he'd trusted her from the start.

"Maybe—" She hesitated. "But on one condition."

"Name it."

"That you don't tell anybody."

He nodded. "No problem."

"And then," she added, "you have to let me see what the city looks like from your window."

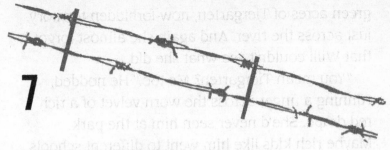

7

KAPITEL SIEBEN

THE VIEW FROM WILLI'S PLACE

The following afternoon, Sabine stood in Willi Stumpff's fifth-floor apartment, staring out the window at the divided city and the Spree River.

"What a great view. I've never seen a better one. And it looks totally different up here," she told him, "compared to down on the street. The East and West sides of Berlin look like different worlds from up here!"

Willi nodded as if he agreed, though she wasn't sure. He couldn't see the new buildings and shops on the other side of the fence and the bombed-out buildings on their side. Could he? The bright signs and lights on the other side, the gray on their side. It was almost as if the war had never ended in half of the city.

And they were in the wrong half.

"I used to play in that park." She pointed at the

green acres of Tiergarten, now forbidden territory, just across the river. And again she almost forgot that Willi couldn't see what she did.

"You mean Tiergarten? Me too." He nodded, running a finger across the worn velvet of a rich red drape. She'd never seen him at the park. Maybe rich kids like him went to different schools.

"What does your father do?" she asked Willi. "I didn't see him at the hospital."

"Oh." His face fell. "Well, yeah, I don't see him much, either. He used to work for the government. Now he works on cars."

Nothing wrong with that. But the way Willi said it made her feel as if it were, well, embarrassing. Willi's father paced in the next room, talking on the telephone in hushed tones. Sabine wished she hadn't asked.

But Willi seemed to shrug it off. He pressed his nose to the window as he had at the hospital. Without taking his eyes from the view, he asked her to describe everything she could see.

"Everything?" She wondered whether she'd get home for dinner in time. When he nodded, she started by telling him about the people walking through the park and the people riding bicycles along their side of the border. She told him about the little shops on both sides of the fence, about the church and the graveyard. She described the soldiers patrolling with guns and the men laying a brick wall next to the barbed-wire fence.

"And look there!" She waved one arm wildly while balancing her crutches with the other.

"What are you doing?" Willi grabbed her wrist and tried to pull her away from the window. "Someone's going to see you!"

"That's the point!" She wrestled her arm free. "I see a couple of American soldiers, over on the other side of the fence...Yoo-hoo! Over here!"

Willi held his head in his hands and looked alarmed. But never mind him. And never mind that his father would probably hear her. She continued to wave as wildly as she could, hoping to catch the Americans' attention.

"There, see? They're stopping!" She waved again, just in case one of the soldiers happened to look up. She prayed the American soldiers could do something about their prison city. Her brother had told her stories about when he was her age, when the American planes flew into the city, bringing food and coal, even candy for the kids.

But that was a long time ago, and these were not the same soldiers. They wore the same uniforms, though, with the same pretty red, white, and blue flag on their jeep. *Come on, look up!*

But a moment later, she let her hand fall.

"What happened? Did they see you?" Willi still hid behind his hands. "Do they have guns? Are they looking up here?"

"Willi, they're Americans, not the Stasi." Not the feared secret state police. She watched, disappointed, as they started their jeep. "Aww. There they go. They just stopped to talk to somebody down there."

She watched the Americans until they had driven out of sight, up their side of Bernauerstrasse.

"See anything else?" Willi finally asked after she'd stayed quiet for a few minutes.

Ja, she did. She continued telling him about the people outside the window: A couple trying to maneuver a baby carriage over a curb. A serious-looking man in a dark gray coat (even in the summer heat!)...probably a secret agent. That's what secret agents wore. She even told Willi about the couple strolling close to the fence, and—

"Wait a minute. He's walking right toward the fence." *What was he doing?*

"What? Do you mean he's trying to—"

"I think so." She nodded. She didn't even need to say the word *escape*. They both knew.

"What about the woman? You said they were a couple."

"She's grabbing his arm, like she doesn't want him to go."

"But he's going anyway?"

Sabine lowered her voice, hoping Willi might do the same. She didn't want Herr Stumpff to come investigate.

"He just shook her off. Now he's trying to climb over the barbed wire."

"What about the guards?"

"One of them is—" The words just wouldn't

234

come. They'd all heard World War 2 stories about the Nazis, the Blackshirts, the Brownshirts, the villains, the men who blindly followed Hitler. Now here in the People's German Democratic Republic, Soviet-controlled East Germany, they had Vopos. The men who knocked on doors in the middle of the night, who kept people from escaping to freedom in the West. The men now pointing their guns at the man trying to scale the fence.

"Are you sure he's trying to escape?" Willi leaned against the window as if he could see for himself. "It's not even night yet. He must be crazy."

Sabine nodded but could not take her eyes off the scene below.

"Come on, Sabine. You have to tell me."

But Sabine's throat had gone dry, and she could barely speak. "He, he's...climbing, now. The woman is on her knees on the sidewalk. I think she's crying. Motioning to him. Telling him to stop, probably."

"And?"

"Another guard just ran over."

"He's got a gun?"

Sabine nodded.

"Sabine?"

"Yeah. He's...pointing his gun. He's—"

She winced. A muffled *pop-pop*, like fireworks from a distance, reached them. Seconds, maybe a minute ticked by before Willi spoke again.

"Do you think he's alive?" he wondered quietly.

"There's an ambulance down there. They're

carrying him off." *Did he move? Maybe.* "I think maybe he is. It looked like he moved his arm. I think."

Or she prayed that he did. Suddenly she hated the wall that now divided their city: allowing free people on one side, trapping people on the other. The free could travel and laugh and buy things in the West; the trapped faced dreary gray cement apartment buildings and limited supplies in the East. No wonder the man had risked his life.

Sabine's shocked tears had begun to dry, and she gripped her crutches until her hands turned white. Wasn't this the kind of thing Corrie ten Boom and Anne Frank had lived through? She'd read books about both of them—books that weren't likely on the "approved" list. Maybe World War 2 hadn't really ended sixteen years earlier, in 1945. Maybe she had just seen it begin again, right outside Willi Stumpff's fifth-floor window.

Sabine couldn't watch anymore. She wanted to throw up. And she hadn't realized it before, but she'd bitten her lip so hard that now she could taste the blood.

"I have to go," she finally told Willi. He didn't ask about seeing her car. Good. Some other time, maybe.

"See you at St. Ludwig's tomorrow?" he asked. He looked as shaken as she felt.

She nodded.

Maybe tomorrow.

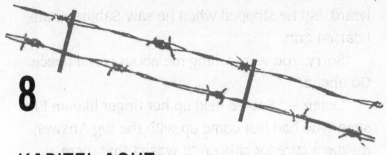

8

KAPITEL ACHT

THE IDEA

"I've been thinking, Willi." Sabine leaned against the wall, near the empty nurses' station.

"That's scary."

"No, really. I think I know how the last war happened."

"Let's hear it for the world-famous Sabine." He raised his voice like a circus announcer. "The girl who's unlocked the key to world peace."

"You're making jokes. I'm serious." She checked to make sure no one was listening.

"Oh, you want a good joke? How about this one: When does a Trabi reach top speed?"

"Willi, I don't think—"

"Come on; it's just a car joke. When does it go the fastest?"

She sighed. "I give up."

"When it's being towed away."

He cackled as if his joke about the clunky East German car were the funniest thing he'd ever heard, but he stopped when he saw Sabine's half-hearted grin.

"Sorry. You were telling me about world peace. Go ahead."

"Listen—" Sabine held up her finger like an Einstein who had just come up with the Big Answer, maybe a cure for cancer. "It wasn't that there weren't enough good people. The problem was that they were all too afraid to speak up."

"That's it?" Willi raised his eyebrows at her.

"Right." She nodded. "And the same thing's happening today. Everybody's too scared to say anything about the wall. But if we all worked together, we could stop it."

"We could, huh? How?"

She scratched her head.

"I haven't figured that part out yet. But I do know how we can bring people together. Right now they're just standing around watching the wall go up, acting like a bunch of sheep."

"Baa."

"Would you quit it?" She punched him on the shoulder. "Do you want to stop the wall, or don't you?"

"You know I don't like it any more than you do." He sighed. "We used to visit my cousins in the American sector and my grandparents. Everybody's over there, and we're stuck over here for the rest of our lives."

Sabine told him her plan, but he didn't seem convinced.

"What if somebody finds out?" he asked. "Do you know how much trouble we'd be in?"

"First of all, nobody's ever going to find it down in the bunker. And second of all, if Anne Frank could do it, so can we!"

"Who's Anne Frank? Somebody you know?"

"You're kidding me. You didn't read that book?"

He shrugged. And for a moment, she wondered if boys had half a brain.

"It's this diary, see, and—"

"I'm not into girls' diaries. Boys write journals."

"Would you stop? I'm trying to explain. Anne Frank was Jewish, and she had to hide in someone's attic the whole war, and she was really brave, and she wrote a diary, which they turned into a book. Got it now?"

"Got it. So we write a journal."

"No. I'm just saying she was brave, even when people were out to get her."

"Oh." Willi scratched his head. "Okay."

"So tomorrow night we meet in the bunker, and we don't tell anybody else."

He raised his right hand. "On my honor as a Junge Pioniere."

"Ohhh." She rolled her eyes. "Anything but that."

"Scout's honor, then."

"You're not a Scout. How do you know what they do?"

"They have them in England. And America. They go camping. I read it somewhere."

"I thought you didn't read."

"I do too. Just not girls' diaries."

"All right. But forget the Pioneer honor." She held out her hand for him to shake. "We have to make a pact."

"Sounds serious." He wasn't smiling anymore. "What kind of pact?"

"To do whatever we can, for as long as we can. For freedom."

Willi rubbed his chin and thought for a moment, then nodded and shook her hand. "For freedom," he said, echoing her words. Time to get down to business.

"So how much money do you have?" she asked him. "We're going to need it to make this plan work."

And the plan would work just fine, as long as Uncle Heinz didn't hear her leave the apartment.

"Who's that?" he mumbled from his dark corner.

Sabine quietly pulled her little backpack on, glad no one had turned on the light.

"Just Sabine," she whispered. "I'm going down the hall."

Which was true, and nighttime visits to the washroom at the end of the hall weren't unusual. She waited a moment at the door, wondering if her uncle would respond. He just grunted and launched back into his snoring. Good. Now she just had to get out of the building and down the street without anybody else stopping her.

"You'd better be there, Willi Stumpff," she whispered as she slipped onto the dark street. The stairs didn't stop her, though she had to admit it took her a little longer to take them one at a time. But now she didn't stop long enough to let goose bumps climb the back of her neck. She just might turn around and scurry back to bed rather than make her way to the bombed-out apartment building on Bergstrasse.

What was that? Someone coming down the street? Sabine dived into the shadows, crutches and all. A dog barked, and a door slammed.

But no one came toward her.

After a minute, she breathed again and picked up her backpack. *Keep going. There it is.* She slipped through the crumbled entry and felt her way into the maze of rooms.

"Willi?" she whispered. Losing her concentration for a moment, she tripped over a loose brick but caught herself before falling on her face. When she looked up, she could make out a flickering light up ahead.

"So I finally get to see this car of yours," Willi announced from the shadows. Light from his candle glittered and reflected off his glasses, casting weird shapes on the broken walls around them.

"There you are," she greeted him. "I was afraid you weren't going to show."

"Didn't I say I would be here?"

"Yeah, but—"

"Or did you think I was too blind to find my way around the neighborhood?"

"You said it, not me."

He just smiled and pulled a little round compass out of his pocket, holding it up to the light.

"I don't get too lost. But where's your car?"

"All right, Mr. Boy Scout." She led the way to the trapdoor. Five minutes later, Willi walked all around the Volkswagen, leaning closer with the candle for a better look.

"Whoa." He whistled. "Too bad it doesn't have an engine, or wheels, or a windshield, or . . . let's see. What *does* it have?"

"It has seats. But now you've seen it. Did you bring the stuff?"

"Patience. I brought it." He unloaded his own small backpack. "One hundred eighty-seven sheets of paper. That's all I could find in my father's office. And the ink. What about you?"

Sabine pulled out her box.

"It has three different sizes of letters, and they snap together like this, see?" She showed him how the printing kit worked, the one she'd bought with Willi's money at the *Schreibwarenhandlung*. The stationery store owner had even shown her how to work it. "First, you arrange all the little rubber

242

letters into words. Next, you ink the letters up with the roller, then you press it against the paper like so."

"An underground printing press."

"Just like in this book I read about the Danish underground movement," she told him as she started sorting letters. "They did this kind of thing during World War Two."

"Another book, huh?" He picked up one of the novels she'd left in the car before tossing it back. "Let's just figure out what we're going to say and get out of here."

"How about *Liebe Freiheit, Keine Mauer*?" Sabine asked.

"'Up with Freedom, Down with the Wall!' Yeah, I like it."

Sabine set up the headline while Willi worked on the rest.

"Done yet?" she asked him five minutes later.

"Come on. You just have four words. I have forty."

"You can do it."

"Didn't say I couldn't. How about this: 'We must protest until the wall comes back down.' Does that sound—"

"Perfect." And for the next hour, they printed sheet after sheet of their protest papers.

"Hey, we're getting pretty good at this," Willi told her as they worked their way through the paper supply.

Well, sort of. Some looked smudged, others crooked, but they kept working. Roll ink on the letters, press against the paper, peel it off...paper after paper.

Willi brought his hand up to meet a yawn, and Sabine giggled. Even in the candlelight, she could see the inky fingerprints on his cheek.

"We're done," Sabine announced as she pulled the last paper off. "Do you know what time it is?"

"Don't know; don't want to know." Willi gathered a handful of papers. "Let's just get this over with. But—" He hesitated. "What about that guy, Wolfgang, who's always watching you from his apartment window?"

"What about him? Most of the time he's there; sometimes he's not."

"Have you actually ever met him?"

"You don't want to know, Willi." She pushed away the memory of Wolfgang waiting for her at the foot of the stairs.

"Well, maybe he's asleep."

And maybe not. Sabine just followed Willi up the stairway and back to her neighborhood. She held her breath, but Wolfgang's window looked dark; nothing moved.

"Up there?" Willi followed her gaze, and she nodded. If Wolfgang were watching, well...Sabine squared her shoulders and prayed he wasn't. They still had work to do.

Their first stop: the townhouse apartments

down her street. Sabine felt a tingle as she slipped the first few leaflets under the doors. What would people think when they read them?

Willi had crossed to the other side of the street, working his way toward Sabine's apartment at twice her speed.

Willi! She wanted to scream but could only freeze in terror and melt into a dark doorway. A Vopo policeman had rounded a corner, and Willi had stumbled right into his path. Though the boy wiggled and protested, the Vopo held him tightly. Sabine's heart nearly beat out of her chest as she tried to think.

But Willi acted; he planted a good kick in one of the man's shins—just enough to loosen his grip. In a heartbeat, Willi whirled free and sprinted down the sidewalk, leaving the policeman in a cloud of flying protest papers.

"Halt!" The Vopo drew his gun, but he was still hopping in pain. Willi had already darted around a corner.

Sabine stared in amazement. That kid could get around! He couldn't see clearly ten feet in front of his own face, but he could run like the wind.

Sabine's grin melted, and she nearly choked when the Vopo seemed to look straight at her, as if he could hear her heart beating.

Could he? She stood lamppost-still in the dark, not breathing, not blinking. She still clutched the "Up with Freedom, Down with the Wall!" papers that would send her straight to jail. She could only watch as the man lit a match and held it to a stack of their papers. When he seemed satisfied that they would burn, he tossed the whole lot in the gutter.

Sabine buried her face in the brick wall as a flickering light groped the shadows. Surely he would discover her. She waited silently, the blood pounding in her ears, the sound of the Vopo's laugh echoing down the street. She could not fight and run, the way Willi had. But maybe if she screamed someone would help her. Maybe Mama would even hear her. Armed with a plan, she turned to face the Vopo—

Who had disappeared. She caught her breath and looked down the street.

No one. All he'd left behind were paper ashes and a few embers, flickering orange reminders of their protest. She walked over and poked the burned pile with her crutch. All that work—

Sadly, she straightened up and instinctively looked over her shoulder at Wolfgang's window. Did the curtain move? She didn't wait to check. She and Willi would just have to think of a better way to get people's attention.

She just had to slip back into her apartment without waking anyone up. She couldn't help yawning as she realized how long she'd been awake. This felt like the longest trip down the hall she'd ever made. As she quietly entered the apartment, she immediately knew something wasn't right.

Aunt Gertrud's voice hissed out of the darkness. "Where have you been all this time?"

Sabine squinted as the probing beam of a flashlight searched out her face. At least she'd slipped the leftover flyers into her backpack.

"Oh, it's you." Sabine yawned like Miss Innocent, ignoring her aunt's question. "I was just going back to bed."

"You most certainly were not down the hall all this—" began Aunt Gertrud. Another sleepy voice interrupted.

"Sabine?" her mother asked. "What's all the noise?"

"Sorry to wake you," Sabine whispered as she used the chance to get into her bed. She pulled the sheets to her chin and decided she could take off her shoes later. Hugging her backpack under the sheets, she closed her eyes.

With a disgusted sigh, Aunt Gertrud switched off the flashlight and shuffled back to bed.

And Sabine did her best to keep from shaking.

9

KAPITEL NEUN

VISIT FROM THE STASI

"What about all the printing stuff?" asked Willi, and Sabine shushed him. She waited a moment while a doctor hurried by, his white smock rustling.

"It's still safe down in the bunker, if we need it again."

"What?" Willi leaned closer to hear.

"I *said*—"

A hospital orderly gave them a curious look as he walked by pushing a laundry cart. Sabine recognized him, one of her brother Erich's friends. Dietrich, wasn't it? He smiled at them. But after a quick nod, she turned away so he wouldn't hear her response to Willi.

"Listen," she said as she pulled him back into a corner stacked high with white sheets and thin blue hospital blankets. "We have to come up with a better plan."

"Yeah," he agreed. "That was a little too close last—"

"Hey, there you are!" Erich walked up and ruffled Sabine's hair. She'd tried to duck but was too late.

"What do the doctors say about Oma?" she asked, not sure she wanted the real answer.

Erich's shoulders fell a bit.

"You see her, same as the doctors. She's getting a little worse each day. But she's hanging on—"

Sabine nodded. She kept hoping the news would change for the better.

"Can you do me a favor?" he asked. "I need you to carry a message home for me."

Sabine couldn't help yawning as she nodded.

"Late night, huh? Well, just tell Mutti that I have to work a bit late, but I should be home by seven. Can you remember that?"

"By seven," she repeated. *Late again?*

Dietrich came back down the hall, this time with his arms full of blankets.

"Hey, back to work!" he teased, a smile breaking through his long face. "Or have we gone on strike today?"

"That's it!" Sabine snapped her fingers and grabbed Willi's arm. "I don't know why I didn't think of it!"

"Did I say something?" Dietrich asked them.

"Gotta go," Sabine said. She tugged on Willi's sleeve and started toward the exit. She stopped only long enough to wave to Erich and the puzzled orderly.

"Already I don't like it," Willi protested, following her. He tried to put on the brakes when they got to the street, but Sabine had set her course and had no intention of slowing down.

"You can't not like it. You haven't even heard my idea."

"I don't need to hear it. I just know that it's going to get us in trouble, like we were in last night."

"Oh, come on. Remember our pact? This is foolproof. Now, here's the plan—"

A half hour later, Sabine repeated the steps in her head as they neared their first target. They'd find plenty of people, probably cranky in the summer heat, standing in lines this time of day. For eggs, one line. For meat, another line. For carrots, yet another line. Working people, on their way home. Perfect. But could she convince Willi?

"You really think everybody's just going to agree? 'Yeah, that's a great idea, we hate the wall too.' Why would they go along with this—"

"This brilliant idea?" she finished. She stepped aside as an older woman hurried out a shop door, bells tinkling. "Of course they'll go along with it. Everyone hates the way we live in this half of Berlin. Everyone hates these lines. And everyone hates the wall. All they need is someone to tell them what to do."

"Baa." Willi did his sheep imitation just under his breath, and Sabine elbowed him as they entered the shop. But he knew what to do, and like a good soldier, he shuffled into one of the lines. Sabine took her place in the other.

At the front of Sabine's line, a squat, frowning man studied his tiny piece of sausage. The butcher hadn't given him enough meat to feed a toy poodle. And so Sabine made her first move, planting one of her crutches far enough into the aisle to trip the retreating customer.

"*Entschuldige!*" she whispered, afraid to look up. "Excuse me. But did you hear about the strike tomorrow? No one is going to work. To protest the... wall."

What else could she say? The man's worn leather shoes paused for a moment next to her crutch then stepped carefully around and continued out the door. When she finally looked up, Willi shrugged and gave her an "oh, well" look. His turn came as a middle-aged woman approached from the head of his line.

"We're having a strike," he blurted out, way too loudly. A couple of people turned, eyebrows raised, and his cheeks flamed red—as if he'd just belched, or worse. "That is, I mean—"

The woman breezed by him. But an older woman ahead of him crossed her arms and turned to face him. She seemed almost as wide as she was tall.

"What are you babbling about, boy?"

He glanced at Sabine before taking a deep breath to answer.

"A strike. You know. No working. To pro-test...lousy food. And the w-w-wall."

The woman just glared at him for a long moment, then she harrumphed and turned her back on him.

And so it went: at the *metzgerladen* that had little meat, at the *bäckerei* that offered little bread, at the *milchladen* that had almost no milk. When Sabine and Willi got kicked out of one shop, they tried another. And another. But in the end, it didn't seem to matter. Sabine grew more and more discouraged as everyone responded like sheep, sheep, sheep.

"What is wrong with these people?" she demanded. After an hour, even Sabine had to admit that her plan wouldn't work.

"I don't know." Willi shook his head and started counting on his fingers. "I had about a dozen people walk by like I didn't exist, even more who just growled or gave me what I can only guess were dirty looks, and at least eight who threatened to call the police."

"And you did better than I did." Sabine batted a chunk of concrete from the sidewalk with her crutch, sending it skittering into the *strasse* like a hockey puck. "But at least we didn't get thrown in jail."

"Well, I don't know about you, Sabine, but I'm done." He turned off at his corner. "Pact or no pact. Maybe I'll see you at the hospital tomorrow."

She nodded and let her shoes drag on the sidewalk, even though her mother always told her not to. It scuffed the sides and the toes. Maybe she would just end up like Anne Frank—captured by the soldiers in the end. As she rounded the corner of her floor's hallway, she froze at the sight of two men in dark leather coats leaving Frau Finkenkrug's apartment.

Stasi! One of them slammed the door shut.

"Republikflucht," muttered the other one, a tall man with a goatee just like Comrade Ulbricht's. They obviously hadn't noticed Sabine—yet. So she backed up as quickly as she dared. Before she backed around the corner, she silently watched the men apply an official-looking red seal to the wood just above the doorknob. It was obviously meant to keep anyone from opening the apartment again soon. As if Frau Finkenkrug had come down with some kind of terrible sickness, like smallpox or black death.

But Sabine knew better. She liked the sound of that word: *Republikflucht.* Flight from the Republic. The frau had escaped! And it would sound even better if people would say it of her and her mother.

"Come on," she heard one of the men say.

"We're going to be here all night if we don't get these interviews done soon."

She heard the men rap sharply on Herr Gruhn's door, hardly waiting for the old man to answer before they pushed their way inside. Sabine knew the pattern: the Stasi would search each apartment, looking until they found something they could use as an excuse to arrest someone, to blame that person for helping the frau escape. A radio tuned to the wrong station? A piece of forbidden *Westliteratur*, like a magazine from the other side of the border? That would be enough. Sabine shivered. When she heard Herr Gruhn's door close, she hurried past it to her door.

"Mama!" she whispered as she pushed inside. "Your fashion magazines! They're coming!"

Frau Becker dropped her spoon in the soup kettle and ran to snatch up the forbidden literature. Sabine could think of nothing more silly than hiding magazines from the Stasi. She hardly had time to grab two magazines off the table and replace them with a couple of Communist brochures—the kind Uncle Heinz brought home from his tractor factory—before the familiar sharp knock on the door made her jump.

"*Um Himmels willen!*" Aunt Gertrud declared, stumbling out of the front room. She looked as if she'd just rolled out of bed. "Heavens! Who is making all that noise?"

She froze in horror when the two Stasi pushed the door open.

"Aack!" She grabbed at her hair and spun around to scurry through the doorway.

"Excuse me," Frau Becker said, "but that door was closed."

"We knocked," said the man with the goatee. He barged into the kitchen and inspected the Communist brochures. Hmm, that made a good first impression, but maybe not good enough. Sabine gripped her mother's magazines behind her back and leaned against the wall. Had one of these men stopped Willi last night?

Too bad Uncle Heinz was out with his friends at the pub.

"My husband and I are loyal party members," stated Aunt Gertrud as she returned to the room, her hair swept into a hasty bun. But they only waved her off as they yanked several books from the bookshelf and let them drop to the floor.

"If you're looking for something—" Sabine's mother didn't have any better luck talking to the men. Finally the taller man straightened up and stared straight at Sabine.

"You knew the woman down the hall, didn't you? Finkenkrug?"

Sabine felt her mouth go dry, but she managed to nod.

"Then you knew she was planning to defect." The statement sounded like an accusation.

"No, she didn't," her mother responded. "How would a child know such things?"

He dropped another pile of books to the floor, never taking his eyes off Sabine.

"Your older brother, the intern. Where is he? He's not at the hospital."

"What do you know about my son?" But the question only brought a frown from the Stasi interrogator.

"You tell him we will be back to speak with him. We have a few questions for him."

"My husband can help," offered Aunt Gertrud, but the men ignored her. They turned together to leave, as if pulled by the same leash. The tall one neatly stepped over a pile of books on his way to the door.

"You tell him," he repeated, pausing only long enough to see Frau Becker's white-faced nod.

And that's when Sabine knew—more than ever—that they could not stay in this place.

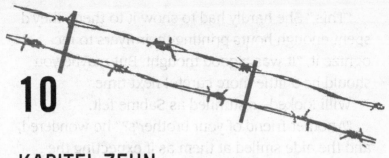

10

KAPITEL ZEHN

AN UNEXPECTED FRIEND

"Do you know that guy?" Willi whispered as they walked the hospital hall from his mother's room to Sabine's grandmother's. Sabine glanced to the side without moving her head.

"Oh." She returned the smile. "That's just Dietrich, Erich's friend."

"So what was the thumbs-up for?"

"I have no idea."

As they passed the nurses' station, a college-aged girl in a white trainee's uniform looked up from her clipboard and winked.

"Good work, you two," she whispered, just loud enough for them to hear as they walked by.

"Pardon me?" Sabine stopped short. The nurse's aide cautiously checked the hallway before she reached into her pocket and pulled out a folded piece of paper.

"This." She hardly had to show it to them; they'd spent enough hours printing their flyers to recognize it. "It was a good thought. But maybe you should be a little more careful next time."

Willi looked as stunned as Sabine felt.

"Another friend of your brother's?" he wondered, and the aide smiled at them as if expecting the question.

"Sorry to be so mysterious," she told them, her voice still low. "I'm Greta. There's a group of us here at the hospital. We get together for a Bible study every week. I guess you could say we stick together."

"So how do you know about us, and—" Sabine wasn't sure how to finish the question without admitting everything. But something about Greta's friendly expression made it easy to trust her.

"Well, for one thing, you and your friend talk a lot here in the hospital. I'd be a little more careful if I were you."

"Oh." Sabine felt her cheeks go red, and she glared at Willi with the big mouth. He looked as if he had no idea what Greta meant. As in, *Who, me?*

"Don't worry about it. Just find something else to talk about. Not everybody here at the hospital is on our side."

And what side is that? Sabine wanted to ask.

Greta went on in her low voice. "Besides that, your brother tries to keep track of you, you know. He thinks you might get into trouble."

"Who, me?"

Greta nodded. "*Ja*, and he wouldn't want me to say anything to you, but"—her smile had disappeared—"we need to ask you about something—"

A doctor approached them, obviously looking for something—or someone. When he motioned for the aide to follow him, Greta pinched her lips together and nodded. Right away, of course.

She pointed at them as she left. "Don't go anywhere." The young aide hurried after the doctor, leaving Sabine and Willi to wonder.

"What was *that* all about?" asked Willi. Sabine could only shrug her shoulders as they made their way to Oma's room.

"I have no idea," she finally said as they neared her door. "But maybe she was right. Maybe we do need to be more careful."

"I thought we already *were*. Didn't you?"

This time Sabine didn't answer. She paused to take a breath, praying that God would keep her, once again, from screaming and fleeing this place. It wouldn't take much to send her running.

She looked at the unscrubbed floor and the beds filled with sick and dying people. The limp sheet showed that man's missing left leg. She tried not to see the woman with the black, sunken eyes who, day after day, stared silently at the ceiling and waited to die. Sabine tried not to look at any of them. Finally they came to Oma's bed, last in line. But her heart sank when she looked at her grandmother. Sabine kept thinking that maybe, if she prayed a little harder, Oma would look better, not so frail.

Was this really the same Oma she had known all her life? This woman lay curled like a helpless baby, her cheeks hollow as if she hadn't eaten in weeks. The left side of her face sagged as if it had been painted on a wet canvas and the colors had all run.

The Oma she knew had fiery eyes that grabbed you and wouldn't let go. This woman looked from one face to the next, confused and frightened.

She didn't even sound like Oma. This woman moved her lips and groaned, forcing out jumbled bits of words.

"Hi, Oma. Sorry I couldn't come see you yesterday." Sabine tried not to let her emotions show. She reached out to take her grandmother's hand. Slowly the light returned to Oma's eyes, but she shook her head and strained to speak.

"Nein...nein...nein..." was the only word she could manage. As Sabine leaned closer to hear, her grandmother's grip tightened.

"No-no-no what, Oma?"

Oma resorted to sign language, and it seemed to take every last bit of the old woman's strength to point to herself.

"Es...tut...mir...leid...," she said, wrestling horribly with each word.

"You're sorry?" Sabine wasn't sure she'd heard

her grandmother right. But she looked back at Willi, and he nodded. "You don't need to be sorry for anything."

Oma shook her head with an effort that made her moan.

Sabine thought she muttered, "Your father—" But it might have been something else. She couldn't tell for sure.

The older woman in the next bed suddenly began ringing her little bell, a signal for the nurse to come quickly. That only made Oma moan again. Sabine squeezed her hand to comfort her.

"What's going on here?" a nurse in an over-starched skirt demanded as she scurried into the room. "Who are you children, and what are you doing in here?"

"They're killing her!" screamed the woman in the next bed. "They're Stasi agents, and they're going to strangle her in her bed!"

Sabine rolled her eyes.

"We're not killing anyone." She moved closer to her grandmother, as if to shield her. "We're just visiting with my oma."

"Well, you're just *done* visiting," snapped the nurse. Sabine didn't recognize her. "I will not have you disturbing the patients."

"She's not disturbing anything," Willi said, coming to Sabine's rescue. "Her brother works here. And she's just—"

The nurse whirled to glare at him. Then she

brought her attention back to Sabine, roughly helping her to her feet.

"I'm sorry, young lady. Out. Now. We do not allow exceptions to visitation hours."

But Oma would not let go of Sabine's hand. She clung to her granddaughter as if for life. The nurse struggled to separate them, and Sabine could not help crying out.

"Bible, Sabine." Oma's words came clearer now. "Read...the...Bible."

At last, Oma let go, and Sabine let the nurse propel her out of the room while she puzzled over Oma's words. Of course she would read her Bible. Willi quietly followed, and Sabine couldn't help looking back at her grandmother, couldn't help wondering if she would ever see Oma again. In heaven, yes, but until then—

Oma had leaned her head back on the pillow and closed her eyes, looking much as she had when they'd first arrived. Once again, she had become that other old woman, that dying woman. Not Oma. And as the nurse escorted them toward the exit, Sabine thought she heard her oma cry: "So, so sorry. Oh, my Savior, sorry!"

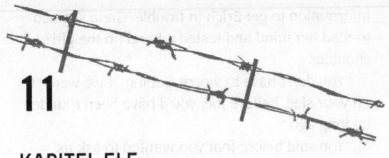

11

KAPITEL ELF

TRUSTING GRETA

"I don't understand what just happened in there."
Willi scratched his head as he stood with Sabine
on the front steps of St. Ludwig's.

First the mystery message from Erich's friend,
then the heartbreaking apology from Oma. What
did the girl want to talk to them about, and what
was Oma so sorry for? And finally their quick exit,
thanks to that rude nurse. Sabine crossed her arms
and looked at the ornate front door, wondering.

Especially about Oma.

The door flew open. "*There* you are!" Greta
exclaimed. "I was afraid you'd already left!"

She stopped next to them and caught her
breath.

"Oh, well, no, we—" Sabine wasn't sure how
much she should tell this girl, even though she'd
said she was Erich's friend. What if she worked
for the Stasi as an informant, a snitch, like half
the city? She could be pretending, looking for

information to get Erich in trouble. Greta seemed to read her mind and rested a hand on the girl's shoulder.

"You don't have to worry, Sabine. If we weren't on your side, believe me, you'd have been rounded up long ago."

"You said before that you wanted to ask us something?" Sabine wasn't going to believe just anything.

"Right." Greta nodded. "But first I need your word that you'll keep this just between us." The older girl looked first at Sabine, then Willi. And Sabine gave her friend a warning look, though she couldn't say it out loud: *Don't you dare mention anything about "on your honor as a Junge Pioniere."*

He held up his hand and opened his mouth, but Sabine beat him to it.

"Fine."

Whoops. What had she just promised?

Greta nodded seriously. "All right, then. We need to know about the underground...the *hole* you fell into."

"Oh, you want to know about *that*?" Willi perked up. "I've been down there. It's dark and musty, actually. And the car isn't as nice as she made me believe at first, and—"

"Willi!" Sabine interrupted. "She doesn't need to know all that."

"A car?" Greta's eyebrows registered her surprise. "Actually, all we want to know is how you managed to get down there again. By the time we figured out that's where you printed your flyers, the workers had already sealed up the street. You know of another way?"

Sabine bit her lip. "Why do you want to know?"

This time, Greta looked nervous, and she checked the door behind them. Did she really trust them or not?

"We're planning to dig a tunnel under the wall," she finally whispered. "But we need a place to start from and someplace to pile all the dirt. We want you to show us the hole because it might be the perfect place to start digging."

"Oh!" Sabine could hardly believe Greta's words. "I've heard stories about people escaping that way. I just didn't know if they were true."

"They're true. And we're going to do it too."

"But through the sewers and such. That's what they're trying now, isn't it?"

"A few have tried. But the Stasi have begun welding the manhole covers shut. Three of our friends died down there before—"

She wiped a tear with the sleeve of her blouse.

"This isn't a sewer, though," Sabine said, trying not to imagine Greta's friends in the sewer. She took a breath and explained about the underground rooms, the passageways, the way down through the bombed-out building. Greta nodded as if she were taking notes.

When Greta asked her to take them into the

bunker, Sabine hesitated. Finally she said, "I guess I can. But…what about Erich?"

"Well—" Greta looked away as she straightened the little white nurse's hat pinned to her hair. "He doesn't like getting you involved, but he'll get over it."

"Yes, but is he planning to—" When Sabine closed her eyes, all she could see was the Stasi agents putting the seal on Frau Finkenkrug's door, going from apartment to apartment. Next time, it might be their mother. "Is he planning to escape too?"

The question hung in the air, and Greta swallowed hard.

"You'll have to ask him yourself. But look, I have to get back to work. Thanks for helping."

And without another word, the nurse's aide turned to go.

"Wait!" Sabine held up her hand. "Do you want me to meet you somewhere? You didn't tell me."

Greta paused in the doorway without turning around.

"Erich will let you know when it's time."

Which turned out to be sooner than Sabine expected. As in, that night just after dinner.

"I'm going for a walk." Erich rose from the table first. As usual, Uncle Heinz was just reaching for a second helping. "May I be excused?"

Uncle Heinz lifted his eyebrows at his nephew

and kept chewing as he spoke. "I'm just curious; you're not spending time with anyone special at the hospital, are you?"

Erich stiffened, and Sabine nearly choked on her last bite.

"Would it be a problem if I were?" asked Erich.

Uncle Heinz stretched, making his chair creak and groan. "Maybe. I hear some of the staff there are, uh, under observation."

"You mean being watched by the Stasi? The way they've been watching me, stopping me, asking me dumb questions all the time? Every time I go out the door, old Wolfgang reports back to them!"

"I would be more careful, if I were you," Uncle Heinz warned. He frowned and kept eating while Erich went on—hotter than ever.

"What kind of a country is this? First it built a wall to keep its own people in. Then it expects everyone to spy on each other to keep people from disagreeing with it?"

Aunt Gertrud closed her eyes as if she felt another headache coming on.

"Erich." Their mother turned pale. "Let's not talk politics at the table. Please."

Uncle Heinz tossed his fork to the table and pushed back.

"I'm just telling him that he needs to be careful who he talks to, that's all. The Stasi are only trying to do their jobs. And I'm trying to do Erich a favor."

"Thanks, Onkel Heinz." Erich leaned over to dip

his hands in the bowl of sudsy water in the sink. "I'll keep that in mind."

Case closed—for now. A few moments later, Erich brushed by Sabine in the hallway.

"Follow me in ten minutes," he whispered.

Nine minutes later, she was standing on the street in the early summer evening, wondering what her big brother was up to. It didn't surprise her when he stepped out from behind Fegelein's *Bäckerei*.

"All right, now listen"—he leveled a finger at her in a big-brotherly way—"I didn't want to bring you into this, and I told them so. But we couldn't see a better way. So all you're going to do," he continued, "is show us the way in, and we'll take it from there."

"Nein." She kept going. "I told Mama I'm going to check up on Willi. So that's what I'm going to do first."

"But I told them we'd meet them in—"

"I'm not going to lie to Mama. Besides, Willi's in on this too."

Erich grumbled something about how they might as well show Wolfgang a big sign announcing their plan to build an escape tunnel. She did her best to ignore him, and a half hour later, three of them approached the bombed-out apartment building.

"We're not just all going to march right in, are we?" Willi looked around nervously. The streets were still full of people at 7:00 p.m. on a warm summer evening.

"And what about your friends?" asked Sabine.

"You just show me which part of the building." Erich ignored their questions. "Keep walking, tell me in a low voice, and don't point."

Okay. She could do this.

"About in the middle, past those two walls that fell on each other, around the back side and—"

"Good enough," he said, interrupting her. "Stop behind that pile of broken bricks, then go in first. I'll follow when nobody else is walking by. By the way, how'd you ever get in there from this direction without anybody seeing you?"

"I don't know." Sabine shrugged. "I guess I was just careful about it. And the first time, as you know, I sort of fell into it."

Another groan from her brother. But Sabine did as he'd said, climbing carefully through the rubble until she stood once again in the room with the crumbled walls and the flowery wallpaper.

Not bad for a girl on crutches! She congratulated herself as she looked around. What had this room once been? A living room? An office? Hard to tell. With all the walls tumbled upon one another, it looked like the inside of an earthquake site.

"You're sure this is it?" her brother asked when he joined her a couple of minutes later.

Then two others seemed to melt out of the shadows: Greta and Dietrich.

"Whoa." Willi whistled as he joined them, not as

quiet. "You guys really must be serious about this. Wait until I show you the car."

"Where is it?" asked Dietrich. Sabine knew he meant the trapdoor, not the car. She pointed to his feet. He stood on a low pile of crumbled cement blocks.

"You're kidding." He lifted first one foot, then the other. "We would never have found this on our own."

"We covered it back up with junk last time." She got down on her knees and started to brush away the rubble. "Here, let me show you."

"You don't need to do that." Erich put his hand on her shoulder. "All we needed was for you to show us the place. We can take it from here."

But Sabine didn't stop.

"If you're building a tunnel, we're going to help."

She glanced at Willi out of the corner of her eye to see him nod. Erich only laughed.

"What are you talking about? You're going home before Onkel Heinz reports you to Comrade Ulbricht. And you can't go home all dirty again."

"What about you?"

"That's not the question. Besides, this is going to be dangerous, you know."

"I know. That's why you need my help."

"You're crazy. And you can't just leave Mutti here in Berlin with Oma."

"But you can?"

"Listen, I'm helping my friends. That's different."

"I say it's not."

"And I say you need to go home before you get hurt."

"I'm not a little kid. I'm thirteen, you know."

"Doesn't matter. I say no."

Sabine wasn't surprised. But Dietrich looked over at Greta, who nodded.

"They already know where the entrance is," Dietrich told Erich quietly. "And we could use the help, Erich."

"What are you talking about?" Erich's voice rose a few notches. "She's my sister, and I say she goes home."

But it looked as if Dietrich could be just as stubborn. Or rather, Dietrich and Greta. Two against one.

"You remember how we agreed to do things," she said. "Dietrich leads."

"But if we disagree—" Erich wasn't giving up just yet.

"If we disagree, the three of us vote."

Sabine looked from her brother to the others.

"They can stay, if they want," Greta finally announced. "As long as they keep quiet about what we're doing."

Willi zipped a finger across his lips and grinned. But when Sabine had a chance to think for a second, she wasn't so sure. Not about keeping quiet. But as she looked down at the hole they'd opened in the floor, she wondered: what had they gotten themselves into?

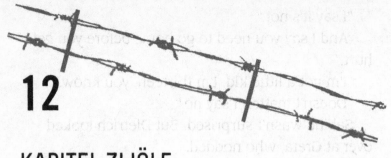

12

KAPITEL ZWÖLF
TUNNEL FELLOWSHIP

"All right, everybody, listen up." The flickering candle behind Dietrich cast a weird monster shadow on the opposite wall of the bunker. Sabine and Willi sat on the back end of their car, watching. Four, five, six...Sabine wondered if they were all from the hospital, and if they could all keep the secret. And the older guys—all about Erich's age or a little younger—glanced over at Willi and Sabine with looks that said, *What are* they *doing here?*

"I'm glad you're all here," Dietrich continued. "Anton and Albricht—"

Sabine looked twice when a candle flicker illuminated the two faces. Unless she was mistaken—

"And yes, Sabine, they're twins."

Sabine nodded, and Willi chuckled.

"I noticed," she told them. "Only, is there any way to tell you apart?"

Anton grinned and flexed an impressive set of arms. "I'm the better-looking one."

"You always say that." Albricht jabbed his brother with an elbow. They could have been a wrestling team, with square shoulders and big chests. "But the only way to tell us apart is the scar."

He leaned close to the candle he was holding and pointed to his jaw.

"There. See? Ouch!"

A little *too* close to the candle.

"Albricht, scar; Anton, no scar," he finished, rubbing his chin.

Sabine smiled and nodded. "Okay. Great. Don't burn yourself too."

The others laughed while the third newcomer kept looking over his shoulder, over his head, down at his shoes. He took off his glasses, put them back on—

"And everyone knows Gerhard, right?" Dietrich made the introduction. "He works in the linen room."

Gerhard nodded but narrowed his eyes at Sabine and Willi.

"No one told me there would be little kids," he began, giving his head a good scratch.

"We're not little kids." Sabine stood up to the challenge. "And we found this bunker in the first place."

"Hmm." Gerhard crossed his arms.

"She's my sister," announced Erich. "She's...okay."

Sabine relaxed when her brother defended her to the group.

"So now that we have that settled," Dietrich went on, "let's lay down the rules of the Tunnel Fellowship and what we're going to do."

Greta brought out a handful of cold candle stubs, giving one to each of them.

"We're going to need to depend on one another down here," Dietrich told them, his voice growing more serious. "Even for our lives, maybe. So now's your chance to leave."

No one moved.

"We dig together. We escape together. No one is left behind."

Sabine didn't dare look at her older brother. Did that include their mother and Oma? What about Willi's family? Dietrich lit Greta's candle with his.

"We pledge to one another that we will never reveal this place, this plan, or this fellowship to anyone outside this room."

Greta turned to light Erich's candle.

"And if any of us has to drop out of the fellowship, we still pledge to keep the secrets—all the secrets."

Erich turned to light Albricht's candle—or maybe it was Anton's. And so Dietrich went on about always coming to the entrance alone, making sure no one discovered the bunker, where they would pile the dirt, how they would keep watch. His words echoed through the underground rooms until they all stood facing one another, flaming candle stubs in hand.

"We're all agreed, then?" asked Dietrich.

"*Ja.*" Greta nodded. Each, in turn, promised as they went around the circle.

At his turn, Willi nodded solemnly. "*Ja*...ouch!" he cried, sending his candle stub flying. He shook his hand wildly. "Hot wax! Right on my hand."

Everyone burst out laughing, even Dietrich—for a moment. Then he brought them back to business.

"All right, then, let's get to it. The twins will be our main diggers, and Gerhard and I will give them breaks when we can. Erich is our engineer and safety man, and Greta will make sure we're tunneling in the right direction."

"What about us?" Willi wanted to know.

"Oh, right." Dietrich held up his finger. "One of you is going to help dump dirt away from the tunnel, and the other is going to watch the entry."

Willi nodded.

"And in a few weeks—" Dietrich looked at them, and Sabine felt a stab of excitement. Yes, in a few weeks. If no one saw them coming and going. If no one leaked the secret. If no one discovered what they were doing. If, if, if—

Her excitement exploded into fear. Everyone froze as they heard someone moving in the ruined building above them.

"Shh!" Erich snuffed his candle first. A moment

later, the darkness wrapped around them like a cold blanket, and Sabine shivered at the sound of someone scratching at the trapdoor. Willi grabbed her arm. "What...was...*that*?" he whispered in her ear. For a minute, she thought he was going to climb up on her shoulders. She didn't answer, just peeled off his fingers and headed for the bottom of the spiral stairway.

"Sabine?" Her brother could not have known it was her climbing the stairs, praying they would hold her one more time. But she had to get to the top before it was too late. She could see the weak light filtering through the cracks. And she could hear the whimpering and scratching—and she knew her guess had been right. Using her crutch for balance, she dug her shoulder up and into the door, popping it open.

"Woof!"

"Hey!" Erich cried from below, and Sabine felt the stairway groan and creak, as if it would give way any moment. She held on to the floor above her, just in case, while Bismarck happily cleaned her face and motored his tail in eggbeater circles.

"Easy." She did her best to wiggle away, but Bismarck kept right on her. Meanwhile, everyone below wanted to know what was going on—as if she alone could see the enemy through the submarine's periscope.

"What's up there?"

"What is she doing?"

276

"Close the door!"

"Get her *down*!"

Voices boiled and blended into full-scale panic, until Sabine felt a pair of hands grab her ankles. She had to grab something too, to keep her balance, and when her hands missed the edge of the opening, she connected with Bismarck's two front legs. Off balance, she felt the mound of moving dog fur fall on top of her, while strong arms wrapped around her waist and eased her toward the floor.

"Wow. You're heavier than I thought!"

That's when all three of them tumbled backward. Erich probably took the worst of it; Sabine had her brother-cushion behind and the dog-cushion in front. Bismarck yelped in surprise (Sabine didn't blame him) while the door above their heads slammed shut once more and darkness reclaimed the bunker.

"I'm okay." Sabine had lost one of her crutches, though.

"Glad to hear it." Erich groaned. "But did we just drag down what I think we just dragged down?"

That only jump-started the Tunnel Fellowship panic squad again:

"Did you bring something down here?"

"I'm getting out."

"Did somebody follow us?"

"What's going *on*?"

Finally Dietrich brought a match to life, and the

pool of light seemed to quiet everyone. Bismarck stared at him with his tongue-wagging happy face.

"*That's* what caused all this commotion?" asked Erich.

"He was just trying to find us," Willi said, defending Bismarck. He scratched the dog behind the ears. "Good boy."

"Your dog?" Dietrich asked as he relit a couple of candles.

"He seems to think so, but no."

"What if someone followed him here?" Count on Gerhard for the dark side. "We need to get rid of him, now."

"No!" Sabine and Willi both shielded their adopted pet.

"Gerhard has a point," Dietrich agreed. "He could give us away."

"He'll work for us." Sabine tried to think fast. "He can be a guard dog, or pull a cart, or—"

Erich shook his head and stared at the floor, thinking.

"I'll probably regret this," Dietrich said, taking his candle and heading for the far rooms. "But he can stay—for now. If he makes any noise or gets into any other trouble, though, that's it. No second chances."

Sabine nodded seriously and reached for her dropped crutch, but Bismarck had already beaten her to it. Taking one of the handles in his mouth, he wagged his tail and dragged it closer.

"See?" she told them. "He's already helping out. And he's really gentle."

"He is kind of cute," Greta admitted, holding her hand out to the dog. "Floppy ears means he's not all shepherd, though, right?"

As Sabine nodded, the hair on the back of Bismarck's neck stood up, and he gave a low, throaty growl. Greta gasped and pulled her hand back.

"What—," she began.

But Bismarck had pointed his attention back toward the hole the street workers had opened—where Sabine had fallen.

"That's it," muttered Gerhard. "I'm not working down here with a growling beast—"

"Shh!" Sabine interrupted. She hugged Bismarck tightly. The dog quieted as well, though he kept alert.

In the silence, they could all faintly hear a worker in the distance.

"I think it's somebody working on a pipe up there," Erich told them.

"Did anybody else hear that?" asked Sabine. When they all shook their heads no, she continued, "See? If we have Bismarck around, he can hear things we can't. And he wasn't growling at Greta. He was just protecting us."

Of course that seemed like a good thing to Sabine, even as they worked their way back out a half hour later. Willi and Sabine stood with Bismarck for a minute on the street.

"That's where we're going to end up, right?" Willi pointed at the small church cemetery on the other side of Bernauerstrasse, on the other side of the wall—the other side of the world.

"Just forty-two feet of digging." Sabine quietly echoed her big brother's words. He was the project engineer, after all; he and Greta would figure out how to come up in the right place, not in the middle of one of the graves. But what if they didn't measure right? She shivered.

"Back away!" The Vopo guard's harsh command made Sabine jump as the guard pushed his way between them and the fence. She saw him finger the trigger of a wicked-looking weapon and quickly grabbed Bismarck by the collar to stop his growl.

"Sorry. I didn't realize we were too close." Sabine did her best to backpedal, but she caught the tip of one crutch on her heel and almost fell.

The soldier's face softened as he pushed the helmet back off his forehead. "You need to find another place to walk your dog," he told them, and he bent down to pat Bismarck, who'd quieted. "A person could get hurt on this fence."

"We were just on our way home," Willi told him, but his voice cracked.

"Well, your mother's going to be upset with you." The soldier bent a little closer. "How did you get so dirty? Digging a garden or something?"

Uh-oh. Sabine looked down at the grime on her

pant legs. Sure enough. Bismarck's paws looked just as filthy.

"Uh, it's the dog," she said, thinking quickly. "He likes to, um, roll in the dirt, and he always gets me dirty."

The man studied them closely.

"Well, I'd clean up a bit before I got home, if I were you." And he waved them off with the end of his gun. "Go on now."

They didn't wait for another invitation.

13

KAPITEL DREIZEHN

SIGHTED

"Day Two of the Tunnel Fellowship—" Willi held his school notebook nearly pressed to his face, his pencil nearly poking him in the glasses. "Digging begins under Bernauerstrasse."

"I don't understand how you can write like that," Sabine told him. She finished off the last chunk of French bread she'd brought along as a mid-afternoon snack.

"You get used to it."

"And besides, I don't think it's a good idea to write about what we're doing. What if someone finds it, like your father?"

Willi flipped the page around to show her. "Does that answer your question?" he asked.

"Looks more like Chinese than German," she answered as she peered at the horrible chicken scratching of tiny letters.

"It's backward, skip a word, and…well, that's the secret part of the code."

"Hmm." She hadn't expected that from Willi, but then Willi kept surprising her. So he kept writing, checking back and forth between his notes and his compass. Sabine returned to the little telescope they'd set up in Willi's window, near the curtain, so they could quickly hide it if anybody looked up.

"Don't move it. I think I found a good spot," he told her.

"All I see are gravestones over there. That is *not* a good spot."

No matter what, she would *not* tunnel up through a casket, through a dead body. *Nein. Durchaus nicht!* No way!

"I mean closer to the church building. There's a little spot of grass, I think. You tell me."

Sabine squinted through the eyepiece. "Okay, I see it," she told him. "There's a bench, then a patch of grass, then the building. I don't know if anyone can see it from the street."

"Perfect. We'll tell your brother?"

"I guess so. I don't know if he'll listen to us, though. We are just the lowly dirt carriers."

Willi shrugged. "I don't mind. I guess I've learned to be content with whatever's going on around me."

"That sounds like something from the Bible, not you."

"Hey." He grinned. "You caught that."

"Yeah. But are you content enough to stay on this side of the wall for the rest of your life?"

Willi didn't answer right away. When he did, his voice sounded softer. "My mom wants us to leave, really badly. Even lying there in the hospital, that's all she ever talks about. For her children, she says. She makes Papa crazy."

"But she's getting better, right?"

"Well, the baby is still tiny, but she's healthy. The doctor said they can come home in a few days."

"That's great. What about your dad, though? Why is he so—"

"Papa...Papa is, uh...Look, Sabine, I don't really want to talk about it."

"But we have to talk about it. What if we dig the tunnel, and they won't come?"

"I know, I know. But you should see Papa every time he hears about someone escaping."

"Not like Onkel Heinz?"

"No, no. He hates it here, but he acts like...like they died of a horrible disease, and we can't talk about it, or else we'll catch the disease too."

"So what happens if you try to say anything?" she asked.

"I can't...I'm not like you, Sabine. You don't care what other people think. Me, I—"

Willi's voice trailed off, and Sabine looked over at her friend. His thick lenses made his eyes look way too big for his face, sort of like fish eyes. He took off the glasses and wiped them on his shirt. She wished she knew what to say to him.

"Don't worry about your family," she finally managed. "We'll figure something out."

"Hope you're right." But he couldn't know that a scared little girl hid behind all her big talk and big promises. She just put the telescope back to her eye. Looking busy and in charge was the best way to not look afraid.

Down on the street, she could actually see the tight curls, tucked beneath a somber gray hairnet, on a passing woman's head. "This is kind of fun," she told him. "I can see—"

The scowl of a very irritated Vopo guard, looking straight at her, filled the view of the telescope.

"Uh-oh." Sabine ducked. "Not so good."

"What?" Willi obviously had no idea what she had just seen.

She pulled the curtain shut. "We have to get rid of this telescope, quick."

"Are you kidding? My father gave me that for Christmas. It's—"

"It's going to get us in a lot of trouble if we don't hide from the Vopo who just saw me with it. *Now!*"

"Why didn't you say so?"

Willi quickly looked around and pointed under the kitchen sink. They squeezed together behind a checkered skirt that hid stuff like the scrub brushes, soap flakes, and a waste bucket.

"Have you even emptied the garbage since your mother went to the hospital?" Sabine whispered, wrinkling her nose in distaste.

"Sorry." He sneezed once, then again. "I just thought maybe no one would look here."

Maybe the Vopo would, and maybe they wouldn't. But Sabine knew she and Willi had to keep silent when the Vopo broke down the front door of the Stumpffs' apartment.

"On Day Two, Willi and Sabine find a safe place for the tunnel to end," Willi whispered, as he planned his next journal entry. "Except—"

They expected the Vopo to break in any minute to capture them. They'd be tried as spies. And Willi had just pulled out his journal again to fill it with more chicken scratching.

"Would you put that thing away?" Sabine hissed. She stiffened when she heard the sound of boots coming up the stairway.

"There!" Willi whispered. "You hear it?"

She nodded silently.

"We don't answer the door, right?" Willi asked, panicked.

Sabine just sat with her knees in her face, waiting for the man who had seen her to burst into the apartment and drag them off. Strangely, the door didn't pop off its hinges; it just squeaked open the way it always did. "Willi!" a man called, followed by a whistle.

"Oh, no." Willi rolled out of his hiding place, sending a glass vase skittering across the lino-leum. "It's my dad."

Good thing Sabine managed to crawl out from under the sink before Herr Stumpff came into the kitchen.

"So you're the Sabine I've heard so much about." Herr Stumpff looked like a grown-up version of Willi, only bald and a little grease-stained. He smiled and held out his rough mechanic's hand. "Willi tells me your grandmother is in the same hospital as my wife and daughter."

"Yes, sir. Different floors, though." She wondered what to do when the Vopo pounded on the door. Herr Stumpff looked at the mess on the floor, then at her shoulder.

"Er, can I help you find something?"

"Oh—no, sir. We were just...that is—"

That's when she noticed the week-old potato peel stuck on her shoulder. "Actually— She felt her face heating up as she flicked the peel into the trash. "I was about to help Willi...get dinner started."

Which explained everything, right? Willi stooped to pick up a runaway scrub brush as his father gave them a curious look.

"That's very nice of you, Sabine. But I thought Willi and I would eat at the hospital tonight and keep his mother company. Of course, you're welcome to join us—if it's all right with your mother, that is."

"Oh." Sabine replaced another scrub brush

and vase. "I should head home. But thank you for offering."

She resigned herself to being arrested in the hallway. But Herr Stumpff kept her from leaving.

"I'm sorry, Sabine, but you should know something before you go out there. You too, Willi."

Sabine nearly choked on her spit. *What did he know?*

"There's another empty apartment on the third floor. The police have sealed it off."

Oh. *Another* one.

"Do not stop there to look," he went on, "and don't ask questions. Just walk on by."

Willi's father looked dead serious as he let her go and went to the sink to wash his hands.

"In fact," he said, "just pretend it's not there and stay out of trouble."

"Yes, sir." She nodded, but her stomach knotted up. Pretend it's not there? That's exactly what was all wrong with this mixed-up country!

Pretend he's not there. And Hitler will go away.

Pretend it's not real. And the war will soon be over.

Pretend you don't notice. And the wall won't matter so much.

Pretend, pretend, pretend. And the Stasi will be nice to us.

Well, it never worked that way. But she tried her best not to glare at her friend's father, no matter how silly he sounded, as she told them good-bye and let herself out.

"Thanks again," she called back, knowing she would run straight into the guard as he made his way up the stairs.

But the fifth floor looked deserted, just like the fourth and third floors. Oh, and she caught a glimpse of the empty apartment, the one that wasn't really there. And though she hadn't known the people who had lived there, she prayed for them.

On the second floor, a couple of stooped men marched home, never looking up from the worn carpet runner. So she worked her way down the last few steps to the street level, one at a time, the same way she always did—but holding her breath, ready to flee. As if a girl with crutches could have outrun a soldier with a gun.

Sabine carefully pushed the outside door open and looked up and down the street.

No Stasi. Not even any Vopos.

14

KAPITEL VIERZEHN
PANIC ATTACK

Sabine stumbled through the chamber with her wooden buckets full of dirt and grunted as she passed by Willi going the other way. Carrying buckets with crutches was quite a trick, but she managed by hanging them on both ends of a makeshift yoke—a stout board—balanced on her shoulders.

And no, she wasn't going to let anyone tell her she couldn't do such a thing. Willi knew better than to even mention it.

"One hundred forty-two," she told him.

"And that's just today."

Right. By the end of the first week, it was getting harder and harder to find room in the underground garage for more tunnel dirt. Even with all the rooms! She paused for just a minute to catch her breath.

"You're lucky," she whispered to Bismarck, who sat and watched them from his favorite spot on the front seat of the Volkswagen. "You don't have to drag all this dirt out. But then, I asked to help, right? So who's complaining?"

Bismarck stopped chewing his bone to look up at her, his head tilted sideways. The nagging little signal bell on the car's windshield frame tinkled once. They'd tied one end of a kite string to it and rolled the string into the tunnel, where Anton and Albricht dug away for several hours at a time. One ring meant "Come and get more dirt." She forgot what two bells meant. But three bells meant "Help!"

"Coming, coming!" Sabine picked up her buckets again, closed her eyes, and headed in. Good thing she'd worked through her claustro-whatever. Fear of dark closets and closed-in dark places. Or dark, damp places like tunnels, where the sides could collapse and bury you alive. *What would Mother think if I didn't come home to dinner?* Already she'd used just about every excuse she could think of, trying her best not to lie to Mama. But how did her clothes get so dirty, even when she made an effort to stay clean by changing into scrubs from the hospital?

And, heavens, look at those fingernails! *Du lieber Himmel,* they'd gotten so dark and dirty. And the candles Erich placed on little stands every few feet don't really help, either, since the tunnel was hardly wide enough to crawl through or turn around in, and the sides brushed against you as if they were alive, grabbing, clawing at you, squeezing the breath out of you—

"Sabine?"

She opened her eyes. Erich stood staring at her in the candlelight, his hand on her shoulder. She blinked her eyes and tried to remember. Had he just said something, or had he just sneaked up on her for fun? And how did she get back in the main room?

"What's wrong, Sabine? Why are you ringing the bell out here? Are you hurt?"

Well, of course not. But that didn't explain her sobbing and shaking. Greta and Willi had come running at the sound of the bells, while Bismarck tried to lick her face.

"Sabine?" Greta took her wrist, the way a doctor would have done. "Sabine, relax. Slow down. Your heart is racing."

And her head wouldn't stop spinning.

"I don't know—" Sabine tried to explain, but nothing came out. She saw herself back inside the closet at the hospital, and she knew Nurse Ilse would keep the door locked until she stopped crying. But she also knew how to stop.

"I'll be good," she whispered. "I promise."

"I'm taking you home," announced Erich. And by the tone of his voice, she knew better than to argue. She let him lead her to the trapdoor.

When they reached the street, she made Erich stop while she waited for the tightness in her chest to settle down, for the crawly feeling on her skin to go away. She took a deep breath as a Trabi sputtered by, and the car's nose-curdling fumes made her choke. At least the afternoon sun felt good on her face.

"I don't know if you should go down there again," Erich said quietly.

What are you talking about? And who do you think you are, some kind of doctor? Just because you work in a hospital— Sabine's mind screamed.

Sabine swallowed the bitter taste in her mouth, sniffed, and wiped away the tears with her sleeve. There. Enough baby-bawling. She set her jaw, adjusted her crutches, and shrugged her brother's hand away.

"Thanks for your help," she told him as she headed down Bernauerstrasse on her own power. She navigated around a tree, full in its summer umbrella of leaves. And she *did* appreciate his help, except— "I can make it from here. But I'll be back tomorrow."

So he let her go, and a few minutes later, she stopped at the faucet in the alleyway beside their apartment building. If she looked up, she could probably see her mother through the living room window, just above her head. Instead, she spent a few minutes cleaning up in the cool water. She hoped she'd rinsed away the tracks of her tears—and the mud. The sound of footsteps made her turn.

"Glad you made it back home." Erich stepped up to the faucet and began to wash up himself. Sabine rested on her crutches, glaring at him.

"Told you I would. Why'd you follow? Didn't you believe me?"

"You can be pretty stubborn sometimes. I just wanted to make sure."

"Fine. But I'm still going back tomorrow. You can't talk me out of it."

He didn't answer, just scrubbed his hands like a surgeon, over and over.

"Did you hear me?" she tried again.

"I heard you. I'm just going to have to talk with Greta and Dietrich. I don't think it's a good idea. Especially not after today."

"What do you want me to do, stay home all day where it's safe, the way Mama wants me to?"

"Don't bring her into it," Erich snapped back. "If it wasn't for Mama—"

"I know, I know. I'm sorry. I just don't want to end up like all our neighbors."

"Not *all* of them, Sabine."

"No? The only ones who have any guts have already escaped. And then everyone else tiptoes by the sealed apartments, like they're not allowed to look. It makes me sick, Erich."

"I know how you feel, Sabine. And I'm helping my friends because they need me. But maybe, some-times, God calls us to stay."

"Not me. Every time I look across that fence, I know where I'm supposed to be. Free. Over there."

"Then what about our family, Sabine? Or is this just for you?"

Low blow. She fought hard to stop her angry tears. And she gripped the handles of her crutches, wishing she could use them to knock her big brother across the side of his head.

"That's not fair."

"Why not?"

"Because this is finally something I can *do*, something that will actually make a difference. Not just passing out stupid flyers or trying to get people to strike. But you've decided to swoop in and say it's 'too dangerous.'"

She didn't mean to sound quite as sassy as she probably did. But Erich didn't miss a beat.

"I'm just thinking about what's best for you and what's best for our family. Maybe you haven't thought of it that way yet. But I have."

"Well, then, tell me something: why are you mixed up in this?"

"I told you. They're my friends, Sabine. I want to help them. I *have* to help them."

"Yeah, but are you going too, or not?"

Erich studied his shoes and pressed his lips together. He did that when he got upset. But Sabine didn't care. She had to know.

"So will you go with your hospital buddies, or stay?"

"Keep your voice down, all right?" Erich hissed.

"All right." She lowered her voice a notch or two. "But you always told me God put you in the hospital for a reason. Right here in East Berlin. Did he, or didn't he?"

Again Erich didn't answer right away. Was it all boys, or just Erich that had to think so long before responding? Sometimes it almost made her want to strangle him. She looked straight at Erich, waiting.

"I've asked myself the same thing, Sabine."

"And?"

"And I don't know, for sure."

"Well, thanks for nothing." She turned away.

"I never said I had all the answers."

And then he burped, just like Uncle Heinz, like a bullfrog. Why did boys always have to do that? Disgusting.

"Excuse you," she told him, glancing back over her shoulder with a frown.

"That wasn't me." He put out his hands and looked up, and her stomach flipped. Just above their heads, the breeze caught a corner of her mother's lacy window curtain. When had Uncle Heinz opened the window?

15

KAPITEL FÜNFZEHN

HOMECOMING

"Your mama and the baby finally get to come home? How exciting." Sabine did her best to keep up with her friend as they walked to St. Ludwig's. "After a whole month in the hospital!"

"Five weeks. And sure I'm excited." He squinted both ways at the corner of Invalidenstrasse. Sabine grabbed his sleeve just in time to keep him from stepping into the path of a speeding Trabi. "I'm just not sure anybody's going to get any sleep at home anymore. Have you heard that kid scream since they brought her out of intensive care?"

"I've heard." Sabine smiled as they crossed the street. Not that she had any idea how having a new baby sister would change things. Sabine couldn't wait to see them "graduate" from the maternity ward.

"Do you think they'll let me hold little Effi?" she asked. "She's about the cutest baby I've ever seen."

"I don't know. They've pretty much had Elfriede

under lights for the past few weeks. Remember? Like a little plant in a greenhouse."

Sabine laughed. And for one happy moment, she wished she could skip through the street, maybe dance a little. Instead, she swung high on her crutches. Watch out! She could still kick up her heels...sort of.

"What are you *doing*?" Willi didn't get it. "You're crazy."

"Maybe," she answered as he opened the hospital's front door. A nurse wheeled Frau Stumpff toward them, baby bundled in her arms. Good timing! Herr Stumpff kept pace alongside.

"She's beautiful," Sabine cooed when the wheelchair came near. Yellow mottled skin, button nose, bright little blue eyes, little curly tufts of dark hair— "And so tiny. Like a little baby doll."

Sabine offered her pinky to Effi and laughed when the baby's miniature fingers curled around it. After all the little one had gone through, Sabine did her best not to breathe on the baby. Willi's mother smiled weakly as she watched her daughter. Herr Stumpff walked away for a moment to sign some papers at the front desk.

"It will be good to get home, won't it?" his mother asked. "I hear Sabine's taught you to cook since I've been in the hospital."

Willi sort of coughed. Well...if you called burned boiled oatmeal *cooking*.

"Willi, could you do me a favor?" Herr Stumpff

looked up from the paperwork. "We left your mother's suitcase in her room. Could you—"

"Sure." Willi nodded and hurried away. And since Sabine knew she couldn't help much, she decided to check in with Greta and Dietrich. Erich wouldn't report to work for another couple of hours.

"I'll be right back." She stroked the baby's cheek before following Willi. But by the time she'd reached Greta's second-floor duty station, Willi had already picked up his mother's suitcase and beaten her there.

"You're sure she's not working today?" she heard Willi ask. He looked puzzled. "She always works Mondays."

But Frau Ziegler, the supervising nurse, didn't even look up. She just chewed on the end of her pencil and flipped open a notebook. Sabine noticed the woman's knuckles had turned white, gripping the edge of the desk.

Odd. She'd always had a smile for them.

"What about Dietrich?" Sabine wondered as she neared the counter.

"Dietrich no longer works here, either."

Either? Finally the nurse looked up at them. The dark panic in her eyes nearly made Sabine's heart stop. "Please. I must ask you to leave right away. This is not a good time for you to be here."

Wait—what had happened to Greta and Dietrich? The shock must have registered on their faces, but Frau Ziegler only snapped her pencil in half as her face turned pink, and she pointed to the exit. Her eyes, however, looked in the opposite direction. How strange. As if she were pointing at something they should know about, something she couldn't tell them about.

"Please go," she hissed. "Or they'll arrest you too. Go now, and don't come back."

But they didn't move quickly enough. A dark-haired man in a starched shirt emerged from a storeroom down the hall—the direction Frau Ziegler had pointed with her eyes. He held several large folders stuffed with papers. An older-looking nurse with her own armload of folders matched him step for step as they came down the hall, deep in conversation.

Sabine had never seen the woman before, but she looked like some kind of supervisor. They heard her say that she would do everything she could to help out the government. And that it served those two interns right for thinking they could get away with something so outrageous. The dark-haired man thanked her and said she'd been extremely helpful, and if she suspected any others—

A chill ran up Sabine's spine; she knew at a glance everything she needed to know about the man.

A Stasi *agent!*

With wide eyes and a quick nod of thanks to

Frau Ziegler, Willi and Sabine turned away and hurried as fast as Sabine's crutches would allow them. Greta and Dietrich—arrested! Sabine and Willi had to warn the others, now! Anton and Albricht worked in the cafeteria; Gerhard collected linens from all over the hospital. But Sabine had no idea whether they were working today, or in the tunnel.

Erich would know.

"Oh, great." Willi stopped short at the top of a flight of stairs. "I left Mama's suitcase at the desk."

Sabine moaned. But what else could they do? She sat down in an empty wheelchair for a moment to think, then looked up at Willi.

"Push me back there," she told him. "I look more like a patient here than you do."

"But all the nurses know us."

"Not the one with the Stasi agent. And I don't think they saw our faces. They'll just think I'm another cripple, out for some fresh air."

Willi rolled his eyes and planted his hands on his hips. "I don't know how I let you talk me into your plans."

"You're the one who forgot the suitcase, not me."

Willi couldn't argue with that, so he pushed Sabine back toward the nursing station. Frau Ziegler looked up in alarm, but the agent and his nurse didn't seem to notice them as they rolled up.

"*Um Verzeihung bitte.*" Sabine cleared her throat and tapped the man's leg with her crutch. "Excuse me, please?"

"Oh. *Ja?*" He glanced up from his papers.

"Would you please hand me my case?" Sabine smiled and pointed at the floor next to him. As he bent to pick it up, she gripped the armrests of the wheelchair to keep her hands from shaking out of control.

"*Danke schön.*" She smiled sweetly as she thanked him and took the suitcase from his hand. But inside she screamed: *Turn this thing around, and get us out of here!*

As if he could hear her, Willi spun her around and nearly sprinted away.

Once they'd gotten far enough to talk safely, Willi said, "I have to stay and help my mother." He waved the suitcase.

"Of course you do. But I have to find my brother before the Stasi get to him too. I hope he knows where to find the others."

Twenty minutes later, breathless, she found her brother in the hall, just leaving their apartment.

"Erich! . . . Wait. I need to talk to you."

"Sorry, Sabine, I'm late," Erich said, distracted by the time. He almost brushed by her. "Can we talk when I get off my shift, tonight after dinner?"

"No! You have to listen—right now!" She swung her crutch and nailed him in the leg to get his attention. "Please!"

"Hey, you don't have to attack me." But he stopped to listen. With each word, he looked more worried.

"You're sure the guy was Stasi?" He rubbed his chin.

"Yes. Who else would wear a jacket like that in the middle of summer?"

"And you're sure Greta and Dietrich didn't just change shifts or something?" he asked.

"I *told* you what Frau Ziegler said! They've been arrested, Erich. *Arrested*."

"Okay." Erich's shoulders fell. "I believe you. And Ziggy's on our side. But she doesn't know what we're doing. She doesn't even know who's involved."

"Erich, you can't go back there. You'll be next."

"Maybe, maybe not. Greta and Dietrich won't tell them anything. And I need to warn the others. The only question is—"

"No, Erich, can't you see? This is serious."

The apartment door creaked open, and Uncle Heinz signaled for them to join him. How much had he heard?

"You should listen to your sister," their uncle said gravely once they'd followed him inside.

"What are you talking about?" Erich narrowed his eyes as if seeing his uncle for the first time.

"Let's not play games here." Uncle Heinz ran a hand through his hair as he paced across the room and pulled down the window shade. "I can't help you unless you cooperate."

Uncle Heinz had heard everything!

"My poor innocent nephew," Uncle Heinz sighed

when Erich stayed silent. "The boy who disappears at night and comes home late with dirt under his fingernails. Wolfgang told me all about your comings and goings, and it's getting embarrassing."

The words sent chills down Sabine's spine, and she thought back to the argument she'd had with Erich in the alley. Uncle Heinz had probably heard every word they'd said then too.

Suddenly he sprang into action, grabbing Erich by the loose collar of his shirt and pulling him closer.

"Now you listen to me," he wheezed, as if it took all his breath to move so quickly. "I know you're not a loyal party member, and I know you don't pay attention to Comrade Ulbricht's speeches. I've made excuses for you, and I've looked the other way because you're my little sister's boy. I promised her once a long time ago that I'd watch out for you. And I keep my promises."

"Onkel Heinz!" Sabine reached out for her uncle's hairy arm. "Don't hurt him. Erich hasn't done anything wrong."

Uncle Heinz stared at her for a second before he laughed nervously and let Erich go.

"Nothing wrong, eh? I wish it were true. But let's talk about your pitiful choice of friends, shall we? The ones who have gotten themselves arrested? In fact, they're all in custody right now, charged with treasonous activity."

All? Treasonous activity? What did that mean?

Sabine stared at her uncle. He sounded so unfamiliar, so Stasi-like.

"You have no idea who my friends are." Erich obviously wasn't admitting anything...yet.

"Let's see. How about Dietrich Spiller?" A little smile curled the man's lip, as if he held a winning hand of cards, and he knew it. "How about Greta Rathenau, or the Lueger twins? Oh, and Gerhard Fromm has proved quite helpful. Very informative."

He let the meaning behind his words sink in: *We know what you're doing. We know when you're doing it. And we know whom you're doing it with.*

It seemed Uncle Heinz had connections they hadn't even imagined. Much bigger than phone calls from the neighborhood spy.

"Oh, and by the way," he added, "even if they're released, your friends will stay on the state's watch list. But here's the good news: I'm not sure if you're on it—yet. That of course could change, depending on what you do now."

Erich didn't answer, so Uncle Heinz went on.

"Look, I'm trying to give you the break of a lifetime. In fact, I've even promised my friends that you won't make any more trouble. A second chance. Free and clear. What do you think of that?"

"I think you shouldn't have made that promise," Erich whispered back, never lowering his eyes.

"Why can't you understand this?" Uncle Heinz's cheeks turned flame-red. "The game you and your friends were planning, it's all over now. Done. Finished."

Erich silently crossed his arms.

"And because I keep my promises, here's my deal for you. You tell me you'll stay out of trouble from now on, and we'll forget we ever had this unpleasant conversation. Agreed?"

Incredible. Did Uncle Heinz really think Erich would agree to such an offer? Yet when he held out his pudgy hand to shake, Erich actually seemed to think about it. Finally he just shook his head and turned toward the door.

"I'll do my best, Onkel Heinz. But I really need to leave, or I'm going to be late for work."

"I can't help you if you run away, boy."

Erich left without another word. Sabine tried to follow.

"Wait a minute." Her uncle planted his foot in front of her right crutch. "The same goes for you, my girl. Whatever you've been doing lately ends here and now. *Verstehen Sie*?"

"Yes, I understand. But I have to go too, Onkel Heinz."

"You know it would kill your mother to find out you're mixed up in some kind of trouble, Sabine. I don't want to have to tell her, but I will."

A threat? Sabine pressed her lips together. Lifting her crutch over his foot, she hurried out the door.

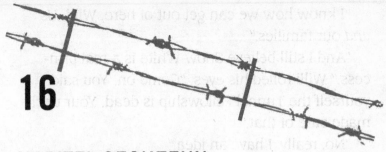

16

KAPITEL SECHZEHN

OUR FATHER

"The weird thing is, I think he really believes he's doing us a favor." Sabine stood in Willi's window the next morning, watching for American patrols on the other side of the wall. Anything to lift her spirits after yesterday's disaster.

Willi tinkered with his telescope, cleaning one of the lenses.

Sabine's mind raced as she looked down at the churchyard where they had planned to tunnel up to freedom. To *see* it from your window, but not have it? This was the worst torture of all.

"At least we don't have to schlep any more pails of dirt out of the tunnel." Count on Willi to try to make a joke. She punched him in the arm.

"That's not the point. The point is that—"

As she gazed at the churchyard, Sabine felt an idea start to bubble. She sometimes felt this way as she fell asleep, or in her dreams.

"I know how we can get out of here, Willi. Us *and* our families."

"And I still believe Snow White is a real princess." Willi rolled his eyes. "Come on. You said yourself the Tunnel Fellowship is dead. Your uncle made sure of that."

"No, really. I have an idea."

"*Ja, ja.* Your ideas always get us into trouble. What is it this time? Dig the tunnel ourselves?"

"Exactly."

Willi stopped chuckling at his joke. His mouth fell open when he realized she was serious. "I was just kidding, okay? We can't do it." He frowned. "Can we?"

She shrugged.

"You're saying this," he prodded, "even after the way you melted down the other day?"

She took a deep breath. Yes. Even after that.

"Well, let's think for just a minute," she said. "The tunnel still has about three meters to go, right? Ten feet?"

"I don't know. Could be a little more, could be a little less. I'm not sure. I'd have to measure it again. Neither of us has gone down there for a couple of days."

"But you know it's close, so we wouldn't have that much farther to dig, right?"

"I don't understand why you're trying to talk me into this. Sabine, the tunnel made you bawl. Don't you remember?"

She nodded quietly. "I remember. But what choice do we have?"

"Well, we could just forget the whole thing."

"After everything we've seen?" she demanded.

"I don't know, I—"

"After we saw that man get shot trying to escape?"

"You saw him. I heard him."

"After the Vopos stopped you for passing out our protest flyers?"

"Well—"

"After the wall went up in the middle of our city?"

He didn't answer.

"Besides, if we don't finish it now, someone will discover it. All that work will go to waste. It's not going to stay a secret forever, especially not with all the others in the fellowship being arrested."

"I hadn't thought about that."

"And so far, Onkel Heinz doesn't know we've been helping with the tunnel. He just thinks we've been hanging around the wrong people."

"Maybe we have."

"I'll pretend you didn't say that. Listen, Willi, we're the only ones who can finish this. Not even my brother can help now. They're watching him everywhere he goes."

Willi took off his glasses and rubbed his eyes.

"Do you know how they planned to come up exactly in the right place?" he asked.

"Not really. But you're smart. I know you'll figure it out."

Willi sighed. He couldn't argue with that, could he? He watched her. She sure knew how to put on a good face.

Most of the time.

But she couldn't keep the brave face on a few minutes later, when the telephone rang.

"Sabine? It's your mother," Willi's father said as he held the receiver out with a puzzled expression. She took it, knowing that her mother would not have called unless something was very wrong.

"It's your grandmother, Sabine." The voice on the other end of the line hardly sounded like her mother. "You need to come home right away."

Sabine closed her eyes and held on to her mother's hand as they sat in the first row of pews. Sabine had never attended a funeral in the big *Zionskirche* before. They'd sung a slow, solemn hymn. Then she'd watched the Reverend Karl Philip Speer ascend to the pulpit. He wasn't the regular pastor of the Zion Church. And surely he wasn't talking about their oma, was he?

Dedicated to our socialist ideals?

Someone who stood in the face of the capitalist West?

An example to the East German community?

Oh, she was an example, all right. But not the

kind you're talking about, Sabine thought. *Who wrote this sermon—Onkel Heinz?*

At least he had shown up. Well, he'd lived in Oma's apartment for years, hadn't he? Aunt Gertrud sat next to him, stiff, bored, and with totally dry eyes. She checked her wristwatch more than once. And Sabine guessed she was probably skipping for joy under her cool mask—Oma was finally dead. She'd most likely start moving into Oma's bedroom as soon as they got home.

Sabine rested her head on her mother's shoulder, and she could not stop the tears from dropping like rain. She knew without a doubt that Oma was with Jesus—though the pastor hadn't yet mentioned their Savior's name. Oma Poldi loved and lived her life for Jesus. Sabine smiled through her tears at a memory of her grandmother praying with her when she was a child. She'd just come home from the hospital. It seemed as if she could still feel the older woman folding her wrinkled hands over Sabine's skinny ones, praying, *"Vater unser im Himmel—"*

"Our Father, which art in heaven—"

But that seemed so long ago. Now Sabine and her mother recited the prayer through their tears—and the memories would not stop: the little extra sweets Oma saved for her, just because. The laughs and the cookies, Berliner pretzels and *Mandelschnitten*—when they could find a few precious almonds. The way Oma slyly threw away socialist newspapers and then acted surprised, as if she couldn't find them! And how she opened her worn Bible and read to Sabine. She especially loved the stories of David and his friend Jonathan, or of Ruth—the faithful woman who stayed with her mother-in-law, Naomi. And of course the stories of Jesus.

If only this pastor would tell some of those stories. Oma would have liked that.

"—*vergib uns unsere Schuld*—"

"—forgive us our trespasses—"

Trespasses? Sabine couldn't help wondering why Oma had gotten so upset the last time they'd spoken in the hospital. What had this sweet, stubborn saint done to make her plead so for forgiveness? Sabine might never know. The secret had likely died with her in the hospital.

Listening again to the pastor, Sabine could tell he didn't know the real Oma. She was certainly not a Communist hero—

"—*wie auch wir vergeben unsern Schuldigem.*"

"—as we forgive those who trespass against us."

Sabine knew her mother believed as strongly as Oma. She'd often talked about growing up and how her mother, Sabine's other grandmother who had died years earlier, had shared her love of Jesus. Without moving her head, Sabine tried to glance at her uncle, just to see if he knew all the words. How could he not? Though he had rejected his mother and sister's God and replaced him with this country's un-god, had he really forgotten everything his mother must have taught him?

No—there! She saw his lips move, just barely.

"Erlöse uns—"

"Deliver us—"

Sabine peeked up at her mother. She knew that things had changed forever for her. The main reason she and her family had stayed behind in this bleak prison-city now lay in the simple wooden casket before them. And this modern-day Ruth and Naomi story would have a different ending from the one in the Bible.

In the Bible's version, Ruth stayed with her mother-in-law, Naomi, even after Ruth's husband, Naomi's son, had died. "Your people shall be my people, and your God my God." In the end, a nice rich guy named Boaz fell for the young widow, they got married, and everybody lived together happily. Sabine liked the story.

In their real-life story, the widow (her mama) remained as loyal to her mother-in-law (Oma). Maybe more. But Sabine wondered what had happened to the happy ending. Now she knew that their lives could change in just a few days, in a big way. And though she couldn't tell her mama about it yet, pretty soon she would have to.

Very soon.

But what about Willi's parents, sitting just one row behind her? How could she and Willi convince them to crawl through a tiny tunnel under Bernau-erstrasse and escape to freedom through a grave-yard? They'd have to leave their jobs behind. Their home. For what? Freedom? She shook her head. What was she thinking?

Uncle Heinz caught her eye, and his mouth snapped shut. Well, he could pretend not to pray, if he wanted to. She waited for him to nod, or wink encouragement at her, or shed a tear, or do some-thing a person might do at a funeral. But he only held her gaze for a moment longer before turning away and whispering something to Aunt Gertrud. And for the first time, Sabine hurt for her uncle, for what he had become, and for whom he had chosen to follow.

Because when Sabine looked up at the altar of the church, she did not see a figurine of Comrade Ulbricht hanging on that cross.

"—in Ewigkeit, amen."

"—forever and ever, amen."

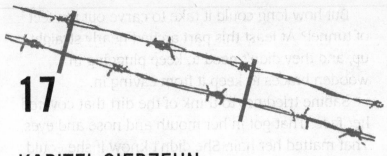

17

KAPITEL SIEBZEHN

BURIED ALIVE

"I don't know how Anton and Albricht dug so far." Sabine squinted as she hacked out a shovelful of dirt and let it fall behind her. She balanced awkwardly on a box as she reached up, praying she wouldn't come face-to-face with a coffin.

At least no one had talked about the tunnel. Not yet. If they did, Sabine and Willi would find out in a hurry.

"Just another couple of feet." Willi's voice sounded muffled. "We should be near the top."

After three days of digging, she sure hoped so. Sabine wiped the sweat from her forehead and tried to breathe. But her head spun and her stomach tumbled, almost as if she'd been playing on a playground carousel too long. When she closed her eyes, she saw stars around the edge of her vision instead of their flickering candlelight. And she knew if she didn't open her eyes soon, she would pass out.

But how long could it take to carve out ten feet of tunnel? At least this part arched nearly straight up, and they didn't need to keep plugging in wooden braces to keep it from caving in.

Sabine tried not to think of the dirt that covered her face. That got in her mouth and nose and eyes. That matted her hair. She didn't know if she could keep moving her arms, but she'd long ago stopped crying about it. And she tried to ignore the blisters that covered her hands. It seemed like the ground had changed a bit. More rocks and roots that made it hard to dig.

Never mind all that. She pushed again with the shovel, muscled past a couple of rocks, and widened the tunnel enough for her shoulders plus a couple of inches on each side. No telling who might use this escape, certainly not Uncle Heinz. She wondered what he would think, though, if he ever found out. Maybe he had already and was just waiting for them to come home so he could have them arrested.

"Well, that would be interesting, wouldn't it?" she asked herself. She could see how coal miners go crazy underground.

"What did you say?" Willi must have crawled in just below her to gather another bucketful of dirt.

"Nothing." She shook her head. "Tunnel diggers always talk to themselves, you know. Keeps them from—"

She didn't finish her sentence as she heard

movement above her and tried to duck. No! She felt herself fall into a blender of dirt and rocks and roots. She didn't even have time to scream or to breathe. The tunnel just roared around her like a hurricane, twisting her head and sending her down.

At first it sounded like a dream. Like a ghostly *"Say-Beeeee-nuhhhh!"* over and over again. Sabine decided she must be dreaming, because she couldn't move her arms or legs. An awful, familiar feeling. Like waking up in the hospital all those years ago...in the starched bed that Nurse Ilse tied her to. In the dark closet that Nurse Ilse locked her in.

This dream had haunted her for years. But she knew that she could trade the dream for a better one. She could fly over the Swiss Alps, over the snow and the meadows, and the reddish-brown cows below would look up at her and moo.

"Please help me get her out of here, Lord!"

But the cows in her dreams had never prayed before. How odd. Someone grabbed her shoulders and bellowed into her face.

"You've got to breathe!" Actually, the voice sounded less like a prayer and more like pleading. "Wake up, Sabine!"

Just when she'd begun gliding over the nice, white snow?

But the shaking would not stop. Sabine

blinked through a dirty crust to open her eyes. How unpleasant. Then she began to focus: Willi Stumpff, upside down, tears making tracks down his dirty cheeks, staring straight into her face—a lot closer than she would have liked. She tried to back away but couldn't move her head. And which side was up, really?

"You're alive!" He still sounded slightly like a cow.

"Haven't I always been?" She coughed and tried to wiggle her shoulders, then her arms. She blew through her mouth like a horse and tried not to spit dirt in Willi's face. As some of the dirt loosened, she rolled a little. And ouch, her shoulder felt like a pretzel.

"You must have loosened something up there," Willi told her. "Are you broken? I mean, is anything broken?"

"Twisted." She took stock of her body. "But I don't think broken." So Willi helped wrestle her out of the dirtslide. When she finally crawled free, something seemed different about the tunnel. They both looked up to find a sliver of light from a smallish hole.

"I meant to do that," she said with a smile. In her excitement, she didn't even notice all the dirt she'd swallowed. "Now we have to clear away this dirt and see where we came up."

But she stopped herself. First she had to tell him.

"I think you saved my life," she mumbled.

"Thanks. But at first, I thought you were a cow in my dream."

"I thought I was supposed to be a sheep," he kidded, trying not to think about Sabine trapped in the dirt.

"You're not a sheep." She felt her voice catch, a tickle in her throat. "You...you dug me out, didn't you?"

"What else was I supposed to do?" he cracked, not allowing her to get mushy on him. "Now go see what's going on up there before somebody walks by."

Sabine could just imagine it: a pastor decides to take a walk near the graveyard, steps into the hole and—

"Come on, Sabine." Willi pushed her from behind. "Unless you really *did* break a bone."

If she had, she couldn't feel it now. She *could* feel a trickle of clean air coming through the opening, though, and she pointed her nose right at it. After breathing the damp, dead underground air for so long, it smelled delicious.

But she couldn't just poke her head up like a mole, could she? Willi pressed something into her hand.

"What's this?"

"You didn't think about it?"

She looked down at the small mirror. It looked like the one her mother used to put on makeup. Oh.

"Just hold the mirror up through the hole, and look around," he told her. "If we tunneled right, you should see the hedge. It should shield us so nobody can see us from the fence."

So while Willi waited, Sabine raised the mirror, like a submarine periscope. But instead of the hedge—

She pulled her hand right back down, as if she'd been burned.

"Can't be!" she whispered, and now she worried that someone might hear them. After all their work—

"What's wrong?"

"We're not where we thought we were." She looked like she might cry.

"Close?"

"Not close. We're in another part of the churchyard, too close to the wall. I don't know what will happen if we try to climb out right here."

"But if we don't?"

"But if we don't—and soon—someone's going to find the tunnel for sure."

18

KAPITEL ACHTZEHN

LAST CHANCE

"Hold it, hold it, hold it." Sabine pulled up short. "We've got to think this through. We'll only get one chance to do it right."

Well, they always looked around before they left the ruins of the bombed-out apartment on Bergstrasse. Just to be sure. And that afternoon, she couldn't see any Vopos, but that really didn't mean anything.

"Right." Willi nodded. "So I'm thinking the only way we're going to convince my father is if both my mama and yours tell him they want to go."

"Maybe." Sabine tried to think through all the angles. "But I wonder if we should find a few more people and help them escape. After all that work Anton and Albricht did in the tunnel. We hardly did anything, compared."

"Yeah, but what are we supposed to do, march around the street with a sign: 'Freedom Tunnel: Open for Everybody'?"

"I just feel guilty, keeping it to ourselves."

She peeked out at the sidewalk once more, wondering. And even after changing into the clean set of clothes she'd stashed in the Volkswagen, she hoped she didn't actually look as if she'd just crawled out of a hole. Oh, well. Their first stop: St. Ludwig's.

"You did *what*?" Erich swiftly faked a smile and gave Sabine a hug when a dozen people in the hospital cafeteria turned to look.

"I said —," she started to explain.

"Little sisters," he said with his broad smile, but Sabine could almost see the steam coming out of his ears as he cut her off. "Always full of surprises."

He steered her to a quiet place in the hallway where he faced her and Willi. He looked like a parent who had caught the kids with their hands in the cookie jar.

"Tell me you're joking," he hissed, this time not so loud.

"It's done, Erich." Sabine crossed her arms and held her ground. She decided they had nothing to apologize for, no matter how mad her big brother sounded. "We finished it."

Erich's mouth hung open as he shook his head. "Do you have any idea how dangerous that was? You could have been buried alive! And who would have known?"

"Ja, Erich," Willi said. "You should have seen it. Sa—"

Sabine jabbed him in the side. They didn't need to tell that story just now.

"It's done, and we finished it, and that's all there is to it," she told her brother. "There's a little opening by the church."

Of course she didn't mention exactly how close to the church or to the wall, because Erich didn't give her a chance.

"An opening, already?" He rubbed his chin with worry. "That's not how we planned to do it. We were going to wait until—"

"We know, we know. It just, well, sort of happened that way."

No use telling the whole story about the cave-in. He already looked like he could have a heart attack any minute.

"Ja, but didn't you think someone could step right through it? Then we'd have Stasi swarming all over this side of the wall until they found the entrance. Did you even think of that? They're already breathing down our necks. One of the older nursing supervisors here watches everything I do. I think she helped get everybody arrested."

"Yes, we thought of it, Erich, and I don't need you to scold me. We just came for help."

Erich paced a little circle around them, but he didn't answer right away.

"And we wanted to ask you if we should tell anybody else in the fellowship," added Willi.

"Nein." Erich scratched his head and settled down a little bit. "I haven't talked to any of them since the Stasi swept through here. It's way too dangerous."

"So, what are you saying?" Sabine parked her hands on her hips. "That Willi and I did all that digging for nothing? Look at my hands! You want us to forget everything, because it's 'too dangerous'?"

That *wasn't* what they'd come to hear.

"Dangerous, yes. Forget everything, no."

"Excuse me?" Willi whispered out the side of his mouth, but Erich ignored him as he went on.

"Maybe you and Mutti should take this chance to escape. I think she'll leave now that Oma is...gone. She hates what this place is doing to you."

"Uh, you might want to look down the hall." Willi tried once more. "Is that the nurse you were talking about?"

The older woman had already started walking briskly toward them, clipboard in hand.

"You there!" the woman called as she approached. "A word with you, *bitte.*"

"Go now," Erich commanded. "I'll take care of this."

"But—" Sabine objected.

"Go." He lowered his voice even more and checked his watch. "I'll meet you at home in an hour. Not a word to Onkel Heinz or Tante Gertrud. And be careful who sees you."

"What do you think she wanted?" Willi asked as he checked over his shoulder for the tenth time in the past block. Sabine didn't want to think about it. But she had a pretty good idea.

"You heard him. Everyone's being watched."

"*Ja*, but why didn't they arrest him, like everybody else?"

"I'll tell you why they didn't." She sighed. "My onkel. I think he's trying to use Erich to find the tunnel, so he can get all the credit. Maybe a pat on the back from Comrade Ulbricht."

"From the Goatee? How do you know that?"

"I don't, for sure. But I can't think of any other reason."

If she'd guessed right, though, the screws would tighten fast. They would have to make their move even sooner. So she kept up her pace for home. Bismarck loped along behind them as if he knew to stay close by. But she paused when they came to Willi's corner.

"You're coming," she told him, without looking up. "Nine o'clock at the Beetle. So we don't need to say good-bye. Okay?"

"Okay. But listen: you know my father might not... well, you know what I mean. So I want you to have something, just in case."

"Willi, I don't think—"

"Just wait here, all right?"

He disappeared into his apartment building before she could answer. In a couple of minutes, he returned with his telescope.

"Here." He held it out to her. "It's yours."

She wasn't sure how she would carry it. But what was she going to do, say no?

"Well, um, okay. Maybe just a loan. I'll borrow it until—"

Until what? They both knew that Willi might not come to the tunnel later. But Sabine wasn't ready to give up—not yet. She turned away, so Willi couldn't see her get blubbery, and hurried home. They didn't have much time.

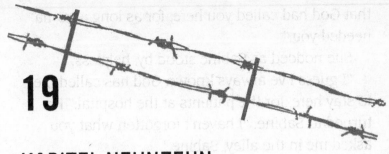

19

KAPITEL NEUNZEHN

THE CALLING

"You *have* to go, Mama." Erich could sound very convincing when he wanted to. "I promise, you'll never get another chance like this one."

"How can you promise that?" She sat in a kitchen chair with her arms crossed. "How can you know things won't open up again?"

"The wall?" He shook his head. "No, Mama. They're building it stronger every day. Adding more guards. More barbed wire. More no-man's-land. It's going to stay for a long, long time."

"Then why don't you come with us?" Sabine knew the answer before she asked it, but she hoped. And Erich looked at them with the saddest eyes she'd ever seen. Sad, but with a sparkle all the same.

"Remember how you always told us your place was here with Oma?" He leaned closer to his mother, his hand on her cheek. "You knew that God had called you here, for as long as Oma needed you."

She nodded as Sabine stood by, helpless.

"I guess I've always known God has called me to stay here, for the patients at the hospital." He turned to Sabine. "I haven't forgotten what you asked me in the alley, Sabine."

Neither had she. He didn't need to explain, but—

"When you asked if I still had a reason to stay in East Berlin. Well, I do. It hasn't changed. I'm staying."

Of course that only made their mother cry. Erich tried to dry the tears from her cheeks, tried to tell her not to cry.

"Mutti," he finally asked her, "don't you think this is what DeWitt would have wanted you to do for his daughter?"

Their mother gasped at the mention of Sabine's father, the American airman whose plane had crashed just weeks before Sabine's birth.

"He would have wanted me to do it a long time ago," she said as she reached out to take their hands. And with heart-wrenching sobs, she finally nodded.

"Good," Erich said. "But we'd better move quickly, or no one's going anywhere."

Sabine jumped when she heard the front door slam, the way it slammed when Uncle Heinz came in. Instantly they all straightened up and dried their tears.

"When's dinner?" he asked, poking his head into the kitchen. And his eyebrows rose when he saw them sitting together by the kitchen table. "Or are we just playing cards?"

Sabine's mother took a deep breath and stood up, though her brother had already returned to the other room.

"I need to tell you something," she announced. Erich shot up like a rocket.

"No, Mutti. Don't—"

But she held up her hand. She had decided, and there was no arguing.

"We're not just going to disappear without saying a proper good-bye," she told him, her chin set. "They're family, even if we don't always agree."

"We could write them a note," Erich suggested quietly. "A fond farewell, or—"

She shook her head firmly.

"We will tell them face-to-face, and that's all there is to it."

Sabine looked at her brother and felt like a leaking balloon, deflating slowly.

Mama has no idea what she's about to do—

An hour later, Sabine stood still in shock as she watched her mother and uncle hug.

"We're going to miss you," said Uncle Heinz. He rubbed his three chins and nodded as if he understood their decision.

Sabine couldn't believe what she heard. *Is this*

really Onkel Heinz? His face looked almost like it had in the church, when he'd quietly recited the Lord's Prayer. Just for a moment. Good thing Aunt Gertrud had gone out that evening to visit her sister.

"And we'll certainly miss you too," replied Sabine's mother. She looked as if she meant it. Sabine had packed her toothbrush and a few small things, including Willi's telescope, in her backpack. They couldn't drag much with them through the tunnel.

"Don't get me wrong," her uncle replied, wagging his finger at them. "I don't like it, and I don't approve. And I'll probably regret this later, but—"

He stuffed his hands in his pockets and studied the floor. "But you're family, and I won't try to stop you."

Incredible. Sabine could hardly believe her ears.

Erich looked at his watch again and shifted on his toes. "It's dark," he announced. "We have to go now."

Sabine and her uncle nodded at each other; that was as close as she could come to a good-bye.

"We should wait for Gertrud," Frau Becker said as she looked out the window, hoping to see her sister-in-law. But Erich shook his head.

"We can't, Mutti. We only have thirty minutes. We have to go."

"I'll tell her you said good-bye," Uncle Heinz

offered as he peered into the darkness over her shoulder.

"We'll write," promised Frau Becker. Of course, no one knew whether the letters would get through. Uncle Heinz nodded once more.

"I'll take care of everything. Even"—he hesitated—"even Wolfgang. Now go."

Sabine and her mother shouldered their bulging bags, as if they simply planned to go visit friends. And Sabine looked back at the kitchen once more, at the only home she could remember. Where would they live, over in the West? So near—only a few blocks away—but so far. Still Germany, but another country.

She waited impatiently to give her mother a head start. They couldn't walk together tonight. And she wondered as she watched Erich shake his uncle's meaty hand. Their sudden friendliness made her uneasy.

"I'm trusting you to come back tonight, nephew. And don't forget. You've got half an hour. After that, I guarantee nothing. If you're still there, you'll be arrested, just like anybody else. I won't be able to do a thing about it."

"Don't worry," Erich told him. "I'll come back. And you can take all the credit for finding the tunnel. That was our deal, and I'll stick to my end of it."

"See that you do."

Sabine gulped at their conversation. But it

explained why Erich had watched the clock so closely. And now they had only twenty-nine minutes.

Ten of which they spent walking the long way around, down Bernauerstrasse and past the *bäckerei*. Then they doubled back behind the bombed-out apartment building. They'd all agreed that they couldn't look hurried, or worried, or anything of the sort. In her nervous excitement, Sabine fought the urge to look up and wave at the mysterious Wolfgang—the Watcher she wouldn't miss. But the last thing they needed was to have a Vopo stop and search them. She wondered if her bulging backpack might make Wolfgang suspicious anyway. The more she thought about it, the more she wished they hadn't packed any bags at all. Too late now. Erich and Sabine had reached the bombed-out apartment building and found their mother in the shadows. Quickly they showed her the trap-door and helped her climb down. Sabine looked into the pitch-dark tunnel and sighed.

"I told them no later than nine." She looked out toward the street. "I thought for sure he would come."

Erich held the trapdoor open and shook his head.

"I'm sorry, Sabine. But—"

"I have to check." Maybe if she saw Willi and his family coming, she could hurry them up. "Just another minute. Give us one more minute."

"No, Sabine. There isn't time!" But Sabine had already started out, and Erich didn't want to drop the trapdoor, leaving their mother alone in the darkness below.

Sabine assumed he didn't follow her because he didn't want to risk making a scene on the street.

Unlike Willi, apparently—Sabine stared in surprise as she watched her friend stumble toward her, dragged along by—

"Bismarck! Come here, boy!"

Bismarck nearly bowled her down in his excitement as he showered her with sloppy dog kisses.

"Sorry we're late." Willi grinned all over. "We had a pretty long discussion, and—"

"You have no idea how late we are," she interrupted him. His parents followed at a short distance, just a couple with a new baby, out for a summer evening's walk. "What time is it, about nine-twenty?"

"I don't know. But the dog found me again, and—"

"Okay, okay. We've *got* to hurry. Get your parents to hurry up. The police will be here any minute."

"Go! Follow the tunnel, and don't look back," Erich whispered urgently as each person slipped through the trapdoor. He paused as Willi pulled the dog closer. "You can't take him."

"You know what he's like if we try to leave him up here," argued Willi.

Erich could only groan and shake his head. "Of course, he'll just whine and bring the Vopo right on top of us. Fine, take him. Just hurry!"

Last to go, Sabine stopped to hug her big brother one more time. She could hardly let him go.

"Change your mind," she whispered into his ear, burying her tears on his shoulder.

He held her close for another moment, then pushed her away.

"I'll see you again, little sister." His voice sounded teary too. She couldn't see his face clearly in the darkness. But she could hear the wail of a siren getting louder and louder.

And then she felt Willi's hands tug her through the trapdoor. Together, they raced through the darkened tunnels she knew so well. She knew every wooden brace, every curve.

"Sabine, are you coming?" her mother called back. Sabine could see her candle flicker up ahead.

"Right behind you, Mama."

"Come on, you. Move it." Willi poked at her. How had he gotten behind her?

"Going as fast as I can. I'm disabled, remember?"

"No, I forgot that."

Sabine gasped for breath as she finally got to the end of the tunnel. When she reached toward the opening, strong hands reached down to help her out.

"Come!" a strange man's voice insisted. "Follow the others, over there by the church." Willi popped up behind her, and the stranger hauled him out of the hole.

"Thank you," Willi said, breathing heavily. "Let's go. I'm the last one."

And a good thing too. They had hardly taken a step when headlights from the other side of the fence lit up the churchyard. Sabine stumbled, momentarily blinded by the light.

"Run!" she told Willi. "Leave me."

But he pushed her crutch out of the way and circled her waist with an arm. Off they ran, a three-legged race. They heard three pops, three shots, and Sabine knew the next one would be aimed straight at them—such a slow-moving target.

But they'd made it to the right side of the fence, right? Maybe that didn't matter. Bismarck had scrambled out of the hole and nipped at their heels. Sabine's mother ran back to help Willi and her daughter. But Sabine had to see, she had to know what happened. She looked over her shoulder and stumbled again.

"Sabine!" her mother cried as many hands grabbed at them, pulling them behind the protection of a large gravestone. But still Sabine had to see. She leaned out beyond the headstone.

Erich stood in the stark headlight glare, alone

where God had called him to stay, surrounded by a swarm of Vopos leveling machine guns at him. What could he do but raise his arms in surrender? Sabine leaned closer, as if that would take her to her brother. But her mother held her back.

Jesus! she prayed silently. *Please keep him safe!*

They could only watch in fear from their little foothold in freedom. A policeman grabbed Erich from behind and forced him to his knees. Yet Erich held up his free hand and waved at his family.

"Oh, Erich." Sabine couldn't turn away as the Vopos dragged him off.

And then she stood with her friends and mother on the free side of the wall, and they hugged one another in a tearful celebration. One that had cost them too much.

"Welcome to West Berlin," the stranger who had helped them said. Sabine noticed for the first time that he wore a police uniform. As he led them away from the chaos of the wall, he added, "Congratulations. You're free now."

EPILOGUE

This story is dedicated to the memory of the 171 people who lost their lives seeking freedom from East Berlin. That's how many people were killed between 1961 —when the wall went up—and 1989—when the wall came back down again. Those twenty-eight years were some of the bleakest in German history.

One of the bright spots came when an American president, John F. Kennedy, visited a divided Berlin in June 1963. He told a crowd of thousands in front of the Berlin City Hall that "when one man is enslaved, all are not free... [so] all free men, wherever they may live, are citizens of Berlin. And therefore, as a free man, I take pride in the words *'Ich bin ein Berliner.'"*

I am a Berliner.

But despite the speeches, the wall remained for many years. And just as in our story, people tried to escape from East to West in all kinds of ways. In the beginning, before the fence became a wall, they ran across or swam across one of the rivers or canals that ran through Berlin. They jumped from buildings that looked over the line. Some made it; some didn't. Some even escaped through the sewer system and dug tunnels. In fact, one of the first tunnels actually came up through a grave-yard, until a woman accidentally discovered it by falling into the hole! And one of the most successful tunnels began in a basement near the line, just like in our story. Twenty-nine people made it to freedom through that tunnel.

One of the most interesting escapes came when two families—the Wetzels and the Strelzyks—secretly built a hot-air balloon and floated to freedom.

What does this tell us? That people will do just about anything to be free. And that sometimes, out of love, people will give their all so others can have that freedom. Dietrich Mendt, an East German pastor, used to quote Psalm 18 to explain why some East German Christians stayed behind the Iron Curtain, serving their neighbors and friends. "With God," the psalmist wrote, "one is able to leap over walls!"

These Christians didn't think the psalm told them to just jump over the wall, though. To them, it was a little more simple. They would stay and serve, and they would work for freedom.

Because for God, there really *are* no walls.

QUESTIONS FOR FURTHER STUDY

1. How has Sabine's childhood disease affected her as she grew up? How did she compensate, or make up, for her physical condition?
2. In chapter four, what did Sabine's mother say was their reason for staying in East Berlin? Do you agree or disagree with her decision? Why or why not?
3. In chapter four, Sabine gets in trouble for reading a book the government doesn't like. Are there times when we should tell *ourselves* not to read or watch something? When might that be?
4. In chapter six, why was it especially hard for Sabine to visit her grandmother in the hospital? Can you think of times when you've been afraid to help someone else? Look up Philippians 2:3. What does the Bible say about this?
5. In chapter seven, what happened to people who wanted to escape from East Berlin to West Berlin? Why do you think they would risk their lives to do so? Would you?
6. In the beginning of chapter eight, Sabine explains why she thinks the last war happened. What was it? What do you think of what she said? Do you think her idea could

still apply today—not just to wars, but to anything else?

7. When Sabine asked Willi in chapter thirteen how he liked digging, he answered with a Bible verse. Which other situations might that verse apply to, as well?

8. Why did Sabine get mad at her big brother in chapter fourteen? Do you think she was right? Why or why not?

9. In chapter sixteen, which Bible story did Sabine compare to her mother and grandmother's situation? What changed when Sabine's grandmother died?

10. What was Willi's gift, and why did he give it to Sabine in chapter eighteen?

11. In chapter nineteen, why did Erich decide to stay behind? What would you have done if you were in his position?

12. Read in the "How it Really Happened" section about the Psalm often quoted by an East German pastor (Psalm 18:28–33). What do these verses have to do with our story?

SMUGGLER'S TREASURE

CONTENTS

PROLOGUE

THE BRANDENBURG GATE, WEST BERLIN
JUNE 12, 1987

The American president's words echoed over the heads of thousands of West Berliners, all crammed into the historic *Brandenburgplatz,* the public plaza in front of the Brandenburg Gate. And while eleven-year-old Liesl Stumpff didn't quite understand the gathering in the huge plaza, she knew it had to be important. Why else would so many people come to hear this man speak? She cupped her hands over her ears every time the crowd clapped and cheered.

"In the Communist world, we see failure ..."

Liesl knew he was right. Nothing seemed to work on the other side of the wall, and everyone always seemed grouchy or afraid. And strangely, that Communist world started just through the big beautiful stone arch of the Brandenburg Gate, the symbol of their divided city, Berlin.

"Even today, the Soviet Union still cannot feed itself ..."

Neither could the Soviet Union's puppet country, East Germany. That's where Liesl's Uncle Erich lived, in the apartment his grandmother, Poldi Becker, had once owned on *Rheinsberger-strasse*—Rheinsberger Street. Just through the gate that divided their city, Berlin, in two.

"Do you think Onkel Erich can hear the speech from his window, too?" she wondered aloud. How could he not, with the huge loudspeakers turned toward the east?

"Maybe." Willi Stumpff, her father, shrugged. "Or maybe from the hospital where he works." If so, he would hear the American president declare: "... *Freedom is the victor!*"

Was it? Liesl and her parents could briefly visit her uncle in East Berlin every three or four months. He, on the other hand, could never leave. The barbed wire, the armed guards, and the wall itself made sure of that. What kind of country had to fence its people in to keep them from escaping? Maybe she was only eleven, but she'd known things weren't right for a long time.

The crowd cheered as the president went on. *"Are these the beginnings of profound changes?"*

"What does *profound* mean?" asked Liesl, and her father tried to explain. Big, he thought. Important. Though she didn't quite understand all of the president's English words, she liked his voice. Smiling and strong at the same time, like her papa. Looking up at her father, she wished she were small enough to ride on his broad shoulders. She wasn't tall enough to see over the crowd yet.

Papa smiled at her. "Maybe they'll show Mr. Reagan on the news tonight."

They did, indeed, show Mr. Reagan on the news. One line especially. Over and over, until Liesl had it memorized and could deliver that part of Mr. Reagan's speech with passion and pizzazz:

General Secretary Gorbachev, if you seek peace ... Come here to this gate! Mr. Gorbachev, open this gate! Mr. Gorbachev, tear down this wall!

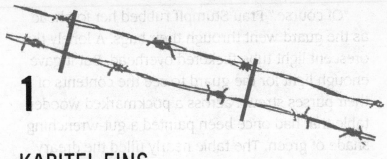

1

KAPITEL EINS

EAST BERLIN CHECKPOINT

MARCH 1989—NEARLY TWO YEARS LATER

Of course it's me. Who else?

Liesl bit her lip and did her best not to look guilty as she waited for the East German Vopo border guard to check her I.D. papers. Again.

Hair: Brown. Eyes: Brown. Date of Birth: 12 *März* 1976. And yes, that would make her thirteen years old today.

Liesl's mother tried to explain. "It's my daughter's birthday, and we're just visiting my half brother for the occasion—"

Frau Stumpff's voice trailed off at the guard's withering stare. He would surely hear Liesl's heart beating, and he would find out everything. Surely he would find out.

"You will simply answer my questions," he snapped, still clutching Liesl's I.D. "Nothing more."

"Of course." Frau Stumpff rubbed her forehead as the guard went through their bags. A lonely fluorescent light tube flickered overhead. But it gave enough light for the guard to see the contents of their purses strewn across a pockmarked wooden table that had once been painted a gut-wrenching shade of green. The table nearly filled the dreary interrogation room, barely leaving them enough space to move. And the guard towered over them across the table, blocking their way to the door. A Russian-made clock kept time on the bare wall.

Ten minutes slow. Liesl checked the clock against her own watch, a nice gold Junghans model Papa had given her a few days earlier, before he went to Stuttgart, again, on business. She pushed her sleeve down before the guard noticed. No telling what he might ask of them.

Liesl's mother gave her an "I'm sorry" look. But what could they do about it?

They could ignore the grimy two-way mirror on the wall behind them. Everyone knew an inspector of some kind sat behind it watching them, waiting for them to say something that could be taken as a "crime against the East German State."

Well, she wouldn't give anyone that chance. The guard methodically picked through their things, thumbing through appointment books, opening up wallets. He even took the rubber tip off her mother's crutch and looked inside. Imagine that!

And Liesl knew she would faint if the guard

moved on from searching their purses to searching anything else. She prayed the small bulges in her socks and the one taped under her blouse would only make her look as if she had eaten a few too many *eierkuchen*—pancakes—perhaps filled with a bit too much sweet marmalade. Wouldn't he just assume all West Berliners were fat and greedy, lazy and overfed?

Some people might think so, but only if they listened to Radio DDR *Eins*—the East German government broadcasts. She closed her eyes and leaned against the table.

Bitte, bitte. Please, please, get me through this, she prayed silently, biting her lip until she was sure it would start bleeding.

Was the guard leading her off in handcuffs? No. Her mother gently squeezed her elbow. "Answer the man's question, dear."

Liesl's eyes snapped open. *What?* The guard faced her, his frown growing deeper. He held out her I.D. papers but wouldn't give them back until she answered.

"Oh, *ja.* Of course." She lit up a smile and bobbed politely, as she might in a ballroom, only this was no dance. She must have said the right thing; his hollow-cheeked expression thawed a couple of degrees as he released the papers.

"*Gut,*" he told them as he glanced once more at the mess on the table. "Enjoy your stay here in East Berlin."

There. Almost like a travel agent—only his words didn't fool anyone. He pivoted like a robot and stepped toward the exit, pausing only a moment as he reached for the doorknob.

"And," he added, still facing away from them, "Happy birthday."

Pardon me? Liesl was too startled to say "thank you." And she couldn't have brought herself to say anything like that to the nasty guard anyway. Not even when she was pretending to be Cher, her favorite American singer and actress. Her hands shook as she shoveled her things off the table and back into her purse. Right now they had to get out of that dirty border-station checkpoint, past the dreary shops on *Friedrichstrasse*, and on to her uncle's flat.

She fought the temptation to check her smuggled cargo, to touch the bulge in her sock. No one must know, not yet. Not even her mother.

"Mutti," she whispered as they turned the corner. "What did I agree to back there?"

Frau Stumpff shook her head as she continued limping along with her crutch. Liesl was used to walking at half speed.

"Oh, just that you should go through the *Jugendweihe* ceremony while you were here." She held a glove to her face, partly because of the chill wind, partly because of the other people on the street. "Just like all the other good young socialists, dedicating their lives to the state."

Oh, bombig! — Great! Liesl groaned at what she'd done without knowing. But she was an actress, just like Cher. An actress played the part.

"You'd better be careful what you agree to around here." A smile played at the corners of her mother's lips. "Or you'll be defending socialism and the Soviet Union before you know it."

Liesl nodded. After what they had just been through, she couldn't help jumping when she heard a man's voice boom at them, "You two!"

Liesl turned and saw the guard who had searched them. He raised his hand as he ran closer. "Stop right there!"

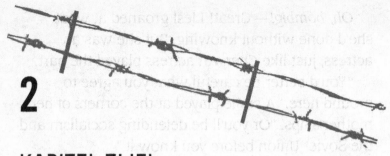

2

KAPITEL ZWEI

THE ANNOUNCEMENT

"Stop right there."

Nick Wilder did as he was told. He gripped the end of the loose control cable and inspected the instrument panel of the big C–54 Skymaster cargo plane as he waited for the next instruction.

"You got it?" he wondered aloud.

Fred grunted as he always did. But the sixty-something man got away with all kinds of rude noises as they worked on the old airplane.

"Keep your shirt on," Fred mumbled.

So Nick waited while Fred fumbled a little more. Who knew getting caught a year ago in the belly of the old C–54 would lead to this unlikely friendship?

And who knew Nick would get to help resurrect one of the ancient warplanes parked on the edge of the Bighorn County Airport in the Middle of Nowhere, Wyoming? Someday, when they got the proud old bird off the ground again, they would look back at all the grunt work and know it was worth it. But for now...

"There!" Fred finally announced his success. "Now pull me out of here. I mean all of me, not just the legs." Fred had two artificial legs, a war injury, Nick thought.

Nick grinned and gently grabbed the man's plastic ankles to help him inchworm out from beneath the panel. In a car, this would be the dashboard. A moment later, they both leaned against the wall and surveyed their day's work.

"Too bad we can't recruit your dad to help with this." Fred wiped his brow with a pink rag. "Would go a lot quicker."

Sure, but the airport's chief mechanic didn't have time to mess with the old museum airplanes—not with all the smoke-jumper planes and small jets he had to work on. But that was okay with Nick and his older friend.

"Not that I don't appreciate *your* help, you understand," Fred said.

Nick nodded. Fred didn't need to explain. But what help was he really, showing up after school and weekends, in restoring a fifty-year-old transport plane?

Oh, well.

"How much longer do you think it will take, Fred?" Nick looked at the impressive panel of dials and gauges in front of them. Thanks to their hours of effort, some worked—though many still did not.

Fred just ran his greasy hands through his bristle of gray hair and shrugged the way he always did. He gave Trouble, Nick's mutt, a scratch behind the ears.

"Like I said, kid, I'm not too good with the future. That's why I stick to the old stuff. Like these planes."

Not that Nick expected an answer. But still it was his job to ask—like a kid in the backseat who had to whine, "Are we there, yet?"

As far as he could tell, they might not be there for a long time. But in a strange way he felt okay with that.

"Anybody home?"

Nick recognized his father's voice coming up through the plane's belly hatch.

"Hey, stranger," Fred greeted him, wiping a hand on his shirt before offering it to Nick's dad. "Decided to join us, after all?"

"Well, I am joining," Mark Wilder grinned as he pumped the older man's hand, "but not the museum staff. Sorry."

Nick sized up his dad from the worn leather pilot's seat, his favorite spot in the airplane. His father didn't usually act all smiley and weird like this.

"Dad?"

"Here, read this." Nick's dad pulled an envelope from the pocket of his coveralls and held it out.

Nick noticed the return address—Department of the Air Force.

"I don't get it." But his stomach knotted as he pulled out the letter and began to read.

Pleased to inform you...

Reinstated to your former rank...

Assigned immediately to...

Nick didn't need to read it all the way to the end. He handed back the letter , feeling as if someone had punched him in the gut.

"I thought you were done with the Air Force, Dad. Just weekends and that summer thing you do."

"Your mom and I have talked about this for a long time." For a moment Mr. Wilder's forehead furrowed. "It's a chance we can't pass up."

"We?" Nick didn't mean it to sound as snotty as it came out.

"Of course *we*. You read the letter. They're assigning me to the Rhein-Main Air Base, which is near Frankfurt, West Germany."

Nick said nothing, just let his father go on. The guy seemed so excited, after all.

"And besides, how many kids your age get a chance for an experience like this? Don't you think it could be a good move for us?"

"Join the Air Force, see the world," Nick said. But by this time he felt totally numb. And instead of backing him up, Fred only chuckled. This was funny?

"Good for you, Mark. Backwoods Wyoming, here, probably wasn't a great step on your career ladder."

"Right. I mean, no. It's not that." Mark Wilder stumbled over his words. "This place has been great for our family. It's just that—"

"Hey, don't apologize on my account." Fred held up his hands. "Believe me, I understand." Both men gave Nick a curious look.

You expected me to jump up and down? But Nick couldn't say it out loud, not here in front of Fred. Instead, he pretended to adjust one of the loose throttle handles while the two men chatted. Trouble snoozed behind the co-pilot's seat.

"He'll get used to the idea," Fred said. How did he know what Nick would get used to? "Course, I'll miss his help here on the plane. Sure you won't let him stay?"

Really? Nick looked over at his dad, hoping for an instant that it might be so. But both men were smiling at Fred's joke. Oh.

"I report in four weeks." Mr. Wilder turned serious. *"With* my wife and kid. Nobody's staying behind."

So that was it. Just like that, no questions asked. Not even a "What would you think if we …" No nothing. Just "We're leaving in a month whether you like it or not." Nick would have punched his dad in the nose, if he could have. Instead, he turned the wheel until it jammed to the side. What would it take to get this bird flying, right here, right now—in the opposite direction of this Main Rhyme or whatever that silly air base was called?

Fred snapped his fingers as if he'd just remembered something.

"Wait right here." He started for the rear of the plane, hobbling slightly as he always did. "I've got something I think you should have, considering where you're going."

Whatever. Nick didn't answer. He just sat in his pilot's chair staring out at the runway, saying nothing, scratching Trouble's ears and trying not to cry. His dad studied the instructions on the side of a half-assembled radio set as if his life depended on it. And Nick let himself wonder how this Wyoming airfield had looked when filled with wave after wave of military planes, filled with crew after crew of military men like his dad. Now it only welcomed the firefighters in the summer (who strutted around the tarmac like soldiers), crop dusters in the spring, and the little private planes when the weather allowed. No matter who they were, though, they always seemed to be passing through on the way to somewhere else. And, as it turned out, so was Nick.

The story of his life, right? Passing through on the way to someplace else. Funny thing was, Nick really *should* have been jumping up and down. And maybe he would have been a few months earlier. Now? He stared at the Bighorn Mountains shimmering in the distance and gripped the steering wheel. Now Fred would have to finish this job alone. Truth was, the older man would probably die before that ever happened.

Fred emerged a minute later from the back of the plane and held out a small, newspaper-wrapped bundle.

"What's this?" Nick took the package and held it up to the light.

"Okay, so it's more of a favor, actually." Fred scratched his head, as if he were still thinking it through. "It's not a present, if that's what you're thinking. Take a look at it."

Nick unwrapped the yellowed newspaper to find a tarnished old cup with a stem—like a small, old-fashioned wine goblet. Very fancy. The side was engraved with a delicate swirly pattern and some funny writing. Nick couldn't make out the words; all the letters looked doubled over with too many elbows. Not a present, though? Fred would have to explain this.

"I got it a long time ago," Fred told them. It was his turn to stare out the window, and his eyes seemed to go misty. "It's a communion cup out of a German church."

"So how did you get it?" asked Mr. Wilder.

"Long story. I won't bore you with all the details." His shoulders sagged as he sighed. "But I didn't steal it, nothing like that. It's just that I can't keep it anymore."

How odd. But Fred had a little more explaining to do.

"See, I could have sent it there myself, only I wasn't sure exactly where to send it, or who to send it to. I'd feel a lot better if ..."

Fred's voice trailed off as he seemed to dip into some old emotional well.

"What do you want us to do with it?" Nick wondered.

Fred still stared outside. "Give it to a church over there if you can, would you? Or just give it to somebody over there. I don't care. Maybe they'll appreciate it."

Nick turned the communion cup over in his hands, afraid to ask anything else. But he couldn't help feeling curious about how this piece of silver had come all the way to the Bighorn County Airport in Greybull, Wyoming.

And he figured he'd probably never find out.

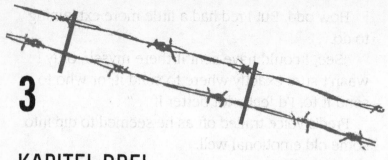

3

KAPITEL DREI

UNEXPECTED GUEST

"I think he liked you, Mutti," Liesl told her mother as they headed up the stairs to her uncle's flat. "Maybe that's why he kept us so long at the checkpoint."

"Please, Liesl. Not even joking. It was bad enough without him coming after us."

"But weren't you happy he returned your makeup mirror?"

Her mother dismissed the teasing with a wave.

"I'm sure someone else could have used it. And they were more than welcome to it."

How clumsy, really. Had he truly found it on the floor, the way he'd said, or had he kept it in his pocket as an excuse to follow them? Liesl couldn't be sure. But she grinned with relief when they finally knocked on her uncle's door.

"I don't know, Mutti. A Vopo friend at the border? Maybe that wouldn't be so bad."

"Shh! Enough, Liesl. Sometimes you don't know when to stop!"

The door opened with a click and Erich Becker gave them a puzzled look as he greeted them.

"Is there a problem here?" He opened his arms wide and greeted his "two favorite girls in all the world."

"No problems, big brother." Sabine Stumpff returned her half brother's hug.

And naturally Liesl would expect her mother to say so. But Onkel Erich probably heard every word they'd said before he opened the door. So did the nosey neighbor, who pulled quickly back in her apartment when Liesl glanced down the hall. Welcome to East Berlin, where every wall has ears, and neighbors care so deeply that they will report everything you do to the Stasi—the secret police. Even now Frau Nosey was probably calling the authorities at the Ministry for State Security to warn them that *Herr Doktor* had visitors from the West—again—and that they looked awfully suspicious.

Liesl waved down the hall, just for fun, as her uncle pulled them inside. She always thought he smelled of the hospital where he worked—of operating rooms and disinfectant—even through the pleasant tang of his Tabac cologne.

He would not be in danger—not as long as he promised to live in East Berlin, the way he always had. As in, *forever*—he would die here. That's the way things worked on this side of the wall.

"So nothing happened at the checkpoint?" he asked. Perhaps he sensed his sister and niece were more flustered than on other visits.

"Just the usual." Liesl's mother shrugged off the question and her coat, and yes, she said, it was very warm in this apartment building. Liesl could have laughed, and her uncle gave her a big smile.

"Is that true, Liesl?"

"Sure, if you call a full-scale shakedown 'usual.' The only thing the Vopo didn't do was ask Mutti out for dinner." It was a good enough joke. But as Liesl thought more about it, she knew what *could* have happened. Her knees began to shake, and she quickly sat down so no one would notice.

Too late.

"What's wrong, *mein Liebling*?" No use trying to hide anything from her mother. Frau Stumpff kneeled by the chair and took hold of Liesl's feet. "You look like you are about to faint."

"No, no." Liesl couldn't pull away. "Nothing like that."

But her mother had discovered the stash of booklets bound tightly around her ankles.

"Liesl." She patted her daughter's legs for more. "What is this all about?"

But she knew—she must know. Liesl pressed her lips together and looked away.

"Is this what I think it is?" asked Frau Stumpff,

and the storm clouds gathered on her face. She looked over at her brother. "Erich, have you been talking to her again about smuggling these things?"

"Don't look at me!" Onkel Erich held up his hands in surrender. "I thought she looked a little well fed, but I wasn't going to say anything. Not polite, you know."

"Oh, come on!" Sabine rose to her feet and planted her hands on her hips. "You two act as if this is some kind of game. Liesl, you know what could have happened to you if the guards had searched you. To us!"

Liesl unpacked twenty-two of the slim New Testaments from her socks, with more to come from her other hiding places.

"It's not the way it used to be, Sabine." Onkel Erich could usually calm his younger sister. "Now they just throw you in the same jail cell with heroin smugglers and—"

"Erich!"

Erich nodded and led his sister to the window. "I know what you're saying. But I didn't ask her to do this."

"And that makes it all right? Because it was a surprise?"

"You know the government still has us in a straitjacket. Even today, when people say communism is dying. *Glasnost* and Gorbechev. But is it really any better? We can still use all the Scriptures we can get. And right now we just can't get them over the border or printed fast enough. There's too much red tape."

"And you would put your own niece in danger to get them?" Her voice cracked and Liesl knew her mother would start crying if they didn't do something.

"Mutti," Liesl said quietly. "Nobody was going to find out."

"That's easy for you to say now!" Her mother's tears began to overflow.

Onkel Erich tried to wave Liesl off with a little shake of his head, but she was determined. "I'm sorry, Mutti." She put her arm around her mother. "I was just—just trying to do the right thing. Obeying God instead of people, right? Isn't that what you've always said I should do?"

"But not like this—"

"Then how?"

Well, that pretty much stopped the conversation in its tracks. That, and an urgent knock on the door. Liesl's mother jumped and her uncle sprang into action.

"Liesl!" He pointed at the pile of smuggled Bibles, then motioned with his finger for her to stash them under his threadbare sofa. His expression told her *now!*

"Coming." Her uncle answered in his usual relaxed voice, though Liesl could tell from his face he felt anything but relaxed. "Who's there, bitte?"

Bitte. Please. And that was just like her uncle, polite to anyone who pounded on his door—even to the men with guns who guarded this prison city. Would the Vopos announce their visit or just push their way in? Or could it be the dreaded Stasi, even? Frau Stumpff grabbed her daughter's hand and perched on the edge of the only other chair in the room. Try to look casual.

Again the pounding, even louder.

"Just a minute, bitte." Erich took his time pulling back the deadbolt. The Vopos had to know whose door they were pounding on. Herr Doktor Erich Becker, one of the few intellectuals who had neither joined the Communist party nor escaped to the West. Didn't that mean anything to them, when so many other surgeons and engineers and scientists had already jumped ship? Anybody with a brain, really. And that clearly didn't include these police, still pounding on the door.

"Oh, it's you, Hans!" Erich opened the door and an out-of-breath man about the doctor's age tumbled in. Not a guard, after all. "Why didn't you answer me?"

"Sorry." Hans, the taller man, brushed himself off and nodded his hello at the others as Erich closed the door. "Your neighbor lady was listening to every word, so—"

Frau Nosey! Erich seemed to understand as they continued their conversation in whispers.

"Come on, Liesl." Frau Stumpff rose to her feet. "Let's go see what your uncle has cooking."

Liesl followed but couldn't help peeking at the strange visitor. She could see everything from the safety of her uncle's small eat-in kitchen. The two men had bowed their heads and seemed to be praying.

"You're just as bad as the woman down the hall," Liesl's mother said as she pulled her daughter away from the doorway and handed her a paring knife. "Here. You can help me peel these potatoes."

Peel? More like *rescue*. Some of the spuds were already sprouting, and maybe it would be a better idea to plant them in a garden. But here in East Berlin—

"Just cut out the parts that are still good," her mother instructed.

Liesl sighed as she worked at the kitchen sink and filled a paper sack with peels and bits of potato they couldn't eat.

"Potatoes, always potatoes," she whispered as her mother busied herself gathering plates to set the table. "I hate potatoes."

"So do I." Her uncle slipped up from behind and grabbed one out of her hand. "And here you are on your birthday, doing all the work."

"Oh!" Liesl dropped her knife in the sink, splashing potato water all over them. She had to giggle. "I didn't hear you. Who was that?"

"Oh. Hans? Just a guy from church." He started

juggling a couple of the potatoes. Onkel Erich, the circus clown. "He and his wife are going through some, uh, tough times."

And so he came to a bachelor for help? Liesl knew her uncle was different that way, that everybody liked him. Even so—

"I gave them one of your little Bibles. See? Already your smuggling comes to good." He clamped a hand on his mouth and lowered his voice. "Don't tell your mother I said so."

Her mother had gone in the other room to look for a tablecloth. Liesl smiled and shook her head. She started to answer but her uncle cut her off.

"But she's right, you know. It's very dangerous, what you were doing."

"But you said—"

"I know what I said. Of course, if you were to take a book back the other direction, that would be a different thing."

Liesl looked at him in confusion.

"See that Bible up there?" He pointed to a shelf piled to the ceiling with papers, magazines, and books. "It belonged to your great-grandmother, your *Uhr-Oma* Poldi Becker. She gave it to me before she died, and I've just kept it, like some kind of memorial. Since I prefer my smaller Bible, I've never used hers. I think you should have it to remember her by, especially since it's your birthday."

Liesl stared at the book. "I don't know much

about Uhr-Oma Poldi. I'd love to have her Bible. Thank you!"

"Then get it down for me, if you would, please."

The medium-sized Bible, caked in a thick layer of dust, rested on a pile of papers. Liesl could barely read the old-fashioned gold lettering—*Die Heilige Bibel*—on the cracked black spine. Her great-grandmother's? Really? She'd never seen anything that had belonged to Uhr-Oma Poldi. She pulled a chair over and quickly climbed up to reach the book.

"Liesl," her uncle warned her, "be careful, that chair's a bit wobbly—"

Too late. Liesl grabbed for the shelf as she teetered, but only managed to grab a fistful of papers. The papers brought with them a pile of books, which knocked over a stack of newspapers, which brought down nearly everything else on the shelf.

Including Der Heilige Bibel.

"Oh, dear!" Liesl tried to catch some of the paper avalanche, but she only came up with a handful of brittle newspaper
clippings as they snowflaked through the air. The Bible crashed to the linoleum floor with a resounding *thunk!*

"I am so clumsy," Liesl moaned as she jumped off the chair and tried to gather the mess.

"Are you two okay in there?" her mother called

from the other room. Erich told her they were fine and hurried over to help Liesl pick up.

"I'm so sorry," she kept repeating.

"Don't worry about it. That shelf needed a good cleaning," he laughed.

As Liesl handed the clippings to her uncle, she couldn't help noticing the photo of a little boy standing beside an American soldier. One of the "Candy Bombers," the headlines called him. During the Berlin Airlift, she read, the soldier had helped to drop handkerchief parachutes weighted with candy over the city for hungry kids. It had helped to raise people's spirits during the tough times.

Neat story. But something about the crooked smile on the little boy's face told her—

"That's you, isn't it?" She knew the answer as he quietly took the clipping from her and replaced it carefully in a photo album. Liesl's mother limped into the room as he did so and froze when she saw the album in his hand.

"I was just going to show her Oma Poldi's Bible," he told his half-sister. "The one she gave me. In fact, I thought perhaps Liesl should have it."

Liesl's mother didn't answer.

"Listen, Sabine, it was just an accident." Erich quickly returned the album to the shelf. But a chill had already fallen over the room, and Liesl's mother handed Liesl a tablecloth without a word.

"She has a right to know what happened, don't you think?" Erich asked. But Liesl's mother simply walked over to the little gas stove and busied herself frying some onions. He went on, "She's thirteen, for goodness' sake. Why is it still such a deep, dark secret? It's ancient history! If you don't tell her about him—"

Him? Liesl felt confused. *Weren't we talking about Uhr-Oma Poldi?* she wondered.

"If I don't, you will?" Frau Stumpff turned on her half brother with tears in her eyes, and Liesl didn't think the onions had caused them. "No."

"Mutti?" Liesl's mind raced as she looked from her mother to her uncle and back again. Could they be talking about her grandfather, the American soldier who had died before her mother was born? The one her mother would never talk about.

What didn't Liesl know?

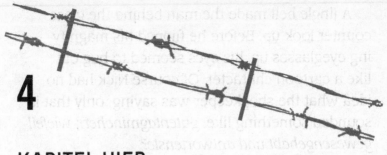

4

KAPITEL VIER

FOR FRED

Nick clutched his backpack under his arm and looked up at the shop sign, then down at his *How to Speak German in Thirty Days* phrasebook to be sure.

S-i-l-b-e-r-s-c-h-m-i-e-d?

But "silberschmied" wasn't in the list. Seemed like everything else was, but not this.

"Forget it." The little sign, besides the terribly long German word, had a picture of a ring on it, so that probably meant the person inside was a jeweler or silversmith. Nick read the sign once more: "Martin König, Silberschmied." He closed the book and looked in the little window. Well, okay, he'd give this place a try. But if this didn't work he would just go to a church and give them the cup.

Why am I doing this? he asked himself again as he pushed open the shop door. But he knew the answer.

For Fred.

A jingle bell made the man behind the glass counter look up. Before he flipped his magnifying eyeglasses up, his eyes seemed to bug out like a cartoon character. Of course Nick had no idea what the shopkeeper was saying, only that it sounded something like: *gutentagmineherr, wiefeilgewesengehabt und antwortensie?*

Excuse me? Nick could only hold up his hand and say what he'd been saying to everybody since they'd arrived in Frankfurt a week ago. "Uh—do you speak English? Sprechen sie English?"

"Oh. Ja, of course. A little." The man switched gears with a friendly nod and looked around Nick toward the door.

"My dad's in the Air Force, and we just moved here."

"Air Force, ja." The man nodded as if he understood every word.

"And I'm trying to find out something for a friend back home in Wyoming."

"Wyoming Cowboy, USA?" The man's grin grew even bigger, as if John Wayne had walked into his shop instead of Nick Wilder, Typical American Kid. "Capital, Cheyenne. Cowboys and Indians. Buffalo burgers."

"Uh—sure. I guess." Nick wasn't sure how to answer the German version of a human atlas. "We didn't have too much of that around where I lived. We did get a Burger King, though."

The man's face fell, but only for a moment. He

seemed to know more about Wyoming than Nick did.

"You know the Old Faithful geyser?"

"Saw it once. My folks took me. It was pretty cool, all the geysers and bubbly mud and stuff. But I was wondering—" He pulled the tissue-wrapped chalice out of his backpack and set it on the counter. "Could you tell me where this came from?"

"Oh! I see. Ja, *natürlich*. Of course." The man nodded as if saluting the item and flipped his jeweler's magnifying glasses back over his face for a better look. With a faint "hmm, ja, ja" he turned the cup around and around in his hands, delicately holding it up to the light. Nick listened to the tick-tock of a wall clock.

"It's a very gut piece," Herr König finally announced as he set it down and flipped up the lenses once again. "Very fine. Very old. Could be quite valuable. May I ask where did you get it?"

"A friend in the States. He wanted me to find out where it might have come from, and—" well, no use telling the *whole* story, but—"he wanted me to return it for him."

The man's eyes narrowed. He didn't believe it. "I see."

"It's not like you think. He didn't steal it or anything. It's just, I don't know—"

"Natürlich." Of course Herr König didn't look convinced. And Nick could just imagine the guy's thoughts: This American, whoever he was, probably had a guilty conscience, and now he wanted the boy to return a stolen chalice. A war trophy. Ja, that was it.

"It was a big deal to him." Nick tried one more time. "To get it back to where it came from, I mean."

Herr König nodded and ran his finger around the edge of the cup.

Time to change course. "Do you know how old it is?" asked Nick.

Ah, yes. At that Herr König held up a finger and squinted at the silver cup.

"This is the interesting question. I cannot be sure, but the design tells me more than 200 years old, perhaps older. Late 1700s."

Nick whistled softly. That kind of thing had to be worth a lot of money. But Herr König held up a finger, like a professor explaining an important point.

"As you can see, however, the inscription is much newer." He flipped the glasses back down to read, while he traced the words with his finger and read: "Presented to Rev. Ulrich Becker, *Versöhnungskirche*, 12 June 1936."

Nick leaned a little closer to see. *Really?*

"I don't see how you can read that stuff." He rubbed his eyes, and Herr König laughed.

"I think your Mark Twain was right about some things."

Nick didn't make the connection, and it must have showed on his face. "I'm not following you."

"Following me?" Now it was the jeweler's turn to look confused. "But I go nowhere."

"No. I mean, I'm not sure what Mark Twain has to do with anything."

"Ahh!" The grin returned to Herr König's face. "I thought all American young people read Mark Twain."

"Well, sort of. I read Tom Sawyer when I was in the fourth grade. Does that count?"

"I don't know who is counting. But it was your Mark Twain who said it is easier for a cannibal to enter the Kingdom of Heaven through the eye of a rich man's needle than it is for any other foreigner to read the terrible German script."

"He sure got that right." Nick had to smile, too. "Mark Twain, huh?"

"Ja, ja. Twain." Herr König returned to the engraving. "But now what about this Ulrich Becker? He is someone you know, perhaps?"

"No." And he had no idea about the church, either.

"Versöhnungskirche." Herr König scratched his chin and furrowed his brow. "This means in English, 'Church of Bringing Back Together.' But you have a better word for it, I feel."

"Pretty weird name for a church," Nick said. But when he thought about it, maybe it wasn't after all. Maybe that's what churches were for. Bringing back together. He tried his best to think like a dictionary. Bringing back together—

"Reconstruction Church!" Herr König was thinking, too. But no. Not quite. "Recondition Church."

"Recondition Church? That's even weirder."

But then the jeweler snapped his fingers and smiled.

"Reconciliation Church. That is the name. Reconciliation."

He said it carefully, like it didn't roll off his tongue very easily. Well, it didn't roll off Nick's very easily, either. Almost as bad as the German version, and Mark Twain would've liked that one, too.

"I was kind of getting used to the Church of Bringing Back Together. You think it's here in Frankfurt?"

They should be so lucky. But the jeweler shook his head no.

"*Nein, nein.* There is no such church here. But now you make me *neugierig*—curious?"

"You mean you think we can find it?"

Herr König nodded. "I will find it for you. And your friend will feel not so guilty, ja?"

"He's not—" Nick sighed. Oh, well. "Right."

And it seemed pointless to ask now, but it would have been nice to know—

"And you wanted to ask how much it was worth?" The jeweler wrapped up the piece and handed it to Nick with a smile.

"That's not why I brought it to you. But—"

"Exactly." The man laughed. "So just in case you're curious, the newer inscription probably cuts the value in half, I would say."

"Half of?"

"Five hundred American dollars, maybe. You will take care of it, then?"

"Until we find out where it belongs."

Nick wrapped the tissue around it one more time and patted his treasure. If he'd known it was worth so much, he might have packed it in a couple more socks on the way over.

"I'll inquire about this Versöhnungskirche," Herr König told Nick with a wink. "You come back in a few days."

5

KAPITEL FÜNF
FIRST DRAFT

"I take pride in saying, *'Ich bin ein Berliner.'*"

Liesl sat at the kitchen table. She stopped her cassette tape player and hit *rewind* once more to hear the famous last line of that speech from the American president. Only this speech didn't come from Ronald Reagan. Twenty-four years earlier, John F. Kennedy had stood in front of the city hall to deliver his own bit of history.

She studied her history book for a minute—the one with the old photo of Kennedy and his wife—then began to write her paper.

Even after President Kennedy told us he was a Berliner, she scribbled, *the wall still stood. And even after President Reagan asked General Secretary Gorbechev to "tear down this wall," it continues to stand today. But now the question is not if, but when it will come down. How much longer? And who will finally give the wall that push it so deserves?*

She chewed on the end of her pencil, wondering

how many others in her class would write the exact same stuff. Yeah, it was okay for starters. She liked the last line especially. Nice touch. Trouble was, everyone knew about Kennedy's speech in 1963. And for sure everyone knew about Reagan's challenge two years ago. She still remembered the crowds that pressed around her and Papa. Most of the kids in her school were probably there, too. So what was new about any of this? If she wanted to be a good news reporter, she had to learn to find another angle, something new that no one else would have. A personal story, maybe?

She leaned back in her chair and glanced at her mother, knitting in the den. No. Mutti would never talk about that sort of thing, even though Liesl knew her mother could probably tell all kinds of great stories, if she wanted to. But she always said, "What's past is best forgotten, dear." And then of course there was the scene on her birthday at Onkel Erich's. Mutti wouldn't even let Liesl say her grandfather's name.

Yeah, whatever. What was he, some kind of Mafia crime boss? Liesl crumpled up her first try and tossed the paper at a wastebasket in the corner. Close.

Her father, on the other hand—*he* might be talked into helping her. Once in a while he'd slipped and told her little bits and pieces about the tunnel they'd dug to escape from the East, the secret bomb shelter her mother had discovered when she was Liesl's age.

But only bits and pieces and only when Liesl's mother wasn't listening. Otherwise—

"Liesl, could you turn that oven on, please? Your father should be home any minute, and he's going to be hungry."

Liesl looked up at the kitchen clock. By eight-fifteen, well, he ought to be. In a way it served him right for working late so often. And as if he could smell the bratwurst, five minutes later Willi walked through the door with his usual bird-chirp whistle.

"How are my girls?" He leaned down to kiss his wife, then stepped into the kitchen and mussed Liesl's hair the way he always did. Never mind how many times she'd told him that she was too old for that sort of thing. She would never admit it, but she didn't move away fast enough on purpose.

"What's the project?" he asked as he retrieved his plate and nearly dropped it on the table.

"Careful." Liesl pushed her papers out of the way so her father wouldn't splatter them with mustard. "That's hot."

"Now she tells me." But Herr Stumpff was smiling, and he bowed his head for a moment to pray before digging in. A few moments later he looked up and studied her through his thick glasses. "History, right?"

"Mutti says not to talk with your mouth full." She could get away with that kind of teasing once in a while. He pointed his fork at her and winked, as in, you got me. But she quickly explained the paper to him before her mother had joined them.

"Sounds to me like you're looking for family stories again." His low voice matched hers. "But you know how sensitive your mother is about—"

"But it's not like he was her husband. He was her father. Why does she have to make everything so mysterious and—and terrible?"

Her father shrugged. "I think it was just hard for her, not having a father when she was growing up. Kids used to give her a rough time. And not just because of her polio and needing crutches to walk."

"What, then?"

"Oh, you know, all the bad jokes about GI Joe, the American. Her father who was never there. You know what I mean, don't you?"

"But her parents were married!" Liesl knew that much, at least. "It wasn't like that!"

"Ja, even so. But silence is just the way your mother has learned to deal with it."

"Was she always like this?"

"Maybe not always." He shook his head and took off his glasses to clean them on the edge of the tablecloth. "I think she used to try to make up for her legs by being sort of a tomboy."

"No way! Mutti, a tomboy?"

"People change." He smiled and replaced his

glasses. "Especially when they have kids of their own."

Yes, but that much? Liesl tried to imagine her mother as a tomboy (and couldn't) as Frau Stumpff joined them in the kitchen.

"Either I'm going deaf," Sabine said, resting on her crutch, "or two people are whispering in here."

Liesl's father moved his mouth as if speaking, but nothing came out. Liesl took up the joke, gesturing with her hands, as well.

"Very funny." Frau Stumpff looked over Liesl's shoulder to check out her paper but said nothing.

"It's for history," Liesl explained once more. "Our teacher is letting us write about the wall."

"That's good, dear." Frau Stumpff nodded as if she had a hundred other things on her mind. "But—"

"I mean, what's better?" Liesl rambled on. "It's history. And here we are, right in the middle of it. Kind of like your church society stuff, right?"

"Well ..." Her mother sighed. Something obviously weighed on her mind. "It just seems like there are so many other things to write about, without getting into—"

She didn't finish her sentence.

"You mean without getting into all the trouble you did when you were my age?" Liesl knew she shouldn't push it, but still she did. "That kind of stuff?"

But Frau Stumpff merely pressed her lips

together. Papa signaled Liesl with his eyes and a shake of his head to stop before she said something she would regret. But she was just getting warmed up.

"Well, even if I can't find out much about when the wall went up, I thought I might write something about the groups protesting the wall today."

Whoops. Why did she say that last part? Big mistake. Her father stopped chewing for a moment and studied her through his thick glasses, as if he expected something to blow. The room felt eerily like her uncle's kitchen had on her birthday.

"You mean the groups of criminals we see on the news, I assume," said Liesl's mother, the fire growing in her eyes.

"No, I don't mean criminals, exact—"

"Then you mean the people who throw beer bottles at border guards or pose for the American news cameras, making big, violent scenes, is that it? That kind of protest?"

Well, at least they were doing something. And Liesl didn't think it was like that, at all. She felt her face turn a light shade of pink before her father came to the rescue.

"You know, dear," he told his wife, "you shouldn't be so shy. If you have an opinion, maybe you should just come right out and express it."

"And you think you're so witty sometimes." Sabine grabbed a dishtowel and swiped him over the head. He held up his hand to defend himself.

"Watch out for this woman, Liesl. She always says her society is against violence, but she's armed with knitting needles!"

Liesl smiled with relief. She'd put her foot in her mouth, badly, again. She was a master at saying just the wrong thing at just the wrong time. But she still had a paper to write, and obviously her parents (meaning, her mother) wouldn't help much. But she couldn't stop digging until she found out what had *really* happened in her family. Even the parts her mother refused to talk about. If it ended up that she couldn't use her history for this paper, well, she still wanted to know.

And if her parents wouldn't tell her, she knew someone who might.

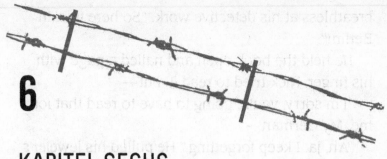

6

KAPITEL SECHS

FIRST CLUES

"Come in, come in, mein *Amerikanisch* friend!" Herr König scurried around the counter waving a book in his hand. "Wait until you see what I have found for you!"

Nick paused just inside the shop as the jeweler took another customer by the arm and led her to the door.

"Come back in an hour, Frau Putzkammer," he told her. "I will have your watch cleaned and ready by then."

"But—" Frau Putzkammer didn't seem ready to leave, but she didn't have much choice. Herr König slammed the door behind her with a jingle of bells before he locked it and flipped the sign in the window from *Geöffnet* to *Geschlossen*. What was this all about?

"Now, I told you I would find out about this church for you, did I not?" Herr König was almost breathless at his detective work. "So here it is. In Berlin!"

He held the book open and nailed a page with his finger. Nick tried to read it, but—

"I'm sorry, you're going to have to read that for me. My German—"

"Ah, ja. I keep forgetting." He pulled his jeweler's glasses over his eyes, as if preparing to clean Frau Putzkammer's watch. "I shall translate for you: The history of the Reconciliation Church ran not straight-lined, but breaks experiences. Thusly, with the *jahr* 1894 Empress Auguste Victoria participated in inauguration place of worship donated of their, which offered one thousand humans seats. The empress—"

"Wait a minute, Herr König!" Nick held up his hands. "Excuse me."

Herr König looked up as if Nick had just interrupted the performance of a symphony.

"I'm sorry." Nick didn't quite know how to say it. "But I'm not following a word of what you're saying. Are you sure that's English?"

"What?" Herr König paused for a minute to reread his book, then flipped up his glasses. "Of course it's English. Only sounding a little bit like the German, perhaps. Translation is—not always so easy."

"Yeah, I'm finding that out. Why don't you just tell me what it says, without—I mean, you don't have to read the whole thing."

"Hmm." Herr König looked at Nick as if he thought Nick were cheating. The building, the first years, the war years—more than Nick wanted to know. But still he listened politely. Finally he had a chance to ask a question.

"So this church was right on the line between East and West Berlin, and it was already called the Church of Bringing Back Together? That's pretty cool."

"Ja." Herr König nodded. "Cool, as you say. Unfortunately, it was damaged by Allied bombings during the war."

"Oh." Nick wasn't sure if he was supposed to apologize for that sort of thing, or not. "That's not so good."

"I said *damaged*, not *destroyed*. Many other buildings were destroyed, turned into piles of bricks. Not this one. It was beautiful, the steeple so tall. Some damages, ja, but it was repaired some years later and used again as it had been."

"That's good."

"Ja, except for one problem." He jabbed at his book and read—or translated—once more. "It says here that a 'Minister Hildebrandt tried 1960 to energize building and add community center. But before this could happen the East German government created other facts.'"

"Facts?" Once more, Nick felt lost.

"They built the wall in 1961."

"That's not so good. But I knew that. Did that mean people couldn't use it anymore?"

"They tried, but it was no good. And so in 1985—four years ago—the government finished what the Americans and the British had started." He closed the book and put it aside. "They tore it down."

"Oh." Nick turned away. "I guess that pretty much ends the story. Maybe I'll find someplace else to take Fred's cup."

"Nein, nein. But here I am forgetting to tell you the best part of what I have learned!"

"The church is history. What else is there to tell?"

Herr König opened the book once more, this time to the end, to a part that looked to Nick like an index. He pointed at a name and address as if it meant something important, along with one of those German words that seemed to go on and on, out the door and around the block. "See here?"

"Uh—" Nick squinted at the printing, trying to make out any familiar words. And there! "Isn't that the start of our church word? Vers ..."

"*Versöhnungskircheerinnerungsgesellschaft.* Which means, The Reconciliation Church Remembrance Society. 'Dedicated to the Future of East-West Relations, Not the Past.' Well, at least that sounds—forward-thinking, no? And look here: This is the name of the society's president and her office address. It appears she's a social worker of some kind, works for the Ministry of Church Affairs, or some such agency."

"No kidding? So all I have to do is talk my folks into taking me to Berlin, and we can give this to—"

"Frau Sabine Stumpff."

"Frau Stump, okay. Maybe you could write that down for me?"

"Didn't I tell you I would find out?" Herr König beamed as if he had just cracked the mystery of the century. He went to the door, pulled back the lock, and turned the sign back over with a flourish and a bow. "I only wish I could have had the chance to buy that chalice myself."

The American boy tried to make sense out of his tourist guidebook, but all he understood were the little black-and-white photos.

"Wish they'd make these things in English sometimes," he mumbled, "for all us non-German types." Oh, well. He was the foreigner here, and he'd better get used to it. His father would be stationed here for a few years, at least, before they could get back to the States. He wasn't sure he would call that "bad" news, exactly. But the good news was that after eight weeks he could recognize a number of German words, thanks to Herr König's help.

Ja meant yes and *nein* meant no, of course. Everybody knew that from watching old World War

2 movies on TV. *Okay* meant okay, which seemed pretty convenient, and then there were *bitte, danke,* and *bitte,* again. Please, thank you, and "don't mention it."

So far, so good. If he only knew that much when he started at the American Academy in the fall, he'd do okay. But a couple other phrases might come in handy. He studied his dog-eared little copy of *How to Speak German in Thirty Days* and tried out a phrase.

"Ikh fer-shtay-e nikht!" He looked up from his book with a smile. "Did I say that right?"

His mother looked over at his dad, who had lifted the top off a frying pan for a sniff of pork chops. He breathed in deeply but shook his head. "Don't look at me," he said, replacing the lid. "Although—that sounds an awful lot like 'I don't understand.' I think I've heard that one a lot around the base."

"Bingo!" And possibly some of the best words he could learn. Even so, Nick graduated to the next page, stumbling through the foreign words one at a time. *"Gehen wir nach Berlin?"*

His parents both stared at him blankly this time. Not a clue.

"That just means, 'Are we going to Berlin?' Pretty good, huh?"

"Oh, I get it." His dad chuckled.

But it was supposed to be a hint, Dad. Nick

waited with an expectant expression, and his mom stepped in.

"I think he's trying to tell you something, dear." She picked up his uniform jacket and hung it in the little hall closet. "Since we've been here nearly two months and we haven't seen anything more than the street between here and the base."

"We all knew it was going to be tough these first few weeks." Mark Wilder—Master Sergeant Wilder—plunked down in an easy chair and propped his stocking feet up on the coffee table. "It's not a vacation, even if it is summer. This is my job now."

"But not twenty-four hours a day." She stood at the kitchen entry, hands on her hips. And Nick held off from adding to the argument. He'd run out of German words. And his mom was doing just fine on her own.

"You know how much it means to him, dear." When she started talking like that, she could sweet-talk a camel out of its hump. "With his friend's—er, artifact, and all. And it would be an interesting trip for all three of us, don't you think?"

Nick did his best not to smile. But Dad would lose this one, no doubt about it.

7

KAPITEL SIEBEN

FOR AN EXTRA COOKIE

"Anything interesting happen at the office today?" Liesl picked through the small pile of papers and mail her mother had dropped on the kitchen table.

Frau Stumpff had already slipped out of her street shoes and headed for the bedroom. "We got a letter that might interest you."

Liesl looked at the top envelope, which carried a Frankfurt return address. But what kind of name was Nick Wilder?

"The one from a British man?"

"American." Her mother's voice drifted into the hall from behind the door. "And it's not a man. It's a boy your age."

"Oh?"

This could be interesting. She looked at her mother's name and the Reconciliation Church Remembrance Society scribbled in messy boyish handwriting. Wonder what made him write?

She unfolded the letter to find out. And she

hardly noticed when her mother came back into the kitchen dressed in jeans and a comfy black sweater.

"Someone found a war trophy in an attic," her mother began. "I think it's—"

But Liesl hardly heard her mother's words as she read about the chalice, possibly from her great-grandfather's church? It sounded interesting.

"Apparently he's coming to Berlin with his parents for a few days," Liesl's mother explained as Liesl read the same thing in the letter. "And he wants to return the chalice."

Yes, but that didn't explain everything. For instance—

"How did he know to write you?" Liesl wondered aloud.

"We're not hard to find." Frau Stumpff leaned in for another look at the note. "You know the society is listed in all those directories and local history books."

"Yes, but—" The mystery swirled in a fog around Liesl's head. "Why do you think he wants to bring it to you in person?"

"I have no idea. There's obviously more to it than what he says in the letter."

Obviously! And that made Liesl wonder, "Are you going to answer him?" She hurried on, not giving her mother a chance to reply. "Because if you're not, it would—well, it would give me a chance to practice my English."

"Well," Frau Stumpff hesitated. "That's not exactly why I brought that letter home. I don't know if—"

"It's just a kid my age, right? And doesn't he say his family is planning to visit Berlin?"

"Well, yes, but—"

Frau Stumpff narrowed her eyes and pressed her lips together the way she did when she and Liesl started to argue.

"But what?" Liesl pressed.

"Nothing."

Liesl tried not to smile. Not that she cared much about an American boy. Boys were boys, after all, American or German, and mostly a pain in the neck. But the chalice!

"Oh, and did I mention?" Liesl thought she'd better say so. "I told Oma Brigitte I'd visit her Saturday morning."

Which should have pleased her mother, but the frown only stretched a little longer.

"Hmm. Social call, or research for your school paper?"

"Uh, both, I guess." Liesl wasn't going to lie. "Papa said it was okay."

"That doesn't surprise me. Just don't go asking her too many uncomfortable questions. You know what she went through."

"I know, Mutti. I won't make her uncomfortable. But you never tell me anything. I just want to know, sometimes."

Well, that pretty much shut down the conversation-turned-argument. Liesl nearly added, just for the record, that when her mother said *uncomfortable,* she meant something entirely different from what most people did. Then she wisely decided to hold her tongue. When she tried to hand the letter back to her mother, Frau Stumpff shook her head.

"No, you answer it. I said you could."

With that, her mother grabbed the handle of her crutch and hobbled out of the kitchen. End of discussion.

Liesl's grandmother sipped her tea after she settled into an easy chair in her den. Liesl looked around the tiny apartment on *Hermannstrasse*—Hermann Street. It was less than an hour away by U-Bahn, the subway, from Liesl's apartment, and on the same side of the wall.

"So, your mother tells me you're on another one of your missions," Oma Brigitte said. But she didn't say it quite the same way Frau Stumpff would have.

One of your missions. It was just a statement. Nothing more. How much did she know?

"That's what Mutti always calls them." Liesl smiled and tried not to burn her tongue on her tea. She added another sugar cube to her cup. "She is always teasing me. She's always worried about something."

That made her grandmother smile.

"Does she have a good reason for this, perhaps?"

"Well—" Liesl thought about it. "Maybe sometimes. But not this time. All I'm doing is working on my school history paper, trying to get more information than just 'The Berlin Airlift happened in 1948, as everyone knows,' and 'The Berlin wall, as everyone *also* knows, went up in 1961.' That is so totally and completely boring. I *refuse* to just write what everybody else is writing."

"Well, that doesn't surprise me. So that's why you came today?"

"Oh. Not a hundred percent. I came to visit, too." Liesl pulled out her portable cassette tape recorder and found a place to plug it in the wall.

"That's quite a fancy machine," observed her grandmother. "I imagine your father gave it to you?"

Liesl nodded. "It's what newspaper reporters use, so they can go back and write down their interviews. I hope it's okay."

"It's okay, ja. I just don't know if I've ever spoken into one that was quite as fancy as that one. You'll have to promise I get to listen to myself afterward."

"Sure!" Liesl smiled. This was already going better than she'd hoped. So she pressed the "record" button and held the microphone between them. *Ahem!* She cleared her throat.

"This is Liesl Marie Stumpff and it's Tuesday, the

twenty-sixth of September, 1989. I'm speaking with Brigitte Becker, my grandmother on my mother's side, and we'll be discussing family history."

"My, don't you sound just like a television news reporter." Oma Brigitte wasn't supposed to say that sort of thing. But what could Liesl do, except plow ahead with her prepared questions?

"Frau DeWitt, tell us where you lived and what you were doing in 1948, after the war."

So Oma Brigitte talked about the food stamps and rationing and the soldiers and how hard they worked to rebuild the city. Which was all very good, but nothing Liesl hadn't already learned in her history books.

"Those were difficult days—"

But oh, she could talk about them! As Oma Brigitte went on Liesl's arm got tired from holding out the microphone for so long, so she switched it from one hand to the other. Maybe this reporter stuff wasn't as easy as she'd thought. Of course, she still had a few more questions to go.

"Tell us about your family after your first husband was killed—how you survived."

Oma Brigitte paused, as if deciding how to answer. Then she nodded and went on, talking about their apartment, how they lived, what kind of work they did. But with each sentence she paused more between words. She waved her pudgy hands in the air and pulled her handkerchief from where she had parked it in her blouse, fussing with its edge. Was this what Liesl's mother had meant about making her grandmother uncomfortable?

"Could you tell me how you met my grandfather?" Liesl asked, finally daring to bring it up. And after a long silence Oma Brigitte looked straight at Liesl with brimming eyes.

"We never talk about him, do we, Liesl?"

Liesl could only shake her head and study her recorder. That side of the tape had nearly finished. She would have to stop and turn it over.

"I'm sorry, Liesl. It's wrong of me. Wrong of your—Is this still recording?"

Liesl hadn't meant to time it this way, but the tape had finished and the record button popped up. She left the machine alone.

"Go ahead, Oma." She'd had enough of playing the reporter for now.

"Are you sure you want to hear this? Of course you are. Here, thirteen years old, and all you know about your grandfather is that he was an American soldier and that he died before you were born. Is that right?"

"And that it was a plane crash."

"I see. Your mother gave you the whole story, didn't she?"

Liesl's throat went dry as she gripped her chair and listened to Oma Brigitte.

Oma Brigitte said, "I don't blame her. She had a lot to deal with as a child. Her missing father and who he was. Her polio. We found out later a nurse in the hospital routinely locked her in the closet when she couldn't endure any more physical therapy and started to cry. Maybe you know that part."

Liesl's mouth fell open.

"All right, then." Oma Brigitte wiped her eyes with her handkerchief. "It was a hard time. Many people didn't survive. But you asked me about your grandfather, Sergeant DeWitt, from Cleveland, Ohio, America."

Liesl nodded and scribbled a few notes in her notebook. She would look up how to spell the American names later.

"He was—he was a very good Christian man." Oma Brigitte made a brave attempt to smile as she dabbed at her eyes again, and Liesl wondered if maybe she should have listened to her mother. But it was too late now. Her grandmother had started her story. "Always happy, always smiling. Very gentle. He spoke German as well as you or me. And he loved your Onkel Erich almost as much as he loved me."

That brought a smile to the old woman's face.

"But look at me now! Can you believe an old widow crying like this—after forty years?"

"It's okay, Oma." Liesl took her grandmother's hand. "You can cry if you want to."

"No, let me tell you something." Oma had a point to make. "You know I've never told anyone this, and I only tell you now because you are a special granddaughter to me. My only granddaughter!"

True enough. And even though Liesl's hands had begun to hurt in her grandmother's grip, she could only nod and wait. Oma Brigitte took a breath and went on.

"I don't cry because my American was killed before we could have a life together or because he never met his little daughter." When she shook her head the barrette fell out of her hair, and the bun at the back of her head unraveled. "That's all in God's hands and I have no right to complain, but—"

Liesl couldn't make herself say anything. Finally her grandmother let go of her hands and pointed to a small dresser crowded into the corner of her apartment.

"In the top drawer there is a small bundle. Go and get it for me, please."

Liesl did as requested, returning with a stack of envelopes tied neatly with brown packing string.

"The letter on top." She pointed again, and the string fell apart at Liesl's touch. These notes obviously hadn't been read in years. And for the next hour Liesl learned what had really happened, the mystery she had wondered about that her mother had never wanted her to know.

She read the letter from the American's parents in Ohio, USA, telling her that Fred had died in a New Jersey military hospital. And then the letter from the Department of the Air Force telling her that they had no record of any marriage.

"I couldn't even call myself his widow."

Liesl saw the hurt in her grandmother's eyes, and she began to understand.

"But couldn't his parents help?"

Oma Brigitte shook her head. "No one wanted us to get married, child. Not his commanding officer, not his parents, and especially not my first husband's mother—the one you know as Uhr-Oma Poldi. Then, when he died, it was as if we'd never married. Except—"

A whisper of a smile crossed her face as she stared out the window at the bustle of Hermannstrasse below. Did she keep watch over this street, remembering the past and its pain?

"Except for your mother. There was my proof that I had once been married to my Sergeant Fred DeWitt. But even then, the military would not believe me. They thought I was just trying to sneak my way in—pretending to be a military widow to get a free ticket out of Berlin to the United States. Isn't that the way it goes?"

She chuckled, but in a sad kind of way.

"I'm so sorry," Liesl said as she handed back the bundle of letters. Her grandmother glanced at her.

"Ja, ja." The old woman shrugged. "I should think after all these years I would not feel so angry anymore. I suppose mein Gott is not through with me."

Liesl smiled. "You're okay just the way you are, Oma."

"Ach. You're just saying that to get an extra cookie."

Cookies? Now that Oma mentioned it, a cookie sounded like a very good idea.

"I don't suppose you'll want to use any of this story now for your school report?"

"Nein, of course not." Liesl hadn't written anything in her notebook for the past hour. She snapped it shut and put away her pencil to make her point. Newspaper reporters called it "off the record."

"There is, though, a happier part of this story."

Liesl raised her eyebrows, wondering what her grandmother would tell her next.

"But I'm afraid it is your onkel's to tell, not mine."

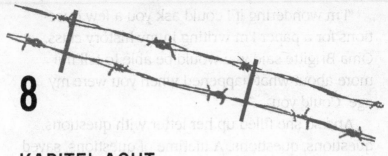

8

KAPITEL ACHT

DEAR ONKEL ERICH

Liesl never got over how odd it seemed, writing a letter to someone who lived so close—and yet so far away. She chewed on her pencil eraser for a moment. How far away did her uncle live? Two kilometers? Three? Close enough to walk. But the ever-present wall made it seem much farther.

So she started and stopped, wondering how to begin. She had decided to write a letter instead of calling, in case what she wanted to ask him didn't quite come out right.

"Dear Onkel Erich," she wrote, reading the words aloud as she used her best handwriting. "How are you? We're doing fine. It's been a couple of months since Mutti and I visited."

Well, he knew that already. She crossed out the last sentence and started over.

"We've missed seeing you."

No. That sounded dumb. She crossed it out and began one more time.

"I'm wondering if I could ask you a few questions for a paper I'm writing in my history class. Oma Brigitte said you would be able to tell me more about what happened when you were my age. Could you ..."

And so she filled up her letter with questions, questions, questions. A lifetime of questions, saved up for as long as she could remember. Why were the Americans here, and how did people feel about them? How did the Americans treat people on the street? How did you feel about it? About him?

She tried twenty different ways to ask the same thing, trying to find out how he got to know Sergeant DeWitt and what kind of a man he was—but never mentioning his name. A couple of times she came close but decided—no. She hoped her uncle would see what she meant. Even though Oma Brigitte had given her a green light more or less, she still remembered how her mother had acted on her birthday.

She folded the letter and stuffed it in an envelope, addressed it, and prayed it would get across the border in one piece. Letters didn't always. Even if it did, she really had no idea what her uncle would write back.

On the other hand, hadn't he meant it when he'd said she had a right to know? She believed he would tell her.

He had to.

"That's the craziest idea I've ever heard!"

Liesl stopped, puzzled. The voice came from down the hallway next to the *St. Matthäuskirche* sanctuary. But her mother's evening council meeting at the St. Matthew's Church should have ended by now.

So who was shouting in the side room?

"Oh, come on. You know better than that."

"Well, even if *you're* afraid to take a stand, *I'm* not."

It sounded like a couple of teenage boys ready for a fistfight. Should she call the pastor? First she tiptoed a little closer to see what she could figure out.

"Nobody's afraid here, Jürgen," a quieter voice said. "We can't just march out and make a scene when the time isn't right."

"And when will it ever be right? You'll always find some reason to wait!" responded the first voice.

"Think about what happened to that East Berliner kid yesterday. The one who was shot. Doesn't that tell you anything about how dangerous it's getting?"

"You can whine and complain about how dangerous it is. But if we don't do something big, more people will just get killed. More kids. Don't you see?"

"But—"

The voices echoed down the hallway, louder

and louder. Liesl peeked into the room to see what kind of meeting—or battle—she had stumbled on.

Turned out to be about twenty intense-looking kids sitting in a big circle on wooden folding chairs. Mostly boys but a few girls, too. She thought most of them looked about sixteen years old; a couple looked older. And they had to be *a little bit* official since they were meeting in the church, and she didn't think just anybody could do that. But they sure couldn't agree. And the argument was so hot, no one seemed to notice her watching from the doorway. And she could pass for fifteen or sixteen, couldn't she?

"Listen, we're not going to solve this tonight." One of the girls spoke up. "So the wall will just have to stay up for one more day. Why don't we all go home and think about it, then come back tomorrow night to decide?"

Well, that sounded like a good idea to Liesl, judging by the way the conversation was going. And now she knew what kind of group this was.

These were the "criminals" her mother had been so angry about the other day. Kids who were trying to bring down the wall any way they could. A protest group that could possibly help her write the best paper in history—if she could just talk to some of them.

"Everyone in favor of voting tomorrow?" The five girls all raised their hands, as did a number of the boys. They outnumbered the hotheads—but barely. And that's when someone noticed Liesl.

"You're too late," one of the kids called at her. "We're just finishing up."

"Oh!" Just then she remembered her mother was waiting for her, probably wondering why she hadn't come by the council office yet. "Well, I have to get going, anyway."

"Wait!" The girl who had wrapped up the meeting ran to follow her. "You don't have to take off just yet."

"But your meeting's over."

"Ja, but we usually hang around for a while after. The pastor doesn't come around to lock the doors for another hour. Were you here to—"

"To meet my mother. That's all."

"Oh. I thought—"

"But I heard what you were saying," Liesl blurted out, even as she kept a close eye out for her mother. "Are you planning to—I mean, is this a protest group?"

The tall, dark-haired girl's expression turned serious, and she didn't answer right away.

"That sort of depends."

"Depends? On what?"

"Depends on who's asking. We're not an official church group, if that's what you mean. Just a bunch of kids trying to—well, you can probably guess. Could you hear Jürgen all the way down the hall? He is *so* obnoxious!"

"Well—" Liesl wasn't ready to answer that question, considering who was joining them.

"Did someone mention my name?" Jürgen strutted up like a peacock. Liesl resisted the urge to reach out and wipe the smirk off his face. A couple of other boys had gathered around them, too.

"Hey, Katja, do we have a new recruit?" asked Jürgen. "Or maybe a spy?"

Katja stepped in front of Liesl like a shield, while the rest circled around as if for the kill.

"I'm no spy." Liesl straightened her shoulders and stood a little taller, the way her mother always reminded her to. As if that would help against this school of sharks. "I've even—"

They waited for her to finish.

"I've even smuggled some things across the border to East Berlin. Actually, more than once."

Oh, brother. How was that for a crash landing? She realized she'd sounded a whole lot sillier than she'd hoped. Not a smooth delivery, not like Cher singing "Gypsies, Tramps, and Thieves" on stage, though she wondered why she'd compared herself to Cher just now. Nobody was about to applaud her performance.

"Like what did you smuggle?" Jürgen, his face serious, stepped around Katja as he challenged Liesl. "Drugs?"

A few of the other boys snickered, and Liesl felt her cheeks flush. She wished she hadn't opened her big mouth. Then she thought, *What can it hurt to tell the truth?* She crossed her arms and faced him.

"Bibles, actually."

What do you think of that?

At first no one said anything. They just stared at her. Jürgen had finally picked up his jaw from the floor and cleared his throat, when they heard the sound of steps clicking down the hall coming toward them.

"Liesl?" Her mother called as she got closer. "Liesl, are you down here?"

Extremely good timing—sort of. Or maybe not.

"I've got to go." Liesl wasted no time bailing out of the little room. So much for her prize-winning paper filled with firsthand accounts of the West German protest movement! But she didn't want to have to explain *this* group to her mother, especially considering the argument she'd heard them having. Before she slammed the door behind her, though, Jürgen's in-charge voice reached her: "Hey! Don't forget we'll meet again tomorrow night, Bible smuggler. Same time, same place."

But Liesl had no idea what to tell her parents the next day. How could she convince them to let her go out alone—and did she even want to? She could imagine the scene:

Mutti, I'm going out to get into deep trouble with

a gang of insane kids who want to get themselves killed in a foolish protest against the wall.

Really? That's nice, dear. How do you plan to do that?

We're talking about maybe charging the barbed wire with signs that say "Give Peace a Chance."

Oh, that would be perfect, wouldn't it? Liesl stabbed at a sausage on her dinner plate, sending a little spray across the table—whoops—as she twirled it through the gravy.

"Aren't you hungry?" Her mother could read minds, which in this case could be pretty dangerous. As a defense, Liesl immediately stuffed the big piece of sausage into her mouth, way more than she should chew at one time.

"I guess you are." Frau Stumpff shook her head. "Mind your manners, bitte. I can't be here all the time to clean up after you. In fact, I'm running a little late now. I told you I have a commission meeting tonight, didn't I?"

"Now you have." Liesl's father wiped his mouth with his napkin and scooted his chair back. "And I have to meet a client in," he glanced at his watch as he stood, "twenty minutes."

"I'll clean up," Liesl volunteered.

"Danke, *Schatzi.*" Her mother smiled and gave her a peck on the forehead. She didn't call her *sweetie* very often. "You'll be okay by yourself tonight? Neither of us will be home too late."

"Oh, don't worry about me." Liesl did her best

to sound breezy, maybe a little breezier than she should have. "I'll be fine, really. Take your time."

She still didn't know whether she had the courage to go back to the church, though. Weren't those kids *doing* something, though? Not just talking and talking about it.

Maybe she'd go just for a few minutes. Maybe they really thought she was sixteen.

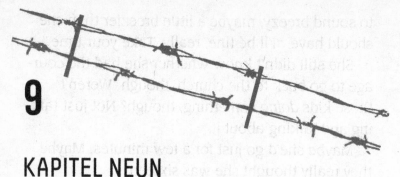

9

KAPITEL NEUN

INSANE

"Slow *down*, Mark!" Mrs. Wilder dug her finger-nails into the dashboard of the little rental car. "We're all going to *die!*"

"Nobody's going to die." Nick's dad clutched the wheel and pulled around a slower truck in the right lane. "Just relax. This is the autobahn, remember? No speed limits on this highway."

"Are you sure?" She peeked over at the dashboard. "We're going 120!"

"That's kilometers, Mom." Nick thought he'd add that bit of helpful information as he pointed at the speedometer. "And since there are 1.6 kilometers in a mile, we're going way slower than that in miles per hour."

"That doesn't make me feel any better." His mom still covered her eyes, as if she expected to crash any moment—or to take flight.

"Smart kid." Nick's father grinned. But Nick couldn't remember holding on to the back of the seat this tightly, either. He looked down at his white knuckles and tried to convince himself to let go, one finger at a time.

"Uh, Dad, maybe we should slow d—"

Whooooosh!

Something flashed by them on the right, a blur of black metal that nearly spun them off the road. Nick's mother screamed and Nick reflexively ducked his head.

"What was that?" Nick looked up as the back end of a car disappeared down the highway ahead of them. His father wrestled the little car to the side of the highway and screeched to a stop. His parents looked at each other as if they'd seen a ghost.

Actually it had looked like a Mercedes. That, or a low-flying Air Force jet.

"Okay," Mark Wilder said, taking a deep breath and putting the car back in gear. "No harm if we get to our hotel a few minutes later."

For the rest of the trip they practically rolled down the shoulder of the autobahn, and even the delivery trucks honked at them as they passed by. At least Nick's mom started smiling again, once in a while.

"You have the address of the office where you want to take your chalice?" she asked Nick, and he nodded.

"I've got it. But I'm thinking there's no way

anyone will be there. Seems like most offices are closed on Saturdays."

"I apologized for that. I couldn't arrange as much time off as I'd hoped." His father didn't take his eyes off the highway as he spoke, and he kept the speedometer needle glued to thirty-five. That would be thirty-five *kilometers* per hour, which would of course be a lot slower in *miles* per hour. With the window rolled down he waved for a farm tractor behind them to pass.

"You can go a *little* faster, now," Nick's mom whispered, "can't you, dear?"

"Slower, faster—" Nick's dad pressed his lips together and kept his eyes on the road. The little car shook every time another autobahn racer flew by, and the speedometer nudged up to forty kilometers per hour. Nick took up a post as the tailman, watching out the back window and warning them every time a high-speed car approached.

"We'll get there, Dad."

And they did—over an hour later, and after asking directions no fewer than three times.

"Don't know how anybody finds anything in this crazy city," the master sergeant mumbled. But the tree-lined streets, the huge stone churches, and the busy shopping districts made the trip worthwhile. After circling for what seemed like hours, they finally pulled up in front of an average-looking three-story office and apartment building next to one of the city's churches.

"This is the right place?" Nick squinted at the brass sign next to the main entry, trying to read the ten-foot-long German word: "Versöhningskirche—"

"Forget it. You'll never get the pronunciation right. This is the place." Nick's dad climbed out and led the way to the front door, while Nick grabbed Fred's cup and followed. He hoped they'd find someone.

Nick's dad tested the door, and a moment later they were standing at a reception desk, wondering what to say to the twenty-something woman sitting behind it. A nameplate announced her as Renate Schultz.

"I'm sorry," she told them in English. Did they look *that* American? "We're not open today. I didn't mean to leave the front door unlocked."

"That's okay, Miss, uh—" Nick's dad looked down at the nameplate. "*Fraulein* Schultz. We expected to get here yesterday, but we ran into a little bit of a delay. Anyway, we'd just like to leave something that belongs, well—Nick, you explain it to the fraulein. This is your thing."

Nick cleared his throat and began to unwrap the treasure.

"A girl named Liesl Stumpff wrote that we should just drop it off here." He held up the cup briefly. "See, a friend gave it to me back home, and it's kind of a long story." He stumbled on, wondering how much to say. "But we thought it might belong here, so that's why we decided to bring it."

The young woman stared at them with wide eyes as she took the cup. "You've come such a long way, all the way to West Berlin—just to bring *this*?"

"Oh!" Nick understood what she meant. "No, actually my dad just got assigned to Rhein-Main Air Base, and we brought this ourselves, since we were already here. So it wasn't out of our way or anything, well, except maybe this little trip to West Berlin, which isn't really that far, except we almost got killed on the highway. Those cars were just *booking* past us. I mean, people drive fast back home in Wyoming, but this is nuts! This is like a Mercedes-Benz test track or something. You know what I'm saying?"

The woman paused for a minute before blinking and nodding, as if it took a little while to catch up with Nick's words. "Of course," she said then. She taped a note to the package and tucked it behind her inbox. "I will be sure to tell Frau Stumpff that you stopped by. And I am sure she will appreciate it very much."

Okay, then. What else could they say? Nick smiled and his step felt tons lighter than when they'd come.

"Mission accomplished, huh?" his dad said with a grin and a salute as they folded themselves back

into the little car where Nick's mom waited for
them.

"Right." Nick saluted back, glad that he had
delivered Fred's—well, whatever it really was. He
would write him back and tell him the cup made
it back to the Reconciliation people. Back where it
probably belonged in the first place, the way Fred
had said it did. But still he couldn't help wondering
why it had been so important to Fred.

Was that really all there was to it?

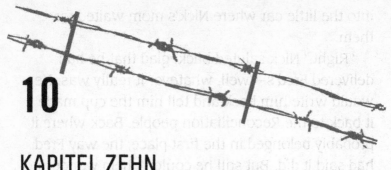

10

KAPITEL ZEHN

QUARK

Liesl looked at herself in the mirror and smoothed her hair back once more. There. Not bad. If she decided to show up at the meeting with all the older teens again, she figured she'd better look the part. A little touch of lipstick, maybe? No, forget it. With a quick glance around the room she started for the front door, just as someone buzzed the intercom from downstairs.

"Oh!" She hadn't expected anyone tonight, had she? She pressed the intercom's talk button and said, "Hello?"

"Liesl, it's Renate, from your mother's office. Is she in?"

Liesl explained about her parents' meetings. She liked Renate Schultz, but she didn't know her well.

"Well, I had planned to leave this until Monday," Renate explained, "but I've got something kind of unusual. Do you mind if I come up?"

Intrigued, Liesl pushed the buzzer that unlocked

the street door and waited while her mother's secretary hurried up the stairs to their apartment. As soon as she entered, she carefully unwrapped a parcel.

"The boy unwrapped it and showed me, I didn't. Honestly." Renate looked at the floor as she stood just inside the apartment door. "At first I thought it was none of my business, and the boy with his father looked perfectly normal. A little nervous, but normal. But you never know these days. It could have been something—well, you know, *criminal,* Or it might be something important to your mother."

But as Renate spoke, Liesl stared at the chalice and at the ornate inscription. She sat down hardly believing she read it correctly.

"Could you read this for me, bitte?" she asked Renate. Because maybe she was just imagining.

"Sure. Of course." Renate took the chalice, balancing it carefully in her hands, and held it up to the light. "It's very pretty, don't you think? I wondered if it could be valuable, which is why I thought I should bring it over tonight, rather than leave it in the office until Monday."

"The inscription. Please, what do you see?"

Liesl needed to hear it from someone else's lips, just to be sure it actually said what she thought it said.

"Oh, right." Renate squinted. The inscription took some concentration. "It says, 'Presented to

Reverend Ulrich Becker, Reconciliation Church, 12 June 1936.'"

The secretary looked up and handed the chalice to Liesl.

"I can't believe it," mumbled Liesl as she traced the inscription with her finger.

"Yes, it's a very nice artifact, isn't it? I feel better knowing it's not in the office over the weekend. You'll tell your mother when she returns home that I made an extra effort to—"

"My grandfather." Liesl didn't mean to interrupt. She just couldn't help herself as the name Ulrich Becker rang in her ears. The secretary stopped mid-sentence and looked from Liesl to the chalice, then back again.

"Pardon me? Your *grandfather*?"

Oh! Liesl bit her tongue, wondering how much she should tell this woman. But yes, she had said it. The *other* grandfather, the one she had known about, Onkel Erich's father. He was Oma Brigitte's first husband—who had also died young, during World War 2, before she had met the American. Liesl only nodded.

"I had no idea." Renate ran her fingers through her dark hair and studied the chalice once more. "And I even work at the Reconciliation Church Remembrance Society."

"If it makes you feel any better, Mutti hasn't told me much, either."

"Then how—"

"I started asking questions for a history paper. I'm starting to learn a lot more than I expected."

"Hmm, yes. I'd like to see that paper sometime." Renate headed for the door, but stopped short.

"I'll be sure to tell Mutti how much of a help you've been," Liesl said.

"Oh, it's not that. I was just thinking. They said the package was from a 'friend.' But I think maybe they just wanted us to *believe* it was from someone else."

"You don't believe them?"

"They're Americans, you know. Big talk, little do. And if you ask me, they had something to hide. I think they wrote the note, too, then made up that story to point the finger at someone else."

"The note?"

"Oh! I almost forgot." Renate reached into her purse and pulled out a small piece of paper, ragged around the edges. "This was taped to the outside of the package. I put it in my purse so it wouldn't get lost. You understand, I'm not trying to be nosey, of course, but—"

Liesl barely heard her. Her hand shook as she took the paper and read the tiny, precise handwriting: "Sorry for taking so long. I hope this belongs to you. Signed, a friend."

What? Liesl turned the little note over and over again.

"See what I mean?" Renate sounded sure of herself now. "Just a phony note to cover themselves."

"How can we get in touch with them?" Liesl asked. She had to know. She thought back to the note her mother had gotten from the American boy, Nick something. He must have delivered the tiny cup. She rolled the note around in her hand, looking for clues.

"I didn't think to ask." Renate cleared her throat and started out the door. "They didn't actually say very much to me. Only that they were staying in the city on holiday. And that the father is stationed at Rhein-Main. Of course, who can believe that? After all, they're—"

"Americans, yes, I know," Liesl repeated.

She'd forgotten all about the protest meeting.

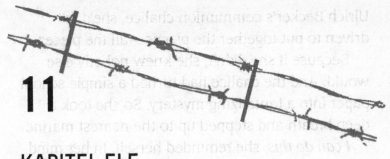

11
KAPITEL ELF
FALSE REPORT

This is getting complicated, Liesl thought as she stood outside the impressive compound at Clay-allee 170. According to the bronze sign over the door, the old building housed the General Lucius D. Clay United States Headquarters. Oh, and the American embassy, complete with grim-faced U.S. Marine guards who stood at attention inside the main entrance. Liesl guessed the only rifle that wasn't loaded was the one held by the American soldier in the bronze statue, also inside the high-ceilinged reception hall.

But she couldn't think of any other way to get what she needed for her paper. Sure, Oma Brigitte had told her bits and pieces, and Onkel Erich had finally mailed her a few newspaper clippings about his experiences with her grandfather, Fred DeWitt, as a "Candy Bomber." Maybe DeWitt had even worked in this building once. But she had to know more than just maybe. Ever since they'd received

Ulrich Becker's communion chalice, she'd felt driven to put together the pieces—all the pieces.

Because if she didn't, she knew nobody else would. And the chalice had turned a simple school paper into a tantalizing mystery. So she took a deep breath and stepped up to the nearest marine.

I can do this, she reminded herself. In her mind, she heard Scarlett O'Hara in *Gone with the Wind,* the old American Civil War movie she'd seen at least ten times.

"Excyuuuuz me?" She poured on her best Southern U.S. accent, the one she'd been practicing for months in front of the mirror. "But can ya'll die-wrecked me to summun who kin help me dig up sumthin 'on a relashin o 'mine?"

She smiled as sweetly as she could and held her breath. That's how Scarlett did it. Or at least she thought so.

But the tall American soldier only looked down at her, obviously puzzled.

"I'm really sorry," he told her, "but I don't think I understood a word you just said. Do you speak English?"

"I reckon that wuuuzz Englush." She would try one more time. "And I'm lookin' for some infoMAYshun."

The marine rubbed his chin and looked around, then waved another man over to join him.

"Hey, Rickles! You gotta come listen to this! Sounds like a bad recording of Jimmy Dean played backward. Totally bizarre. Maybe you can make it out."

A moment later the two soldiers huddled over her, and she realized she couldn't back down now. Bravely she tried to tone down the Scarlett and convince them to let her talk with someone inside.

"I get it!" Marine Number 2 finally said. He looked at Marine Number 1. "I think she wants to know about a relative of some kind who was killed in a plane wreck—one of ours—back in the forties."

Marine Number 1 seemed to ponder this. Then he turned to Liesl and said, "That's military, Miss. We can't help you with that. You understand?"

Liesl nodded but decided these guys would help her whether they liked it or not. She stood her ground until Marine Number 2 finally gave up and led her inside. "None of us were even born back then, you understand," the told her over his shoulder. "But maybe Mr. Marshall can help you find what you're looking for."

Mr. Marshall turned out to be Mr. Thurman Marshall, press attaché, who politely removed his feet from his desk and stubbed out his cigar when she entered his office.

"Sorry about the smoke." He waved his hand then cleared a pile of foreign-language newspapers from a chair before he motioned for her to sit. "What can I do for you?"

This time Liesl decided to leave Scarlett behind,

and Mr. Marshall nodded as she explained her story.

"So you're looking for the scoop on this DeWitt fellow, sorry, I mean, your grandpa, and you think he died back in '48?"

She nodded and showed him the notes she had taken when she'd talked to Onkel Erich.

"Here's the date." She pointed. "What my onkel told me."

He took the notes and held up a finger, picked up the phone, and dialed out. A few minutes later he sat chatting with his friend somewhere, talking baseball—how 'bout them Yankees—about the mess old Reagan's speech was still causing, and oh, yeah, can you dig something up in your archives for me?

He nodded and scribbled, scribbled and nodded. Waited a few minutes, then asked, "Are you sure?" Finally Mr. Marshall thanked his friend, hung up the phone, and held up his hands.

"Well, that wasn't so hard," he told her. "That was big news back in '48. Fella I talked to remembered everything."

"About my grandfather?" She leaned forward.

"That's the funny part. My guy said three men died in that crash." He looked at his notes again. "Zablowski, Aimes, and Nicholson. No DeWitt."

"You're sure about that?" Liesl asked, puzzled.

"Everything else lines up." He waved his hand across the notes she'd given him. "The crash, the place, the plane. We're talking the same one, all right."

"Maybe you didn't hear about him because he didn't die until a few days later?"

"Maybe. But Zablowski was apparently in the hospital for three weeks. Either your grandpa didn't die the way they said he did, or—"

He stopped trying to make a joke and handed her back her notes.

"I'm sorry I couldn't help you, Miss. You go back and ask your uncle to explain it to you one more time. There's got to be some kind of mix-up. I couldn't say where, but there has to be."

He was right about that. But as Liesl waved at the marines on her way out, she knew her story wasn't finished yet.

In fact, it had hardly started.

"Liesl!" The boy caught up to her as she crossed *Kurfürstenstrasse*, nearly home.

Oh! From the protest group. What was his name? He must have seen the blank look on her face.

"It's Jürgen. Remember me? From the—uh, *study* group."

"Sure I remember." His penetrating blue eyes were impossible to forget. Like a snake charmer—she broke away from the thought with a shake of her head.

"You didn't come back. Everybody said it was my fault for scaring you off. That's not true, is it?"

Nothing like a direct question, eh? Jürgen had a way of making her want to run and stay at the same time. He also had a way of tying her tongue in knots. And he had to know how young she was. Or did he?

"N-no, of course not. Nobody scared me off. Something just came up and I couldn't get there, is all."

"That's good. Really good. Because—" On a sunny day, he could have used his front teeth as a bright white emergency signal mirror. "Because we could still use you."

"Are you kidding? Why me?" She couldn't imagine what he wanted from her. But she knew she wanted to end this conversation before she got close to home and her parents saw her talking to a sixteen-year-old boy.

"Why you? You don't know?" Jürgen laughed, a low, easy chuckle that made her feel more at ease, in spite of the danger she felt. It almost made her forget they were only two blocks from her apartment. "Let me tell you: We need a few more people who are willing to go all out for what they believe—people who aren't afraid to actually *do* something about the wall. Like Bible smugglers, for instance."

Liesl felt an odd chill run up the back of her neck. And it wasn't even that cold this afternoon.

"But you don't even know me," she answered back. "Maybe I'm not who you think I am."

"You're not fooling anybody, Liesl." Again he showed his brilliant teeth, and it was hard not to be pulled in by his smile. "And you're not at all like Katja. She's always running around rubbing her hands together, saying, 'Ahhh, let's think about this. Let's pray about that. Let's be careful.' Nothing against praying, you understand, but—"

"Careful is good." Liesl remembered the girl who had tried to protect her. "Isn't it?"

"Careful is *quark*. Total baloney. Careful only gets you in trouble. If you're careful you miss your chances in life."

That didn't exactly sound like something her parents would say, for sure not something Pastor Schmidt would say in a Sunday sermon. But something about the way Jürgen said it—something about his emotion—made Liesl want to hear more. Without thinking, she turned onto *Genthinerstrasse* and around another block, taking the long way home.

"Is it just me," asked Jürgen, "or are we going in circles?"

Liesl didn't answer. What if they were? She still had questions. "Tell me what happened at the—*study* meeting," she said. "Did you decide what to do, or just argue some more?"

"See, that's what I mean." He grinned. "You're not afraid of anybody. I knew that the first time I saw you. Fearless, right?"

Again the back of her neck tingled. But if she turned red, Jürgen ignored it.

"What about the last meeting, though?" She still wanted to know, sort of. Well, yes, of course she did. She could use it for her paper. She could use all of this. In fact, she probably should be taking notes.

"The meeting, right. Sure, I guess you could say we discussed our plans some more."

"And?"

"And people have finally begun to see things my way."

Liesl bit her lip as she wondered exactly what he meant. But he hadn't finished explaining yet.

"So we're all meeting at nine tomorrow morning in front of the wall, where it meets *Leipzigerstrasse*. You know the place?"

Liesl nodded. Sure she knew it.

"And you want to actually do something that makes a difference, right? Not just talk about how unfair things are?"

Again she nodded. As long as he put it that way, sure she did.

"Then you'll come?"

"Uh, actually, maybe I should think about it."

"Now you're sounding like Katja. Thinking is quark."

"But I have to write a paper. And I have to present it next week in front of everybody."

She didn't say everybody in grade eight. But who needed to know?

"It's Saturday morning. No school. No excuses. Understand?"

Liesl finally nodded, maybe just so he would smile again, which he did. Well, why not? Jürgen had asked *her,* hadn't he? He'd even gone out of his way.

"Good," he told her. "I knew I could count on you."

He turned to head back the way he'd come.

"Oh, and by the way, kid," he tossed the comment over his shoulder like a bone to a dog, "I wouldn't say anything to Mutti and Papa if I were you. That'll just make things more complicated, right?"

Kid. The word stung, but Liesl swallowed hard and nodded. She could barely force out the word.

"Right."

12

KAPITEL ZWÖLF

PROTEST

The next morning Liesl shivered in the light drizzle as she dodged the spray from passing cars and hurried to the end of Leipzigerstrasse. The rain had pounded the city during the night, filling the streets with angry gray puddles. She pulled the hood of her jacket farther over her face, but the walk from home had already soaked her.

And even when she reached the end of the strasse, she couldn't stop shaking—maybe not just from getting soaked. She felt in her pocket for her notebook, hoped it hadn't gotten as wet as her clothes.

A group of about thirty teens huddled under sheets of plastic and a few umbrellas just around the corner from the western side of the wall. Here, in the shadow of the wall, a person could spray paint slogans (and many had) or even shout at the guard towers. But what difference did it make? Now, if they could spray paint the *other* side, that would be something. But of course the machine guns and mines and barbed wire lay just over there, daring anyone to try to escape.

"Liesl, isn't it?" Katja, the girl who had protected her at the meeting, met her with a smile. "Nice to see you again, but—"

"Jürgen said you decided to meet here at nine. I thought I'd just stop by, see what happens."

Katja took Liesl's sleeve and turned her away from the group.

"Listen, are you sure you want to be here? I mean, did Jürgen tell you about our plan for today?"

"Not really, but I can guess. Some kind of protest, right? A few signs? I'll take some notes for my paper. The one I'm writing for history class."

Katja looked around the group, opened her mouth, and then closed it. As if making up her mind, she said, "Right. Well actually, Liesl, it's going to be a little more than that. So if I were you, I think I would turn right around and—"

"Hey, look who's here!" Jürgen plowed into the group like a movie star schmoozing for the press, ready to grant autographs to an adoring public. "Is everybody ready for this?"

The group murmured and parted to either side, leaving Liesl to face their leader.

"I've called the press," someone offered. "Reporters should be here any minute, if they don't mind the rain."

"Perfect." Jürgen nodded. "And the ropes?"

"In my bag."

Wait a minute. Ropes? Liesl wondered, as one of the group dropped a sack at Jürgen's feet. Another couple of teens arrived with protest signs shouting in big letters: *Gorby: Tear Down That Wall!* and *The Wall Is History!* And a dozen others Liesl couldn't read, stacked in a pile.

"But—why in English and not in German?" Liesl wondered out loud.

"Oh, come on." Jürgen grinned. "If we had just German signs, none of the Americans watching their TV news would understand what's going on, here. *Verstehen Sie?*"

Yes, she understood, and she began to see that maybe this was more than she'd bargained for. Too late. A couple of shopkeepers glanced out at them through their windows, but nobody smiled. Probably they'd seen this kind of thing before. Jürgen unzipped the duffel bag, pulled out the end of a rope, and looked straight at Liesl.

"You wanted to do something to make a difference?" he asked her.

"Leave her alone, Jürgen." Katja stepped up to the rescue once more. "She doesn't have any idea what's going on."

"Makes no difference to me." Jürgen shrugged. "I just thought she wanted to be involved."

"Not like this, Jürgen."

Jürgen sighed and picked up a sign.

"We don't have time for this. Here." Jürgen shoved one of the signs into Liesl's hands. "Stay away from the wall and don't get hurt. You can manage that, can't you?"

Just then Liesl felt she could have managed to break one of the *Amerikanisch* protest signs over the older boy's head. Instead she nodded and joined the others holding signs. But nothing seemed real—not the yells of the protesters, not the shouts of the small group throwing ropes weighted at one end so they'd fly over the wall. What were they thinking? Surely they'd get the attention of the East German border guards.

And they did, just as the news photographers arrived in three cars and started snapping photos of everything that happened. The East German Vopo guards fired warning shots from their towers. Jürgen and his friends tossed ropes into no-man's-land. A curious crowd gathered, watching from a safe distance. Kids held protest signs—even the petrified thirteen-year-old wondering what to do with hers. Liesl tried to turn away from a photographer but couldn't tell whether he'd caught her. Maybe he had.

She *could* tell that the photographers snapped plenty of shots of West German police headed straight for Jürgen, Katja, and three others holding ropes.

"Join us and pull down the wall!" Jürgen yelled louder than anyone, as if he had a built-in megaphone. "It must come down now! Our friends in East Berlin must be heard!"

A television news crew arrived in a Volkswagen van, wheels screeching to a stop. Liesl took the chance to blend into the watching crowd, just in front of a florist's shop. Most of the other protestors had also dropped their signs and sprinted down the street to safety, but the police didn't seem interested in following. Liesl could only watch in horror as officers led Katja and Jürgen and a couple of others to waiting cars. She tried to look away when Jürgen made eye contact with her and winked, just as an officer shoved him into the car. What was she still doing there? And why had she really come?

"I'm so sorry, Lord," she whispered. No one heard her above the two-tone wail of sirens. No one but God.

"Crazy kids," said an old man in the crowd. He must not have seen her join the onlookers. "They're on the wrong side of the wall. What do they think they're going to prove over here?"

Yes, what? Liesl wondered how she would answer that question in her paper. Why had she let Jürgen sweet-talk her into showing up for this circus? Had they really done *anything* about the wall? As the flashing lights of the police cars disappeared down Leipzigerstrasse, she pressed her back against the brick wall of the flower shop, let herself slip to the sidewalk, and felt the tears of relief and frustration run down her cheeks.

Back home that night she discovered that the rain had soaked through her notebook and smeared her notes. Maybe it was just as well. She realized she had to ask herself, how *did* she want to focus this paper, really?

Was it about the protest, about kids throwing ropes over the wall in a strange demonstration and getting themselves arrested? She had plenty to write about that. Maybe the protest could add something to her paper, if she could sort out what had happened.

But maybe it should be about the beginning of this stupid Cold War between the East and the West, between the Russians and the Americans, between East Germany and West Germany, East Berlin and West Berlin. Or maybe she should center her report on the American grandfather she had never known—the one who had helped drop candy to the hungry kids of Berlin but had died in a fiery plane crash. At least, that's what Oma Brigitte had always believed—the man at the American embassy must have the wrong information. Didn't he?

Or maybe she should write about the brave pastor, her grandmother's first husband, Ulrich Becker, and the mysterious communion cup engraved with his name. He had died during World War 2 fighting his own walls. Surely she could get more information about him from Onkel Erich and her grandmother.

After thinking it over, she had no answers, only more and more questions. But by this time she knew one thing: it all fit together, somehow. And she also knew—*I could have been taken away today, too.*

And maybe she *should* have been. She couldn't shake the guilty feeling. It had followed her all day as she'd gone through the motions of cleaning windows for her mother, sweeping the kitchen floor, finishing all the Cinderella chores she had to do each Saturday.

Later that evening after dinner, her mother came to check on her as she scrubbed the kitchen sink. Liesl had hoped that somehow she could scrub away this guilty feeling. But the harder she scrubbed, the worse she felt.

"Ouch!" She scraped her knuckles against the faucet and pulled her hand back in pain.

"Careful." Her mother looked at her with concern.

"I'm okay," Liesl said, keeping her face brave, debating once again whether she should say something to her mother about the American who might not have died. How could she keep it to herself? "Er, Mutti? There's something I want to tell you."

"Hmm?"

"It's about—" But no. Her mother had always refused to talk about him. And Liesl couldn't bring him up without knowing for sure. Because if the man at the embassy had it wrong—"I mean, I'm almost done with the sink."

A pause, as Sabine tried to figure out what she'd just missed.

"That's what you wanted to tell me?"

Liesl nodded. Now it was.

"I see," her mother told her. "Well, thank you."

In the den the TV blared, and it was a good thing no one but Liesl was there to watch.

"A gang of young protesters were arrested near the wall earlier today," the announcer told them, as if such a thing happened every day. "Four were detained briefly on charges of disorderly conduct and trespassing on government property, while at least twenty others fled after police arrived on the scene. Authorities say the young people are part of a growing sympathy movement with protestors on the other side of the wall, and that—"

Liesl's face flamed red as she prayed the cameras hadn't caught her, too. She didn't want to listen anymore. She finished her chores and quietly found her way to bed. She pulled the covers over her head and plugged her ears—but it didn't help. She even listened for God but could only hear a TV commercial in her mind for a detergent that left dishes sparkling clean. An hour passed, then another, and she lost track of time. But even after the house got quiet, the echoes from that morning would not let her sleep. They just played over and over in her head—the warning shots, the Vopos, the reporters, the sirens.

"I didn't belong there." She began to pray, but she didn't have much of an excuse to offer God. She thought back to the photographers snapping shots of her and the others holding their silly signs. And she couldn't fight off her worry. "What if someone sees me in the paper? What will Mutti and Papa say?" If they had caught her on film, well then, what would happen if the photos were actually printed in *Die Welt* or the *Berliner Morgenpost?* The thought made her almost ill, and she lay for another hour worrying whether she'd managed to avoid the photographers' lenses.

Well, it's too late for that now, she finally told herself, but it didn't make her feel any better.

It was about midnight when she snapped on her reading light and pulled Uhr-Oma Poldi's Bible from the shelf above her pillow. She realized with a start that she hadn't even opened it since bringing it home from Onkel Erich's.

"I'm sorry for not keeping in touch, God," she whispered as she leafed carefully through the well-worn pages. She read some of her favorite psalms, then skipped over to the words of Jesus recorded by his friend John. And she began to hear God once more, at first in a whisper, then louder as she read the record of Jesus' life—Jesus forgiving the woman everyone wanted to stone to death, Jesus teaching in the temple, Jesus arguing with the religious people. And the one line she found herself reading over and over and over:

"Then you will know the truth, and the truth will set you free."

Free? She asked herself. Who's free, around here? In a weird sort of way, only Onkel Erich, who had chosen to live behind barbed wire. And Liesl? Living in a nice apartment, in the "free" half of the city?

Was she free?

As if God heard her question, the answer came right back to her as she read another verse, one underlined in her great-grandmother's wavy pencil:

"So if the Son sets you free, you will be free indeed."

If this had been one of her great-grandmother's favorite verses, Liesl could understand why. It made a whole lot more sense to her than trying to scrub her way to feeling better, or forgiven, or whatever she was missing. And now she knew she was missing *something*. She took a deep breath and kept reading.

"What's this?" Several pages fluttered out, like pressed autumn leaves, and settled on her lap. At first she thought the Bible had actually started to come apart. Then she realized they were letters, written on thin onionskin airmail letter forms, the kind that folded up into their own envelope. And there were two—no, three.

I wonder if I should be reading these? They looked—private, somehow—personal letters. But she couldn't just throw them away without even looking at them. Her great-grandmother had saved them for a reason. She unfolded one and held it up to the light.

The first was dated 1948 and addressed to Mrs. Brigitte DeWitt in the precise, feminine script of the American nurse who signed the note. Liesl caught her breath as she read: "Your husband is struggling bravely, even after losing both legs."

What?

"Though he remains in critical condition, you should know that he asks for you often. We hope that you can leave Germany soon to join your husband."

Liesl wrestled to put the words into place, strained to make sense of them. For one thing, the letter was dated *after* her grandfather supposedly died in a plane crash. And for another thing, how did they end up in Uhr-Oma Poldi's Bible?

No. This was the kind of thing that happened in the movies, not in real life. She picked up the second letter, obviously scrawled a couple of months later by a man with not-so-neat penmanship.

"Dearest Brigitte, I am not the man you married anymore, and I understand why you might have second thoughts about us. But won't you please write back?"

Liesl read it through to the signature at the end ("Your Fred") but still couldn't believe she was holding letters her Oma Brigitte should have seen many years ago—but clearly never had. How could this have happened? Not even the third letter, dated two months later, explained everything.

"Dear Brigitte," Liesl's breath caught as she read her American grandfather's message, "I received the note from your mother-in-law, and I want you to know that I will not contest the annulment."

Annulment? Liesl wasn't completely sure of the English word, but it became clear when she read the next sentence:

"I understand your decision to end our marriage, though I never thought it was a mistake. I guess you deserve better than taking care of a crippled American for the rest of your life. I wish you had written me yourself, but I also wish you all the best in your new life with your new husband-to-be. Love always, Fred."

Liesl read each of the letters again and again, still trying to put the story together. If they meant what she thought they meant, her great-grandmother had pulled off a horrible lie. Or maybe Oma Brigitte had known all along? Either way, she had to tell someone, right now. Was this part of the truth that was supposed to set her free?

Letters in hand, she slipped off her bed and padded down the hall toward her parents' room.

Never mind that her clock said 2 A.M.

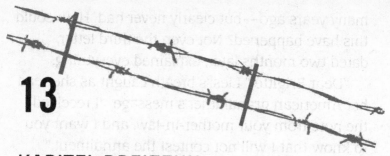

13

KAPITEL DREIZEHN

SECRET TOLD

"But this is crazy. Absolutely crazy!" Willi Stumpff paced the living room floor the next morning, waving the evidence in his hand. "If I hadn't read these letters myself, I would never have believed it. I'm still not sure I do."

"We have to believe it, Papa," Liesl said. She glanced at her grandmother. But Oma Brigitte merely stared out the window, far, far away. She'd hardly said a word.

At least the *Berliner Morgenpost* hadn't splashed Liesl's photo all over the front page. She looked down at the paper on the coffee table again to reassure herself.

"We'll have to verify the information Liesl has found." Her father sounded like a businessman now, or a lawyer making sure of the facts. "This will take some time, you know. We'll need to go through the right channels."

Verify. The right channels. As if anybody really

doubted what he held in his hands and what she'd learned at the American embassy. The pieces had begun to fall together and make sense.

"Mutti?" she asked her mother. "Are you okay?"

Liesl's mother looked as numb as Oma Brigitte. Who knew? The bomb that Liesl had discovered in her great-grandmother's Bible had blasted apart so much of what they'd believed for the past—what, forty years?

Liesl had told them what she'd learned at the embassy, which these letters confirmed, right? As far as the information went, that is. But this was Oma's Brigitte's husband they were talking about. The dead husband who might not have died after all. Her mother's father. The father Sabine had never known—the father who had never even known about her. Liesl had a hard time imagining what it must have been like growing up without a father.

"Is there any chance the letters aren't real?" her mother wondered. Her voice sounded weary, so far away.

"They're real, Mutti," Liesl told her. "I wish they weren't, but they must be."

Of course life would have been much easier if this turned out to be someone's idea of a cruel joke. But chances weren't good for that. And now they had to figure out what had *really* happened.

"So let's get this straight." Herr Stumpff looked

like a lawyer in a courtroom drama on the American TV station.

"Willi—" Sabine interrupted her husband with a glance at Liesl that seemed to say, *Should she really hear this?*

But it was far too late to shield her, and they all knew it. They couldn't just pretend that Liesl didn't already know everything—even if she didn't quite understand it all yet. Her father shook his head and went on, and that was as much permission to stay as Liesl would get.

"Fred DeWitt's plane crashed in 1948," he continued, "we know that much, right?" He looked at Oma Brigitte for confirmation, but she continued to stare out the window at nothing. "But then he was taken to a hospital in the United States, where his life was saved but he lost both his legs."

Liesl winced at the chilling thought, while her father went on, unfolding the mystery.

"Only you were told he didn't survive, that he'd died with the other three crewmembers."

Oma Brigitte's shoulders began to shake, and Liesl nearly pleaded with her father to change the subject. She couldn't bear to see Oma so upset. Please. Her mother walked over to comfort Oma.

"Did you know any of this, Mother? Even a little bit?"

At first Oma Brigitte didn't answer. But she couldn't possibly hold it all inside. A few moments later the tears began to come—a trickle at first, eventually a flood.

"Of course not! I believed he had died. Do you think I would have stayed here if—"

If—She couldn't finish.

"This is the part I don't really understand." Liesl puzzled the pieces around in her mind. "It doesn't add up."

Maybe not yet. But her father still had more of his case to make.

"His grandparents hated the thought of their Fred marrying a German, isn't that right, Oma? Wasn't that true?"

Another pause. But she took a long, ragged breath and drew herself up straight, determined to answer as best she could.

"They said they would never allow it." She held her head in her hands. "They thought I was trying to trick him, use him as a way to escape to America. And they were very bitter, too. Over the dead body of Fred's brother, they said. He was killed in the Battle of the Bulge."

A World War 2 battle. Killed by German soldiers, of course. Right.

"But you got married anyway."

Oma's cheeks turned a little pink, and she looked at the floor.

"I had a son; he needed a father. Fred was a good man, a good Christian man. He cared about us, and he really seemed to love little Erich. Fred was—"

Fred. The Amerikaner had a name, didn't he?

"But what about the American military?" Maybe Willi was too much the lawyer now. But they *did* want to know. "Didn't you expect something more official from the government? Something more than just a letter from his parents?"

Oma began to shake her head, then slowly answered, "I didn't know what was supposed to happen. All I knew is what Fred's parents told me. That he had died. That they had already buried him. And that they never wanted to see or hear from me again."

"But how could they—" Liesl didn't know how to finish her question. Her grandmother shrugged and dabbed at her eyes with a handkerchief.

"They even sent me money. Three hundred fifty American dollars, which was a lot of money in those days." She took her daughter's cheek in her hand. "I used it to take care of you and Erich until I could get a decent-paying job."

Liesl looked around the room and realized they all had tears in their eyes.

"I can see how they misled you," Liesl said. She took the letters from her father's hand and looked hard at them. "But he knew it wasn't true. I mean, Fred knew he wasn't dead. Why didn't he ever come back?"

"Maybe because he believed Oma Brigette

got remarried. He never got an answer from her directly," Willi guessed as he rubbed his forehead. "But Brigitte never wrote to him because—"

Liesl knew that someone had to say it. But it seemed so hard to comprehend.

She quietly finished her father's sentence. "Because Uhr-Oma Poldi didn't like the idea of her son's widow marrying an American, just like his grandparents didn't want him to marry a German. Is that right?"

The silence in the room told her yes. This felt so weird to Liesl. If not for the tears all around her, she might believe they were just talking about some characters in a story.

"So Oma Poldi kept the letters he sent. She could have set the record straight when Brigitte got those letters from his grandparents, but she didn't." Willi was winding up his case. "She even went so far as to send Fred DeWitt a letter saying Brigitte had found someone else, to keep him from writing again."

"Ooooo!" Liesl pounded on the table with her fist. "That is so—I mean, how could she do that? I thought she was supposed to be a *Christian!* Why—"

"We'll never know why." Liesl's father didn't have all the answers, after all. "All I know is she wasn't perfect, like we aren't … ja? She must have thought she was doing the best thing for Brigitte."

"The best thing," Liesl mumbled as she looked

around the room. Yes, she knew that Oma had tried to apologize, how it didn't make sense at the time. Was this what she had meant? Her grandmother—betrayed. Her family—cheated. And Onkel Erich, well, he lost as much as everybody else—a stepfather who loved him.

"I can't imagine what Fred went through," Herr Stumpff said sadly.

"Learning to live without two good legs." Sabine had suffered from polio as a girl. She limped over to the couch and sat down, letting her crutch fall to the floor. "I think I can understand how that might have felt."

No one spoke for a moment. Oma Brigitte broke the silence with a surprised gasp. Liesl followed her gaze as Oma asked, "Where did that come from?"

She meant the communion cup, which she recognized at once. "I haven't seen that since the day Fred and I married."

Liesl retrieved the little cup, along with the seed of a plan.

"I think we need to track down the Americans who brought us this cup," she decided, taking it to her grandmother. "They'll just have to tell us where it came from, and then—"

If Fred DeWitt was still alive, they had to know. *Brigitte* had to know, more than anyone. And if not—well—they should know that, too.

"Do you still have the letter from the American

boy?" Liesl asked her mother. Relief flooded through her when her mother nodded. At least they had a starting point.

"I'm going to look for him," Liesl announced.

Her father started to say something, but didn't. Her mother looked as if she might faint, her eyes closed tightly. So Liesl looked to her grandmother for permission, the question clear on her face.

Oma nodded weakly before burying her face in her hands.

14

KAPITEL VIERSEHN
THEY KNOW

"I'll get it!" Nick ran for the phone, though he knew it was probably for his dad. You never knew, though. Maybe Fred had received his letter by now.

But Nick knew in an instant his friend wasn't on the other end of the line.

"Sabine Stumpff calling." Oh. A woman. Probably for Mom. Maybe somebody from the air base wives' club. "I'm from the Versöhningskircheerinnerungsgesellschaft, and—"

It took a moment for the monster word to register in Nick's brain. Well, he'd only heard it pronounced once before, by Herr König. Meanwhile, the woman at the other end of the line said something he didn't catch.

"Huh? I mean, excuse me, I wasn't following."

"I said, am I speaking to Nick Wilder? You wrote a letter to me regarding a chalice and enclosed your phone number. I wanted to thank you for what you did, returning the cup. The family especially is quite grateful, as it has great sentimental value."

"Sentimental? Sure. I mean, that's good. No problem." Nick wasn't sure what he was supposed to say to that.

"I do have a request, however. We would very much like to trace how the chalice came to be in your possession, perhaps find out where it has been all these years."

Uh-oh. Nick stopped for a second to think. She wanted to know where he got it and how. He'd been afraid of that. And he wasn't sure if that's what Fred wanted or not. Or if Fred could get in trouble.

"Herr Wilder?"

"Yeah, still here. I was just thinking. The friend who gave it to me, well, he kind of wants to keep it anonymous, if you know what I mean. He just wanted to see the thing get back to where it came from. Is that okay?"

After a slight pause, the woman said, "I understand, but the family is quite intent on finding out as much as they can. You are certain you cannot help us?"

Nick swallowed hard, not totally sure what he should say next. Fred hadn't said absolutely positively don't tell them his name, had he? Just something about "keep it low key, would you?" Well, he'd tried.

"I just don't want to get anybody in trouble," he

finally said. "Not that he did anything wrong. He's not that kind of guy. It's just that—"

Nick hesitated. Maybe he'd already said too much.

"Please tell me if I'm wrong." The woman's voice sounded shaky, like Nick's mother's voice when she was about to cry. "But are we talking about a man missing both legs? Are we talking about—a man named Fred DeWitt?"

Holy guacamole. Nick almost dropped the phone when he heard that name.

"Whoa, lady. How did you know? I didn't say anything about him—"

But Frau Stumpff couldn't speak. Nick heard what sounded like a sob, then another voice came on the line.

"Hello?" This time a girl spoke to him. "Sorry about that. This is Liesl, Sabine Stumpff's daughter. You're probably wondering what's going on."

"As a matter of fact—" Nick felt totally confused. That confusion turned to amazement as Liesl told him about her grandfather, Fred DeWitt, what they thought had happened to him in 1948, what they had just found out, and how hard it was on her mom, who had fallen apart at the news. This girl called her mom "Mutti," which Nick thought was hysterical, but of course he didn't dare laugh. Besides, the story sounded too bizarre. Fred had never told him anything about this, nothing about a family back in Germany, or even what he had done when he was in the Air Force. In fact, Nick hadn't even been sure Fred *was* in the Air Force. But then, Fred never talked much about himself, period.

"Nothing more than that?" Liesl pushed him, after he'd told her what he knew about Fred.

"Like I said, he doesn't talk about himself much. He always asked me stuff about what I liked to do, about school and stuff. My dad was always busy, so we did stuff together. Worked on the plane, mostly. Took care of my dog when we moved. But I got the impression he didn't really have a whole lot to brag about, if you know what I mean."

How else could he explain it? Fred was a cool guy. He just wasn't the most talkative person in the world. But this Liesl Stumpff didn't seem to care about that. All she wanted now was his phone number back in the States, so she could call him and tell him he had family here in Germany.

"I don't know. He might not believe you. And if he does, he might have a heart attack if you just call him out of the blue. You know?"

Liesl paused.

"I'm sorry. My English. Sometimes I'm a little slow. I'm not sure what *blue* has to do with anything."

"Oh!" He chuckled. "Sorry. I just meant, just coming out of nowhere. You know? No warning? He's not like a really young guy, you know."

"Of course I know. But I still must have the number."

Whoa. Now this girl was getting a little too pushy.

"Well, listen, Leezuhl Stump. First of all, I don't have his phone number. All I have is his mailing address, back in Greybull, see? And second of all, even if I did have his phone number, I'm not sure Fred would want me to give it out."

"Not even to his granddaughter?"

Right. Nick almost forgot.

"Well—maybe. I still just don't want you to scare him out of his wits. You know, like 'hi, I'm your long-lost granddaughter you never even knew you had, since you never even knew you had a daughter? Remember me?' I just think he's going to freak out. You should just write him a letter. Give him a chance to, you know, soak it in a little."

Liesl chewed on that one for a minute.

"A letter takes too long," she nearly whispered. "And I don't have enough time before I have to present my paper. But thank you anyway, Nick Wilder."

15

KAPITEL FÜNFSEHN

FEIGLING

Liesl wasn't kidding when she'd told Nick she didn't have enough time. Two days later she looked out over the classroom full of faces and wondered why her hands were shaking this much.

After all, it's just another day in history class, right?

Two other classes had joined them, filling the room to overflowing. But so what? If she were Cher, this crowd would seem small. And Liesl Stumpff loved to perform, didn't she?

"All right, now." Herr Reinberger rapped on the edge of his desk with his ruler and looked over his funky half-glasses. "I've asked Fraulein Stumpff to present her paper first, simply because it's one of the best I've ever seen."

Yeah, right. If he knew what was missing from this paper, he'd know what a sham it really was. One of the best? Ja, the paper without an ending. But Herr Reinberger kept going on and on to everybody about what a fine job she and the other top writers had done, and blah blah...

" ... And believe me, in the past twenty-two years I've seen plenty of papers. Some of them excellent, others *nicht so gut*."

Great. Nothing like a little pressure. Herr Reinberger ran a hand through his spikey gray hair and explained something about their evaluations and grades. On a normal day Liesl rather liked Herr Reinberger. But today she saw him as the enemy, putting her through this stinking trial. Never mind that all five of the top writers had to read their papers. Maybe they'd have an easier time of it, once she made a fool of herself up here.

What an honor. Liesl could have kicked herself for spending so much time on this paper, so many rewrites, so much—*ach, ja.*

"She will read it to you as an oral report, and then she will answer your questions. And I expect you all to pay close attention, because you will fill out evaluation papers. Go ahead, Liesl."

That's when their headmaster, Frau Goudsmit slipped into the back of the class. She did that once in a while, just to watch what the class was doing. And any other time, it would have been fine with Liesl. But today her tongue stuck to the roof of her mouth as she looked at her teacher, hoping he would take it all back and tell them he was joking. Instead he smiled and nodded at Frau Goudsmit, as if he'd been expecting her. *Vielen Dank.*

Thanks a bunch.

On the other hand, a kid in the second row looked as if he had already settled in for a mid-morning snooze. Well, let him. What did she care? She stood up straight behind the podium, the way her father had coached her. This was no big deal, really. Read each word slowly, and pronounce her words carefully. She could do this, and if some people chose to sleep through it, all the better.

"My paper is about a family split apart by the wall," she began. "And it starts back in 1948, when my Onkel Erich was thirteen years old. Our age. He told me that—"

But as she gathered her papers together they somehow slipped from her grip and—

No! She might expect this to happen in a bad dream, but not in front of the headmaster and a hundred snickering kids. She felt her face steaming as she stooped to collect her pages off the floor, in random order. Oh, please. She could find page one easily enough, but after that—why hadn't she written page numbers on them? She straightened up and tried to put the report back in order, but everything looked blurry.

"Take your time, Liesl," Herr Reinberger told her, and that helped a little, but not enough. She took another deep breath, because her head had started to feel a little lighter than usual.

Make that *way* lighter than usual. But another deep breath didn't help any. Herr Reinberger's voice had turned fuzzy, and the room began to spin around her like a carnival ride. She gripped the edge of the podium for balance. The last she remembered, her knees buckled as she fell to the floor.

"Liesl!" Jürgen came running behind her on the sidewalk. How did he always find her? "Where have you been?"

She didn't slow down, just kept walking. He'd probably heard about her fainting in class. Hadn't everyone?

"Hey, hold up." He tried to grab her shoulder, but she shrugged away. He jumped around in front of her and held his arms out, forcing her to stop. "I'm only trying to be friendly, huh? What's wrong with you?"

She looked straight at him and did her best to keep her voice steady.

"Nothing's wrong with me. I'm just on my way home. Excuse me."

She started walking again, forcing him to walk backward. What was he thinking?

"Sure. Well, I just thought I'd tell you we've planned another protest. Thought maybe you'd want to tag along again."

Tag along? Liesl shook her head no, but he wouldn't give up that easily. What was with this guy?

"I thought you wanted to make a difference."

"Of course I want to make a difference. Just not the same way you do. The kind of difference you're making will just get people hurt."

"Come on. When has anybody ever gotten hurt?" He held up his arms again, as if she had called him a criminal. She didn't answer, but that was apparently enough for him.

"Fine. You know what you are, Liesl?"

"I have a feeling you'll tell me."

"You're a *feigling*, Liesl." He kept up with her, still walking backward down the sidewalk. "You say you want to do something important, but when someone hands you the chance, you run."

A coward? Wasn't that something boys called other boys? But by this time Liesl could feel the steam erupting from her ears. And though she could see the lamppost getting closer and closer, she said nothing. Three steps, two, one—

"Ohhh!" Jürgen crashed backward into the post and stumbled.

So sorry about that. She took the chance to hurry past.

"Feigling! Do you hear me? You'll never get what you want by being sweet and nice. That's not the way the world works."

Liesl stopped for only a moment, not turning.

"I don't care how the world works, Jürgen. And besides, I don't know how old you thought I was, but guess what? I'm only thirteen."

She kept walking, and this time Jürgen had nothing to say. Good thing, too.

16

KAPITEL SECHZEHN

PITY PARTY

"How was school today, Schatzi?"

Liesl had hoped to slip into her room unnoticed, maybe bury her face in her pillow and have her own private pity party. She deserved a good cry. But no such luck.

"Okay for most people." She decided to try for a middle-of-the-road answer, something that wouldn't get into the details. She would show them the note from the school nurse later.

She cheered a bit when she realized that her mother had parked herself in front of the television with a box of tissue and hadn't even looked up. Another episode of *"Schwarzwaldklinik,"* her mother's favorite daytime soap opera? But it didn't quite sound like the Black Forest Hospital.

Maybe it was just an automatic question, and Mutti wasn't really looking for an honest answer.

As in, "Oh, I fainted in front of the entire eighth grade, and I'll never be able to face my class again so now we have to move to Antarctica where no one knows us." Good thing she hadn't bumped anything on the way down and hurt herself. At least she wouldn't have to explain any bumps or bruises to her mother. They told her afterward she had looked just like a limp noodle or a rag doll—folding up on the floor in front of everyone.

So much for the best paper Herr Reinberger had ever read. If he wanted anybody else to hear it, he would have to read it to them himself.

"That's good." Sabine didn't take her eyes off the TV screen.

Well, maybe Liesl didn't blame her mother. But she couldn't help stopping in the hallway to see what held her mother's attention. Once again she saw a demonstration at the wall—the arrests, the shouting, the protest signs. Only this time several people looked like they were bleeding. Liesl winced as a video clip showed some teenagers lighting a fire beside the wall, climbing the wall, yelling and screaming. Of course the police grabbed them, and Liesl couldn't tell if the grainy picture was of Jürgen or Katja or one of their friends. She remembered Jürgen's words. No one was getting hurt?

But Liesl had her own walls to climb, and as she turned away she nearly stumbled on Oma Brigitte's purse. Oh! Had it been there since they'd practically had to carry her home, after everything about Fred DeWitt had come out in the open?

Maybe I should go see her, Liesl thought, *and take her purse back.*

Maybe. Unless her Oma asked about the paper, and—*forget* about the paper. The good news about fainting was that she'd learned one thing: it really wasn't about the paper. In fact, without the ending to the story about her American grandfather, the stinking paper wasn't finished.

So what am I doing here? she asked herself, feeling a pang of shame. *Am I the only one who understands how big this is?*

She watched her mother for a moment longer and it became pretty clear. It was all up to Liesl. Sure, Papa said he would help, and he had sent out a few letters requesting information about the American. But letters took time, and besides, he'd left this morning on another business trip to the factory in Stuttgart. Perhaps he could make some calls from the hotel, he'd said, in between his meetings.

Sure, everything could wait until he got back. But when would that be—next week?

And if the American boy wouldn't help, either, she'd just find what she needed on her own. Well, why not? Newspaper reporters figured out people's phone numbers all the time, didn't they? Even halfway across the world. All she had to do was—what, exactly?

Forget about the pity party. She padded into her father's den, skimmed through his phone book, and dialed one of the "help" numbers in the front of the book.

"Hello?" She hoped she was talking to the right operator. "I need a telephone number for Herr Mister Fred DeWitt ... Oh. Where? Amerika ... Yes, I know that's a big place. I was just getting to that. He lives in Greybull, Wyoming state, USA ... Yes, I'll wait, danke."

As she did, she almost hoped there would be no number for Fred DeWitt, but she knew she'd feel cheated. And after twenty minutes and almost as many calls to operators and directory assistance (half of whom she could hardly understand—so many different odd Amerikanisch accents!) she still didn't have a number for Mr. Fred DeWitt.

Or should she call him "Grandpa" DeWitt? Not yet. And maybe not ever, if she couldn't reach him. She might have to write a letter, after all, the way Nick Wilder had suggested.

No. She sat by the phone trying to think of a way to find this number, if there was one to find. She knew her call wouldn't give him a heart attack. She would—she nearly fell off her chair when the phone rang! Speaking of heart attacks. She grabbed the receiver and squeaked, "Ja—hello?"

"Oh, yeah. *Guten tag* and *wie gehts?*" The American boy did his best to say "Hi" and "How's it going?" Give him credit for trying, anyway.

"This is Liesl Stumpff." She kept her voice down so

she wouldn't disturb her mother in the next room. "I speak English, remember."

"Liesl Stumpff! That's great!"

He hardly took a breath as he went on.

"Nick Wilder. Remember me? I was afraid your mom had answered."

Ja, she remembered. And she waited for him to go on.

"So I—" he began into the silence, just as she'd decided to ask what he wanted. Like a dance where both partners try to lead. Finally she told him to go ahead.

"Okay, fine," he said. "Anyway, I just called because I told my parents what you were doing, trying to track down Fred, I mean, your grandpa."

He paused, as if waiting for some kind of drumroll in the background. Couldn't he just come right out and say what he wanted to say?

"And?" she asked. This American kid was driving her crazy.

"They thought it was a great idea."

"Er, what does that mean, bitte?"

"It means that my dad called the airport guys back home in Greybull to see if they could tell him how to get hold of your grandpa. And I've got a number for you."

Another pause. Enough with the pauses, already.

"Fred's phone number."

17

KAPITEL SIEBSEHN
FINDING FRED

Liesl knew this phone call would take courage. She stared at the string of numbers Nick had given her. He still seemed pretty annoying, but he could be nice, too. About the number, she meant. So, okay.

She dabbed at her eyes, trying not to get all emotional.

"Stop it, stop it!" she whispered fiercely to herself as she fanned her eyes. "Leave the crying to Mutti." Determined, she reached for the phone and carefully punched in the numbers. The international code, the area code, and all the rest. And at first, just silence. Then the line started ringing—three, four, five times. Finally a click told her someone had answered.

"Hello?" Liesl waited for someone to say something. Instead, she heard the phone fall—*thud*—some scuffling, and finally a far-away, thick-voiced "Yeah?"

Did all Americans answer their phones this way? Maybe Nick had given her the wrong number!

"Er, am I speaking with Fred DeWitt?"

"Hard to say." The man cleared his throat and sniffed. "Four in the morning, I have no idea who I am."

Four—what? Liesl's face flushed in confusion as she checked her watch. But it was noon—oh, no! Noon in Berlin. She had totally forgotten about time zones. How stupid of her, forgetting that Wyoming state, USA was—she did the math in her head—eight hours behind!

"So who wants to know?" he asked, as she nearly hung up in panic. But something in his voice told her not to. She hesitated as she listened to her grandfather's voice: "Only time someone calls this early in the morning is to bring bad news. Like somebody died."

"Nobody died, I don't think." Her voice cracked as she pressed the receiver hard to her ear, as if she could feel her grandfather through the line. "And I am so sorry. I didn't realize—didn't think. I'm calling from Berlin."

"Yeah?" She heard him snort and cough, and imagined him fumbling for the light. She'd better deliver the line she'd rehearsed for hours, before he hung up on her.

"My name is Liesl Stumpff. My mother is Sabine

Stumpff, and her mother is Brigitte—Brigitte
Becker DeWitt."

"Brigitte?" This time his voice went cold.

"Your wife."

"Used to be."

He said nothing for a long while. The soft hiss
of the phone reminded Liesl of the sound of listening to a seashell.

"Are you still there?" she wondered.

"Still here," he finally answered. "But—how do I
know this isn't some kind of—scam?"

"Because it's not." This wasn't going as well as
she'd hoped. "And because I have some letters you
sent to my grandmother, to Brigitte. One a nurse
wrote for you after you were—hurt."

Hurt, not killed. She hoped she could read it
without breaking down. The other end of the line
grew very quiet, just that quiet hissing sound,
slightly louder now, like wind through a tunnel.

"And you need to know," she went on, "that she
read them for the first time just three days ago."

"I'm not following." Now his voice sounded flat,
maybe angrier than before, as if she had no right
to tell him such things. "Where did you get these
letters?"

"I found them in my great-grandmother's Bible.
She died before I was born and my Onkel Erich
had the Bible, but he never used it. He gave it to
me for my birthday, and I just found the letters. We

think she kept them from Oma Brigitte—I mean your wife. Please don't be mad."

When he didn't answer, Liesl took a deep breath and read from the first letter in his handwriting, the one that started "I am not the man you married, anymore ..." But her voice quivered, and she felt very small as she read the lines. It felt wrong to give voice to something so sad and personal. These were, after all, the pleading words of a broken man—though they had never reached the one who should have read them so many years earlier. And now—

And now when she finished she ignored the tears streaming down her cheeks. She could hear ragged breaths coming from the man in Greybull, Wyoming state. She waited for him to say something, anything, and it seemed like the longest silence she'd ever sat through.

"Are you saying—" He swallowed hard and started over. "Are you saying I have a daughter, and I didn't even know it? A granddaughter, even?"

She tried to explain what she knew—the letters, the lies, the wall that had separated her family. She even told him how she'd talked to Nick Wilder and about the communion cup. Of course, he already knew that part of the story. Maybe that would help him believe her.

"But what about the other fellow?" he finally asked.

"What other fellow?" Liesl replied.

"The one her mother-in-law told me she wanted to marry?"

"That's just it!" she said, anger tingeing her voice. "There never *was* another guy. No one else. It was all a horrible lie!"

"Forgive me if a guy has a hard time believing that. After all these years, I mean."

"But it's true. Oma Brigitte never married again. She raised Erich and Sabine, your daughter, by herself."

"Sabine. That her name?" He sighed, long and heavy.

"Wouldn't you even want to talk to her? Meet her?"

Should she have asked that? He must have thought about it for a moment.

"Listen," he finally answered. "This is all pretty sudden. I'm not quite sure what to do with this kind of stuff."

"I understand." She didn't. She couldn't.

He went on. "See, a guy like me gets used to the way things are, and it's not so easy to change gears, just like that. Especially not when someone calls out of the blue at four A.M., tells you she's your long-lost granddaughter."

Out of the blue. She understood this time.

"But that's who I am," she whispered.

"Okay. But even if what you say is true, and you really are, I can't just ..."

His voice trailed away. Maybe she should have

listened to Nick. Maybe she should never have called him like this. She should have written him, given him a chance to ease into the idea of a family a little more slowly.

"I could mail you the letters, prove to you—"

"You don't have to do that, Lisa—Liesl. That's a nice name. But tell me something: why are *you* calling me, and not your mother, or—?"

"I-I'm not sure." Her tears let loose again, and they nearly choked her next words. "Maybe they're too afraid because it's been so long."

"Hmm."

"Or maybe they're just afraid they'll discover that you had your own family and kids and grand-kids, and that you wouldn't want to, you know, hear about us."

"But you're not afraid?"

"Ja, I'm afraid."

Afraid, and she wondered what to say next. Maybe he was wondering the same thing in the silence that followed.

"May I write to you?" she finally blurted out. He didn't answer right away, but he did answer.

"You can if you want. You probably have my address, I'm guessing."

"Greybull, Wyoming state, USA." The words echoed back at her across the long-distance lines.

"You got it."

So was that it? As she said good-bye and hung up, Liesl could have kicked herself. What could she have said differently? At least she knew he hadn't died. But this conversation hadn't turned out the way she'd hoped. Maybe she shouldn't have tried to do this on her own. She'd only made a mess of things.

She could only think of one person who could help her make this right—and he didn't live on this side of the wall.

18

KAPITEL ACHTZEHN
LONG-DISTANCE CALL

Nick looked up from his homework when the phone rang.

"I'll get it," his mother said, leaving their hamburgers frying on the stove, sputtering and popping in a familiar sort of way. The warm smell kind of massaged his nose, made him grin without really knowing why, like a secret untold, or a joke. And for just a moment, if he didn't look around too much, he could almost imagine himself back in the States, Dad heading home from work, Mom fixing dinner, him doing his math homework at the kitchen table.

Just like back home in Wyoming.

So was anything really different, living here in Frankfurt? All the American kids went to school on the base, so most of the day he swam in a sea of American kids, teachers, and books. On the surface, who could tell the difference, really? Sure, they learned German in school. And of course everybody off the base was German. So the accents sounded thick and hard to understand sometimes, and once in a while he had to use a little sign language to get his point across. But other than that—

He heard his mother's voice from the den, almost shouting. She always did that when someone called long distance, no matter how good the connection. Maybe that made sense when his grandma from Dallas called. She had a little trouble hearing anyway. But everybody else?

"I'm so glad to hear it, Mr. DeWitt, and—"

Nick's ears perked up even more. Fred? Calling here? He walked into the den to see what was up, and his mother waved him over to the phone.

"Yes, and here he is. I'm sure he'll be pleased to hear from you."

She nodded and handed Nick the receiver.

"Hey, Fred ... Yeah, I miss hanging around the airport, too ... Oh, pretty good. It's actually not so bad here, I guess ... Yeah, lots of cool planes to watch on the base."

He twirled the phone cord around his finger as they talked about what he was doing (not much), whether he missed Wyoming (he did), and how his parents were doing (just fine). But of course, that wasn't the real reason the man had called. Fred said he guessed Nick might be wondering.

"Well, sure—I guess you could say that. Not every day I get long-distance calls from the States ..."

He listened for a moment.

"That cup?" he said. "Sure. I was going to write and tell you all about it, too ... Yeah, it was pretty weird how it turned out. A little confusing, but I think the lady who—oh ... You know all that already?"

Nick nodded as his friend explained about the call from Liesl Stumpff.

"Right! She told me about that, too. Yeah, I know it sounds weird ... Uh-huh. I guess there are a lot of scams out there. But all I know is what she told me."

The hiss and sputter on the other end of the line told him Fred hadn't hung up.

Into the silence, Nick ventured, "So does this mean maybe you'll come visit Germany? Kinda check out your long-lost relatives at the same time?"

Well, he'd thought it sounded like a good idea. Fred had a different way of looking at it.

"Oh. Right ..." Nick agreed. "Sure, I understand it's all pretty sudden. Yeah, I'd feel that way, too ..."

Nick wasn't sure what else to say, except—

"Anyway, if you change your mind you could always stay here. I mean, I could sleep on the couch and you could have my bed if you want."

And what was the chance of that ever happening? Maybe that's why they both chuckled, which seemed a better way to end the conversation, anyway.

"Sure. I've got to go, too. It's probably expensive

to talk like this. Long distance, I mean. My dad's always getting after my mom for calling her sister back in Oklahoma, says it costs big bucks for overseas calls. Yeah. See you, maybe."

Or maybe not. As he hung up the phone, he wondered if he could have said something else.

19

KAPITEL NEUNZEHN

DETENTION

Liesl checked her watch once more. In less than an hour she'd answered most of the usual East German checkpoint questions—name, age, address. And where were her parents this afternoon? No, she hadn't crossed before without her mother or father. But she had to go see her uncle. It was very important.

After the mess she'd made of the phone call to Fred DeWitt, she'd taken the time to think things through before acting this time. She decided to show Onkel Erich the letters she'd found, not just tell him about them. She just had to convince him to help her.

She suddenly realized the guard had asked her another question. Yes, she replied, her parents would know where she was (if they looked in her room, they would see the note on her dresser). But she'd be home before dinner, no problem. She could do this on her own.

But now she fidgeted in her seat next to the

same wooden table where the guard had made her and her mother dump their purses on the last crossing. Today's guard fired questions at her just as she'd expected.

"What is your business?"

She wondered what to tell him. Why not the truth, again? "Well, you see, I was working on a paper for school, and my onkel promised to tell me more about my grandfather. He's the only one who can really explain—well, my grandmother could, too, but she's kind of in shock, since she found out that my grandfather is still alive. But I've never met him, you see, and so last week I tried to call him on the telephone, and—"

"Ja, ja." The guard waved for her to stop. "That's enough."

She almost smiled, but didn't, of course. He didn't believe a word of it, or didn't care. And this time she wasn't worried about getting caught with Bibles tucked into her socks. So what was taking so long?

Another of the border Vopo guards entered the room and squinted at her as if she were wearing face paint or might be carrying a bomb. But this time, she felt confident. *Go ahead and look through my purse,* she thought.

Just as long as they hurried it up. If they did, she could see Onkel Erich and get back before dinner, no problem. And maybe he could help her convince Herr Fred DeWitt of the truth. If her uncle couldn't, then who?

The first guard found her letters.

"These are yours?"

"They're just old family scrapbook things. Old."

He could see that. Liesl sighed with relief when he tossed them aside. Then he pulled another scrap of paper from her purse and held it up to the light.

"Who is this person and what is this number?"

"Oh." Liesl wondered if this might mean trouble. Good thing they hadn't seen where she'd written the matching phone number on her palm. "That's my grandfather. The one I was just telling you about?"

"But this is an Amerikanisch name? You said nothing of this. A telephone number in Amerika?"

"He's Amerikanisch, ja." She shrugged. "It's a long story."

And did they want to hear it? He frowned and called over yet another guard. This was getting to be a replay of the last time she had crossed with Mutti. Only this time she didn't see the guard who had the crush on her mother.

"Is something wrong?" Liesl felt her hands start to shake, though she had nothing to shake about this time. All this fuss over a silly phone number?

No one answered. And they called over a fourth guard, who carried a binder full of photos that they all crowded around. She could only see the corner of the collection, but when one of the guards pointed at a photo, they all looked closely at Liesl, then back at the photo. They nodded in agreement.

"That's her," said the first guard, and there could be no mistake in his voice. The others agreed and straightened up.

"May I see?" They could at least give her that courtesy, and now despite her shaking hands, she could feel the heat rise to her face.

Guard 1 took the photo binder and spun it around in her direction.

"This is you, is it not?"

Liesl gasped when she saw the photo. It must have been taken with a high-powered camera lens—it looked grainy and far away, taken from an East German guard tower, for sure. Yet there was no mistaking Liesl Stumpff, carrying a rather large protest sign, standing near the wall. It looked as if she were scowling, or shouting, or both. Not the best shot she'd ever seen.

"You will come with us to the detention center for further questioning." The first guard pointed at the door. "We've been instructed to detain anyone involved in subversive activities against the state."

"But I'm not an adult."

"We recognize no age limits in this matter."

"You mean, you don't care if I'm only thirteen?"

"You will follow us, please."

"Wait a minute. Subversive activities? I don't

even know what that means, and I'm not East Ger-man. I was born in *West* Berlin. You can't do this to me."

"We will continue this conversation in the detention center."

"But my things —"

"You will not be needing them."

"How long will this take?"

"You will be fed and accommodated, if that's what you're concerned about. For the time being, consider yourself a guest of the East German government."

"But what about my parents? They'll be worried."

Maybe they'd already found her note?

Back by 5:30. No worries. Love, Liesl.

"They will be notified in good time," replied the guard, who didn't know about any notes and wouldn't have cared if he did know. "But per-haps you should have thought of that before you attempted to cross the border."

Liesl thought of all the times she had crossed smoothly. Now her first solo crossing was going so wrong. What would they do to her now?

"Can you at least call my onkel, tell him I'll be late?"

As if he knew she would be coming.

"No calls. No more discussion."

This time the Vopo meant business. He grabbed her arm — hard — and dragged her through the door. Okay, okay! She looked back at her stuff and wondered why she had decided that crossing alone was a good idea.

Liesl remembered waiting for an hour and a half in a doctor's office once. Or maybe at the dentist's office.

But she'd never waited this nervously this long.

She checked her watch once more, just to be sure. Six hours, twenty-three minutes. Already past dinnertime, and still the Vopos hadn't come. She didn't know what to expect, but so far no beatings, no interrogations, no nothing. No one had shoved a light in her face and said, "We have ways of finding things out, you know."

No, they must have forgotten her.

And the "detention center" had turned out to be a miserable little concrete-walled jail cell—with four bare walls, no windows, and a metal door (also with no windows). A previous guest had scribbled his initials in the faded green paint. She pounded on the door one more time, skinning her knuckles on the cold steel.

"I need to use the toilet!" She yelled until her lungs gave out, until she started to sound hoarse. But someone must have heard her. Some minutes later, a prune-faced woman in a gray military-style skirt yanked the door open and kicked a metal bucket into the room. It spun like a top as it skittered across the damp floor.

"What's that for?" asked Liesl.

The woman hardly looked at her, only pointed at the bucket and started to close the door again.

"You asked, so there you go. I trust the accommodations are to your satisfaction."

"No! Wait!" Liesl jumped as the door clanged shut and the lock slammed into place. The bucket reeked of disinfectant and—other things.

"You've got to be kidding me." Now she almost wished she hadn't said anything. "You're not serious, are you?"

The whole day seemed like a bad dream. Liesl kicked at the door and didn't care that it hurt her toe. At least the pain pointed out that she wasn't dreaming. After six hours and twenty-three minutes, she only cared about getting home. What had she been thinking, trying to visit her uncle alone, anyway? She laughed bitterly at how sure she'd been about getting home way before dinner. She faced the door and imagined it had become the prune-faced guard.

"What do you think of Ronald Reagan, huh?" She challenged the closed door, but in a hoarse whisper. She gave it a good kick every few words or so for good measure. "Have they told you about him over here? Born the sixth of February, 1911, in Tampico, Illinois state, USA. Fortieth President of the United States. How do I know this? Because

I've been writing a stinking report on the stinking wall for the past two stinking months, and if I ever get out of here I'm going to write it all over again so it'll be the best stinking report in the whole eighth grade at the *Hans Eichendorff Schule*."

Maybe that was one too many *stinkings,* but in this room that word (which she could rarely remember using before) seemed to make a whole lot of sense. Unfortunately. And she wasn't stinking through, yet, either.

"You remember, now?" She lowered her voice even more, just in case the walls had ears. "You heard his speech, didn't you? Ja, you did. They had the loudspeakers pointed straight at you! Half the people in East Berlin could hear it—especially you people."

She did her best Ronald Reagan imitation, which wasn't very good at all. "'Mr. Gorbechev, tear down this wall!'"

Well, even if they didn't remember those words, she did. And if she could have torn that stinking wall down, she would have, right then and there. With her bare hands. But she could only cry and pray and whisper, until she crumpled to her knees on the cold concrete floor next to the stinking bucket, bawling her eyes out.

"This wasn't quite what I had in mind, Lord," she prayed. "I tried. I give up."

But she figured the Lord had probably let her get

into trouble on her own—since she'd decided she could do everything by herself, right?

Right. And she couldn't help wondering about her parents. She'd long since missed dinner and a whole lot more. By now they'd have found her note and were probably going crazy. She bet they even had the police out looking for her.

Oh, yeah—wrong country. She wasn't even on her own side of the wall! If only her uncle knew, if only they'd let her call him. On the American TV shows, criminals always got one phone call when they got thrown in jail. These people obviously didn't watch American TV shows.

Someone yelled down the hall, and the sound sent a cold, electric shiver up the back of her neck. He didn't sound well.

At least she didn't see any rats in the cold blue-white light of the overhead fluorescent lamp. But it had started flickering as if deciding to go out. The fluctuating light was starting to drive her crazy. Everything was driving her crazy. And she started to understand how people in these kinds of places might confess to all kinds of weird things they had never done. If it would help get them out, hey, sure.

Just get me out of here, Lord. Please. She didn't want to start crying again—if she did she felt she'd never stop. So she shivered and huddled on the floor, afraid to touch anything, afraid, suddenly, that she might never get out of this hole.

She checked her watch again—seven-thirty. A

noise in the hallway got her attention. It sounded like someone running down the outside hall-way, boots clicking fast. And then again and again—then shouts echoed back and forth. Guards yelling? If only she could make out their words. She pressed her ear to the door—and nearly fell over when someone yanked it open.

"Oh!" When Liesl reached out to keep from fall-ing, she ended up grabbing the prune-faced guard around the waist. A little awkward, ja? "Excuse me, bitte. I was just—"

"On your feet." Frau Prune-face brushed Liesl off with a look of distaste. "Follow me. Now." Her voice commanded action.

Liesl hoped she'd get to use the phone now. But the way Frau Prune-face grabbed her arm and half marched, half dragged her down the hall squelched that hope. At least she'd gotten out of that stinking room.

A couple of guards rushed by. Liesl realized they were decked out in full riot gear—heavy black jackets and motorcycle-style helmets with Plexi-glas shields—and guns.

"Ow!" she cried as a guard's rifle butt caught her in the back, nearly knocking her off her feet. But he didn't slow down, no "Excuse me, bitte." And Frau Prune-face didn't seem to notice. She just marched on. Liesl at last gathered the courage to ask, "What's going on? Where are you taking me?"

20

KAPITEL ZWANZIG
RIOT

The prune-faced guard never said a word as she led Liesl down the hall of the olive-drab detention center.

"Please tell me where you're taking me." Liesl tried one more time.

No answer. Not even a grunt. But when they reached a door at the end of the hall, the woman fished out a set of keys, selected one, and looked over her shoulder before jamming it into the lock and turning the deadbolt. The door swung out to reveal a side alley. What in the world?

"I'm doing you a favor," the guard finally said as she shoved Liesl outside. "So go home immediately. Get out of here. Ask no questions. Just run."

Which Liesl would have gladly done, but—

"What about my papers?" She stopped. "My purse?"

The guard deepened her permanent frown, dug

into a pocket, and tossed Liesl's West German I.D. papers to the pavement. *That was it?*

Without another word the woman drew back inside and slammed the door.

"Oh." Liesl said as she heard the deadbolt slide home. She stood shivering in the alley, facing the back of the ugly concrete security building that had held her captive for eight hours. She felt certain she'd never see her purse again, or the letters from her American grandfather. At least she had her I.D. papers. The guard had to know Liesl would need them to get home.

"Well, then, thank you," she whispered, scooping up the papers. "I guess."

If that's all she had, that's all she had. She knew God had answered her. She also knew she should run like the wind back across the border—she should get home any way she could, as quickly as she could. Now. Something big must have happened for the guard to dump her into the street like that. For the others to have on full riot gear.

But—she hadn't waited all this time for nothing. She needed to see Onkel Erich.

After only a moment's hesitation, she hurried down *Invalidenstrasse* toward her uncle's home, not many blocks away. But the farther she went, the more she heard the growing noise of a gathering crowd, like a flood, rolling in her direction.

"*Wir wollen raus!*" she heard chanted over and

over, louder and louder. The words echoed down the street. *"We want out!"*

Out? That could only mean one thing.

She rounded a corner and stopped in her tracks. What she saw made her blood run cold.

A flood of angry people, moving toward her. The last time she'd seen this many people crowded into a city street, they'd come out to hear the American president.

But this crowd seemed very different. Even from a distance she could feel the wild edge, the electricity in the air. No, this looked like a very different kind of protest, nothing like the ones Jürgen and his friends had organized on her side of the wall. Clearly these people didn't just want to get on the evening news. She didn't see any neatly worded signs, any well-dressed teenagers who should have been home doing homework.

These people clenched their fists and marched as if their lives depended on it. The army of workers advanced toward a row of uniformed guards at the Invalidenstrasse border crossing—guards who had planted themselves behind gleaming Plexiglas shields wearing protective black helmets. Just like the guards who had sprinted past her in the hallway, moments earlier.

And Liesl realized she'd put herself right between the two groups.

People in apartments above hung out of windows, watching. Liesl briefly had a vision of ancient times, when Roman crowds watched the gladiators battle the lions. Someone was about to get bloody, or worse, and everyone knew it. Liesl could feel the near panic running through the crowd, the energy of a frightened, cornered animal ready to lash out at anything that got in its way. A young woman pushing a baby carriage down the sidewalk nearly ran Liesl over as she tried to get away from the crowds. The woman's look of white-faced panic confirmed Liesl's thoughts: *Run. We do not belong here.*

Liesl should have listened to the prune-faced guard and headed for the border when she had the chance. Up ahead, traffic stopped for another flood of people. And the street behind her filled with people too, shoulder to shoulder, elbow to elbow. Where had they all come from? They surged with one mind toward the wall. As if taking part in the yearly running of the bulls in Spain, Liesl realized she could hurry on before them, find a doorway, or be trampled. She didn't like her options.

What about this bakery? Surely she could slip in out of the way. She saw the baker, pacing just inside the door with his flour-smudged apron. But when she tried the door—

"Bitte?" she cried as she knocked on the glass panel almost as urgently as she'd knocked on the detention center door. She didn't even notice her raw knuckles. "Please let me in!"

The crowd had nearly reached them, and the

baker had a clear view of the approaching riot. He crossed his arms, backed up, and fearfully shook his head.

Liesl looked frantically for another escape. But the crowds had just about met in the street right in front of her. If she didn't want to get trampled, she'd have to keep moving.

"WIR WOLLEN RAUS!" The chant seemed to fill her. It grew impossibly loud as the various groups merged and rolled that last block toward the wall and the waiting guards. "WE WANT OUT!"

Yeah, so do I, thought Liesl. A couple of college-age guys bumped her from behind. She held her hand out, steadying herself against the person in front of her. The huge number of people forced her to take shuffling baby steps to keep from tripping.

But she realized this shapeless mass of yelling protesters seemed to have leaders. One man raised his hands and they slowed their pace. Another raised a hand-held megaphone to his lips: *"KEINE GEWALT!"* he reminded them. "NO VIOLENCE!"

Liesl hoped the border police advancing on the crowd were listening too. She could only see bits and pieces through the people ahead of her, but she could hear the nervous yells and then screams when the police whistles sounded.

"I should have stayed in the prison," Liesl told herself, but no one could hear her above the riot. And like a school of fish being attacked by sharks, the crowd parted and people ran, scattering. Liesl felt herself shoved backward against a building, and she landed with a thud on the cold pavement. She covered her head with her arms, praying she wouldn't get trampled as the riot passed over her.

21

KAPITEL EINUNDZWANZIG
CELLAR SECRET

"Ja, ja." Onkel Erich nodded as he spoke into his phone. "She is—"

He held up the receiver to look at it, then tried again.

"Hello? Sabine?"

But no. He frowned and listened another moment before replacing the phone in its cradle.

"Dead," he told Liesl. "The lines just went dead."

And that's how she felt, too, thinking about what her parents might do to her when she finally made it home.

"Sorry." He shook his head, as if it were his fault.

Liesl knew the lines often failed between East and West, but they'd chosen a particularly bad time as far as she was concerned.

"Do they know I'm okay?" she squeaked. Erich shrugged and tipped his head to the side.

"I hope so." He poured his niece a steaming

cup of tea and set it on the kitchen table as she sagged into a chair. "I'm just glad you weren't killed in that riot. Look at your knees!"

Oh. Liesl hadn't even noticed that her jeans had ripped. She examined her bloody knees. And her hands. She shook her head and dabbed at her skinned palms with a paper napkin.

"I'm sorry." She didn't know how to explain herself. She just did her best to keep from crying again. She'd already done more than enough of that for one day, hadn't she? "But I really didn't mean to cause Papa and Mutti any worry. I just wanted to make it happen, all by myself."

"Wanted to make it happen—you mean, to bring him here?"

"Well—"

She shrank a little more in her chair, hearing the lecture on its way. She knew she deserved one for making such a mess of things. Her uncle started to say something, opened his mouth, and sighed as his shoulders fell.

"Liesl, Liesl, Liesl. Your parents have been worried sick about you. They called at least a dozen times before you showed up. Your father went out looking for you, too."

She swallowed hard. Home by dinnertime? Not quite. Onkel Erich's kitchen clock showed half past ten.

"Maybe we could just tell them I got caught in traffic on the way to visit you?"

Which was true, in a way—though it might depend on one's definition of *traffic*.

He chuckled. "Nice try."

"Or we could explain that you promised to help me write my paper about the wall? You did, didn't you?"

"I thought you finished your paper."

"I did, sort of. But I never got some of the most important details."

He nodded. Of all people, Onkel Erich understood. He lowered his voice, as if sharing a secret.

"I still can't believe he's alive—your father told me about those letters. I hope you brought them along."

"The letters. Right." She took another sip of tea to buy a little time to think. "Actually, that's a long story."

"Try me."

"Uh—it's just that everything sounds so ... *phantastisch*. Maybe even a little bizarre. I don't know if he believed me when I told him—"

"Wait a minute! Hold everything." Her uncle nearly choked on his tea. "Him? You talked to him?"

Phantastisch. Right. She nodded and explained about the phone call, what he said, what she said. Onkel Erich began to smile, then to laugh. Pretty soon he bent forward, holding his sides, breaking up.

"I don't get it." She couldn't figure out what he found so funny. "Don't you believe me, either?"

"Oh, I believe you." He caught his breath. "It's just that only you would have the courage to call this stranger on the telephone, all the way to America, as if you were calling a school buddy."

"It wasn't quite like that. I just thought that if he came back, and he and Oma Brigitte could get back together, well—"

"Say no more." Onkel Erich smiled again and winked. "After all this, I don't have a choice. I'll have to—"

BAM-bam-bam!

Liesl jumped.

"You've got to see this, Erich!" shouted a voice from the hall.

Erich, recognizing the voice, jumped up from the table and threw open the door.

"They announced it late this evening!" the neighbor yelled over his shoulder as he flew down the hallway. "They're opening the border. Really opening it!"

"You're not joking?"

"Come look out the window!" He pushed up the pane at the end of the hallway and pointed to the ground below them.

It looked like half the city—or maybe more—was streaming down the street toward the border. The skyline blazed with fireworks and some people honked their tinny car horns.

"The wall is gone!" A man leaned out of his window and yelled to anyone who would listen. "The wall is gone!"

Gone? For real?

"Bombig!" Her uncle pumped his fists, the way he did when his Dynamo Berlin soccer team scored a goal. "I thought we might see this in twenty years, fifteen maybe. But never so soon."

Liesl watched the mass of people and a few cars weaving down Invalidenstrasse toward the fireworks. Red lights reflected on the dirty window like a sunset—or in this case, a sunrise.

Onkel Erich snapped his fingers as if he had just decided something important. "Come with me," he said, motioning Liesl to follow. "I have something to show you."

They ran down the staircase as Liesl pulled on her sweater, past the main floor landing, around a corner, and down several steps. She stopped to let her eyes get used to the dark. It looked like a furnace room. And she had to sneeze.

"Sorry about the dust," her uncle said, yanking on a cord. A single light bulb cast a weak yellow light across the middle of the room.

"Are you sure—" she stopped and looked at him curiously.

"I'm sure, all right." He pointed at a double set of barn doors, nailed shut. "Help me get those doors open."

When she hesitated, he handed her a crowbar.

"I'm not kidding," he told her. "We're opening these doors."

Which was easier to say than do. But between the crowbar and a hammer they managed to pry off the boards that held the doors shut.

"These boards have been up for as long as I've lived in this building," Onkel Erich told her. "And that's been quite a few years."

"What in the world is going on down here?" An older woman, her gray hair pulled into a severe bun, poked her head down the last few feet of stairs. "Erich Becker, I'm going to call the police!"

"You can do that, Frau Müller. But I think the police are all down at the wall, celebrating with the rest of the city."

"Hmmphh!" She sounded cranky. "Just because we've had a little disturbance, doesn't mean everyone has to go crazy! I'm still calling the authorities."

"You do that, Frau Müller." Nothing would stop Erich Becker today. "Let me know what they say."

The last board fell away and Erich and Liesl both put a shoulder against the doors, pushing with all their might. The poor old doors finally gave way with a loud creak, and Liesl and her uncle looked out on Rheinsbergerstrasse. The frosty night air made Liesl gasp, but no one on the street seemed to notice them.

"You still haven't told me what's going on." Liesl clapped the dust off her hands and followed her uncle back to a tarp-covered, lumpy shape in the corner. He pointed to the corner of the tarp nearest her.

"Give me a hand," he said, and they gingerly pulled the tarp off, as if unveiling a piece of art. And, well—

Not exactly art. But close. Liesl stared at the machine and Erich beamed like a proud father.

"What do you think?" he asked, polishing the fender with his sleeve. It looked like an old German army staff car, a convertible, older than anything she'd ever seen.

"A Volkswagen?" she wondered, and he nodded. "Where did you get this?"

Liesl knew that even doctors didn't own Volkswagens in East Berlin. The few people who owned cars drove the small East German Trabant, a horrible little smoke-belching machine. But of course even those were rare.

"It's a long story. But just before the wall went up, your mother discovered this thing in a cellar-turned-bomb shelter of a nearly destroyed building. We figured it was left down there during World War 2."

"Cute. But—" Something didn't make sense. "Did you say a *cellar*?"

"A cellar." He smiled. "When your parents escaped to the West—through a tunnel we dug from that cellar—I stayed here. Later I brought the VW to this garage piece by piece. I've been working on it for twenty-eight years. And now we're going to drive it through the Brandenburg Gate."

No kidding? The car looked like it was held together by chewing gum and a little glue, with springs sprouting from every seat and nice airy openings where most cars had doors. "Will it start?"

He held up a finger at her question.

"Oh, ye of little faith. I told you how long I've been working on this thing, nights and weekends, practically all my life."

"And you've never had it out on the street before?"

After working so hard to open the barred wooden doors, she knew the answer.

"This car and I have been waiting for this day, Liesl. Just sit in the driver's seat and do what I tell you."

And she did, while he held down a throttle or something in the rear engine compartment. She smiled and pressed down on the gas when he told her to, and—

22

KAPITEL ZWEIUNDZWANZIG

BOMBIG!

"Turn the key! Now!"

Liesl obeyed her uncle's shouted instructions, but the car just groaned and whined and rattled. Uh-oh. She let go of the key.

"No, no!" he hollered. "Keep cranking."

So she did, sending the ancient Volkswagen into a fit of coughing and sputtering that should have sent Frau Müller scurrying to the police once again. Come on! One more time, and—

rrrrrrrrrrommmmm!

The old Volkswagen rocked to life with a throaty gusto, making her uncle disappear in a thick black cloud of smoke. But he emerged with a laugh and a shout and a jubilant hug for Liesl.

"It's alive!" she yelled, caught up in the moment. She had never really paid much attention to cars before and didn't quite see the appeal of a hunk of metal on wheels. But she could see the glow on Onkel Erich's face.

Or maybe that was soot from the exhaust.

"Drive you home?" he offered with a grand sweep of his arm.

He pointed to the passenger seat and she slid over—avoiding a healthy spring. He climbed in, put the car in gear, and they lurched down Rheinsbergerstrasse toward the wall.

"I never dreamed I'd get to do this so soon," he told her over the uneven roar of the VW. Clearly the thing didn't have a proper exhaust pipe. It sure could *roar!*

The horn worked too—sort of—and they honked their way west along with the tide of thousands. To Liesl, it looked like everyone in East Berlin was headed for the wall, through the open checkpoint, past guards with their hats pushed back, scratching their heads in wonder. Some of them covered grins with their hands, and none of them attempted to check I.D. papers or stop anyone from traveling in either direction through the border crossing.

I could have saved myself a major headache, Liesl told herself, *if I'd just waited one more day.*

True, but it didn't seem to matter now. Just beside them, a boy with straight-up Mohawk hair (obviously from her West side of the wall) laughed and shook hands with a gray-shirted old man (obviously from Onkel Erich's East side of the wall). A man in a leather jacket shook up a bottle of champagne and let it spray—all over the front of the car.

"Windshield wipers even work," Onkel Erich bragged, flipping the wiper switch. The crowd cheered all around them, and some slapped the side of the car in congratulations as they inched along. Surrounded by thousands of walkers, they passed under the towering old stone arch of the Brandenburg Gate. Once it had stood as the symbol of a city split in two. But tonight?

Neither of them could stop grinning. Midnight on the border. And look at this! Hundreds of people had climbed to the top edge of the old wall, where they stood arm in arm, as lights and fireworks played over the whole fairy tale scene.

Bam! Everyone clapped and cheered as a red rocket exploded into a thousand sparkles above them. A few of the wall hoppers had brought along sledge hammers and chisels, and they had begun to take swings at the concrete. One held up a chunk as the others cheered and blew an assortment of old trumpets and noisemakers. And for a moment Liesl caught his eye—Jürgen!

Liesl waved to him from the Volkswagen. Why not? What had he once called her?

Feigling. That's right. She crossed her arms and stared him down, as if daring him across the crowd to call her a coward again.

Go ahead and try.

But of course he couldn't. Instead he gave her a thumbs-up and a smile before he turned back to the celebration. And through all the noise Liesl heard the echoes of the American president's speech.

"Mr. Gorbachev, tear down this wall!"

Maybe the others heard it, too. Thousands of West Berliners had also gathered, cheering and waving, singing and shouting, celebrating as they'd never celebrated before. It looked like Christmas and New Year's and the soccer championships all rolled into one. The crowds grew and closed in more tightly, barely leaving enough room for the car. And then the VW sputtered, shook—and died.

But no matter. The crowd behind simply pushed it along. Erich shrugged his shoulders.

"Well, I'm a doctor, not a mechanic."

Liesl giggled and stood on her seat, holding onto the windshield for balance and waving like a grand marshal in a parade. The eyes of dozens of television news cameras waited for them on the other side, but tonight she didn't mind. Let them take their pictures! She even recognized one of the American news anchors, surrounded by lights, delivering his lines to the cameras.

"Good evening," the Amerikaner boomed above the celebrations. "Live from the Berlin Wall on what may be the most historic night in this wall's history. We have a remarkable development here tonight at the Brandenburg Gate ..."

Remarkable, what a perfect word. Liesl glanced down at the faded phone number barely visible on the palm of her hand. She wished Fred DeWitt could share this with her. But she realized she might never meet him.

After nearly an hour of searching and honking and celebrating, Liesl spied her parents in the crowd. Jumping up and down, she waved her arms to get their attention, amazed that she had found them in the sea of people.

"Over here!" yelled Liesl. "We're right here!"

As if on cue, the VW allowed her uncle to coax it back to life, gassing the crowd behind them with a puff of thick black smoke. Nobody seemed to mind, though. They just waved their arms and laughed—just one big, fantastic joke. Liesl caught the stunned look on her mother's face as she recognized the car, and a minute later Liesl jumped out. Working her way through the crowd to her parents, she wrapped her arms around them. Only then did the tears start. Her mother held on as if she'd never let go.

"Thank God you're safe," her mother cried, "but Liesl, you have some explaining to do!"

Liesl ducked her head, then smiled through her tears as Oma Brigitte wrapped her in a huge hug.

"I just wanted him to be here," Liesl told her grandmother. Had it all been for nothing? The report, the search, the prison—Oma Brigitte wiped a tear from Liesl's cheek.

"Shh, it's all right." Oma held her granddaughter at arm's length, and a little smile played on her face. "I want you to meet a friend."

The older woman shifted so Liesl could see a shy-looking boy in a blue windbreaker, shivering in the cold November night.

"This is my granddaughter, Liesl," she announced in English, which could only mean the boy didn't speak German. "She's the one I told you about."

When? Liesl wanted to ask, and Oma must have read her mind.

"He tried to call you this afternoon." Liesl's grandmother shook her finger. "But of course you were off getting yourself in trouble, so you wouldn't know about that."

"But—" Liesl started to explain.

"Actually," her grandmother continued, "I think you two may have something in common. Oh, and Liesl, Nick Wilder has a surprise for you."

Liesl looked the boy over and gasped at the name.

"*You're* the Nick Wilder I talked to on the phone?"

He nodded, and her mother and grandmother looked at each other as if they knew a secret. Never mind that she had just barely escaped from an East German prison, never mind that she'd nearly gotten trampled to death or that she'd probably get grounded for life. Now they had a *secret!*

"Um, I talked to him a couple of times," the American boy said, looking at his watch.

"You talked to him?" Liesl's father interrupted. "*You're* the one who's responsible for trying to bring him here?"

He'd said *trying*, Liesl realized. Oh, well.

"Well, I'm not really sure." The boy couldn't seem to stop checking his watch. "I told him he should, but I wasn't sure if he actually would. I guess he's a little late."

"Late?" They were just playing with her mind, weren't they? She hated all this mysterious talk—especially when everybody else apparently knew what was going on. "Tell me what you're talking about!"

Nick grinned and pointed his thumb at the sky. Liesl stared, then made out the lights of a small airplane, getting closer.

"There he is." As if that explained everything. And as a matter of fact, it did. As the crowd around them continued to celebrate, a small group stood, heads craned back, as the plane came in view.

Liesl's parents huddled close to each other.

Onkel Erich was still seated in the driver's seat of his classic VW.

Nick grinned as if he'd just scored the winning goal.

And Oma Brigitte's tears flowed down her cheeks. Liesl slipped her hand into her grandmother's and squeezed.

"He's come back?" asked Liesl. She couldn't stop shaking. She hardly dared to believe what she saw. And she felt a strange peace. She knew the plane hadn't come because of something she'd done—she hadn't wrestled it from the sky, hadn't arranged it, hadn't figured it out.

In the end, it had just been handed to her.

Oma nodded just as the plane—a small two-seater—came in low over the crowd, lower and slower than Liesl expected. At any other time, the Air Force might have scrambled to check out the border threat. But not tonight. Tonight the plane belonged. It was just another part of the crazy celebration, like the fireworks and the singing. The people on the wall raised their hands in the air and cheered as the plane dipped a wing.

And Liesl saw his face clearly—though from a distance—as he leaned out the small plane's window and released a handful of—parachutes.

"His aim is still pretty good," Erich declared, laughing and waving up at the man, who waved back before the plane disappeared into the night. They watched the American candy bars raining down, landing in the outstretched hands of the crowd. Liesl hopped back in the car and patted her uncle on the shoulder.

"Think we can get through all these people?" she asked him. He looked over at her and raised his eyebrows.

"Right now? Where to?"

But he must have known the answer. The airport, of course.

"You drive," she told him, "and I'll navigate."

"You mean *we'll* navigate." Oma Brigitte slipped into the back seat with Nick in tow. Sabine and Willi squeezed in, too. Liesl smiled as Onkel Erich revved the VW and put it in gear. No, she didn't have to do it all by herself. And what could she say, but—

"Bombig!"

EPILOGUE

It's easy to see how this series is rooted in real history and real places. Though Liesl and her family are pretend characters, you can actually visit many of the settings where they lived in this story, including the General Lucius D. Clay United States Headquarters, the checkpoints, and the streets like Rheinsbergerstrasse and Friedrichstrasse.

The wall itself is largely gone, though in many places you can see where it once stood and visit museums that explain how it worked back before 1989.

Much of the historical timeline and events from 1989 is real in this story, too. You've read the actual words of President Reagan's famous speech, where he says, "Mr. Gorbachev, tear down this wall!" That's all true. Protests around the wall happened very much as they were described in the story. And the timing of the German people's push to bring the wall down is accurate.

So the wall came tumbling down, and the people of Berlin danced to see their city united once more.

But was it, really?

Because after all the parties and celebrating had died down, people on both sides of the old East-West line woke up to the sober truth: Bringing a divided city back together again takes a lot of hard work and a lot of sacrifice.

That's how it works with people, too. In our story Liesl just *knew* that their family could come back together, and she had the faith and courage to see it through. But it didn't just happen overnight. It took several months of cautious visits, for instance, for her grandmother Brigitte and Fred to announce that they would be renewing their wedding vows and making their new home in Berlin.

So in stories and in real life, reunions are good—especially the ones that bring real people back together after a long time of being apart. We often find that the reasons that separated us really aren't good reasons, after all.

Best of all, though, are the reunions that bring you and me back to God—the way we were created to be. That's why Liesl's favorite part of the Bible would always be found in the Apostle Paul's letter to the believers in Ephesus, the section in chapter two that she would read over and over, even as the wall became just a memory and she grew up herself:

Remember ... you were separate from Christ, excluded from citizenship in Israel and foreigners to the covenants of the promise, without hope and without God in the world. But now in Christ Jesus you who once were far away have been brought near by the blood of Christ. For he himself is our peace, who has made the two one and has destroyed the barrier, the dividing wall of hostility. (Ephesians 2:12–14, TNIV)

QUESTIONS FOR FURTHER STUDY

1. Have you ever had to go through a border crossing or security check at an airport? Did it make you nervous, even if you knew you hadn't done anything wrong? Describe what Liesl must have felt in chapter one, going through the checkpoint to visit the East.
2. In chapter three, why did Liesl have to sneak in New Testaments to her friends in East Berlin? What could have happened if she had been discovered?
3. In chapter five, Liesl had to write a report about the Wall, and she quoted speeches from President John Kennedy, years before. Do you think kids in 1989 knew they were living in historic times? What history are you living in?
4. Google "reconciliation church Berlin" to learn more about the Reconciliation Church you read about in chapter six. Who tore it down, when, and why?
5. In chapter seven, Liesl uses a tape recorder (you know what that is, right?) to interview her grandmother about old stories. What are some ways you can find out more about your own family stories, or stories of older people you know?

6. In chapter eleven, Jürgen says being careful is "quark," or total nonsense. How would you have answered him, if you were in Liesl's place? Remember, she's thirteen and he's sixteen.

7. In chapter twelve, Liesl's grandmother underlined the verse in her Bible that said "if the Son sets you free, you will be free indeed." Compare Onkel Erich and Liesl. In this story, who is really more free, and why?

8. In chapter fifteen, what's the difference between the difference Liesl wanted to make, and the difference Jürgen wanted to make? What is a "feigling"?

9. In chapter sixteen, Liesl feels she's the only one who can track down her grandfather. Have you ever felt like "it's all up to me"? What do you do about it?

10. Why was Liesl arrested in chapter nineteen, and what did she do when she was? Do you ever find yourself praying like she did—only in emergencies?

11. The scene in chapter twenty-two where people from both sides of the Wall climb on it and begin to tear it down is based on real history. Find a video clip (there are many online) and describe what you see and hear. Pretend you are Liesl. What are you feeling, and what does it look like to you?

12. Explain how Liesl's long voyage of bringing her family back together was like the real Berlin wall that eventually fell. Can you think of people or places with real (or imaginary) walls that need to come down? Groups of people with barriers between them? What could you do to help bring down those barriers?

Trion Rising

The Shadowside Trilogy

Robert Elmer

In book one of the trilogy, things couldn't be better for 15-year-old Oriannon and her friend Margus. Life is good on the bright side of the planet Corista.

But when a strange new music mentor begins to teach them a different way to play their songs, she's not sure she wants things to change... that much. Could he really be a Faithbreaker, an enemy, the way Oriannon's father says? And when she finds herself lost on the Shadowside, can the once self-centered Oriannon follow her heart ... and save half the planet?

Available in stores and online!

The Owling
The Shadowside Trilogy
Robert Elmer

In book two of the trilogy, *The Owling*, the planet of Corista has been thrown off its axis. In the midst of global chaos, Oriannon's former music mentor Jesmet miraculously returns and promises a special power called the Numa. Meanwhile Sola, Corista's charismatic head of Security, proposes the "ultimate solution" for peace. Can Oriannon trust either of them?

Beyond Corista

The Shadowside Trilogy

Robert Elmer

In book three, *Beyond Corista*, war is sure to erupt on Corista and beyond—unless Oriannon and her friends can alert space outposts of the coming danger... from a people no one has ever seen. Is Oriannon's vision of Jesmet's warning only an illusion? The exciting series conclusion!

Available in stores and online!

Code of Silence

A Code of Silence Novel

Tim Shoemaker

Booklist 2013 Top Ten Crime Novels
for Youth

"...deliberate, plausible, and gritty
whodunit." - *Booklist* Starred Review

When three friends witness a gruesome murder where the
killers are dressed as policemen, Cooper, Gordy, and Hiro are
left questioning whom to trust. Is telling the truth always the
right thing to do, or in the interest of protecting yourself, is it
okay to lie or withhold the truth?

Back Before Dark

A Code of Silence Novel

Tim Shoemaker

"...sickeningly smart. You will not have any fingernails left by the final page."
- *Booklist* Review

The kids find themselves in the wrong place at the wrong time. It's every kid's worst nightmare, when a ride through the park gets Gordy abducted. Their powers of observation are put to the test like never before, as Cooper, Hiro, and Lunk fight the clock to find their friend. In the dark, things are never what they seem.

Below the Surface

A Code of Silence Novel

Tim Shoemaker

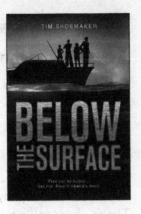

Cooper thinks he can bury his fears, and a vacation aboard The Getaway with his best friends is just the escape he needs. But when they witness a murder Coop realizes his fears are alive and well...just below the surface.

Sudden Impact

AirQuest Adventures bind-up

Jerry B. Jenkins,
#1 Bestselling Author

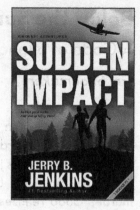

Three books in one, this AirQuest Adventure bindup by #1 New York Times bestselling author Jerry Jenkins combines pulse-pounding suspense, nonstop action, and a message of hope amidst tragic circumstances. Travel with twelve-year-old Chad, his younger sister, Kate, and their fighter pilot father, as the three span the globe helping those in need—and land in more trouble than they ever imagined!

Available in stores and online!